Raising the Blackbirds

Edward J Atherie

PRAISE FOR
RAISING THE BLACKBIRDS

Moncrief deftly braids a complex history with a fictional dramatization—a synoptic account of the draw of Mexican workers to the U.S. is furnished within the story. . . . This is a meticulously researched book that manages both to entertain and edify in equal measure. A worthy union tale for readers in search of poignant historical fiction.

-**Kirkus Reviews** *("Recommended" Book)*

"*Raising the Blackbirds is a dramatic and inspiring novel about the struggle of Sixto Torres, a farm worker who leads his family and entire community in a fight against exploitation, injustice, and racism during the César Chávez era. Moncrief writes with an authentic passion that peels away the myths and shows how much sweat, blood, and tears it took to get every small gain and how the struggle continues today.*"

- **Alan Rinzler**, consulting editor

Most people said San Jerardo couldn't happen in the Salinas Valley of the Seventies. I lived there, in the cooperative, as a young man and today I'm the manager. No one thought that would ever happen either. . . . It all started when we migrants decided we weren't going back to Mexico or Texas after the crop was picked. Why would we? We had our jobs. We had our union. We knew, if we fought a little harder, we'd have a real home right here in the Valley. I think that's the promise of America; to struggle and succeed. We lived that promise. In Raising the Blackbirds, Moncrief tells Sixto's story through Sixto's voice. It's a good story and a strong voice.

- **Horacio Amezquita**,
Manager, San Jerardo Cooperative, Inc.

THE AUTHOR

Born in Los Angeles in 1942, Edward
Moncrief grew up in the rural town
of Redlands, California. As a boy, he
beat the summer heat by sleeping
outside. He awoke in the mornings,
hearing bracero laborers, singing
their alabados among the orange
trees. He spent ten years studying
to be a Franciscan priest, receiv-
ing a solid grounding in the liberal arts. During those years,
he developed a love for literature and the English language.

Moncrief decided to leave his studies for the priesthood
at the age of twenty-three. He married Judi Carl in 1967.
The following year, he entered graduate school where he
earned a Master's degree in Social Work with an emphasis in
Community Organizing and Development; after which, he
moved first to the San Joaquin and then to the Salinas Valley.

Moncrief spent his forty-one-year career directing
non-profit housing organizations and developing new
housing for farmworker families and other economically
disadvantaged people. "Raising the Blackbirds" is based
on his experiences developing farmworker housing.

In 1980, he founded Community Housing Improvement
Systems and Planning Association (CHISPA), a non-profit
housing development corporation operating on California's
Central Coast. Over the years, he has been a guest columnist
and has written editorials and articles for the "Salinas
Californian", the "Monterey County Herald", and "Western
City Magazine" among other newspapers and journals. He
was also a contributing writer to Jill Shook's "Making Housing
Happen", an anthology of stories about faith-based affordable
housing models in the United States. Later in his writing career,
Moncrief was a freelance reporter for the "Salinas Californian"

Raising the Blackbirds

---

*"CRÍA LOS CUERVOS, Y TE
SACARÁN LOS OJOS."*

"YOU RAISE THE BLACKBIRDS,
AND THEY PLUCK OUT YOUR EYES."

Singwillow
PUBLISHING

ISBN-13: 978-1-54393-136-5
LCCN: 2016916094

The lyrics to "Sin Tí" by José Guízar Morfín are used with permission of Memorial-Maya Music.

Printed in the United States of America

Dedicated to the Memory of

BENJAMIN J. MCCORMICK,

priest, professor of literature, counselor, mentor, and friend,
who taught me to love and respect the English language.

This story is based on actual events. In certain cases, however, incidents, characters, and timelines have been changed for dramatic purposes. Certain characters may be composites or entirely fictitious. Except in the case of selected characters and public figures, any resemblance to actual persons living or dead is purely coincidental.

PROLOGUE

The new president, Jaime Robledo, banged on the Formica table. The blows resonated throughout the room, signaling the installation of the board's new officers. I was now officially removed as San Jerardo's president. Despite my continuing anger over the results of the recent election, I had decided to attend this first meeting of the new board. The agenda included an eviction action against the González family.

I stood to speak. Jaime Robledo and the other six newly seated board members stared past me.

"Señores," I said, "Efraín González is not a bad man. You know that it's hard to work long hours from early morning into the night and still maintain control of all that your children might do."

"Why is Torres wasting our time defending this man?" called Adalberto Castillo from his seat at the table. "It was he who put off the eviction of Efraín González all these weeks and months. Who is Sixto Torres to come here at the last moment and address us? He has nothing new to add." The twenty or so people in attendance fidgeted and murmured to each other. Castillo continued, "For ten years we've listened to Torres and his lies, but his time is over. We've heard enough from Sixto Torres."

Each time Castillo spoke my name, he threw his chin forward as if he were spitting into the air. He and his wife, Catalina, had been after me for years. Now they had deposed me—in a way, beaten me. I could no longer speak as president of the San Jerardo Farmworker Housing Cooperative; the new president was there with my gavel in his hand. I was only a man standing to ask forgiveness for a friend, nothing more.

"Can't you give him a little more time to correct the situation," I asked.

"*Señor presidente, por favor,*" Castillo threw a notepad onto the table, continuing his pronouncements, "I move to evict the González family from the cooperative!"

The motion was seconded and the vote taken without further discussion. The decision to evict was unanimous. Not even Juan Alemán, who had once been my friend, supported my request.

Suddenly, Efraín González launched himself from his chair. He shouted at the new president, then at Alemán and at Castillo, stabbing a finger at them.

"*¡Pendejos!*" he screamed. "*¡Pinches pendejos!* I know of many others who break the rules. No one is throwing them out."

I stepped toward Efraín. I grabbed him by the arm and led him toward the exit as he continued to shout. As we reached the door, I heard Castillo call to me. I turned to see him standing and waving his arms, beckoning me to return.

"Hey, Torres, don't leave. I have a second motion for you." He picked up his notepad from the table and brought it to eye level.

"Mr. President," he declared, scanning his notes, "I move that we establish a committee to meet with our attorney for the purpose of drawing up a list of grievances against Sixto

Torres. We all know that he's guilty of numerous violations of our membership documents. It's time we prepare formal charges against him."

I didn't stay to hear the board's response. Efraín had stopped cursing and had flung himself on the bench outside, away from the light. I stooped to place my arm around him, to say something—I did not know what—when the voice of Juan Alemán came from behind us. He had risen from the table and followed us into the night. His darting eyes were now fixed on me.

"You shouldn't have come here tonight, Sixto, *ves*. This is not your business anymore." I stared at him, unable to speak. He turned and walked back into the room.

I sat beside Efraín in silence and shadows. I took out two cigarettes and gave one to him. I raked a match across the rough wooden bench. The smell of sulfur surrounded us.

"They're after you next, you know," he said. "They won't stop until you're gone too."

Part One

CHAPTER ONE

Even as a boy of nine, I knew that I was a strong worker. Each morning, I carted to the river two wooden *baldes*, swinging from a limb pressed against my neck and shoulders. I filled them and carried them back up the dirt road to my father's tanning shop.

"*¡Oye! Camotito morado*, where are you going?" The older boys always laughed as they pushed ahead of me with twice my load of canisters. "That is what he looks like," they said, snickering at their own cleverness. "A baked yam!"

"My name is Sixto!" I shouted back. "Sixto Torres!"

The daily ridicule caused my jaw to tighten. I imagined flinging the canisters to the ground, grabbing the limb at one end, swinging it against their backsides, and before they could respond, ramming my barrel chest into the trio. The eruption would surely topple them and send them back down the hill where they would fall like sticks along the river's shore.

Each day I made as many as fifteen trips to the river, lugging the water up the hill to the door of our home, carefully maneuvering through the narrow opening, brushing past the stacks of calf hides, then dumping the crystal liquid into the designated tub of dye.

"Only two more," I thought. I resisted the temptation to cut the work short and tell *mi papá* that I was finished before I had delivered the last bucket. Some of my friends urged me to try it, but I could not give in. That would mean that I was not a strong worker.

"Your arms are growing like corn, *m'ijo.*"

"*Gracias, abuelito,*" I said, hurrying back down the hallway and past my grandfather.

Into the *madrugada*—the early morning—as the first chill of autumn sliced through my sarape, *papi* and I rode the wagon to cut and lay the corn stocks in rows. I struggled to keep up, sometimes coughing against the dusty husks, always trying to ignore the scratches that the dry leaves, sharper than my machete, served upon me. Later, we returned to wrap the stocks in cupped piles, *los mogotes*; and still later we came again to load and carry them to the pens for the horse, the goats, and the pigs.

Papi said that doing hard labor well was a quality of the soul. Knowing that I was a strong worker sustained me for hours at the shop bench as I stripped the bark from the *timbe* and encina. I pounded it with the butt of a rusty hatchet, producing the powder that my father needed for the leather dyes.

Late in the day, I stood with him at the small sink and watched him rub the stains from his hands, using the milk-colored cream from Señora Alonzo's bodega, one of the many stores in the plaza of my village, San Ciro de Acosta.

"*Por favor, papi*, I need some too," I pleaded.

"*Sí. ¿Cómo no? ¡Haces un buen trabajo!*" My father rubbed the healing *pomada* deep into my palms and along the *marcas* on the underside of my arms.

One night in mid-December—I was perhaps eleven—I awoke to the sounds of my parents talking with señor *y* señora Rosillo. I realized immediately that *mamá* was still in the front *salón* on the sofa where she had been sitting when I had fallen asleep. She was but a few meters away. I could hear her soft voice clearly.

"*Sí*, it was on this day, when I was only six, that *los bandoleros* came to San Ciro."

Then my father said, "Amelia, *mi amor*, you don't have to tell this story."

"No, Fili, I do have to tell it. Samuel and Juana have been friends for enough time now. I want them to know what happened."

I stared at the shadowed curtain that separated my room from the tiny hall leading to the *salón*. My brothers slept against the opposite wall. I lay motionless, breathing deeply so as not to miss any of the words.

"They had ridden through before. *Ustedes saben*, the revolution was starting. *Los federales, los revolucionarios, los bandoleros*, they all came and went, looking for food and money and guns. But by this time, they must have been more desperate."

"Our families were fortunate to have missed all of that," señor Rosillo said. "Juana and I grew up in *la capital. Los federales* ruled there."

After a moment, my mother continued.

"*Como siempre*, early in the morning, the women came from all directions down from the hills, from all of the tiny villages, dressed as always in black, singing hymns to *la Virgen* and carrying our candles; and in front, the *cueteros* were sending up the fireworks, the same as this morning. I was walking with my mother. We came into the plaza and crossed over to the church. We attended *la misa*. Just like today, when we came out, some of the men were already setting up the booths and getting everything ready. My father arrived with a basket of corn and calabazas and told me to husk the corn." The more my mother talked, the more I could hear a sadness growing in her voice. She drew out her words as if struggling with the burden they carried.

After a while, I heard her say, "You were right, Fili, this is harder.... It's been a while since ...but I want them to know ...I will finish." She was now crying softly.

Señora Rosillo said, "It's all right, Amelia, continue or no. It's up to you, but take as much time as you need."

I sensed that my mother was telling a story that she wouldn't want me to hear, but it was too late for me not to listen. She had mentioned her father, which was unusual. When I was younger, if I inquired about my maternal grandfather, I was told only, "He died before you were born."

My mother spoke again.

"You know the ceiba tree that's there in the plaza? Our family always set up near there with our corn and vegetables and the rosaries that my mother made. By noon on that day, the plaza was very full of people buying and selling, everyone moving by us back and forth. Then someone yelled that the *bandoleros* were coming, but it was too late.

"They rode in, raising dust and waving their rifles and shooting into the air, twenty or thirty of them. The talking, the selling, the music—everything, of course, stopped immediately.

The people stared as the riders circled the plaza and as some stationed themselves along each side. My mother grabbed my brother and me and put us on the ground, but my father stood and watched in silence with all of the others. The gang's *comandante* came near to where we were, still mounted and holding his rifle. I remember the wooden butt was cracked."

I heard *mamá* take a long breath in and exhale with a subdued moan. "It's so stupid," she said, "but that's what I was looking at, the butt of his rifle. I was too young to know what was happening. The *comandante* said nothing. He only nodded and a few of the riders dismounted and gathered food and money wherever they could grab them. Then some of our men began an angry murmur and started moving, almost imperceptibly, toward where the *comandante* sat astride his horse near the ceiba.

"I saw my father look around at them. He realized that they were all looking back at him as if he should do something because he was in front, the closest. I heard my father yell, '*Mira, capitán, por favor*, do not do this!'"

"I saw the man look at my father for an instant and hesitate. Just then, others started yelling and the motion among the people grew stronger. I saw the man's black eyes jerk back toward my father. Then he raised his rifle and fired. My father fell in front of us." Again, I heard Mother's voice break into a sob. My own heart was pounding, and my own eyes filled with tears. *Mamá* continued. "Of course we were all screaming, the people were shouting, my mother, my brother, and I were wailing, but no one dared move after the shot. Then two or three of the *bandoleros* came forward with a rope. They tied it under my father's arms, threw the rope over a branch of the tree, and hoisted his limp body above us...."

I heard Doña Juana cry, "*¡Dios mío!*"

A muted shuffle followed. I surmised that the woman had moved to be closer to *mi mamá* and strengthen her as best as she could.

"*Sí*. It all happened thirty years ago today," exclaimed my mother through her sobs.

Her words penetrated my heart, filling my mind with images of my dead grandfather hanging from the great ceiba, the beautiful and embracing ceiba under which I had played as a child. I cried for my grandfather, whose tinted photo even now hung in the *salón*, murdered in front of his wife and children—and for my mother, who had lived with these memories throughout her life and had felt that she must keep them hidden from her children.

My stomach churned with sympathy, anger, and confusion about how and why such terrible events should happen in the world. I was enraged that this injustice could exist. My chest tightened as if a void was sucking away my breath. I couldn't remain in this room with its faint light and intruding nightmares.

I jumped from the cot. My feet hit the cold stone floor as the bed frame lurched noisily against the wall. Barely able to stand, I tottered toward the curtain, nearly blinded by my tears. I flung myself clumsily through the opening and braced myself along the hallway's plastered wall. I steadied myself while wiping my eyes, now squinting against the light of the *salón*. I moved forward past my father and the Rosillos, toward my mother's arms. Upon seeing me, she tried without success to wipe away her own tears.

"Sixto! You're awake?"

"*Sí, mamá.*"

"*Pobrecito*, you've heard me tell about your grandfather."

"*Sí, mamá.*"

"I didn't want you to know of this until you were older, *m'ijo*. I should have been more aware."

By now I was sobbing uncontrollably and clinging tightly to my mother's warmth.

"*¿Por qué, mamá?* Why did they shoot him?" My mother didn't respond. She only drew me still closer to her.

Finally, she said, "I don't know, *m'ijo*. Perhaps there are just evil people in the world."

My own father then rose and walked across the room toward *mamá* and me. He stood in silence. With one hand, he cupped my shoulder from behind; and with the other, he stroked Mother's thick, flowing hair.

As you will see, after that night, I could never again walk near the large ceiba there in the quadrangle of San Ciro without remembering my grandfather's death and my mother's suffering.

Three years later, Padre Joaquín paid a visit. The priest told my father and mother that he had noted my good habits and my faithfulness in helping them at home. He had marked my contributions to the whole parish as an acolyte. The truth is, from the time that I was able to walk, *mis tías* had been there with my parents to ensure that I was properly dressed and ready for *la misa*.

"*Ándele, m'ijo. Mire*, take this comb to your hair," they said. "*Aquí*, put on this jacket," they said.

The priest spoke with animation.

"Your son, by all accounts, is not a spiteful person," he observed. "Granted, he whipped Popo García with a fallen branch a few months back, there among the adobe remnants of the Montoya Hacienda, but only after suffering years of harassment at the hands of that *rufián del diablo*. In my opinion, Sixto showed admirable restraint up to the moment of the beating. Undoubtedly, the bully deserved each *golpe*; and, in fact, he has since stopped his taunting of the younger children." The priest beamed with pride.

In the end, everyone agreed, including me, that I should continue my schooling not in my pueblo's tiny L-shaped building with its five teachers but in the seminary two hundred twenty kilometers away in San Luis Potosí.

That summer my parents bought me new dress pants, a white shirt, and black tie. On the night before my departure, the aunts, uncles, and cousins, together with the *comadres y compadres*, filled the house with food and stories in my honor.

"*Vea, Sixto, le digo*, it's because you're a Leo. This is why you're so strong." *Mis abuelitos* always claimed that being a Leo was the source of my strength and that my sign would serve me well in the great accomplishments that lay before me.

"What will you do, Sixto, among so many people? Here we are only a few hundred. They say there are thousands in San Luis."

Late into the night, I lay on my cot in a half-dream. Tomorrow I would leave. I had never known any other home but San Ciro with its white houses, the river, the shops, the fields and garden, and the lagoon. I had heard of San Luis Potosí to the west, but neither *mi mamá ni mi papá* nor I had ever seen such a place. I had heard of Tampico to the east, through the arroyo of the Sierra Madre; but only a few of our *pueblito* had traveled such a distance, returning with black and white postcards showing the sandy shore and the sea beyond. Before the postcard photograph, the *laguna* was the largest body of water I had seen. In truth, I could not imagine that so much water could exist in this world.

Suddenly, although I could jump out of bed and be there in two minutes, I missed my grandparents' home, *la casa grande*, only two blocks up the street. Almost every day I visited them to sit in the guava tree for hours eating fruit. My aunts and uncles passed by.

"Look at the *chango*," they teased. "Is that a monkey we see, eating our guava fruit?"

I didn't respond. I didn't even know what a monkey was. The truth is, I had never seen one. I thought a monkey must be something like a dog or coyote or, perhaps, a pig. These animals I knew; they lived in the hills near the house or on the *ranchitos*.

In all my life, I had been to only one other *pueblo*, Rioverde. Our family went to Rioverde in May and again in September for the fiestas. My friends and I raced through the groves of mango, lemon, and orange trees. We hid under the branches and ate the sweet Valencia until we could not eat anymore.

In Rioverde, the fog pushed through the mountain gap from Tampico and the ocean, down into *el valle* surrounding the river, but it seldom visited San Ciro. *Mi papá* said that here the weather was hard. The people were able to nurture a few trees and vegetables, along with sugar cane and corn, but nothing like Rioverde. Sometimes San Ciro suffered three or four years without rain. Everything dried up.

Papi said that you had to think of San Ciro in three parts: el plano, el pueblo, y la laguna. When the storms did come, they swept in a torrent down from the Sierra Madre, filling the rivers that crossed the plain. When the rivers were full, the floods pushed on to the lagoon, a vast expanse of land lying like half of a bottle below the *pueblito*. When at last the lagoon was full, the people were happy, for they could look forward to one, maybe two, years of good crop, *buena cosecha*.

The wooden slats creaked as I turned restlessly on my cot. My four younger brothers slept near me. They lay motionless, stirring only when a deep breath took hold of them.

Juanito was almost twelve, yet too small and frail with twisted arms and hands, slow to understand and to speak, always following me as he worked, trying to help as best he could ...*Papi* had told me many times that it was my job to protect Juanito.

Enrique was only nine, but each day growing taller and stronger. Now the task of caring for Juanito must fall to him. Polo always wanted to feed the animals. He was just starting school. Then came Chito, nearly three. Six-year-old Licha and *la bebita*, Mago, slept across the hall.

The September breeze fuffed at the window, carrying to me a vague scent from another time in my short life, the smell of rancid water. It called up the image of a distant black dot in the sky set above the evening sun. I saw mud and broken clouds, smelled again the decaying reeds along a barren shore. The grimy water ...*muy lodosa* ...I was ...maybe ten ...certainly no more than ten ...In September, *por el día quince*, we stood in a circle to watch an old man weaving and wrapping *los globos* ...watching him create the globes ...of wood and paper ...making them in order to fly them ...wood and ...my friend, Rafael— *decimos el* Flaco—said, a paper from China. Some of the globes were very large and colorful. I wondered how they could have produced a paper in so many different colors: blue and orange and green and ...My father could stain the *cueros* in only two shades ...and ...

All of us in the circle watched as the man wrapped the paper around a tiny frame made from strips of *carrizo*. With twisted yet delicate and dark fingers, he attached the canister of kerosene under the globe and brought forth a match to light the fluid.

"*¡Cuide sus zapatos*, Sixto!" I pressed back into the crowd around me, protecting my shoes from the threat of the flame. That morning I had dressed for the fiesta in my new school uniform: all white and pressed with creases down the front. *Mamá* had presented me with a pair of glossy black shoes, the first dress shoes I had ever owned. Always before, I had worn old sandals or work shoes even to school.

"*Tenga cuidado, hijo.*" They are very pretty. Take care." The old man lit the kerosene. The flame shot up from the tin cup.

Now, in the darkness of my room, I smiled as I remembered first seeing the magic of *el globo*, slowly rising with the help of only a little heat ...moving away from us over the booths and the tables, past the stone tower of the church, out beyond the last houses and trees, and into *el plano*.

My schoolmates and I watched in amazement as it was taken higher by that same September breeze that always came in from Tampico and the sea (and that even now buffeted the window above me).

"*Hola, muchachos. ¡Síganlo!* Follow it! Whoever brings back the frame, *un centavo!*" The old man was calling to us. "*¡La armazón! ¡Un centavo!*"

In an instant, I found myself chasing after the rising image, following it with the others, running as if enlisted in a cause of great import, my schoolmates on all sides, my cousins, my friends from Rioverde out past the plaza, past the church, past the grove of encinas, onto the open plain. I was not a fast runner; still, I hoped that I could be the lucky one. Perhaps the globe would drop quickly from the sky and fall right at my feet. Perhaps the others would grow tired before I wearied of the chase. As I ran, I watched the floating object grow smaller and darker above the fading light.

High clouds dropped the hint of rain. We paid little notice. Our parents, alerted by the dampness and realizing our absence, must have marked the position of the sun. They found their way to the edge of the plain and strained to call us back, but we couldn't hear the summons because we were yelling at *el globo* to return. We didn't feel the rain; we paid little attention to the dying sun. We saw only the drifting, darkening ball, each of us holding firm to the hope that it should be ours to retrieve.

We ran for more than two kilometers when a few began to slow. Some of us continued into the open neck of the haggy lagoon, but some turned back from its damp and spongy floor. They stood in silence, eyeing the matted shoreline that curved along the edges up to the crest of the hills.

The globe seemed purposely to lead the rest of us into the lagoon's rank web of grass and tangled reeds. By the time I stopped and looked around me, only five or six of my comrades were left in the chase. We had slogged a hundred meters into the mire when the dot against the sky disappeared with the sky itself.

The others also paused to gather their wits.

"We'd better get back," they said, each of them sensing the danger.

I looked down at my once white uniform and once glossy black shoes. Even through the twilight, I could see how spotted and smeared they were with the *mugre* of the lagoon. Too late, I removed the shoes and tied them around my neck. I rolled my pants to my knees. With only my slimy socks to cover my feet, I began the long trek back toward the town.

Beyond the neck of the lagoon, we prodigals finally heard our parents' calls. Halfway across the plain, we could see the torches lit for us. I remembered, as I fell into a calm sleep, how *enojado mi papá* was, ready to take a brush to my backside because of the uniform and mostly because of the shoes. How glad I was that my *abuelitos* defended me.

CHAPTER TWO

"*¡Bienvenidos! ¡Bienvenidos!*" Padre Joaquín embraced my parents. "'This is the day the Lord has made!'" he proclaimed, grinning. He took his place by the door of the *autobús* and waited to usher in the others and me. Federico, whom everyone called Kiko, and Teodoro, known as Toro, were also to attend the school. They greeted the priest and boarded the bus. My parents, brothers, and sisters hugged me in turn. My *mamá* kissed me through a whisper of tears. Her oval face and ebony eyes reflected a mingling of sadness and pride, each sentiment bleeding into the other like the dyes from my father's shop. Mago clung to my leg, her podgy cheeks and matted hair against my knee. My grandparents kissed me on the forehead, as did Licha.

"*Adiós*, Sixto. Until Christmas."

We three boarded the bus. Padre Joaquín followed. The priest began reading the black book of prayers that was always with him. I peered through the closed window of the *autobús*. My family stood waiting. Their eyes kissed me again as the groaning bus pulled out along the narrow streets. A mix of excitement and fear gnawed at my stomach and heart. My brothers and sisters raised their hands, and I waved back until the bus rounded a curve.

In Rioverde, the padre led us the two blocks to the train depot. We arrived just in time to board the daily and begin the ten-hour ride to San Luis Potosí. Kiko and I held our ears to dampen the noise of the waiting train, but we could still hear Toro's continuing warnings and comments. He had not stopped advising us since leaving San Ciro. He was, after all, an experienced traveler, having been to San Luis on several occasions and to *la capital* twice.

"Oh, that's nothing," Toro observed as he sat across from us. "You should hear the noise in San Luis. Ten trains *pitando* all at once. After a while you just get used to it."

I stretched toward Toro to hear his words while continuing to cover my ears. I was accustomed to my friend's bravado. He was always charging ahead like a young bull. The three of us had known each other all our lives. Toro loved to talk. He was taller and faster than either Kiko or me. He was a better student. His parents owned a large *rancho* beyond the lagoon. Unlike Kiko, however, I didn't allow myself to play the part of Toro's burro.

Long ago I had noted the smooth hands and stringy arms. I had concluded that Toro couldn't survive even ten trips carrying the canisters from the river to the house. Toro couldn't have manufactured the *tinte*. He couldn't have made the *mogotes*. What good was it to know so much about far-off places?

Toro wore a new shirt with colored stripes and a stiff collar. He wore pleated trousers with a black belt that matched his polished shoes and well-groomed head of hair. I listened through the din as he continued with his advice.

"Just wait until it starts to move. You'd better sit back and hold on, Kiko! Just wait. It pushes you against the seat. If you're standing up, Kiko, you're going to fall on your *culo!*"

I braced myself as the train lurched from the station. The noise all around me grew in a panting rhythm that attacked my brain and pushed my shoulders up to my neck. I wrapped my hands tighter against my ears. The train picked up speed, huffing its way through cane fields and orchards.

"*¡Mira!*" Toro shouted, pointing out the window. "In a minute you'll see the river!"

I spied the bowed line of cars ahead and watched the distant engine creep toward the dark outline of an iron bridge. Within a few seconds, black stalks of steel slipped past. Toro stood against the casement, looking straight down.

"*¡Mira!*"

Kiko and I also pressed against the glass. We peered into the gap of space beyond the bridge's charcoal ribbing and saw the rushing water and tangled banks of the Río Verde far below. My heart beat in fervid rhythm with the train's rapping pace. I had never viewed the world from such a height. I shut my eyes for a moment, but when I opened them again, the river was gone.

"Oh, that's nothing," Toro was saying. "You should see, there are even higher bridges up north."

Next, I became aware of a stale and heavy odor coming, I believed, through the floor of the train. Kiko also had noticed it and covered his nose.

"That's diesel fuel," Toro said. "Don't worry. You'll get used to it."

Indeed, after a while, I found that the intensity of the engine's noise had diminished and the once obtrusive smell had dissipated. I watched the passing mango trees and fields of sugarcane spread along the Rioverde plain. I felt the twist of the great iron wheels as they wrangled with the unbending rails. I smiled in recognition at the passing groves of encina. "So this is where the tree grows," I thought, remembering my father's shop and the murky dye.

After two hours, the encina began to thin. A thick chaparral of mesquite and *nopál*, yellow retama, *pirúl*, and eucalyptus covered the land. I caught glimpses of grazing goats and *vacas* beside their calves. Piled corn stalks dotted the landscape like spilled baskets. Rock walls were strung together by woven fronds and poles to hold in the pigs and sheep.

In the afternoon, we felt restless and hungry. The train stopped beside a village. The dirt streets and the adobe houses reminded me of San Ciro. A woman wrapped in a black *rebozo* and two young girls in long gray dresses passed through, selling tacos, enchiladas, and tamales. I thought of my mother and sisters. Padre Joaquín brought us lunch, paid the vendors, and they were gone. We ate as the whistle signaled our departure.

We arrived in San Luis Potosí after dark. I stepped cautiously from the train into the clamor and brightness of the depot. I stood for a moment, awestruck by the muralled walls and lofty ceiling of the great box-shaped station.

"Oh, this is nothing," Toro was saying. "You should see the depot *en la capital!*"

Toro raced ahead, completely at home. I again felt the now familiar mix of excitement and fear as I followed Padre Joaquín. I clung to my valise and stared at each new wonder: the station's thick, square columns, the marble floor, the iron doors, the wooden stairway, the crowds of soldiers in green uniforms carrying rifles and holstered *pistolas*, men in dark suits and ties—clothes *mi papá* wore only to weddings—and young women in dresses that didn't cover their lower legs and shoes.

I had never encountered a priest or a nun who didn't know me and greet me as *el hijo del* señor Filiberto Torres. Now, dozens of clerics and religious mingled through the crowd around me. They took no notice of me. They didn't even pause to greet Padre Joaquín.

Outside I stopped suddenly. Night had come; yet for the first time in my life, I looked up to the sky and saw only a vast emptiness. Where were the silver specks of light? Where was the ball that had always shone like the silken face of a polished hide ready for market? In San Ciro, I knew the stars as trusted companions. They guided me through the evenings when *mi mamá* sent me to throw scraps to the pigs and through the streets to *la casa grande* when my grandfather needed *hierbas* to make medicine.

"Where are the stars?" I asked. Padre Joaquín smiled and placed a hand on my head.

"*Pobrecito,*" he said. "Don't worry. They are there. We simply can't see them because of the lights from the city. You'll get used to it." The cab driver took my valise and box.

"Where are you from, *joven?*"

"San Ciro," Toro informed him, dropping his own bags into the trunk.

"San Ciro, eh? And where is that?"

"Near Rioverde."

"Rioverde!" The driver nodded in affirmation. "Ah, *sí*. I have heard of Rioverde."

We rode through narrow cobblestone streets, past houses, tiny shops, *fábricas*, restaurants, and office buildings. Elevated lights illuminated every street, revealing a chain of signs, murals, and posters advertising strange and unfamiliar products. By now it was after eight o'clock. I saw only a few people along the walkways, some closing doors for the night, others standing on street corners for no apparent reason.

The driver, short and burly, had a face that fell over his neck and onto his shirt. A cigarette was stuck to his bottom lip. It waggled as he spoke to Padre Joaquín.

"If the Germans whip the Allies, Padre, they'll be on our doorstep next. I hear they're burning people over there."

It was the first time anyone had mentioned the war in several days. In San Ciro, once a week the people gathered in the plaza to listen to the radio. "*¡Las noticias de XAUU, radio México!*" I went only twice. They gathered beneath the twisting branches of the ancient ceiba tree in the midst of the plaza, the same branches that still caused *mi mamá* to weep because of a different kind of war from long ago.... If someone purchased a magazine, the people passed it from hand to hand and from house to house, but I had never been able to see one for any length of time.

For many years *mi papá* had been the treasurer *municipal* de San Ciro. On occasion, I had accompanied him to the government building to watch while he worked with the town clerk, signing receipts and authorizing payments. The clerk talked about the Japanese dropping bombs. He said *los americanos* would take care of them.

Kiko craned his neck out of the open window. He pointed ahead as the driver brought us to a wide and brightly lit avenue lined with trees and large glowing signs. "*Mira*, Sixto, that building is enormous!" he shouted. "How do the people get to the top? With a ladder?" Toro laughed at the idea. "Have you never heard of an elevator?"

"No. What is it?" Kiko asked. My eyes followed the upward line of the building's five rows of windows.

"That is Hotel Altamirano," the driver told us. As I stared, my heart jumped in response to a flash of letters that burst through the darkness above the roof. The words *"Carta Blanca"* appeared, disappeared, and appeared again.

"Look at that." Kiko gestured toward the sign.

"An elevator is a box," Toro stated. "You stand in it and it pulls you up to the top."

"How can it do that?" Kiko now pointed to the blinking sign as Toro proceeded to explain the workings of an elevator.

I stopped listening, drawn instead by the enchantment of the electrical wonders all around us. The houses in San Ciro had, at most, one electric bulb hanging in the kitchen or *en el salón*. Everywhere along the avenue, giant words glowed and flashed, lighting the taxi's path: *"Ropa de frio," "Zapatería Canadá," "Banco de México."* The bobbing, chasing light darted into and out of clear plates of glass larger than any I had seen before, revealing shadowed then brightened pockets of leather goods and jewelry, hand creams and soaps, dresses and shoes, furniture and crafts ...I wondered how someone could have time to use it all.

At the end of the avenue, we entered a large square. The taxi stopped. The driver jumped out quickly and circled to assist first Padre Joaquín and then the three of us. We stood silent in the semidarkness before the massive stone facade and towers of *el Santuario de Guadalupe*. Even Toro didn't speak.

Padre Joaquín paid the driver. The priest led us through a side door, down a roughly hewn hallway, and into the flickering and shadowy interior of the church. From my first cautious steps along the dimly lit aisle and then into the expanse of the domed sanctuary, I sensed the shiver within my body.

The faint heat rising from the candles near me didn't dispel this coldness. The barrel of my chest trembled from deep within as Padre Joaquín led us farther into the strangely moist cavern. The interior of the grand church revealed altars, tapestries, statues, endless rows of pews, flaming wax, stained glass, marbled floor, and walls of *cantera* adorned in gold leaf. We genuflected before the altar. I turned, stopping for a moment to peer down the stretch of center aisle to a distant and darkened exit. We knelt.

The wonders of this day—the force of the panting locomotive, the expanse of the train station's arched ceiling, the bustling crowds and glancing lights, the pine forest, even my brief moment hovering like a bird over the crystalline, crawling Río Verde—they all fell away beneath the lofty umbrella dome above us. Padre Joaquín made the sign of the cross, and each of us followed the gesture. I prayed silently, asking God, as always, to protect *mi pueblito* and to deliver my family from evil. In the midst of my prayer, however, the shiver in my chest and stomach continued to confuse and distract me. I eyed again the mottled light darting along the ranks of votive candles. I leaned forward and bowed toward the cold marble floor, hoping to catch a reflection of my face in the whorled pattern. Because the light was too dim, I saw only skipping shadows.

Padre Joaquín stood in front of me. He placed his hands on my head and gave me a blessing. He moved on to Kiko and Toro. He stopped and waited for us to look up. He spoke softly, yet his voice filled the flickering expanse.

"If you work hard and pray, you'll be fine," he said. "Now we're going to meet Father Rector and then we'll eat."

Outside we again followed the pastor through a labyrinth of corridors and archways.

"The cathedral is beautiful," Kiko said.

"Oh, that's nothing," Toro was saying. "You should see the one en la *capital!*"

For nearly three years, I believed that I would be a priest like Padre Joaquín. I rose each day to the clamor of the bell. Its command was followed by the squeak and crackling of iron beds and the thump of bare feet on cold wooden floors. The seminarians raced to the line of sinks set in one corner of the dormitory or to the *baños y escusados* beyond. Within a week I had fallen into the daily routine of Mass, breakfast, class, play, and study. I made new friends but spent most of my free time with Kiko and Toro. Together we explored the seminary's stone buildings, expansive fields, orchards, and well-trimmed gardens.

"It looks like a prison," Toro observed on the first morning as we came from breakfast and into the large quadrangle.

After dinner, we probed the dark hallways and staircases, the towers and cellars, the closets and courtyards. Cautiously and with whispered excitement, we pushed open heavy doors to fuggy storage rooms filled with carved statues of unknown saints, ancient and tattered books, spiraling silver candelabras, and gold-flecked vestments hanging in musty casements of carved oak and tinted glass.

We crept down hidden and probably forbidden passages, spied into the priests' cloistered hallway, then scurried away undetected. Kiko and I watched from a distance as Toro, with precise inflection of movement and poise, followed the upperclassmen through the library's towering stacks, selecting random volumes and giving each an intense examination in feigned study of the meaningless words. We giggled until cold stares sent us out.

For many weeks after we arrived, I lay at night sleepless, crying softly from loneliness for my home and family. I lingered in the hallways between classes, staring out the windows, unable to chase from my mind the picture of my *abuelitos*. Padre Díaz, who taught Latin, paused beside me.

"You'll be late for class, young man." I was struggling with Latin, but I had grown to like Padre Díaz.

"*Dispense*, padre," I said. The priest noted my sad eyes.

"What are you thinking about?" he asked.

"*Mi familia*."

"I'm sure they miss you, as well, but Christmas is just a few weeks off." He paused and put a hand on my shoulder. "Right now you need to get to history class."

"*Sí*, padre."

Later, Padre Díaz found me alone in the woodshop. "You have decided to work with wood for your hobby?"

"*Sí*, padre."

The priest glanced at my nearly empty tool bag. "It looks like you need some tools."

"*Sí*, padre."

"There're always a few from last year's graduates. I'll look around for you."

"*Gracias*, padre."

"What are you making?"

"A ladder for the sacristan."

"Those lines will be easier to draw when we find you a square."

"*Sí*, padre."

"Are you still thinking about *su casa*?"

"*Sí*, padre."

The priest squatted near my place along the workbench, his black cassock folding over his knees and shoes.

"Do you still think you want to be a priest?"

"*Sí*, padre."

"You know, when you miss your parents, your brothers and sisters, and your grandparents, I want you to remember that here we are also like a family. In fact, when you go home for Christmas, you may discover that, after a few days, you will miss your family here too." Padre Díaz rose and turned toward the door. "Sixto, if you are feeling sad and want to talk, you come see me, okay?"

"*Sí*, padre."

Slowly I grew accustomed to the daily routine. I thought less often of my home and family and became ever more familiar with the buildings and grounds, the dormitories and lockers, the classrooms and dining hall, the students and teachers.

Every Tuesday, I met in the woodshop for an hour with Gonzalo Ordoñez, who was two years ahead of me. From Gonzalo, I learned how to cut a board straight and how to use an electric drill—which I had never seen before the day Gonzalo placed one in my hand and made me hold it steady and firm along the stretch of thick, dry lumber. He also showed me how to fit dowels for the rungs of a ladder so that they didn't loosen. Occasionally Kiko and Toro joined me in the woodshop, but Kiko was more interested in plants and Toro in painting.

Late afternoon, Saturdays, each student sat in the chapel examining his conscience in preparation for the Sacraments of Confession and Communion. I had much to ponder. Only yesterday I had had a fight with Moncho Moreno. During *fútbol*, Moncho kicked me more than once after the play had ended and in a way that the referee wouldn't see. My stomach was a cauldron of anger, but I managed to control myself until the game ended, knowing if I reacted I would surely be carded. I searched for Moncho and confronted him as our teams returned to the locker room.

"Why were you kicking me?" I demanded to know, letting my anger build again. Moncho was only slightly taller than me but twenty pounds lighter. Sweat still ran down the offender's tapered face and narrowing eyes.

"Hey, you're the one who throws your weight around, *camote!*"

"Don't kick me ever again, *macetón!*"

"Who are you calling a jarhead?"

We both started pushing and striking each other. Our teammates immediately surrounded us but did nothing to intervene. In fact, they quickly took sides and urged us onward. We were soon wrestling on the ground, which gave me a distinct advantage. Before I could turn Moncho over, however, two upperclassmen caught up with our group and pulled us apart.

"*¡Miren los muchachos, tan avispados!* You are like wasps at play!" they declared affably, hoping to lighten the mood. One of them was tall and athletic. He easily raised Moncho off the ground and set him down again.

"Hey, *torpe*, don't you know? If Padre *Pesca* catches you, you'll be scrubbing floors for a month!"

Moncho and I brushed off our uniforms, still glaring at each other as the older students led our teammates and us into the main quadrangle. There they told us that it would be best to shake hands and forget our differences. We complied, but said nothing more as we departed with our comrades in opposite directions.

Now, I sat on the hard pew. I could see Moncho's long, straight hair and thin neck three rows ahead. The smell of carne asada filtered from the refectory through the open stained glass windows of the chapel as if riding the afternoon's waning light.

Padre *Pesca* was the prefect of the seminary. His real name was Father Valentino. He won the nickname of *Pesca* among the students because of his bulging eyes, round glasses, and cold, fishlike demeanor. I was relieved that the priest had heard nothing of the melee.

I returned to my self-examination. Why did I chase after Moncho that way? Why didn't I just let it go? I hadn't had a fight since the clash with Popo García nearly two years ago at the old Montoya *hacienda*. I was not sorry that I had vented my anger, that I had even fed it. Still, I asked why.

I remember my father coming home from meetings of the *comisión municipál*, feeding his own anger with *tequila*. I lay in my bed listening to *papá* in a rage as he regurgitated the evening's revelations. *El presidente de la comisión* had reported that the taxes—*los impuestos* that my *papá* was responsible for collecting—had been properly sent to the state officials, but the promised roads and gutters, yet again, were to be delayed another year.

"I tell you, *mujer*, the *cabrones* take our money. They pocket it and leave us with nothing!"

Mi mamá listened quietly and pleaded with him to calm himself lest he awaken us children.

Sometimes in the tannery, my father's knife slipped and cut a hide or caught a corner of his own flesh. In an instant, the atmosphere changed from tranquility to turbulence. *Papá* flung the knife to the floor. "*¡Qué chingado pendejo!*" he screamed at the offending tool.

I had to admit that, if I were alone and dropped my books and homework or hit my shin on a workbench even here in the seminary, I disgorged the same words instantaneously. Then I would have to confess to the priest and accept the imposed penance.

Now, waiting for my turn to enter the confessional, I knew the priest would certainly whisper, "You will say the rosary and beg the forgiveness of Our Holy Mother, my son."

I remembered Uncle Neto, who came to live with us for a time. Neto was fourteen. I was only four. Every day Neto teased me and frightened me to make me cry. Once, Neto rolled me up in a mattress and sat on it, pressing it against me. The tight padding constrained my squirming and muted my screams. I fought but couldn't move my arms, my legs, or my head. I struggled to breathe, but the nightmare wouldn't end.... Finally when Neto rose, I pushed my way outward, shrieking madly, kicking, jumping forward, and flailing my arms at him.

"I hate you!" I squealed in a rage. "I never want to see you again!" Perhaps that was the moment my anger began its festering.

I shifted in the pew. I knew I would have to tell the priest about the fight with Moncho, and I would have to promise to try harder to control myself at those moments when someone might taunt me and abuse me.

In mid-December, Kiko, Toro, and I boarded the train for Rioverde and then the bus to San Ciro to celebrate Christmas. On the first day home, we ran through the dirt streets, yelling joyously and greeting friends. We laughed at the small L-shaped school and how tiny the *auditorio* behind the church now appeared. I quickly settled into the family's daily chores, helping my younger brothers who struggled beneath the swinging *baldes* and behind the pounding hatchet.

We also spent our days in the auditorium. Recently, the parishioners had refurbished the building. It smelled of fresh cement and paint. The three of us squatted on the floor in the center of the main room. We worked alongside the women and their daughters, all of them busily preparing festive decorations. Posters, together with cut and painted cardboard figures, rested against the walls or waited beneath wooden tables.

Kiko and I knelt on the cold floor, gently laying strips of papier-mâché over the molds of *carrizo* to form the piñatas. Toro had started the morning working on the other side of the room with some of the women. He was drawing large pictures of sheep and cattle for a crib scene. I had never understood how Toro, with just a crayon and some paint, could make animals and even people and angels look so alive.

Two girls were helping him. It was clear to me that the girls, Toña *y* Chelo, were also impressed with his talent. They urged everyone who came in the door to watch him sketch. I knew them from years before when we played in the streets. I especially liked the shorter one, Antonia, but Kiko had never been a close friend of theirs. Certainly Toro could not have known them very well. He did not even grow up in San Ciro because his family's *ranchito* was four miles outside of town. Kiko and I could hear the girls and Toro across the room joking and laughing like the oldest of friends.

As I lay a wet strip of *papél de chino* across the nose of a Christmas donkey, I saw Padre Joaquín walk over and ask the girls to help the women who were sewing banners near the raised platform across the auditorium. Toro was left sketching alone. It served him right. The rector warned us before each trip home to be careful.

"Your vocation is a very special gift from God that you must not put in danger by associating too closely with girls," he had said before we left, "even those who may have been family friends. After all, they are growing up and becoming *señoritas*." Toro should have known better by now; still, this was not the only time that he had risked losing the gift.

On Christmas Eve, Padre Joaquín, dressed in satin-white vestments lined with gold leaf, walked beside a shaggy burro. The plodding animal carried a young girl covered in a white veil and blue smock. A boy, a modern Joseph in search of lodging, led the burro. Kiko and I, each clothed in a red cassock and surplice, accompanied the priest.

"*¿Y donde está* Toro?" the priest asked just before we began. I had seen him earlier mingling in the crowd and talking with Toña *y* Chelo.

"He was here," I said simply, "but I don't know where he is now."

The parishioners pressed together as they marched through the narrow streets of San Ciro. The dirt paths and plastered walls fluttered in waves of light and shadow cast by the torches and candles as the humble "*familia*" knocked on door after door, seeking shelter but finding only rejection. A ragtag blend of voices rose through the late night sky. The words of the song described the desperate yet majestic journey from long ago. Its wistful chorus floated across the plane to the lagoon and beyond.

"*De larga jornada, rendidos llegamos . . .*"

The procession pushed along the side of the church and into the plaza, near the spreading branches of the ceiba. My torch lapped at the edge of the tree's spindled umbrella inked against the sky, luring my mind into its shadows where the branches, as always, strutted, gawked, and gestured awkwardly at the swinging, lifeless mass. The beckoning umbra reached toward me, drawing me from the brightness of the Christmas pageant and into the bleak, somber story told by my mother of *revolucionarios*, of *federales*, of *bandoleros*, and of their murderous sins.

As the community joined in the chorus of *Glorias*, I became aware that my family had gathered near me in affirmation of my place there in the front with Padre Joaquín. The song ended. The crowd listened for a moment to the priest's Christmas greeting, then entered the church to hear midnight Mass. Later in the hall, Kiko's voice, stern with recrimination, pushed through the noise of the crowd.

"Toro! You were supposed to serve *la misa* with us! Padre Joaquín was looking for you."

"I didn't feel too good," Toro said, drinking a cup of steaming hot chocolate and eating a piece of *rosca*.

The room was teeming with young couples and their babies. Children ran between ranks of bright banners and balloons, each youngster clutching a small bag of candy. Near the platform women bustled over trays of tamales, menudo, mole, *pasteles*, an array of food and drink.

The parishioners waited patiently in line as they eyed all the delicious possibilities. Older couples rested on benches along the walls. Teenagers clustered among the hanging ribbons. The men lingered near the side door, smoking, talking, and quietly ducking in and out for a toast in the shadows of the quadrangle.

I sat with my younger brothers and sisters, keeping a close eye on Chito, who was only three. He was scurrying back and forth to the food table, clutching pieces of *rosca* in each hand.

I remembered how *mamá* used to warn us about drinking too much chocolate and eating too many candies and bread. I knew too well how it felt to spend Christmas day with a stomachache.

"*¡Chito, ya es demasiado!*" I yelled over the din. Toro passed by.

"*Oye*, Sixto, Toña asked me why you're so quiet. She wants you to say hello to her and Chelo. *¡Vamos!*"

"Not now, Toro. I have to stay with my family." I pointed to my younger siblings.

"*Dime, amigo*, are you a woman or a man? *¡Vamos!*"

I shook my head and waved Toro away. Just then, I heard applause in the center of the room and knew that it was time for the piñatas. My brothers and sisters ran to get in line.

We returned to the seminary for the spring semester. Toro and I were in the woodshop with Diego Martínez and Gonzalo. We heard a scratching sound along the wall that separated the woodshop from the kitchen. We looked at each other, eyebrows raised. The scratching came from behind a large painting of Jesus the Carpenter. Gonzalo closed the door to the hallway as Diego removed the painting from the wall. A sliding wooden panel appeared. He tapped on it. Immediately the panel flew back. Two young women stood smiling through the opening.

"Hello, Rosa *y* Chonita."

"*¡Hola!*" they answered, first surveying and then reaching an arm into the shop.

Gonzalo and Diego moved immediately toward the panel, each taking an extended hand and squeezing it briefly. The smell of roasted chicken and menudo filled the woodshop.

"We haven't seen you for a long time," Diego said.

"Our *mamá* had to leave for the store. She'll be gone for a while." The older youth nodded and grinned even as they looked back, self-consciously, at the two of us.

"This is Sixto." Gonzalo stepped behind us. "And Toro."

"*Buenas tardes*," Toro said, smiling broadly. I sat in silence, uncertain how to respond.

"Have you been working hard?" Diego turned back to the guests.

"*¿Como no?* Someone has to cook your meals all day and clean the kitchen."

"*¡Pobrecitas!*" responded Gonzalo, eyeing the visitors with mocked concern.

The two upperclassmen leaned comfortably against the wall on either side of the panel. The younger girl pushed back her long black hair and looked at me carefully with soft, unwavering eyes. I sensed my body swaying with emotion as if I were swinging on the hammock behind my father's workshop. I bowed my head toward the scraped and ragged edges of the bench and then stood up.

"I have to go," I said, gathering my tools into the carry bag.

"Aha! *Camotito* is embarrassed," Diego proclaimed with a quick laugh. "They don't have such beautiful girls in San Ciro, perhaps. Will you leave us, too, Toro?"

"I think I'll stay a while," Toro announced in a matter-of-fact tone.

I nodded politely toward the open panel, then turned and left the shop. Behind me, I heard one of the girls ask, "What's the matter with him?"

Later, in the quadrangle, Toro repeated the question.

"*¿Qué pasó, camotito?* Why did you leave *tan pronto?*"

"They shouldn't be doing that," I replied. "They could get into a lot of trouble."

"For what, talking to the cooks? *¡Estás loco!*"

I struggled with my classes, especially *las Matemáticas y el Latín*. In the evenings, during study period, I pushed myself to complete these assignments early, leaving more time for *la Literatura*. Padre Benito gave us each a copy of the works of Jules Verne. I read *Around the World in Eighty Days*. I couldn't put the book down even after the night bell had rung. More than once, I stole away to the bathroom after lights out to finish a chapter. Then it was *Twenty Thousand Leagues under the Sea*, and then another novel, and another.

Never before had I found myself carried away on journeys stranger even than the one from San Ciro to San Luis Potosí. Never had I witnessed such heroic deeds of great men living in foreign lands, taken to the very bottom of the distant sea to encounter and defeat the terrifying creatures that, I was sure, still existed in those places. I knew if given the chance, I would in some future time meet such creatures, and I, too, would defeat them. I grew to believe that life itself must be a continuing struggle to accomplish such great deeds.

Padre Benito sat at his desk, eyeing the class and glancing occasionally at his notes.

"One must ever pursue Beauty, *mis jovenes*, and overcome Darkness with Beauty's light; but what is Beauty? Certainly, it's hard to describe. Over the centuries, however, great minds have attempted to define it. Beauty is Truth. It is Wholeness. It is the Totality, seeing the Totality of Existence." The priest cupped his eyes with the palms of his hands.

"Some see only what is in front of them. Their vision is limited by the narrow world of what *is*. Beauty is a vision of the Totality, not only what is but the Ought To Be! We must see and strive for what ought to be! In doing so, we find the Eternal. We find the Face of Christ stamped on all creation. We find God. It is the artists—the painters, the sculptors, the writers, the musicians—who show us the way; and when they capture Wholeness, Totality, Beauty, they show us the Divine! When we dream, when we envision a greater good and struggle to realize that vision, we change the world; and in changing the world, we touch Eternity."

I listened to the priest's grand words. My heart swelled with inspiration. I felt transformed. I resolved to spend my life pursuing Beauty, Wholeness, the Ought To Be. Never again would I allow myself to be drawn into the narrow neck of the miry *laguna* while chasing *el globo*. Petty anger, jealousy, lust— none of the Seven Deadly Sins would rule me. I was confident that I would see The Totality and embrace Beauty wherever I might find it.

Early in our second year, on an unusually warm autumn afternoon, Kiko and I were alone in the woodshop. Kiko had agreed to help me finish a wheelbarrow. After a while, I heard again the faint scratching sound from behind the picture.

"What is that?" Kiko asked. I sat for a moment in silence, struggling with the idea of escape. Then I heard the dull scraping of the wooden panel against its track. A girl's voice whispered through the picture frame.

"*¿Quién está ahí?*" I looked at Kiko, who looked back blankly. I walked cautiously to the picture frame and lifted it from its nail. "*¡Hola, joven!* I remember you." The younger of the two girls appeared alone in the pass-through, smiling just as before. "*Déja me* ...I know ...*Camotito, sí?*" She smiled at her astuteness. "I'm Chonita. Remember me?" The beautiful eyes glanced beyond my shoulder. "And who is that behind you?" Kiko gazed at the two of us, his face frozen. He stood, packed his hammer and square into the mochila beside him, and ran from the shop.

"*Sí.* I remember you," I said quietly. The girl had to be at least two years my senior. In some strange way, this thought made me relax a little.

"*¡Está muy guapo, joven!*" In all of my life, no one had ever told me that I was handsome. "Come here." The girl reached toward me. I took one step. "It's okay if we shake hands. *Tu sabes, como amigos.*" I was filled with confusion and panic. I drew back and stammered, "You're trying to make me sin! I am going to tell the rector you're here!"

"You're crazy!" the girl exclaimed. "Are you a baby? I'm just trying to be friendly."

"No! You're the devil!" I shouted as I pulled away and, like Kiko before me, ran from the room.

Kiko would no longer come with me to the woodshop. I explained to him repeatedly that I didn't talk to the girl and that I had told her to go away and had called her the devil, but Kiko was adamant. Later I came to realize that Kiko, perhaps, was wiser than me.

Each year in January, the *pueblito* celebrated *la fiesta de* San Ciro de Acosta. By the fifteenth of the month, a string of battered trucks limped in from Querétaro by way of Arroyo Seco, where they had contributed greatly to opening the New Year. The frazzled convoy dragged flatbed trailers and wagons covered with torn and flapping tarps under which rattled splayed limbs and bundled chunks of metal.

Children and youth gathered on the edge of the plaza. Two- and three-man teams jumped from cabs and unloaded the disjointed pieces of wood and steel, canvas and cloth.

"¡Yo les ayudo!" we older boys called out, moving from truck to truck, hoping to land a temporary job. "Señor, I'll carry those for you! Do you remember me from last year? Can I work for you again?"

"Perhaps later," the crewmen responded without so much as a glance or a pause in their routine. We were unruffled. We knew that the task was more than the men could handle in the time they had. The aggressive and persistent among us would find our reward in work and wages. I chased from truck to truck, eager to spot a friendly face from previous years, someone who would remember that I was a smart, strong worker. Kiko followed. We already knew that Toro and his lanky frame would disappear until Tuesday when all was ready.

For the better part of four days, the younger children sat among the weeds and bushes in silent awe as the men clustered the disorganized scraps in this direction and that. With growing excitement, the children watched the parade of workers, which now included Kiko and me. The smallest of them marveled as, by some incomprehensible craft, these odd chunks and bits and strips were slowly drawn together piece by piece, lashed and tied, pounded and raised, bolted and wrapped until at last there emerged from each cluster an enticing, spinning carrier of danger and ecstasy. They saw that the scattered rails and massive plate on the left had changed into a giant merry-go-round. The arms of steel, wooden benches, and chain on the right had evolved into *una rueda de la fortuna*, climbing nearly as high as the church tower. The sheets of tin and rounded canisters with leather seats in front had been reborn as a roller coaster chasing itself.

On Friday morning, the nine-day fiesta began with its music, its color, its booths, and its *juegos! Los fayuqueros* arrived the same day in the early hours bearing their merchandise. They came from a hundred kilometers around carting goods purchased in Tampico, Querétaro, or San Luis, and some made by their own hands. They, too, rolled into town in ancient trucks and station wagons. As the Sierra Madre dipped against the morning sun, they unpacked and stacked, unwrapped and hung, fluffed and dusted.

Throughout the plaza, the *municipio* had constructed booths made of poles covered with *mantas* of cotton cloth. By ten o'clock, the square was bursting with eager buyers and sellers, hawking tamales *y* burritos, tortillas *y* churros, *sopa y camarones*, fruits and vegetables, mole *y* menudo, *sábanas* for the bed, sarapes and blankets, *ollas* for cooking the beans and rice, *cazuelas* for frying eggs, machetes and knives, belts and boots, shirts *y pantalones.*

By noon, the *lotería* had begun. The old men and women, the young boys and girls, entire families sat along the benches and tables beneath the sparse shelter of the thinning trees. Nervously, they thumbed their kernels of *maiz* and listened intently, guarding the hope that they might be the first to cover the lottery card: twelve squares, each square with the picture of an animal or some desired treasure.

"He who bites with his tail ...the crab!" the caller cried amid sad groans or joyful gasps. "He who sang to St. Peter will sing no more ...*¡El gallo!*" he screeched again as a hundred players dropped kernels of corn on the image of a strutting rooster.

I sat at a table, eyeing my card and watching my father walk through the plaza, moving from booth to booth in his capacity as treasurer *municipal*, collecting the day's fees from each merchant.

Antonia appeared with a bag full of corn and two cards. She sat down across the table. She had grown into a short and feisty young woman with the round face of a full moon whose broad smile lured you to listen to her despite the fact that she was constantly talking. Some part of her was always in motion as she described her latest encounter with a friend or her recently formed opinion on almost any subject. I often marveled at how her words flowed as easily as the Río Verde in the rush of a winter storm.

"You were working on the Ferris wheel yesterday. Chela and I were over there to see if it was ready." Her face lit up as she bounced into her sentences. "But only if I see you riding it will I know that it's safe." The lottery caller's voice rang from his booth at the head of the tables.

"The shrimp that sleeps is carried away by the swift ...*¡El camarón!*" He had started a new game.

Toña and I glanced at our cards. She leaned forward and her breasts seemed to offer themselves to me with the dip in the line of her blouse. I felt ashamed that I had not controlled my eyes as Padre *Pesca* had stated we must. "*Custodia oculorum!*" he had warned sternly. "You must guard your eyes!" I searched my card for the picture of the shrimp.

"That's the tallest Ferris wheel I've ever seen. Have you been to the top? That must be scary," Toña continued.

"*El que cantó a* San Pedro will sing no more ...*¡El gallo!*" came the voice again.

"No," I said. "They wouldn't let us. They were still working on it when we left last night. But it's very high."

"A blanket for the poor ...*¡El sol!*"

"You could probably see over the church from up there."

"I'm sure you could see well beyond the river."

The caller's voice pushed through our conversation.

"If you die I will give you ...*¡La corona!*" I dropped a kernel on the crown.

"I don't think I want to go up alone, Sixto. Will you take me later?"

"*Seguro*," I responded, surprised at my lack of hesitation. I had always found Antonia easy to talk to.

"If you're not careful, friend, he will get you ...*¡El diablito!*"

"And afterward, *la olla grande!*" she said. "Round and round! Just like when we were children!"

"*Sí. ¿Cómo no?*" I responded, smiling at the memory of all of us lying on the wide expanse of the fiesta's merry-go-round.

"The world is a ball and we are having a ball ...*¡El mundo!*" the voice barked.

"*Ayer mi mamá* was very angry at me. She thinks I should cut my hair. What do you think, Sixto? I like it this long. What do you think?" I bowed my head and pressed my lips together. If I answered, I would be only telling the truth.

"Do not go sailing with her song ...*¡La sirena!*" came the voice again.

"I think your hair is beautiful," I said softly, wiping away the tingling that I suddenly felt across my face.

"*¿Sabes qué? Mi papá es un cuetero* this year. He says the fireworks will be the best ever. Chelo *y* Toro want me to tell you to sit with us, okay?"

"*Con placer,*" I said.

The following summer, having completed our second year, we three students were back in San Ciro. I spent my days helping my father. The family business was expanding. My uncles had started a boot factory and were demanding more and more hides from the shop.

On a late Sunday morning after Mass, Toro passed by my house. He was on his way to meet up with a group of old friends. He drove his father's truck. Kiko refused to go along because the boys planned a swim in the river and the girls had been invited. Kiko repeated what Padre *Pesca* had said, that dating girls was like throwing a precious glass in the air.

"*Jóvenes*, remember, it takes only one miss and the glass is broken forever."

"You don't know how to have a good time, Kiko!" Toro chided our conscientious comrade for hanging back.

I respected Kiko's opinion, but I had learned on at least two different occasions how to be with Antonia without letting her feel that we could be more than friends. In the end, Toro and I drove to the swimming beach, changed in the truck, then scrambled down the rocky embankment to the sandy shore. Toña and Chelo were already swimming with eight or nine others. Toña greeted me warmly, but then spent most of the time with Paco Moraga. After wading for a half hour up and down the cooling river, I sat on the shallow beach.

"Hello, Sixto." Toña smiled briefly as she passed in front of me, without stopping, on her way back to Paco's side. I couldn't help but notice how beautiful she looked in her bathing suit. For a long time that afternoon, I tried staring just at the trees.

When we were about to return to the seminary for our third year, Toro announced that he would not be going with us.

"You two should stick it out. ¿*Ven*? But I can't stay. ¡Ustedes saben, *las muchachas!*" He waved the palms of his hands apologetically and bade us good luck.

Kiko and I made the trip with four new students who stared out the window of the train in quiet amazement. Padre Joaquín had appointed us, as upperclassmen, to act as *chaperones*. We traveled in silence most of the way. Although we were good friends, without Toro, Kiko and I found very little to talk about.

We had just ended the first game of *fútbol* to start the new semester. I was still in my uniform. I toiled in the woodshop mending the very same wheelbarrow that Kiko had helped to build the year before. Marco Acuña had tried to haul rocks with it and had broken one of the supports. Aurelio Costa was also in the shop, making picture frames. He heard the scratching first and was already removing the painting before I even noticed. I heard Chonita's voice.

"*¡Hola!* How is my little boy?" she asked, glancing toward me.

Aurelio never allowed himself to get excited about anything. He smiled both at me and at the girl with a casual disregard, then started talking to her. I continued my work, trying to be polite while also trying to ignore their quiet conversation.

After a very few moments, Aurelio surprised me by announcing that he had to leave. He gave a friendly gesture of goodbye and walked calmly out of the room. I looked at Chonita and smiled awkwardly. Her face reminded me of the seminary's black-on-brown cat that sat comfortably near the door of the refectory, its dark pupils afloat in a buttery light.

"*Hola, mi Camotito,*" the girl began, tossing her head back and casting her voice across the workbench, "you've been playing soccer. You look suave in that uniform."

"*Gracias,*" I said cautiously.

"Do you still think that I'm the devil? You see ...I've not forgotten."

I had rehearsed this moment in my thoughts many times so that I could say what I needed to say

"I think you're dangerous," I told her as calmly as I could.

"And why am I dangerous?" Chonita challenged amiably.

"*Usted sabe,*" I said.

"No. I don't know."

Now, I felt confused. I wasn't sure if she was mocking me or was sincere.

"We're studying to be priests. We shouldn't be talking to girls alone."

"So priests don't need to know anything about women?" Chonita folded her arms in front of her as if she had just won the debate. "That's where you're wrong, *muchacho*. That's the trouble with priests. They don't know anything about life."

My thoughts were muddled. I didn't want to argue with her, nor did I wish to offend her. I regretted that I had never told Padre *Pesca* about her, yet I wasn't sorry that she had found me here today. I knew that I should leave; but I thought maybe she was right. Maybe I was too scrupulous.

Padre Tomás had warned us about girls, but he had also told us that we shouldn't be afraid to live in the world. If only I were able to relax and talk to her as I could with Toña ...perhaps if I stayed a while. No, she was different. I rose and gathered tools.

"So, you're going to run away *otra vez?*" she asked blithely. "*Mire*, Sixto, before you go, you want to see something? *Venga, acá.*" The girl was smiling mischievously now and beckoning me to the pass-through. I slung the mochila over my shoulder and moved first toward the door and then, at her invitation, back toward the opening. This once, I thought, I would simply shake her hand and leave. As I approached, however, the girl's eyes danced in a way that dissolved the space between us.

I considered returning to my desk or scurrying back to the dormitory; but I knew if I left, this moment with her would end. I was surprised to discover that I didn't want that to happen. "We are alone," I thought. "No one will come into the woodshop so late in the afternoon. What harm to spend a moment more?" As I made the decision to stay, I turned away from the door and toward the girl. I felt my heart beating faster, and the drive to enter into the aura of her eyes was growing stronger.

She continued to smile. I took another step. My stomach was drawing in on itself; and, with the stirring of my blood, I no longer resisted the urge to move closer to her. I dropped the satchel on the floor as she reached out and gently took my hands and placed them in hers.

"You see," she said, pressing her lips contentedly, "we're just friends. Now give me a friendly hug, eh?" I hesitated, but then stepped still closer to the pass-through. I let her draw a circle around her waist with my right arm. Then Chonita leaned toward me and spoke in a casual whisper. "*Mire, Camotito*, would you like to feel something more?"

She cocked her head and again compressed her lips, waiting for an answer. I stood motionless, absorbing her words and curious to know her intentions. I did nothing to escape the cold shiver within my gut and the pounding heat below.

"*Sí. ¿Cómo no?*" I said simply. The girl led my left hand to her breasts. She cupped and rolled my fingers, silently instructing me, pressing my arched palm against the warmth and softness beneath her blouse.

"I like that. Do you?"

"*Sí*," I replied, looking down into her unwavering eyes and sensing that I was treading along the edge of a world that she already inhabited, a world of special knowledge, of power, and of dangerous yet triumphant joy. My lips were now very close to hers. For a moment, I thought that I might kiss her, but then she turned.

"Do you want to see?" she asked. I hesitated, paralyzed in a tangle of desire and fear. The shop behind me had disappeared. I had no thought of courtyard, classroom, or cathedral. I hung motionless, afloat only in this moment, expectant, willing. "Do you?"

"*Sí. ¿Cómo no?*"

My voice, though barely audible, filled the space between us. The girl raised her eyes to the ceiling and rolled her head, slowly easing my hand and arm away from her. Then with a quick move of her fingers, she drew the string on her blouse. With a second move as deft, she cupped her exposed breasts in each hand and raised them to me.

"Here, Sixto," she said, "now you can know something about women!" For the briefest of moments, I stared at the girl's beauty, the raised nipples and honey smooth orbs.

"¡Chonita!" A voice erupted from a corner of the kitchen.

"*¡Mi mamá!*" the girl gasped, tying her blouse and turning toward the wall opposite the direction of the voice. "*¡Ahorita vengo!*" she called over her shoulder. "*Adiós*, Sixto," she whispered, then pushed the panel door closed and was gone.

I stood for a long moment staring at the cream-colored partition. At last, I picked up the picture and hung it over the pass-through. I walked to the door and out into the hallway. My heart had ceased its pounding. The cool shaking within and the hot race of my blood had subsided.

In the days ahead when I thought about Chonita, I experienced neither guilt nor regret over my brief moments with her; still, after that day, I never again visited the woodshop.

I never again saw her, nor did I ever again feel with the same
confidence that I would someday be a priest like Padre Joaquín.

In the middle of our third year, we again came home for the
Christmas holidays. Kiko and I helped as always in the parish.
We worked in the auditorium on the banners and piñatas. We
set up the tables and benches and hung the decorations.

On a Saturday morning after mass, I entered the rectory
for breakfast. Padre Joaquín's mother and his younger sister
were there visiting from Rioverde. The girl, Verónica, was my
age. I had seen her before, but we had not talked more than
three times. She was very friendly and very beautiful with the
chiseled features of an Aztec queen.

"Have you been practicing the piano, Sixto?" Padre
Joaquín asked as the housekeeper and his mother rose to clear
the plates.

"*Un poquito*, padre," I replied.

"Verónica plays very well. *¡Venga!* She can entertain us."

I followed the priest and his mother and sister into the
living room. The lamps and furnishings, the shelves, the books,
and the pictures had always made me feel comfortable ever
since my days as a young acolyte. I sat and listened quietly
as the young woman played Christmas songs, including "*A la
nanita nana*," my favorite. After a moment, the housekeeper
summoned Padre Joaquín. He did not return for half an hour.

"Would you like to learn one?" Verónica asked. Her mother smiled at me and nodded approval.

"The first one," I said.

I sat next to her at the piano and watched her hands caress the keys, drawing from them the melancholy lullaby. Her fingers were as fragile and smooth as those of the delicately carved saints near the main altar in the church. She took my hands and guided them on the keyboard as I struggled to learn the patterns; but I had not practiced enough to play the chords and the melody together as she could.

Despite my fumbling, her gentle warmth encouraged me. My fingers followed the lead of her touch. "*A la nanita nana, nanita ella, nanita ella.*" She sang the words softly, and I joined her. Then I pulled back my hands to listen and watch. She played with elegance more direct and powerful even than the vast expanse of the *santuario* in San Luis, more beautiful than the song and ritual of a midnight *posada*, more eternal than the speckled sky above San Ciro. "*Mi Jesús tiene sueño, bendito sea, bendito sea.*"

As our voices blended, I rose from the chair and stood behind Verónica; and with feelings of comfort and courage that until then I had not known, I placed my hands on her shoulders and sang the words. I sang, as Padre Benito would have described it, without fear and trembling.

This moment fell upon me, like the final blows of *el palo* against the swinging piñata. My emotions released a wellspring of questions and doubts about the path of my life. I acknowledged to myself for the first time that perhaps I would not, after all, exchange the very real mysteries of a woman like Verónica for the mysteries promised in *el Santuario de Guadalupe.*

No sooner had Christmas festivities ended than, once again, we began our preparations for the feast of San Ciro. The celebration, with its carnival and dances, parades and rodeo events, continued for nine days.

In the mornings, the riders, some spinning their lariats to ready themselves for the coming competition, filed through the plaza on their way to the *charreada*. The slap of hooves against the pavement overwhelmed the voices of children playing and the trumpets and drums from a distant band. In the midst of the clatter, I wandered through the crowds, revisiting in my mind the warmth of Verónica's body next to me as she had played the piano. I couldn't subdue the questions and doubts she had raised.

I knew that I must make a decision to return. How could I abandon the gift that I had been given? It was impossible to think that I wouldn't return; yet, unlike previous years, the thought of returning did not make me happy. More and more, I had been struggling with the decision. More and more, I had been thinking about what my life might be like if I were to decide not to become a priest.

In the evening, under a string of dim yellow bulbs, I stood apart, watching the couples dancing and pausing between songs to laugh and chat, to hug, to kiss.

Pera approached. She was another childhood friend who was becoming a young woman. Her amber eyes met mine. I had never before noticed that she wore lipstick.

"Sixto, I'm running for queen! Will you buy a ticket?"

"Of course," I answered, pulling twenty *centavos* from my pocket.

"*¡Gracias! ¡Te amo!*" she said, laughing. Then without warning, she raised herself up and kissed me on the lips and brushed by me. Startled, I turned to watch her moving happily through the plaza, my mouth tingling with a strange sweetness. Esperanza Estrada, whom I had known all of my life, had just given me my first kiss, my first real kiss from a girl, from a girl my own age.

I turned back to watch the couples dancing, savoring the scent of steaming bathwater and perfume that had, for a brief moment, engulfed me and had at the same moment quashed the dust and the noise around me. I stood in silence, my heart beating too fast.

Padre Joaquín never failed to warn us when we arrived for the Christmas holiday.

"When you see a pretty girl, don't think about her. Pretty girls are not for you. You must guard your eyes to guard your vocation. You must be especially careful of the lint pickers. They are the friendly ones who will pinch your sweater to remove a speck of lint or a thread, and pretty soon, they'll take your arm and want to go for a walk...."

As the dust and noise of the fiesta slowly returned, I found myself asking: Why must I always feel like an outsider? Why must I be the one who is different? Maybe I'm not really different. Maybe I just haven't thought enough about what I am doing and why.

Again, I ambled through the crowd. I decided to pretend that I would not return to the seminary just to see what it would feel like to be independent, free to do as I pleased, to dance with Verónica, or Pera, or Toña; but the experiment changed nothing. I couldn't really dance with them, or touch them, or kiss them.

I left the crowds. I walked past the *zócalo* where the band had settled for the evening. Two of my uncles sat among the *conjunto* with their horns ready. At the corner of the square, I trudged up the stone steps and pulled the iron ring on the church's heavy wooden door. The dark interior, with its smoked stone walls and hanging tapestries, held the smell of time passing. I pushed myself forward down the aisle, clasping my heart as if to surround and buttress its onerous burden. I was alone in the expanse of the apse. All was quiet. All was still except the wavering candles. I knelt on a front pew and folded my eyes into the palms of my hands.

"My God," I prayed, "what am I to do? What am I to be?"

The emotions of the day welled up. I began to sob without control. Through my tears, I saw myself again as a boy, chasing the globe into the muddy lagoon. My fervid mind fell upon the image of Padre Benito and the stories of the great monsters in the books of literature.

"A priest's life is to overcome the monsters that frighten us all, yet this work is not for the priests alone. It's for the great and small, the visionaries and leaders, the seers, the artists, and poets. They must show us how to look beyond what *is* to the Ought To Be!" The priest's words pounded in my head: "One must ever pursue Beauty, *mis jovenes*, and overcome Darkness with Beauty's light; Beauty is Truth. It is Wholeness. It is the Totality. Some see only what is in front of them, what *is*. Beauty is a vision of the Ought To Be, the Totality. When we dream, when we envision a greater good and struggle to realize that vision, we change the world; and in changing the world, we touch Eternity!"

Even if I am not to be a priest, I avowed, I will not abandon this pursuit of my soul. Beads of sweat lay on my forehead. My shoulders still rocked with emotion. Finally, I wiped away my tears. I sat in the pew, staring at the reredos with its ornamental pillars framing the crucified Christ. The heritage of Spain surrounded me: the dome above, the ancient portraits of dark and bloodied Saints hanging on the rough-hewn walls. The image of Padre Bartolomé, our history teacher, arose.

"For three hundred years, the Spaniards exploited Mexico, then other Europeans did the same, and finally the *americanos*. For the past fifty years, our people have exploited each other! We seem to know no other way of life."

The priest's image faded, but the question remained: What was left for my generation? As a priest, the table would be set for me. I thought I knew all there was to know about the life that Padre Joaquín led. As a layman living in the world, however, with freedom to follow my own path wherever it led, how would I find my way? Would I spawn a new revolution like Zapata or Villa in a country still reeling from the decimation of the centuries? With my temper, my passion, and my thirst for justice, would I encounter the kind of monsters who had slain my grandfather? Would I vanquish them as fully and completely as I had beaten the bully of San Ciro, Popo García?

I returned to the decision at hand. If I leave, *mi mamá y mis abuelitos* will cry. Padre Joaquín will say, "You have come so far. Do not turn back now." I wondered: Is it only the dread of telling my parents and Padre Joaquín that drives me to continue my studies?

That night I lay on my cot, the struggle in my head and heart unrelenting. To my family and childhood friends, I had become a serious and quiet young man. For three years, I had wrestled with the fire in my stomach that I had known to burst forth when provoked. Under the tutelage of Fr. Díaz and the other priests, I had learned accommodation and reflection. I had learned to avoid confrontations and assertions that led inevitably to an explosion of temper. Still, I wondered what I would become without the priests' calming presence to guide me. What would I be without the seminary to enfold me in the fluidity of its daily life of pray, study, and work? The people of San Ciro knew that I had wanted to be a priest.

"Señora Torres, you must be very proud," they said when they met *mamá* on the street.

I was most grateful for all I had learned because of Padre Joaquín; but beneath the veneer of my life, an urgency and passion was growing, was leading me, not to question the past but to question how faithful I could be to the life of a priest. My anger I had always had with me, but now this second fire as strong as or stronger than that first had invaded my loins. This knotted pulse of passion and desire stirred unabated; and, as a priest, would remain unabated until the day I died.

After many nights lying sleepless, at last I acknowledged to myself what my heart was telling me. I must speak the truth to my parents and to the padre. They must accept it. The truth was that I could not go forward. I wanted something else for my life. I could not follow in Padre Joaquín's footsteps. I was not Padre Joaquín. God forgive me! I did not want to be Padre Joaquín!

I awoke knowing that I would have to speak. I was afraid, yet I felt an inner peace because I knew that once I had revealed my decision, my life would change forever. This burden would disappear.

As I left the house, I found that my eyes and my mind were magically recreating my *pueblito*. Every tree, every building, every foot of stone pathway appeared to me new and fresh as if I were seeing it all for the first time, as if I were again making that first journey on the train to San Luis Potisí. The leaves on the trees glistened sharply. Even the dogs barking as I passed filled me with joy and excitement to be alive and moving into an unknown future. Now my world contained boundless possibilities. My life was no longer on a fixed course.

In the evening, I stood among the crowd to watch the fireworks. Kiko passed by with his parents.

"When will Toro return from *la capital*?" Kiko asked. "It would be good to see him before we have to go back ...or maybe he will stop to visit at school."

"*¿Quién saben?*" I responded.

I felt uncomfortable and stared straight ahead. Kiko and his family continued on their way as the sound of a small orchestra, with its trumpet, guitars, and accordion, drifted through the trees and above the noise of the crowded plaza. The clap of fireworks shooting into the sky broke through the music. Then I heard the cheerful lilt of Toña's voice.

"Do you like *los cuetes*?" She pointed to the purple and rose lightning falling above us. She was carrying her shoes. "I shouldn't have worn these heels. They're killing my feet."

The "Aahs" of the townspeople signaled yet another burst of multicolored spikes illuminating the night.

Toña's smile graced her round moonlike face.

"How have you been, *Camotito*? I've hardly had a chance to say hello to you in six weeks. What's been keeping you? Padre Joaquín has you working day and night. Is that it?"

"*Mi papá* has needed my help. It's a busy time of the year for him and my uncles."

"What? You're supposed to be on vacation. And when do you return to your seminary—your monk life?" She made it a habit to tease me until I also would have to smile. I didn't answer immediately and then realized that I needed to say something or risk giving away my secret.

"One more week."

Toña felt the hesitation and eyed me suspiciously.

"So you're going back?"

"That's the plan."

She shrugged and nodded.

"I'm sure it's a good plan. And I'm sure you'll be happy in your chosen career. Take care of yourself, Sixto." With that, she reached up and gave me a quick kiss on the cheek.

"*Nos vemos.*"

She moved into the crowd.

I was sorry not to have told Kiko and Toña, but I felt that they should not be the first to know. Finally, late that night when the rest of the family was in bed, I told my parents.

"I am not going back."

"*¡Ay! Dios mío!*" my mother gasped.

"Are you sure, Sixto?" my father asked.

"*Sí, papi.* I am sure."

"But why? We thought you were happy there." My mother's eyes were already filling with tears.

"I don't know. I just know I cannot go back. I am sorry."

They sat together for a moment without speaking.

"Have you told the priest?" my father asked.

"Not yet."

The next morning, everyone in the household was upset. *Mamá* sat in her room throughout the day crying softly. *Papá* stayed in the hide shop, working in silence with the younger children. I wandered in and out of the house, suspended between guilt and exaltation. I had abandoned the gift. I didn't know how I could turn away after having been so blessed; yet in the very act of turning, a kind of exaltation had lifted me beyond the moment of pain, even the pain that *mi mamá* was feeling. I walked to the rectory to speak to Padre Joaquín. I couldn't put it off any longer.

"But, *joven*," the priest said in an exasperated tone, "you have come so far ...so much to give . . ."

I tried to listen but my mind drifted.

"I'm sorry.... *Lo siento mucho*, padre."

That afternoon, again in the plaza, I looked for Kiko or Toña. My sense of relief and excitement moved me to share the news freely. Couples sat on the benches holding hands, whispering, hugging. My uncles and their brass ensemble played in a far off corner. A group of teenagers had gathered in front of the church. There, as always during the fiesta, a thick trunk of encina had been sunk deep into the ground. It rose twelve feet into the crisp January air.

¡*Veinticinco centavos!*" barked Felipe Gómez, the parish gardener and handyman.

In his hand, he held a thin pole with a glimmering rag tied to the end. He dipped the rag into a bucket of lard set near the edge of the path and smeared the lard up and down the staked and polished shaft as high as he could reach.

"Twenty-five cents for a chance to take home *un peso de plata!*" He finished swabbing and laid the rag on the ground only to grab another thinner pole fitted with a tiny cup at one end. He flashed a silver dollar around the circle of onlookers.

"*Veinticinco centavos* to climb to the top. Nothing to it! Take home the silver dollar!"

I joined the circle between Eliseo and *el* Flaco. They welcomed me readily, laughing and jostling, pushing each other toward the post. El Flaco pulled off his shirt, exposing his bony, adolescent frame. Felipe raised the cup to the very top of the post and neatly dropped the silver piece onto the flat surface above.

"Go get it, Flaco!" The young man approached the smooth, slick pole. He embraced it amid shouts of encouragement.

"Hold on! Tighter! Climb!" Flaco grunted and kicked, but soon fell back streaked with sweat and lard.

"*¡Otra!*" shouted Felipe. Davíd Barajas stepped into the ring of onlookers, struggled momentarily toward the top, but fared no better.

"*¡Otra!*" shouted Felipe. In a fit of exhilaration, I tore off my shirt and kicked off my shoes. Eager hands pushed me forward.

"¡Sixto! ¡Sixto!" they chanted and clapped. "¡Sixto! ¡Sixto!" "*¡Agárralo*, Sixto!"

I grasped the *palo* and pressed the barrel of my chest against it. Slowly I climbed, wrapping my legs and forcing my bare heels along the rounded surface. I was three feet off the ground and making progress. I struggled to four feet, higher than the others had gone.

"¡Sixto! ¡Sixto!" the chant continued.

At five feet, unable to hold on longer, I lunged for the coin. I slapped at the rough lip along the upper edge of the pole, but my fingers fell short of the mark as my grip faltered and I tumbled downward. I lay on the ground, exhausted and grimy. The circle of voices erupted again.

"¡Popo! ¡Popo!"

I pulled myself up in time to see Popo García begin the labored ascent. The crowd cheered as he shinnied upward, reaching four feet in a matter of seconds. I wished I had waited. Popo would have the best chance now that the pole was nearly clean of the lard. His ample muscles and frame churned against the wood. He paused and gathered his strength.

"¡Popo! ¡Popo!" The crowd urged him onward.

In a sudden thrust, he gained another foot. He hesitated again, his face strained, jaw jutting, eyes squinting. At six feet he looked up, set his sights, and flung his arm at the upper edge of the pole. Like the tongue of a snake, his fingers lapped at the coin and held it tight as he fell to earth in a rush of cheers and applause.

"*¡El palo encebado!*" Felipe called as the crowd dispersed.

"Come back in one hour. Try again to climb the slathered pole. One hour from now!"

I walked toward the *lotería*. Toña sat holding her pieces of corn. She watched me approach.

"I spoke with Padre Joaquín. I'm not going back," I said.

"I know," she responded with a gentle and consoling smile.

CHAPTER THREE

Of course, I didn't return to seminary. For a month I worked in my father's shop, but my heart was not there. My mind was full of the larger world beyond San Ciro that I had discovered through my studies. My parents knew that I was restless.

"If you're not happy here, *m'ijo*, perhaps it's best for you to go to Mexico City and stay with your *tía* Chita and *tío* Mayolino." *Mi mamá* smiled softly, her eyes full of love and resignation.

"We called them last night," my father said. "And they're happy to take you in. *Tío* thinks he can find you some work, and you can finish your schooling."

"Thank you," I said sadly.

Chita picked me up at the train station in *la capital*. She was in her late twenties. The youngest and prettiest of my aunts, she had always been my favorite.

"Welcome, *sobrino*!" she called to me from the platform as I stepped off the train. She hugged me warmly. "Now you will see the world's most beautiful city!"

As promised, my *tío* Mayolino found a job for me moving furniture. Each night I returned from work by bus and walked up the sixteen marble steps to their apartment. The couple had no children. They were happy to have me there, to give me support, and share their lives with me.

"And where will you carry the beds and couches today, *mi sobrino?*" Chita asked when I left for work in the morning;" and "Don't let that Macias fellow take advantage of you, just because you can carry twice as much as him;" and "Be careful of your back. No job is worth killing yourself over."

"There is no better way to learn about who is who and what is where than moving furniture, *joven*," my uncle declared, holding their small black terrier. "Moving furniture, you see the whole city. You know everything there is to know. Who's doing what to whom! Who is going up and who is coming down." *Tío* Mayolino laughed louder than anyone at his own jokes. "Sit down. Dinner is not for half an hour. Here, *una cerveza* . . ."

That had been my evening routine for three years and my uncle had been correct on all counts. Now I knew every street in Mexico City and all the corners of every one of the neighborhoods and many of the most important residents. Who knows what might have come from that education?

One evening, near the top of the stairway, I saw that Chita was not herself. Her dark eyes were pink, and her smooth skin was cracked from too many tears. The couple led me in silence into the apartment. Whatever the problem, I thought, *mi tía* had finished her crying before my arrival. I felt her concentrating all of her attention on me. With every step into the living room, I sensed her growing stronger and more controlled. When, finally, she spoke, it was in short firm phrases.

"Sit down, Sixto. We have some bad news. We must leave immediately for San Ciro. Your father is very ill ...an infection ...He is dying. They say ...nothing can be done."

Within a few hours, Chita and I had boarded the *autobús* to Ciudad Valles and then the train. I leaned against the window of our berth as the sleeper rolled through the darkness, toward Tamasopo and Cardenas and on to Rioverde. Chita sat next to

me. I was grateful to have her there but did not wish to talk.
Throughout the long night, I fought against the stark finality
expressed by her words. She had said all she had to say—all that
she knew.

"He is dying. Nothing can be done."

Over and over, these words plagued me. This is crazy ...*está
loco! Mi pa*pá is not dying ...*Mi papá es fuerte* ...the strongest ...That's
what all of his friends always said.... *"Su pap*á is the tallest, the most
handsome, *ve* ...*es el más fuerte* ...Stronger than any man in San Ciro.
He can lift a whole hide when it is soaking wet—over his head! He
can lift seventeen dry ones all at once. Who else can do that, *ves?*
Su papá is a good man, Sixto.... *Su papá* has been elected as delegate
of the *ejidos*, Sixto. No one else could have organized *los ejidos*. You
should be proud, *joven!"*

I remember the elderly men, coming in the dry dusk.

"Fili, *amigo, mire, hombre* ...You know we have had no rain
this year.... Could you spare some corn?"

"*Sí*, Rigoberto. ¿*Cómo no?* Sixto, take our friend to the store
room and get him *un saco de maíz....*"

"Fili, look at how they treat us. *El ejido* has no place to meet....
They push us into this tiny school room like we are nothing...."

"Señores, I want you to listen to this idea I want you to
believe in it. We *can* build our own *centro ejidal....* Each of you must
commit to your share ...*dinero* and volunteer hours. . . ."

"*Tu papá*, Sixto, organized the whole thing. ¿Ve? He kept the
money in a coffee can. You should be proud. ¿*Ve?* The building is
there because of him."

When we arrived at the house, *mi mamá y mis tíos* were there
with my younger brothers and sisters. They greeted me with silent
and distracted nods. *Mamá* hugged me without a word and then sat
listless and subdued. My uncles, agitated, spoke in tense whispers.

"*El doctor* did nothing!" My father's younger brother, Alex, stood between them and the closed door of *papa's* bedroom. "For two days, he did nothing. *¡Nada!* Imagine, a thorn in the foot, and he did nothing! He should have gone for *la medicina*! He did nothing!" My uncle waved his hand at Chita and paced in anger and disbelief. "Now today, he goes, but everyone knows it's too late. The poison has taken hold!"

Chita came to me.

"Your father knows that you're here."

In silence, I followed my mother into *papi's* bedroom as my aunt and the others waited behind. The morning sun brought its warmth and light to the narrow room. My father's hands, large and cracked, lay on the blanket. They were still dark with a burgundy veneer from the tubs and the *tinte*. His eyes were half closed. *Mamá* moved sadly toward the bed. Upon hearing the steps, my father opened wide his eyes and stared at me with a desperate concentration, pushing himself forward and struggling to reach me.

"Fili," *mamá* murmured, "don't move too much." She placed a chair for me. I bent to kiss *papá's* forehead, even as the familiar arms embraced me with unexpected strength. I struggled to speak.

"*Te amo, papi*," I whispered.

"Sixto, how good that you've come! I've been waiting." My father spoke in a strained and dampened voice. *Mamá* cried. He gripped my hand intensely as if to ensure that I wouldn't leave. "Sixto," he said with fervor, "you are *el más grande*, Sixto. I need you to help your mother until the rest are grown. You must take charge of your brothers and sisters."

I stared into his eyes, searching for words that could bring them comfort. I hesitated.

"*Si, papi*," I whispered.

"No! No!" My father's voice, now familiar in its strength, rang with urgency. He let go of my hand and grabbed at my *chamarra. ¡No! ¡Prométemelo!* This pain is nothing to me. Promise me this! Promise me that you will stay with them until they know how to work!" The words burst from deep in his throat. His great chest beneath the covers lurched in a fit of coughing. Still he repeated, "*¡Prométemelo! ¡Prométemelo!*"

I reached for his hand again and was surprised to hear my own voice loud and strong.

"*Sí, papi*, I promise!" My father lay back breathing deeply. He coughed again and spit into a rag. I stared at him, feeling empty and afraid.

Within three days, my dear *papi*, Filiberto Torres, died of blood poisoning from the prick of a thorn in his foot because the doctor did not think it was serious and waited too long to travel the thirty-five kilometers to Rioverde for the antibiotic that surely would have saved him.

Before I arrived at the church that morning, I had thought that I might somehow avoid the funeral, but I knew that I must attend. I would attend. I must be present with my family. I found the service strangely comforting, even as I resented the God that had allowed my father to die so senselessly.

Since returning to San Ciro and with the death of my beloved *papá*, I walked about as if I were an alien in senselessly familiar surroundings. I couldn't imagine life in San Ciro without *mi papá* among us. After the Mass, we trod the five blocks from the church to *el Campo Santo* and watched in silence as my father's brothers lowered his body into the grave.

My mother had wailed and wept throughout the morning. At the graveside, again, she moaned in anguish. It was not until someone handed me the shovel and I had tossed the dry soil and had heard its thrump against the wooden casket that the tears came to me. I couldn't stop my thick shoulders from shaking uncontrollably. Emotion heaved through me as I backed down off the piled earth. Then, Chita was at my side, embracing and filling my senses with her fragrance and warmth, but my tearful grieving didn't cleanse me of my anger.

Later, the mourners gathered at the church hall. I stood outside with my brothers and uncles. The *pendejo* doctor suddenly exited from his car. As soon as I saw him, the rage welled up and overtook me. I moved quickly down the dirt path, grabbed the unsuspecting man by his coat, and shook him, screaming into his frightened eyes.

"Why didn't you go to Rioverde *en su automóvil? Idiota,* sitting here waiting for the *autobús!*"

I threw him to the ground before my uncles finally restrained me. After that, each morning, I felt more lost and empty as I observed both my mother's struggle just to rise from her solitary bed and my family's struggle to cope with its daily routine.

I wandered over the cold brick floors of our home. I passed back
and forth by my mother's room, listening to her quiet sobs. She
was exhausted and inconsolable. My father's sisters and brothers
stayed on as long as they could, but eventually they had to return
to their own homes and to their own families and jobs. Before
departing, some urged me to continue working the tanning shop.

"It's the best way," they advised. "How else can you fulfill
the promise to your father to care for everyone?" I listened but
said little.

My sister, Licha, now twelve, cooked the meals and tried
to hold the daily routine together. She cared for the younger
siblings as best she could while my brothers and I struggled
to fulfill orders for the leather hides that had lain unattended
during our father's illness. Fourteen-year-old Enrique and Polo,
now ten, carried the canisters of water up the hill to the waiting
tubs. Juanito took his place on the shop bench, laboring with his
bent fingers and twisted arms to strip *la cascara* from the trunks
of *el timbe y la encina* as I once had done. He pounded the bark
with the same rusty hatchet to make the dyes.

Through the morning hours, I scudded flesh and hair.
The anger within my gut tore against the scragged underside of
the raw pelts. As I scraped the tissue, Enrique's gangling frame
shuffled through the narrow door. My brother dumped the two
wooden buckets and eyed the latest hide thrown on the pile near
the tubs. He then glanced warily at me as I stopped to sharpen
the fleshing knife. I had not worked in the shop for over two
years. Enrique was not accustomed to having me back.

"You ripped this one!" he snapped, holding up the topmost
skin and exposing a torn center. He knew at once the source of
my blunder. He had watched me earlier in the morning barely
controlling the blade against my now familiar fits of anger.
Enrique feared that I would damage other hides as badly.

"You're not helping doing the job this way!" he barked across the room.

"*¡Chíngate!*" I retorted sullenly.

I turned and scowled at him. He stood silent and stunned at my unfamiliar use of profanity. After a moment, he continued his work. He laid the damaged skin on a corner pile of seconds, which only served to re-kindle my temper and drove me to give full vent to my fury. I threw the knife toward the foot of the fleshing pole and tramped across the muddied cement. I stepped out of the dank shop and into the warming sun.

A dozen brown and yellow chicks peeped at my feet. Bruto, the family's scruffy, shorthaired hound, nosed my trousers and apron. I bent over and scratched the dog's tattered ear. Of course, I knew I had scoured too deeply. Of course, I knew that my father, if he were here, wouldn't tolerate my careless tearing at the hides. I didn't need Enrique to tell me that.... The dog licked my grubby work boots.... I kicked at the mutt awkwardly, missing my mark and sending the chicks in all directions. An anxious mother hen cackled disapprovingly near the egg shed. I stood impervious to the disturbance I had caused. I scalped the ground with one boot. I was ashamed of my eruption. I had never used such language with my younger siblings. I would have to apologize.

My thoughts ran from my *papá* to my life in the seminary, the education that I had received and left behind, *la capital*, *tío* Mayolino and *tía* Chita's home, the daily routine, loading the van with furniture and moving through the back streets of the city. How would I keep my family together? I hadn't even completed my secondary schooling. I stepped again into the shop. I grabbed a fresh hide.

I remembered the courses that I still had to take to receive my high school diploma. Before the day of the telephone call, *tía* Chita had helped me to enroll in evening classes, mainly science and history. Now I was uncertain about everything. I needed no certificate to work in a tiny tannery in San Ciro de Acosta. When Enrique returned with the brimming canisters, I waited until he had emptied them.

"I'm sorry, *mano*," I said. "*Mira.*" I showed him how carefully I had scraped the new hide now hanging on the fleshing pole.

My thoughts turned back to my father's funeral. I had watched Padre Joaquín sprinkle the casket with holy water. I had listened impassively as the priest intoned the "*Dies Irae.*" The padre's voice was no longer as vibrant and clear as I remembered it. His aging body moved more slowly now, and he labored to swing the tarnished silver censer. He encircled the casket with the acolyte following near to grasp the heavy lapel of the black, gold-laced chasuble, thereby freeing the priest's arm as he lifted the smoking bowl toward heaven. The air grew dense with the aroma of burning incense.

I remembered the numerous funeral masses that I had served as an acolyte. How simple and distant was that life. I felt detached from it, although I couldn't say why. My aunt and uncle no longer practiced their faith, no longer appeared at weekly Mass, and I seldom found my way to the worship now that I was on my own.

Mayolino and Chita disagreed with the rest. Before departing, they took me to a quiet corner of the house to say that I should consider bringing everyone back to Mexico City, where I still had a job and where I could finish my education.

"Can you be happy living in San Ciro?" Chita asked. "I think I know you well enough, Sixto, to see what will happen. You will grow very bored and impatient. You are a searcher, *mi sobrino*" She reached up to pat my shoulder, for I was now a head taller than her. "You need a larger space than San Ciro can provide to find what will be your life's work."

The days passed. I came to the realization that the family and I could not stay in this place. The pieces of my father's life—the relationships and the daily routine—were too fragile to rebuild. My father's strength had held them together.

Late one evening, I spoke to my mother in whispers so as not to disturb the sleeping siblings.

"*Mamá*," I said, "I had never thought that you and *papi* would leave San Ciro, but we can't stay here. Without *papi*, *la tañería* will fail. Everything is changing. The Serranos, *usted sabe*, their shop was growing even before *papi* died. Already, some are giving their orders to them. Before long, Licha and the boys will have to return to school. Serrano knows that we can't keep up. Even the uncles will soon grow impatient when we can't meet their orders."

My mother stood at the far side of the table. Her faded print dress hung loosely to her ankles, her hair in a tight bun. Since *papa's* death, her once high spirits had softened. Her cheeks had grown dry. Her mood drifted between thoughtful and elusive. Her spent eyes looked past my shoulder, surveying the tiny sink and stove where she had worked the better part of her life. She stepped forward and settled slowly into a chair. She said nothing. At last, she reached across the table and took my hand in hers.

"The shop was your father's life," she said, her voice barely audible. "I understand that it's not for you, but you must give me some time to decide. Perhaps we'll stay here. Perhaps we'll go. We'll talk again."

Four days later my mother agreed to leave the house and furniture, the animals and the crops, and move to Mexico City. She had already spoken to her brother. She looked at me sadly yet with resolve.

"*Tío* Manuel will take care of things here," she said, "until he can sell it all."

I was surprised that she had accepted the move so readily; yet, within two weeks, we had packed what we needed for the trip and had boarded the *autobús* to the capital, where I could continue my work and where my siblings and I could finish our schooling.

Mayolino and Chita helped us to find an apartment within blocks of their own home. I returned to moving furniture from morning until sunset. I took classes during the evening hours or sat at the table studying. I had a special interest in the history of Mexico with its continuing struggles.

The siblings also enrolled in school. My mother slowly recovered. She grew to accept what she could not change and began again to care for the smaller children and take her place at the stove.

Finally, after four years of intermittent classes and makeup tests, I earned my *certificado*, but it served only to make me restless once again. Day after day, I continued moving furniture; but more and more, I was growing weary of the droning and strenuous routine. I wandered through the house from room to room, planning and waiting for the right moment to share my ideas with my mother. My studies had fed my wanderlust, and my reading of the daily news had convinced me that my family could expect little improvement in our threadbare existence so long as we stayed in Mexico City, so long as we stayed in Mexico itself.

I had heard of the money to be made *en el Norte*, across the border in the United States. I had seen the young bravados returning at the end of the harvest season, parading down *la Calle Princi*pal to show off their Stetsons and Levi's, carrying their battery-operated transistor radios with names like Philco and Zenith, and wearing their gold Timex watches.

"We should go north for the work," I told my mother. "There are more jobs available across the border and higher pay." I expected her to resist; I didn't let up. "I can see what is happening here, *mamá*. The economy is growing a little, but you know as well as I do that in this country, the benefits never filter down to those at the bottom. Even Mayolino agrees. In my job I'm stuck in neutral." Night after night, I continued to push my arguments.

"You have other sons coming along, *mamá*. Soon they, too, will need employment. They, too, have their dreams for something better. They will not find it here.... *¡Vamos al Norte, madrecita!*" My mother sat silent as she had done in San Ciro.

"Everyone agrees there's more opportunity *en los Estados Unidos!* Juan and Enrique and Licha, they will all get a better education. It's a rich country, *mamá*. We'll do well there, and if we don't make it, we can always come back."

After months of late-night conversation, I convinced my mother to pack the cardboard boxes and wrap them with twine, to bundle the children and board the *autobús* to Matehuala and points north. In reality, I believe, she agreed

only because she had relatives in Monterrey and in the Río
Grande Valley. I believe she thought that, in due time, I would
tire of this new adventure and want to return home.

We traveled in crowded, melting buses through the listless
desert in the company of crying children, squalling hens,
squealing pigs, and gunnysacks pungent with the smell of
too-ripe corn and beans. We stopped in Matamoros. After
searching in three directions and wearing out the cab driver
amidst the dusty back roads beyond the city, we found the
home of Don Ramón Yáñez and his wife Josefa, friends of my
mother's sister, Julia, who lived across the Río Bravo in Santa
Maria.

The Yañez couple had seven children. They owned a
modest ranch named La Palma on which they raised cotton
and vegetables. *Tía* Julia had arranged for us to live in the
guesthouse near La Palma's grand *hacienda*. In this way, we
would have work and prepare ourselves for the eventual
crossing into the United States.

That evening, as a cooling breeze swept down from the
Sierra de la Iguana, I met their eldest daughter, a strikingly
beautiful woman named Elida. We eyed each other across
the room while her mother showed us our quarters. We felt
the warmth of our bodies as we brushed by each other in the
narrow hall while the beds were being made up for the night.

In those first moments, Elida's dark, deep-set eyes and her black hair spilling over her shoulders, down the small of her back to her slender waist seized my heart and mind. I watched her movements as, with a quiet confidence, she joined in the preparations and slyly returned my appreciative glances.

I soon learned that although in her mid-twenties, Elida had little experience with men. The ranch was far from town, and few visitors passed by except those looking for work. Don Ramón insisted that no mere worker was worthy of his daughter's attention. Her duty, as the eldest, was to concentrate on the well-being of her family and the household. The years came and went; few suitors were available and none were permitted to pursue her.

The day after our arrival, with the midsummer sun already baking the prickly plants, my family and I worked the cotton. I joined the crew assigned to loading the wagons. My mother and older siblings were strapped with gangly white sacks that straggled behind until each picker had stuffed them with hundreds of white puffs of fiber laced with seed. When the bulky bags were full, the pickers dragged them to the loaders for dumping then waited in silence, fanning themselves against the pitiless sun until the loaders tossed the empty sacks at their feet. Then they returned to the grueling trek up and down the rows of spikey branches.

Within days of our coming to La Palma, Elida and I found moments to meet and converse among the hidden corners of the ranch's outbuildings. Considering our mutual lack of experience in such matters, the conversations flowed easily as we shared stories of our childhood and schooling.

"I studied to be a priest," I revealed to her as we both leaned against the back wall of the shed where the seed was stripped from the cotton.

"You?" Elida cried. "It's not possible!"

I laughed. "I was very young then."

Through the summer, my family and I bore the curse of the workday's choking heat. The unfailing arrival of gentle and cooling sea breezes signaled day's end. Only then might we find comfort and refreshment, sitting on the narrow porch of the modest two-bedroom guesthouse. As the weeks progressed, the moments and conversations between Elida and me grew longer and our meetings grew bolder. Often in the early evening, Elida slipped out to join me for walks along La Palma's dry and weed-lined dirt roads.

On one such evening, as the sun melted beneath a scatter of burnt orange clouds, I asked about something that had become important to me.

"How can it be that you have no boyfriend?"

"There is no one," Elida answered. "Not since I left school. That was almost ten years ago." We noted the darkening horizon and turned back toward the distant ranch houses and sheds. "This is a lonely place," she continued. "*Usted sabe*. My parents need me. Besides, who are you to talk? You're still taking care of your family, as well." She laughed easily.

As we walked, I took her hand for the first time.

"You're a beautiful woman, Elida. I can't stop looking at you, thinking about you, and wondering if I have any chance—"

Elida cut me off.

"My father will never allow it." Her dismissal came spontaneously. "You're just one of his workers. To him, you're a *peón*. You know that. You have no *ranchito*, no wealth." Her tone turned to bitterness. "That disqualifies you."

I took another step, then stopped and faced her.

"I'm not asking about your father. I'm asking if you find me attractive. Do I have a chance with you, father or no father?"

Elida gazed at me.

"I see what is in your eyes, Sixto. I see in them a solemn urgency, a passion, a conviction to find where the path of your life will take you. That first moment, I thought, he's cute ...even handsome." She smiled and stepped backward. She cocked her head and surveyed me up and down. "And despite your sometimes brusque manner, those eyes, the high cheekbones, the curly black hair, the trimmed mustache, the six-foot frame, barreled chest, and rich bass voice all combine to impress and persuade."

By now, I was laughing and assuming a grandiose posture. I affirmed her statement with feigned superiority, holding my head high and pushing my chin forward with an antic smile.

"*¡Cierto!*" I acclaimed. "I am the ideal blend of the ancient and noble Aztec and the marauding and rapacious Spaniard; and it is in this guise that I come to steal you away." Her laughing only encouraged me to continue. "I am the firstborn son of the president of the Municipal Council of San Ciro de Acosta and the grandson of his father, who held the same office."

I finished with a flourish and bowed, grabbing her hand again. Elida smiled and cooed as if she were overwhelmed with my credentials; then she relaxed.

"I like your stories. You make me laugh," she said, removing her hand from my grasp. "Yes, señor Torres, I do find you very attractive." She hesitated. Her smile disappeared, and she choked on her words. "I would love to keep seeing you and talk like this and take these walks ...but my father will . . ."

I took her hand yet again and drew her toward me, even as her tears welled up. I dried them with my sleeve, then brought her body still closer. I was surprised at how light she was and how readily she allowed me hold her. I raised her face to mine and kissed her lips for as long as she would permit and with more passion than I had known before. When we finally pulled away, we walked in silence for a while. We stopped and kissed again.

"We'll have to deal with your father," I said.

Don Ramón was not blind to the exchange of glances and smiles between Elida and me nor the long walks against the setting sun. One evening, shortly after our first kiss, while my family and I lounged on the porch of the guesthouse, Don Ramón's short and angular frame appeared across the yard as he strode toward us. He wore a fusty straw hat soiled with farm swelter and grime. His printed shirt and oily jeans were clammy with sweat.

After the initial pleasantries, he turned to me.

"What are your plans for the future, *joven*? I suppose that you dream someday to own a great ranch like this one."

I heard immediately the man's derisive tone. Such a tone had been served upon me many times before by some of the wealthy customers whose furniture I had hoisted onto the moving trucks and carried to large homes in the suburbs of Mexico City.

"Get that piece over there, *joven*! Handle it carefully," they snapped. "What is taking so long, *joven*? Put it over here. No! Better, over there!"

To be addressed as "*joven*" might be fitting to a youth of seventeen, but not to a man of twenty-four. I sensed immediately that *el patrón* was less interested in an answer to his question than he was in sending the message of his intent to end my strolls with his daughter.

Not waiting for an answer, Don Ramón turned toward my mother.

"Señora Amelia, it's fine you've come to visit and work." He paused, now leaving me entirely out of the conversation.

"But we have many veteran laborers passing through here now and only a few weeks left for harvest. Your boy has a lot of responsibility, a lot of mouths to feed. He had best find some full-time employment in the city or across the border. You're welcome to stay and continue in the fields, but he's not. I don't want him here. We have nothing for him. No work. No lodging. I want him gone tomorrow."

We sat stunned as Don Ramón turned and retraced his steps homeward. I glowered at him but made no reply. So this was how he'd kept Elida to himself. My mother, of course, had been aware of my pursuit of her. She had done nothing to dissuade me. She bowed her head and stared at the faded wooden porch.

No one moved. I burned to race after the man and scream in his face, "Let her go! She is a grown woman! You can't hold onto her forever, *cabrón*! Can't you see that?" I was sick of Don Ramón and his presumption of superiority. Go after him. Confront him. Make him listen to reason. I was ready to jump from the chair when *mamá's* voice broke through my rage.

"What shall we do, *m'ijo*?" she asked.

"I'm going to talk to him," I responded harshly. "I'll make him listen!"

"No, you must not!" she said. "You'll only make it worse." She thought for a moment. "We'll call *tía* Julia," she said. "Perhaps she can help."

CHAPTER FOUR

Although we had journeyed north with the idea of entering the United States, until Don Ramón's pronouncement, neither my mother nor I had planned how or when the crossing might happen. Now necessity led us once again to seek the help of *tía* Julia. Horacio, Elida's brother, drove us to Matamoros to make the telephone call. Julia arrived the following afternoon.

"You're well, *hermana?*" my mother asked, hugging her sister hurriedly as the exuberant woman promenaded into the room and instantly responded with one of her many Mexican sayings.

"'A good life stretches the wrinkles,'" she proclaimed. She plopped her short and plump frame onto the couch. "I should have thought to warn you about him," she continued. "'Eyes that do not see; heart that does not feel.'" She sat to catch her breath and surveyed the room. "He can't expect you to pick up and leave with no notice," she stated. "We'll see about that. I'll speak to Josefa."

Licha and I had settled on now familiar scratched wooden chairs near the front window. *Tía* Julia focused on me.

"Young man," she said, "'lovers think that others have broken eyes.' Too late, you've learned that they don't." As she spoke, she adjusted an earring. "Don't misunderstand me,

I've long felt that Elida should have her own life, and I've said as much to her parents. But, Señor Don Juan, 'before going hunting, be sure you have a house in which to live and land on which to toil.' That is something you failed to do, and now we see the results."

"*Sí, tía,*" I answered respectfully. This was not the time to debate my aunt or challenge one of her endless string of *dichos.* "We'll have to see if what they say is true," she continued. "'Good words allay worry and soften the heart?'"

She was a generous and resourceful woman. Despite her disappointment in the turn of events, she quickly journeyed to the main house and persuaded Josefa to walk with her to the tractor shed where she cajoled Don Ramón to agree to the additional time needed to arrange the crossing. The conversation also provided the opportunity for Elida and me to meet in our familiar place among the piles of stripped cotton. We held each other and kissed for as long as we dared. As Elida darted out the rear door, I pledged that I would find a way to see her again.

Within the following two days, in rapid succession, *tía* Julia deftly arranged for the issuance of temporary work permits and purchased tickets for a ferry ride across the Río Bravo. Don Ramón agreed to allow my three teenage brothers to remain at La Palma and to complete the harvest of the spiny cotton plants. When the season was over, we would arrange for their crossing.

Once the preparations for our own departure were complete, *mamá,* Juanito, Chito, Licha, Mago, and I arose early to bid farewell to the boys. *Tía* Julia drove us to the Río Bravo in her well-worn but spacious town car. When we reached the ragged edge of the river, we crossed a rickety platform of steel. The car's sturdy frame lumbered noisily onto a battered launch. We sat idle until we heard the barge's ratcheting motor. As it pulled away, we exited the vehicle and stood in silence, surveying the opposite shore with its uneven line of paloverde, ash, hickory, and willow.

I placed my arm around my mother's shoulder to comfort her. She was distressed, mostly at having to leave the boys, not knowing when we might be able to return for them. The gravity of our choice to leave our homeland deepened with the river itself. We drew toward the opposite shore and disembarked onto the new and unfamiliar terrain of *Norte América*.

The midday sun engulfed us in a balloon of Texas heat. Julia brought us to the home of señora Raya, an elderly *comadre* in Santa María who had two extra bedrooms and was happy for the company and the additional cash she would collect for room and board. *Tía* Julia hugged her sister goodbye, kissed the younger nephews and nieces, and then turned her eyes toward me.

"'With patience, you gain heaven,'" she stated, sweeping by me and out the door.

We passed the afternoon getting acquainted with our new host, a scraggy and determined woman in her mid-sixties with impish eyes and a playful smile, which she craftily employed to accentuate her many stories.

She claimed to have ridden with Carranza as *una soldada* during the revolution before that famous man became governor of Coahuila and later president of Mexico; and still later, was either assassinated or died at his own hand. No one knew for sure.

"Give me a moment," she said, rising slowly and padding past in purple house slippers. She brought from her bedroom a desiccated leather holster, which she displayed with great reverence.

"This is the one I wore then," she announced.

I watched my mother's already burdened face grow even wearier. The unaware host wagged on, oblivious to the discomfort of her guests at hearing about the valiant *revolucionarios*, who in *mamá's* mind were still indistinguishable from the *bandoleros* who murdered her father.

As night fell, we noticed the lack of any cooling breeze that might give some relief to the stale air. Señora Raya retired. Alone at last, we stared at our surroundings. The kitchen stove and refrigerator were sleek and shiny, the couch a glossy turquoise, the living room walls pastel green with white trim, the lamp stands and coffee table of thin and colorless wood. Nothing was familiar. All had changed. We were among strangers in an unfamiliar country where English was the common language and gringos, about whom we knew nothing, were in charge. We had few belongings, no work, and little understanding of what tomorrow held for us.

To me, the passage itself was secondary to the more pressing issue: How would I continue to see Elida? Our brief *adiós* served only to kindle my passion and to reassure me that I was in love with her and she with me. Eventually, I surmised, I would have to return to La Palma to bring my brothers across, perhaps by the fall when the harvest was over. I would find a way to be with her.

In exchange for the price of replacing the threadbare tires, *tía* Julia and my uncle, Norberto, lent me a tatty and sun-bleached Frazier Vagabond, whose bulky shell, for too long, had sat idle at the rear of their house. The car rattled along well enough. I set out to find work. I landed a job cutting squash, lettuce, and onions, about which I knew very little. By the end of the day, I was exhausted from the heat and sore from the stoop labor, but I'd earned the $6.68 cash in my pocket, and felt myself to be a lucky man.

After two days, I had demonstrated my qualities as a strong worker and quick learner. On the third morning, the foreman directed me to a rig with a disk hitched on the back.

"Ever driven tractor?" the foreman asked, leading me to a dusty red Ford 8N. Muñoz, a lanky cutter from Durango whom I met just the day before, stepped in to translate. Once I understood the question, I sensed an opportunity for higher pay. With feigned competence, I asserted that I could handle the job.

"You'll find a cut lettuce field 'bout a half mile down the road. Git down there and start diskin'," the foreman said.

Fortunately, the man instructed Muñoz to accompany me and to make sure I knew what to do. In Mexico, our neighbor owned the only tractor that I had ever been near. *Papá* hired the man to plow the two hectares of land on which we grew our corn.

Muñoz soon realized that I was a novice. He rode on the tractor with me and taught me how to use the gears and levers.

"Make two passes. Don't forget to lift the discs once you get to the end before you make the turn." After an hour, he said, "You'll be fine. I'll see you later."

At the end of that first day of disking, a day in which the heat and humidity drained my strength even more than the hours of cutting cabbage, I lay under a tree, unable to move. When at last the foreman returned, I struggled to my feet, still stiff and sweaty. The man laughed at my condition, but told me to come back the next day.

At night, I arrived at our temporary home. Señora Raya forbade me to enter until I had knelt on a slubby patch of grass in the backyard and stripped my jeans and shirt from my sweaty body and doused myself in cooling water from the tattered end of a hose. The crowded dwelling had no air conditioning and no fans. Our host tried to make us feel welcome, but she had lived alone for too many years and couldn't refrain from commenting on the smallest intrusion on her daily routine.

We soon determined to move on. We found a more accommodating rental in a Santa Maria apartment building. Once again, we packed and hauled our few belongings, bidding goodbye to the former *Adelita* of the revolution. To our surprise and relief, upon arriving at our new home, we encountered, among our new neighbors, families from León and Zacatecas and even some from San Luis Potosí and San Ciro.

I poured myself into my work, learning all I could about tractors and plows, about rows of steel dishes dragged in endless circles, each attachment precisely designed for disking, furrowing, or planting, and about banks of seed canisters drawn in endless

lines. The September sun cooled. I sat on the metal seat of the
Ford 8N or the John Deere M-60 and inhaled the smell of the
newly turned soil. I admired the machinery, efficient in its design
and compact in touch and feel. At La Palma, Elida's brothers
didn't allow me near the tractors. They were senior to all others;
but here, the foreman had given me full reign, and I savored the
opportunity.

Upon completing a plot five hectares in size, I felt animated,
proud, and even courageous, having accomplished what I had set
out to do. I compared my work with that of other drivers, noting
their pace, their attention to detail as they made their turns, the
precision of their line in forming the beds. I spent my evenings
reading the manuals to learn about the machine's mechanics and
maintenance. I competed with myself and with the others to do
more, to learn more, and, hopefully, to earn more. I strove to
be the best tractor driver, and once I had gained the distinction,
to wear it proudly. I found, however, that no matter how hard I
worked, my pay remained at sixty cents per hour.

I fraternized with the other drivers and mechanics. We
huddled after work beneath a wide pepper tree, drinking *cervezas*,
smoking Lucky Strikes and Camels, and, as always, telling stories
about our childhood and our *pueblitos*.

"*Mire,*" one of them asked, "did you ever see Feliciano
Zedillo? Once I spotted him and his warriors riding hard out of
Rioverde. I was coming on the road, *usted sabe*, an*d phew* ...right
past me *con sus caballos* and all of the loot ...and into the hills.
The soldiers could never catch them." The narrator drew on a
cigarette and drank from his bottle. "One time, I heard, during
the World War, they even tried to drop bombs on them. *¡Bien
tontos, los soldados!* They believed that the thieves were still there
in the *arroyo*, but the bombs only succeeded in killing the horses,
the cows, the sheep, and everything around except the *bandidos*."

"And what happened to Zedillo?" another asked.

"He was long gone to Guanajuato, I think!" The men laughed at the ineptitude of the soldiers.

All the while, I never stopped longing for Elida. Despite the distance and the difficulties of communicating—there was no telephone at Rancho La Palma—I had tried to stay in touch. I sent postcards, not knowing if she would see them. I waited with guarded expectation for a reply.

On a Friday in mid-September with work beginning to slow, I hitched a ride across the border through Matamoros and south into the open countryside. Over the months, I had developed the habit of dressing like a Texan, donning a gray Stetson, printed long-sleeve shirt, jeans held in place by a thick belt and round leather buckle embossed with the horns of a steer. I was especially proud of my boots that were as soft as any that my uncles made.

I walked the last two miles to La Palma. To my good fortune, I found Elida at home alone. She greeted me with an uninhibited burst of emotion as we kissed and embraced in her father's doorway. We held each other for only a moment. At the same instant, we both knew where we would find privacy. By this time, my brothers had moved to Monterrey, Nuevo León, to work with an uncle who managed a large factory for making buses.

I led Elida across the porch to the empty guesthouse and through the sparsely furnished *salón* into the bedroom that my brothers and I had shared. There, we spent the afternoon together, alone at last, free from those who would keep us apart. We made love for the first time; and, despite its small inconveniences, the experience was both joyful and overpowering. All of our doubts disappeared. Our lovemaking affirmed that we belonged together and that no one and nothing would ever change that.

Afterward, we lay in silence, growing in the confidence that this love would survive whatever gaps of time and place might separate us.

"When I brought my family here," I mused, "I thought I understood the reasons. I felt propelled, but now I know the truth. I came to find you. Nothing is the same in my life now."

"It's not the same for me either," Elida concurred. The dark moons of her eyes reflected the late afternoon sun as it sieved through the drawn shade. "For the moment, I must continue to obey my father, but I'm no longer his little girl. I think he knows that. Still," she sighed, "I'm sorry to say I don't believe that he'll ever accept you." We embraced again.

"Never mind your father," I whispered. "He thinks he is strong, but we are stronger."

Elida dressed and brushed back her hair, preparing to return to her housework. She gave me a final kiss and embrace.

"I almost forgot," she said playfully. "Thank you for the postcards. My cousins retrieve our mail for us. They have passed them on, but please understand how difficult it is for me to answer."

Later, as I rode north in the battered pickup of a generous stranger, I looked back on the past years since I had left the seminary. I had kept the promise to my father. Despite the move from San Ciro, I had held my family together. The daily transport of furniture through the streets of the capital had fed and clothed us. I had led us north out of Mexico itself to find greater opportunity.

In Mexico during the evening hours, I often watched my uncle's television, a strange and wondrous new machine from the United States. I listened to the peculiar music coming from that other world, observed the bravados on the streets with their jeans, their Stetson hats, their shiny boots, and their transistor radios. My youthful visions and expectations, my sensitivities, my emotions, even my anger had driven me to succeed not just in a van crawling through the streets of Mexico City but succeed—although modestly—in the expanding world beyond.

Now I had met Elida, a stroke of good fortune that affirmed all of the commitments and abandonments of my youth and early manhood. In all the years since I had left seminary, and despite the stirrings that had prompted that decision, I hadn't seized opportunities to meet with girls and now women my own age. I dislodged my family to come north. Only now did I understand why. Only now had I encountered this woman of beauty and wonder waiting for me.

As I rode to the border in the generous stranger's battered pickup, I rolled down the window and sang unabashedly into the stream of warm air slapping against my flushed face. I crooned a dozen ardent *canciones de amor*, each trumpeting the passion, the pain, and the joy that consumes the life of every lover and that now had engulfed my own.

Sin ti,
No podré vivir jamás
Y pensar que nunca más
Estarás junto a mí.

Without you,
I can live no longer,
And think that never more
Will you be next to me.

¿Sin ti,
Que me puede ya importar

Si lo que me hace llorar
Esta lejos de aquí?

Without you,
What else is there to care for
If what makes me cry
Is to be far away from here?

The generous stranger smiled at me, a youthful Don Juan riding beside him. He joined in each verse lustily.

With the end of the harvest, I obtained work at a dairy in Harlingen. A man named Ray Hollings looked me over.

"Where're you from?" he asked in Spanish.

"Santa Maria," I replied.

"What do you know about cows?"

"I know enough to learn more," I responded, grinning broadly. The man laughed.

"Now that's the best answer I've heard. Come by tomorrow, six sharp!"

I spent the first days cleaning the spacious barn, but soon Hollings recruited me to operate the farm's newly installed milking machines. Each morning I snuzzled the herringbone hose bibs against the udders of sixty-seven seemingly oblivious cows and monitored the flow of milk to the expectant drums. I repaired the machines' hoses and clamps, tossed the hay into the trough, and carried fresh salt licks to the pens.

Meanwhile, *mamá* found a position as a caregiver in La Feria and moved there with the children. Licha also left to keep house for the uncle in Nuevo León. She joined her brothers there.

With all of these changes, I felt that I had fulfilled the promise that I made to my father to care for the family. My older siblings were now supporting themselves. I had earned the right to enjoy greater independence from their daily concerns. I soon rented a small apartment in Mercedes to be nearer to my work.

Each morning I wondered if Elida's response to my postcards would arrive. I had never received a letter from her. It didn't matter what the letter might say; only that she had sent it. I promised myself that if she actually answered my cards, I would leave immediately for La Palma. For two months, I waited, nearly losing hope.

During the third week of November el *patrón*, el señor Hollings, approached me. "You don't need to come in on Thursday," he said, "or 'til Monday. It's Thanksgiving Day comin' up. My son'll be home from school. He can cover for you."

I didn't know what Thanksgiving Day was, but I was delighted for the break. Free of the cows, I drove my green Frazier, with its newly repaired motor, south to be with Elida. The car's hornet-shaped body skittered through the rough and narrow roads of Brownsville and over the *Puente Viejo* into Matamoros. My mind was afire with passion and yearning for her. She was a remarkably beautiful woman. She conveyed the feeling of a wounded yet resilient bird, a loving and sensitive being shaped by the anguish of a lonely existence imposed by her own sense of duty and the requirements of tradition.

"What am I waiting for?" I asked myself as I moved through the morning traffic. "We're in love! We aren't children! We're adults, still living like children. What am I waiting for?" I knew that Elida wouldn't continue her captive existence much longer. During the moments of our first intimacies, she had cried out that she loved me and had been waiting for me her whole life. She was feeling the possibility of freedom and would soon demand it from her family and for herself.

"*¡Despierta!*" I thought. "Wake up! It's time. I must bring her across. *Mi mamá* is fine. Juan and Enrique and Polo have jobs, and now Licha is talking about marrying. I'm a strong worker with an education. If it's necessary, I'll find a way to support my mother and José and Mago and Elida too."

The arrangements for our meeting had been made quickly through the network of Elida's cousins, some of whom lived in Mercedes, Harlingen, and San Benito. The cousins had telephones or could write to Elida without fear of discovery. Some lived in Matamoros. One of the cousins had agreed to bring Elida to that city's *Zona Central*, ostensibly, to shop.

We rendezvoused in front of the statue of Don Miguel Hidalgo y Costilla. We quickly bade the cousin goodbye, having arranged a later pickup time, and slipped into my rumpled auto. We hugged and kissed each other until a municipal policeman told us to move along.

We drove into the cool yet arid countryside, stopping along an isolated stretch of the *Río Bravo*. I had stowed the items we needed for our afternoon together, and we carried them through the low-lying brush. As Elida watched, I staked a sheet of canvas to a fallen tree trunk and branch that lay between the brush and the water. Her hair lifted gently in the autumn wind. An edge of the canvas fluttered against the rising bough.

We threw one blanket onto the sand-cushioned ground and wrapped ourselves beneath the canvas tent in a woolen *cobija*. A flock of seagulls plied against the wind, cackling loudly. We had chosen our trysting place well, noting that the river's ever-bending shoreline protected us from view. We lay on the bank, at last together again with no intruders who might keep us from our joyous passion.

As we rediscovered the wondrous curiosities and sensations of our lovemaking, I closed my eyes. Through Elida, my past and my future had converged. She possessed the sensitivity that I had gained from my years of study and self-examination. She conveyed a quality of determination to move beyond our present lives and define our futures, no matter the cost. I imagined myself swinging above her like a great pendulum rotating upon the axis of the earth, our pasts slowly evolving, turning inevitably toward new choices and new opportunities.

In the months since we had met, Elida had grown to believe that if her father wouldn't accept her independence, she must either continue her submission to him or cut her ties. She told me what her mother had said as they worked together through the midday serenity of the family's otherwise empty home while her father and brothers were away working.

"Your father is very stubborn, *m'ija*. He'll have it his way. I know that he will not change. Your friend, Sixto, appears to be a sincere young man, but he has nothing to offer you. Sincerity and feelings are not enough for your father, not for me either. You know that. We can't stop you from doing whatever it is that you must do; but if it is to go with him, don't ask our permission or our blessing."

Once our passion was spent, we nestled in our small makeshift tent.

"I have my own apartment now in Mercedes. I want you to see it one day soon." I pulled the blanket tighter around us.

"I would like that too," Elida responded, her head lolling on my arm.

"I'm starting to make a little money, although I have been spending much of it on my family."

"I understand. And your brothers are helping too?"

"*Sí*, but they earn so little in Mexico; and, in the US, everything is more expensive. My mother has also taken a job as a caregiver, and Licha is getting married."

"I've heard that."

"Anyway, little by little ...I am doing well enough. It may take a while . . ." I sat up and knelt on the sand, bringing Elida with me. I cupped her face in my coarse hands. "Anyway," I said with uncharacteristic apprehension in my voice. "Anyway, Elida, I . . ." I hesitated again. "I want to know if you will marry me."

Elida blinked and stared back at me in a studied silence, examining my eyes.

"Oh," she said and reached out and touched my lips. Suddenly, a smile came into her eyes but disappeared as quickly. "*¡Ay!* Sixto," she sighed, shaking her head and beginning her response in a confused and desperate whimper. "You must know that I had stopped thinking about marriage. Long before we met, I had lost hope. I know my father loves me, but he had left me without any choice. My only future was to serve my family's needs and the ranch. I stopped thinking about anything else."

She paused and took a deep breath. "Then, one afternoon, you came to La Palma. Because of *tía* Julia, you moved into the guesthouse. That's the only reason we had a chance to talk, the only reason we had this chance to be together. Do you know that my father had never let one of the workers live there before, so close to our home? And now everything has changed ...but not really, not to them." Elida's voice grew louder and stronger as she spoke and as the anger rose within her. "Before, I guess they thought that I was happy," she continued. "Now, I have told him how hard it has been for me to live without you; but still, he wants me to forget you. He claims I don't know anything about love. For ten years, he's been expounding his doctrine: 'There's plenty of time for finding a husband!' Now, he says, 'That man is not for you! That man has nothing to give you!' As if I should care only about cotton and corn. Then, I think, maybe he is right. Maybe I don't know anything about love. How could I?"

Elida folded her hands and laid them on my shoulder. She dropped her head against my shirt, her hair brushing my cheek.

"I'm so confused. I love my family. I don't know what to do about them or how to answer you!"

With the blankets still surrounding her half-naked body, she wrapped my head in her arms.

"I love you," I declared. "Your father has no right to take away our happiness."

Elida now was overwrought with conflicting emotions.

"I love you, too, Sixto," she whispered, "but I need some time. I can't answer now."

"I understand," I said.

Weeks later, as I scrubbed and washed the barn's gray cement floor, Señora Hollings appeared at the door. She walked across the wet surface and handed me a letter.

"This came for you," she said and smiled at my animated "*¡Gracias!*"

I stared at the soft blue envelope with my name on it, "To Sixto Torres, care of Leone Dairy, Harlingen, Texas, USA." I wiped the soap from my hands. I ripped the supple paper hurriedly and read: "Dear Sixto, we are very busy here. Your brothers and Licha are fine. I'm glad you wrote. I must see you soon if you are able. Elida."

Although I noted the sense of urgency beneath the few words, several more days passed before I could return to La Palma. This time, I found that Elida's mother was at home. She skirted behind her daughter and greeted me briefly before disappearing into the kitchen. Elida led me to the *salón*. Until this moment, I had never been invited to enter the house.

Two thick wood-framed chairs upholstered with padded cowhide sat to one side of a modest brick fireplace. Brass lamps hung from the exposed beam ceiling, and a wrought iron and glass table strewn with dog-eared newspapers and magazines stood between the chairs. The house smelled of freshly cooked carnitas and mole. Elida gestured toward a worn leather divan. She sat down next to me.

"I must tell you something," she said. She took my hand, intertwining her fingers with mine. She waited another moment before she continued. "I think that I'm pregnant." As she spoke, she studied my face. At first, I didn't respond. I simply stared back, trying to comprehend. Then, I took a deep breath and exhaled sharply, placing two fingers over my lips.

"*¡Ay, Chihuahua!*" I exclaimed before inhaling again and sighing.

I threw my head backward and covered my eyes with both hands. I found myself thinking of my father. Strangely, the smell of the leather chair near me took me back to the tanning shop and my childhood. What would *papi* say? He would be proud to have a grandchild but perhaps not under these circumstances.

"My mother is sure that I'm pregnant. She insists that I'm at least six weeks."

I leaned forward, my head still in my hands. What will my mother say? My brothers and sisters? *Tía* Julia? I shook my head, realizing that none of that mattered. I moved to the edge of the divan and opened my eyes. My face softened as I peered at Elida and stood up.

"Does your father know?" I asked.

"No."

"Are you going to tell him?"

"Of course. In any case, he'll find out soon enough."

I knew immediately I had to convince Elida to come with me now. We had to confront her father and let him know that she's free of his heavy hand. I gently guided my loved one to her feet.

"Now we've no reason to wait," I said. "If he will accept it, then we can marry and celebrate with him and everyone together."

"I wish for that with all my heart," Elida responded, snugging more deeply into our embrace. "But my mother says my being pregnant will only make him angrier at you and at me."

"Then we must go," I declared. "We'll leave together now and live on the other side. I have work and a home there, Elida."

She sat down again, crying softly into her hands. "I had hoped it wouldn't come to this," she said.

"Someday, Elida, he'll have to accept it."

She dabbed her eyes and stared ahead, deep in her thoughts; then, with the slightest glance upward, she bade me to sit again close to her.

"Sixto, *mi amor, te amo*. I want to marry you. I *will* marry you." Slowly, she nodded her head. I embraced her awkwardly. She continued, "But I can't leave with you now, not right now. I must be here when he comes home tonight. I must speak to him."

At last, Elida had accepted my proposal; yet, I had to wait to take her into my life. My conflicting emotions—desire, love, fear of losing her, anger at the continuing rejection—brought tears to my eyes. I knew that I couldn't convince her to leave immediately, to forsake her family without even a farewell. I understood that her father, once he heard the news, must be given the opportunity to accept me, to accept the two of us as a couple.

"Take the time you need," I said. Again, we sat in silence. We heard a sound from the kitchen and remembered that Josefa had been there throughout the conversation.

Elida stood.

"You must go," she said.

We kissed for a long moment. I retraced my steps through the living room and out into the warmth of the day.

A lonely week passed. I heard from *tía* Julia, who had just received a phone call from Elida's father. Neither Don Ramón nor Doña Josefa would yield. They refused to accept what everyone else had come to believe must happen: a proper and joyous marriage. Elida's uncles and aunts spoke to them. Her brothers spoke to them. Her cousins spoke to them, all to no avail.

Within three days of hearing from Elida that she was pregnant and that I was the father, Don Ramón—still determined to control his daughter's destiny—drove the thirty miles to Matamoros to rent a small apartment, paying three months in advance. He had decided that she would carry the child to term there in the city. She would then return to the ranch and again assume her responsibilities as part of the family.

"I'll bring her tomorrow," Don Ramón told the landlord. "I'll be back when the rent is due."

With these preparations completed, he phoned *tía* Julia to advise her of his decision.

"How is Elida taking all of this?" she asked him.

"She speaks very little, but I think that she'll come to her senses soon enough."

"Don Ramón," *tía* Julia responded, "may I give you some advice?"

"Why not?" he replied.

"'The mule that doesn't kick, bites.'"

Indeed, Elida sat with restrained acceptance when her father informed her of what he had done.

"Your aunts and cousins are there to help if you need anything," he declared, as if that information alone should put an end to any concerns she might have had regarding his solution to her condition. Josefa stood in the doorway, discreetly hiding her doubts. Elida had decided that, for the moment, she would not openly rebel.

Within three weeks of her arrival in Matamoros, however, she and I were exchanging phone calls and plotting our elopement. The aunts and cousins, in fact, were helpful but not in the way that Don Ramón expected. On the assigned day, they provided the taxi fare needed for Elida to ride to the border, where she met me. *Tía* Julia had already arranged for a judge in San Benito to marry us. She, *tío* Norberto, *mi mamá*—and, of course, the two of us—were the sole witnesses to our ceremony.

Once again, Elida's parents called *tía* Julia. She told us that they were furious when they heard of our marriage. During the conversation, she could hear Don Ramón's voice in the background, declaring that he would disown Elida and wanted nothing more to do with either of us.

Elida refused to accept this statement as the final word. She loved her father and mother and believed that they still loved her. She felt confident that, in time, they would relent.

When Sixto Junior was born, she wrote them a letter and sent his picture. She told them about our life in the Rio Grande Valley. She thanked them for all they had done for her as a child and into her adult years. She sent her love to her brothers and sisters. She ended the letter on a hopeful note. "We look forward to bringing the baby to see you when he is old enough to travel."

She waited patiently for a response, but none came. Her cousins told her that her parent's anger with their daughter and attitude toward me had not changed.

Our family grew with the passing years; four babies in the first ten years and four more to follow. With the arrival of each new child, *tía* Julia laughed and repeated her favorite *dicho*: "Where there are children, there is no room for relatives or friends!"

During those early years, I continued at the dairy until Elida and I determined that with her beside me, we made more money in the field. In the spring and early summer, I cultivated and planted cotton and corn for local ranchers. Together, we picked peaches and apricots. When she was not bearing children, Elida joined me in packing tomatoes.

We were hired on at a poultry farm in Weslaco. We packed eggs in Harlingen, making seventy dollars a week between us. Often we brought the babies with us, as was common among our coworkers and friends. In time, we moved to McAllen and bought a modest, three-bedroom home.

Wherever I worked, I often spent evenings with my friends, with our neighbors, with my coworkers, with anyone who cared to join in. Some nights after work, we men leaned against a battered pickup that smelled of damp rust and stale vegetables, our wives at home cooking dinner, putting the children to bed.

Some nights we gathered on a back porch after dinner or under an empty carport, our trucks and cars parked along the unlit streets. Sometimes, especially on Saturdays, we met in the early evenings in La Cantina, El Pilón, or another seedy bar, staying until very late.

On all of these nights, we drank together and smoked together, we told stories to each other. We talked about our work, or our families, or our *pueblitos* left behind. We talked about Mexico and our lives en *los Estados Unidos*, the country that we had come to and in which we still struggled to make a place for ourselves and our loved ones. We talked about *los gabachos*, *los* gringos, the good and the bad.

On this night, Rodrigo, wearing a Dodger-blue baseball cap and a thread-thin Dodger jacket, sucked on a Lucky Strike.

"No," he began, "I don't like the way they act sometimes, you know ...*ustedes* saben." He scratched the two-day growth on his chin. "The way the foremen act. To me, it is—how you say—bullsheet! *¡Es pura cagada! Muy rudo, superiores!* Go here! Go there! Do this! Don't touch that!"

"*Sí, por cierto*, you're right." Sergio took up the argument. "But look, man, think about what you're saying. It's the same in Mexico. At least here you have work. At least here your children have a chance, an opportunity." Sergio lifted a beer from a torn six-pack container lying in the middle of the circle.

"They think all Mexicans are burros, a little more than dogs!" Rodrigo stated. "You will find out soon enough."

I was following the banter in silence, but at last I had to speak.

"Maybe we are!" The men were surprised to hear this. "Maybe we are burros. After all, why are we here?" They looked at me, a hunched shadow in the half-darkness of a canted porch light. I reached for another beer and licked the crevice between my thumb and finger and covered the spot with a dash of salt. "Why are we here?" I asked again, licking the salt and drinking. "We're here to work like burros, *nada más* according to them, according to the *gabachos*." The others shook their heads in quiet agreement. "But *are* we here just to work? No, no, *mis amigos*. Sergio is right. We're here because of opportunity. It's not for us we're here. It's for our children, *por los niños*, señores. What opportunity would they have in Mexico? Nothing. *Nada*. You know well what happened in Mexico, what's still happening."

I remembered Padre Bartolome's lectures in seminary on Mexican history and the classes I had taken in *la capital*, and all the reading I continued to do.

"Mexico abandoned its people more than a hundred years ago. Porfirio Díaz, everyone loved him because he built roads and schools, but it was all fabricated at the expense of Mexico's future. For one, he allowed the *americanos* to come in and buy up millions of acres in the north. The Rockefellers, the Hearsts, all the "robber barons," J. P. Morgan, on and on. You've heard these names, no? Never forget them. They explain why you're here!

"The Anaconda Company, Standard Oil, Continental Rubber, United Fruit, on and on. They stripped it all away: copper, tin, oil, railroads, rubber, silver, cattle, and cotton, on and on. You name it. All gone!" I carried on, as if on a soapbox.

"During the '*Porfiriato*,' the *federales* stole the land and its resources from the *campesinos* and sold it all to American investors. Surely someone has told you what happened to your parents and grandparents, or do you need a lesson in your own history?" Elida had warned me that I became too emotional when I discussed our history. It was true. My anger and indignation rose, especially when I met *paisanos* like some of these men who were unaware. "By 1920," I continued, "the *americanos* owned 25 percent of Mexico and 80 percent of its railroads! The *campesinos* were left with nothing, *nada*!"

"No, no, Sixto, we understand, but it's so long ago," Sergio stated. "I remember my father told me once that when he and my mother got married in 1907, Mexico had to import corn to make its own tortillas."

"*¡Exactamente!*" I affirmed. "And later, when Mexico took back the land from the *americanos*, little changed. The Mexican robber barons took over, and they, too, controlled the land and ignored agriculture in the North. And so it is: the industrialists ran the country and sucked it dry for another fifty years, *y aquí estamos*."

"I'm afraid you're right," Sergio declared with resignation.

"The North is still neglected," I stated, "left dry to rot in the desert sun." I drew deeply on a Marlboro. "All the money is in the cities, and here we are."

Refugio offered a comment from a corner in the dim light.

"It's true. The people have had nowhere to go but to the cities or *a los Estados Unidos.*" Torivio eyed the shadowy group through thick, black glasses set below a thinning hairline. "It'll never change," he observed without emotion. "How could it change?" He looked toward me.

I handed him a beer and announced, "This kind of change must come from the bottom. The people must make the change, but they have no interest."

"Again, you're right," Sergio said. "*Tiene razón, hombre,* but why? Why don't they have any interest?"

"Because," I answered, "they have an out; they can leave. If they couldn't leave for the cities or for the US then, yes, they—I'm talking about us—we would have great interest in changing Mexico."

Rodrigo said, "People who try to change things in Mexico don't live very long." Everyone nodded agreement.

The group sat silent for a long while. At last, Rodrigo said, "The witch is calling for me." Everyone laughed. "*Sí. ¡Por cierto!*" They repeated, "*¡La bruja me llama! ¡Ya nos vamos todos!*"

We rose and drove to our homes.

A few days later, in the late afternoon, I watched Elida sitting on the grass in Porfirio Díaz Plaza in Harlingen. Sixto Junior and Enrique, seven and five, played on the nearby swings and slide. Celina and Moisés were three and two. They lolled with her on a blanket as she nursed the infant, Elida. Shortly after the birth, Celina had tried to pronounce the new baby's name, it came out closer to Gloria than Elida; so, we called her Baby Gloria.

I observed them through the car window. I had completed my work for the day and had come to take the family home. Elida hadn't noted my arrival. I hoped that she was glad to escape the tension and anger that had erupted between us last night. Although she appeared relaxed, I had no doubt that she was still upset with me. She surveyed the children, then closed her eyes and raised her face heavenward, perhaps in a gesture of thanksgiving for their health, perhaps in despair. Nearby gardeners worked on the park grounds.

The smell of fresh-mown grass engulfed the tepid air. Undoubtedly, it called to mind her parents' ranch. Two years into our marriage, with our second child's impending birth, her parents had softened. They were eager to see their first grandchild and to welcome the new baby when he would arrive. Since then, occasional visits to La Palma had helped to mend the family's wounds.

Her father and mother had told her that I could give her nothing; yet now they relished every moment with their grandchildren, greeting them with trinkets and sweets purchased during frequent trips to Nuevo León. Even Ramón neglected his duties in La Palma's fields and barns to hold the babies and shower them with love and care.

Elida relished being a mother. For a time in her life—all of those years after completing her secondary education, living with her parents—she had wondered if she would ever marry and bear children. Now she rejoiced when her doctor would confirm, almost annually, that she was again pregnant.

News from other doctors, however, was not happy. I had been feeling unusually weak and tired lately. I had lost weight and looked jaundiced. The doctor advised me that I had liver disease in its early stages. Elida now worried that I might never fully recover, especially since I tended to take the news lightly and ignored the doctor's advice to quit smoking and drinking.

I wasn't worried. I had always been confident in my ability to support my family. With the medication, I had been able to return to steady work after only a few days of rest.

Of course, most of the time I was away on a job or out searching for something better. Elida was home alone with the growing brood of children. I knew I had to make up for her lost earnings. When I could, I worked overtime or took odd jobs to supplement. Somehow the bills were paid, and we were able to put food on the table each evening.

I had to admit that I enjoyed my drinking with friends and exchanging stories and dreams. Elida told me that I was too much a dreamer, always sanguine—*siempre emocionado*—about the future and always sure that a new opportunity would come along.

"Has it occurred to you that your family is growing and I need your help at home? You spend too much time with your wheedling *compadres* and too much money on drinking! We have no savings and no security beyond the next paycheck!"

That was why, last week while returning from La Palma, she again was angry at me.

"Why, Sixto? Why?" She had screamed with the bottles rattling between Junior and Jose in the back seat of the station wagon. "Why are you buying such things? Twenty bottles of tequila! You're destroying your health, your strength, and your ability to make a living and support us. If we had an extra dime, you would waste it on your drinking companions rather than bring it home!"

And that was why she grew angry again yesterday evening. I had been drinking, but I was not stumbling drunk. I had never come home stumbling drunk. Apparently, while I was gone, she had counted the number of bottles left sitting in the closet.

Elida didn't like to show her anger in front of the children, but at the moment that I returned, she was ready to snap.

"Eleven, Sixto. You and your drunken pals have already finished off eleven bottles!" she yelled. "I won't live this way!" I stood and stared. I opened my mouth to speak.

Mire, bebé," I mumbled.

"*¡No!* I'm not listening to you. You're going to listen to me!" She paused and tried to calm herself, but the anger surged through her and into the sour air. "Do you think I'm angry just because of your drinking, Sixto Torres? No! I've lived with the smell of drinking men all my life. My father drank. My brothers drank. I'm used to it! I'm never judgmental about that! No! No! You know why? Because you're not here when I need you! Look at this place! I can't do it all! *¿Me entiende? Además*, you know very well that you have a health problem! Don't you care that your drinking night after night will only make it worse?" Her voice collapsed. Tears came into her eyes, but she recovered and continued. "How can you spend our money on José Cuervo instead of on food for our children?"

"*Mire, bebé*" . . ." I tried again to speak, to calm her. I realized I had nothing to say, so I sat down to clear my head. "*Mire*," I fumbled about, "you know that I buy them cheap in Mexico. *No cuestan mucho*." I thought surely this was the right answer. Elida stared at me. She stopped yelling. She stood at the sink. Then, she was in front of me, pouring a cup of coffee and speaking very slowly, intently.

"Don't be absurd. I don't care where you bought them, Sixto! Now are you listening to me?" She had exhausted her emotions. I sipped the coffee. "This is what is going to happen," she said. "I'm telling you what you're going to do. Are you listening to me?"

I looked up at her but then stared again at the floor.

"*Díga me, mujer*," I said meekly. "I'm fine. I'm listening."

"You will be here in the evenings with me and your children. You will stop killing yourself every night drinking. *Además*, you have nine bottles of José Cuervo left in the closet. Take them, Sixto. Take them all tomorrow to *la pulga* in Harlingen and sell them. Do you understand? I want you to sell them. You should get at least double what you paid in Mexico. Tomorrow, Sixto!" With that, she turned and walked toward the bedroom.

"Okay," I mumbled as she strode away. I laid my head on the threadbare tablecloth. I felt chastened by her anger. The following morning, I followed through and peddled the nine bottles at the flea market. I promised to rein in the drinking and to spend more evenings at home. I wasn't sure how faithful I could be to the latter pledges.

CHAPTER FIVE

When the Texas rains failed and the crops were poor, I painted houses, worked in a body shop, or returned to milking cows and cleaning out barns. With the harvest reduced because of late rains, I hired on at a bakery in Harlingen. Each morning, I rose at 4:00 a.m. to assist the manager in mixing dough, glaze, and frosting. The *jefe's* name was Conrad Klaus. He demanded a ten-hour day and a six-day week at only eighty cents an hour.

Within moments of my arrival, I observed that the other three assistants said very little to each other. They were all Mexican and Green Card holders like me. I thought it strange that my compatriots neither welcomed me nor asked me for information about my life's journey. Despite the sweet-smelling air, the atmosphere was muted and anxious.

Conrad, in his mid-sixties, was a pinched-face, hard-driving entrepreneur with a balding head and a gut that sagged over his belt like an apron full of dough. He growled English commands with a German accent or, just as often, in fragmented Spanish phrases. We assistants found him difficult to follow in either language. We relied mostly on his juddering hands and arms to understand what he wanted.

After work one evening as I walked to my car, one of the assistants, whom I knew as Jaime, approached me. The man was about my age, but the top of his head reached only to my shoulders. In addition to his slight build, he wore lengthy sideburns to frame his narrow face and balding head.

"Do you know anything about this place and what's going on?" he asked, almost whispering.

"*Nada*," I said.

Jaime looked cautiously back toward the bakery.

"There are six shops between here and Brownsville— this one, and one in Mission, another in San Juan, Weslaco, Edinburg, and La Feria—all owned by this guy and his brother. So, I think you should know something." He eyed the store nervously. "We're organizing a union."

"Really?" I said.

I found the idea of a union intriguing. I had heard about farmworkers in California unionizing. Jaime raised his brow and nodded excitedly.

"We're talking to everyone and trying to sign them up. I'm hoping you'll come to a meeting tomorrow evening, but you can't say anything to him." He gestured over his shoulder.

"Of course not," I promised.

The following night, I attended the meeting, sitting quietly in a stranger's living room and listening to other Klaus Bakery workers. Some spoke guardedly. Others voiced complaints in loud and short-tempered tones.

I knew that a union movement existed in Mexico, but I had never had occasion to participate in one. I followed Jaime to the back of the room with ten or twelve other Mexicans. They leaned toward Jaime's chair to hear his ongoing translation.

In front, a lanky Anglo named Randy addressed the group. He was maybe thirty, with intense blue eyes surrounded by a bushy head of blond hair and a beard. He was from the union office in Brownsville. Eight other gringos and two Negroes occupied the first three rows of chairs.

Randy was holding a yellow tablet. He introduced himself, tapping a pencil on his lips, waggling it in the air for emphasis, or chewing on it when he wasn't talking.

"Okay, so like we said last week, the Rainbow crews went out on strike and had a contract within three weeks. They got a twenty-cent-per-hour raise and medical coverage. Rainbow knew they had no choice, and like we said last week—but for those who weren't here—there's no reason we can't match that."

Randy stuck the pencil in his teeth and pushed the fingers of his left hand through his thick hair.

"So, at this point, the Klaus Brothers are paying below the market and will keep taking advantage of their workers if we let 'em."

That night, as I drove home, I felt animated. I liked the idea of people taking action, joining forces to change their lives. It reminded me of my father, how he took charge to build a community room in San Ciro. It reminded me of Padre Benito: "You must look beyond what *is* and strive for the Ought To Be!"

Two meetings later, I no longer sat silent. I had noticed that Jaime was good at translating, but he contributed very little to the meeting itself. I could see that our compatriots were holding back. They had no reason to distrust the Anglo, but neither did they have a reason to trust him. They sat silent, not asking the questions that concern them most. Finally, I raised my hand. Randy pointed his pencil at me.

"Yes, sir, you want to say something?"

I stood up. I have always had a strong voice. When I spoke, a hush settled over the room.

"Some of us here," I began in Spanish, "hold Green Cards. If we strike, they will fire us. If they fire us, we are without work. They will send us back."

Jaime interpreted, and Randy was quick to respond.

"They ain't gonna fire you. They don't want the publicity. I told you. Rainbow rolled in three weeks. They didn't fire nobody."

Randy shifted on his tall frame and looked away, scanning the small room.

"Any other questions?"

"Excuse me." I had another question. "Rainbow is a big bakery. Maybe bad publicity hurts it more than it does a smaller company like Klaus."

As Jaime translated, Randy shifted again, nodding impatiently.

"I'm telling you all one thing, and let's get it clear. They ain't gonna fire you! Bakeries are local. They need their faithful customers—most of who, by the way, are Mexicans. You guys go out on strike, your wives, your cousins, your *compadres* are all gonna know it. You get fired or replaced by scabs, they're all gonna be pissed off. They're gonna stop goin' to Klaus Bakery. That's called havin' power." Randy paused for Jaime to catch up, then continued.

"You gotta learn to use the cards you hold. That's what we're here for. Figger out what cards we hold and how to use 'em."

I had another question.

"If we have to strike, where do we get money to feed our families?"

Randy rubbed the back of his neck.

"Well, as I have stated before, I don't think we gonna need to strike; but if we do, the union will make sure nobody starves."

After the meeting, all of the Mexicans gathered around me and thanked me for asking my questions. Jaime suggested that I should consider joining the negotiating committee. The others nodded and immediately selected me for the three-man team. Later I saw Jaime and Randy bending their heads together by the kitchen door. They came over and invited me to go with them in making other house visits.

"You kinda threw me there with all your questions," he stated. "But the fact is we need someone like you. We need someone to talk to the Mexicans who are still hangin' back."

I agreed to help. At home, I proudly shared with Elida the news of my appointment.

Elida said nothing. She knew that my excitement meant that, once again, I would be out too often; yet she also understood the need to fight for higher wages. I was soon spending evenings with Randy and Jaime.

One night, we visited the home of Simón Salazar. Randy liked to start by describing the Service Employees International Union and its success with Rainbow Bakery. After that, he talked about solidarity. That was the "Key to Success." Then he advised his listeners that union members "have to put their bodies on the line." Finally, he described the potential benefits of unionizing.

"We'll be going after an increase in the hourly wage and push 'em for medical coverage too."

Jaime translated. Randy finished and nodded toward me. He took the empty chair near a small TV set sitting on a TV tray. Simón had gathered three friends—all Krause employees—for the meeting. I lit a cigarette and sipped coffee. I let the silence in the room sit for a long moment. Then I placed my cup on the table beside me.

"Señor Salazar," I began, turning to address the evening's host, "Jaime tells me you're from Durango."

"I am from Durango," Simón Salazar affirmed proudly. He was in his mid-thirties, a small-boned man, perhaps five six, with delicate arms and hands, gentle eyes, an aquiline nose, and thin lips. "All three of us are from Durango." He gestured toward the two *compadres* seated beside him. "Oh," he said, pointing across the room, "and he is from Oaxaca. His name is Omar Cisneros. And, well, you have already met us, but this is Rafael Murillo and Rufino Reyes."

I acknowledged the two and returned my attention to Salazar. The man's sharp features reminded me of sketches of Atahualpa, the last great Incan King whom Pizarro defeated in 1532 and executed two years later.

"I've never been to Durango," I said. "Tell me about it. What's the food like?"

"*¡Pollo borracho!*" The three men responded immediately, laughing loudly. "Our native dish is Drunken Chicken!"

"I like that!"

"We're also known for our scorpions. But we don't eat those!" The three men laughed again.

"Not even with tequila?" I asked.

"No, no! No one there eats *alacrán borracho!*" Simón exclaimed.

I eyed the three men and was reminded of my youth in San Ciro, sitting with Toña at *la lotería*, placing *un grano de maíz* on the card with the caller yelling, "He who bites with his tail ...*el alacrán!*"

Omar Cisneros suddenly spoke up.

"In Oaxaca, we eat grasshoppers!"

"I have heard that!" I responded. "*Otra vez*, do you get them drunk first?"

"Probably some do," Omar exclaimed, smiling broadly, "but I've never tried it."

The conversation died momentarily. I turned toward a photograph on the table beside me.

"Are these your children?" I asked, thumbing the portrait.

"*Sí. Gracias a Dios*," Simón responded. "Three beautiful babies."

"Señor Gallardo, you have children?"

Randy watched me and nodded his approval.

"*Sí, cuatro*." Omar beamed.

"And you, Cristobal?"

"No. I'm not married."

"But you're looking, No?"

"*Sí, por cierto*. Do you know someone who is also looking?"

The men chuckled.

"Tell me, señor Salazar, in Durango, did you ever hear of unions?"

"*Oh, sí*. We had unions there, but they were very political and full of *corrupción*." I was thinking that noting the children would provide a perfect opening to discuss their future and the need to unionize; but, before I could continue, Simón pushed forward on his own. "I'm a lucky man to have this job. Anita, my oldest—she is twelve—she was born with a medical condition, a hole in her heart. I think they say a 'blue baby.' Señor Klaus, he paid the doctors $2,000 to operate. Out of his own pocket.

Now she is well. My wife and I are very grateful to him." Simón's
voice quavered as he spoke these last words. He shut his eyes and
breathed deeply before continuing. "That's why I can't go against
him now. He's been very good to my family."

Simón's *compadres* sat, attentive to his words. I could
see that they knew about the payment, and they had watched
as little Anita's shadowed life had been transformed by the
healing of her heart over the course of a few months. They,
too, had decided not to vote for the union in deference to their
friend and to what Klaus had done.

The mood in the room changed. I felt at sea. I looked
toward Randy, who was listening intently to Jaime's translation
of Simon's story. Randy decided that he had to take control.
He stood up, his tall frame towering above the host and his
guests.

"Señor Salazar, Jaime here has told me what you were
just saying. I appreciate the situation you're in. And, believe
me, I'm not tryin' to convince you to do anything you feel
you can't do. But may I just say one thing?" Jaime translated,
almost whispering. I squinted at Randy disapprovingly. I was
ready to leave. "Now, I'm sure that Mr. Klaus is a good man.
Please don't get me wrong. His helping your daughter was a
beautiful thing. But what he did was charity. And again, don't
get me wrong, but what we're here to talk about tonight is not
charity but rights, working conditions, and benefits that, once
we win 'em, mean we shouldn't have to rely on charity. And,
well, when Mr. Klaus agrees to medical benefits, he likely won't
have to give charity to his employees."

As Jaime translated, I watched Simón's response. His
meek eyes floated softly around the room as he listened. I
knew that Randy's heartfelt plea made sense in some other
world outside of this room; but nothing that Randy said had

touched Simón's soul the way that Conrad Klaus had touched it with his kind act. I stood up. It was time to end the meeting. I looked at Randy and gestured with two hands as if to say, "Enough."

He thanked our host. He and Jaime shook everyone's hand before quietly retreating. I paused at the door.

"You do what you need to do, señor Salazar. May God care for Anita."

Simón responded, "*Vaya con Dios.*"

On Saturday, I volunteered to leaflet the McAllen Safeway in support of a national boycott against California grapes. The growers in the San Joaquín Valley had refused to sign contracts with a new farmworker union led by a man named César Chávez. The response was to organize a grape boycott across the country. I had been working for an hour when I spied Conrad Klaus crossing the parking lot. Klaus saw me at almost the same moment. We watched each other in silence until Klaus disappeared into the store. For a moment, I found myself admiring what Klaus had done for Salazar; yet I knew that the *jefe's* generosity didn't change the need for a union. Randy was right about that.

A week later, Josef and Conrad Klaus had planted themselves on one side of a scuffed wooden desk in a back room of Klaus Bakery's Harlingen location. I sat opposite with Jaime, Randy, and Toby, a lanky man whose skin and face reminded me of *National Geographic's* photographs of Zulu warriors that I had seen in the doctor's office over in Brownsville. The man's stare was intense. His irises reflected the late morning light, motionless in a fig-tone sea.

Randy began with introductions and then got right to the point.

"We represent SEIU Local 623 out of Brownsville. We've signed up thirty-three of your employees. Now, by our calculations, that represents 91 percent of the total workers you have." He paused. The two brothers waited stoically. "And these gentlemen here represent the group's negotiating committee. I believe they have something to say. Jaime?"

Jaime spoke in halting English.

"Well, we see wha happen at Rainbow. We think if Rainbow pay a dollar why no Klaus pay a dollar? And if Rainbow pay medical, why no Klaus pay medical? Dat's how we feel."

Conrad slouched with his elbows on the tatty table, his large hands cupped under his chin. His brother, a younger and thinner man, leaned back and swiveled slightly on a green, plastic-covered office chair. He wrapped his arms across his chest.

Conrad responded, "Vee are smaller company den Rainbow. More percent overhead of sales. Vee don't have money to pay more. Vee open six shops in four years." His brother nodded slightly. Conrad continued, "No money to pay more."

Randy smiled coolly.

"Yah, we hear a lot of that in this business. But I gotta tell ya', you'll have even less money if we all go on strike."

"Dey tell me strike ees illegal," Conrad announced with confidence.

Randy placed both hands on his thighs with his long fingers running down across the seams of his jeans. He bent in toward Conrad.

"I don't know who 'they' is.... Maybe it's illegal. Maybe it isn't. But say what you like, these men are ready to do what they need to."

Toby spoke up.

"I bin on strike befo'. I kin do it agin. Bin in jail befo' too."

He smiled and looked around at the others. Jaime translated in my ear. Josef and Conrad glared at Randy. Josef lit a cigarette. Conrad's face floated on the roll of skin under his chin.

"Why you come from Brownsville, make trouble to us?"

"Hey, friend," Randy said with a shrug. "These are your employees. They came to us lookin' for help."

I shifted in my chair. I wished I could speak English better so that I could explain what it is like trying to feed my family. Jaime glanced over, gesturing with the slightest move of his head.

"*Dígalo*," he whispered.

"Señor Klaus," I said in Spanish, "you pay only eighty cents an hour. We have children who need clothes and food and a roof."

Jaime translated. Conrad smirked, waved his hand in the air, and sat back in his chair. He stared at Randy.

"Dis man start maybe one month ago, and now he's telling me he wants a raise! Why you bring him here?" Randy said nothing. He seemed surprised that I was a new hire. Jaime translated. There was silence.

"I need a doctor," Toby said. "I kaint affod it. What gonna happen if I git sick?" The others nodded in agreement. Neither Josef nor Conrad replied.

I spoke again in Spanish. "You're paying eighty cents. Rainbow is paying a dollar. We can't live on eighty cents."

Conrad had heard enough.

"Many people lif dat way," he stated in a flat tone. "If you don't like, go work someplace else or go back to Mexico! Maybe you do better there!" With this, he stood up, signaling that the meeting was over. Jaime translated. I also rose, responding as if Klaus had made a serious argument that needed an answer.

"Señores," I declared, "we aren't going back to Mexico! We're here to stay. What we are asking will not be solved by telling us to go back to Mexico!" By now the brothers were moving toward the bakery door. I raised my voice. "Señores!" My expression grew stronger, my tone more urgent. "You say many people live on eighty cents, but we're here telling you it's not enough. Maybe you should listen!" Jaime reached up and touched my arm gently. The others all stood as well. The brothers paused and turned at the door. They stared at me and then glanced at each other.

"Listen." Randy decided to try one last time. "We need to know what you're plannin'. We need to know within ten days. Okay? Here's my card. You give us a call."

Josef and Conrad disappeared through the door. We cleared the room and strode into the parking lot. Randy gathered us around himself.

"That went well," he proclaimed with feigned sincerity as he shook hands all around. My blood was still up, and Jaime looked worried. Randy took note and changed his tone. "No, really," he said. "You all did real good. It's gonna be fine."

"Sonamabeecha!" I grumbled.

Jaime and I waved a listless goodbye at Randy and the others. We walked back into the bakery to resume our chores. Toby headed for Edinburg and Randy for Brownsville.

On Saturday morning, with the day off, once again I joined the *boycoteros* in front of the Safeway store, this time in Harlingen. Randy was there, helping to hand out signs and buttons to the volunteers and telling anybody who would listen about the excitement in California.

"This guy Chávez," he declared, "he's the real deal. Ain't nobody organized farmworkers the way he's been doin' it. The fact is, he's got the growers on the run. This boycott thing has completely taken 'em by surprise. They know they gonna have to pay the price one way or the other. John Q. Public jes ain't gonna buy their grapes if they don't start payin' decent. And next week, Fred Ross from IAF will be right here in McAllen drummin' up support. Chávez has learned a lot from Alinsky and Ross and those guys up in Chicago."

The tension and silence at the bakery continued thick as maple glaze. Conrad said nothing about the meeting, but everyone noted that Josef was coming by to talk more than usual. They huddled in the back room. No one could hear what the two were saying. Then, within ten days, just as Randy had predicted, he received a call. The brothers agreed to a fifteen-cent raise per hour and medical coverage. The union countered at seventeen cents, and the parties reached accord. Conrad Klaus had only one condition.

"Vee must restructure," he said. "Vee must let go three workers."

The Service Workers' Union presented the offer to the members, who overwhelmingly approved it. They all agreed that it was unfortunate that the boss had to lay off three of the newer hires; but what could they do? It wasn't for them to tell the man how to run his business.

I heard one of the workers say, "Don't seem fair, especially for that fellow Torres. Kind of liked him. Seems like he got the short end of the stick."

Jaime came to tell me about the layoffs.

"I'm sorry that happened. I guess they were pretty angry at you."

I stared at Jaime, not quite believing the news. "So this is how it works," I thought. "You stand up for folks, and they watch silently while *el jefe* cuts off *los huevos.*" Jaime was hesitant to say much more. He felt my anger.

"It's bullshit," I said in Spanish. "*¡Pura caca! It's* not right. The union should have protected us."

"Listen, *amigo*, we were lucky to get what we got. They were not going to turn it down. But you did well. You're good at organizing. Where'd you learn that?"

I didn't answer. I wanted to return to the bakery and punch old man Klaus in the mouth.

"I didn't learn it anywhere. You tell Randy I said he is full of shit!" I turned and walked to my car to begin my search for another job.

Shortly after Josef and Conrad Klaus had given all of their workers a seventeen-cent raise and medical coverage while firing me, a terrible calamity struck our family. Afterward, Elida could not bring herself to tell me about it in any detail; but I knew my wife and I knew my daughter. I pieced the moments together in my own mind....

Elida was standing by a pile of clothes lying on the floor. She had nearly finished her first load of wash and would soon be ready for a second. As the machine emptied, she lifted each item from the tub and squeezed out the water by hand. She then fed each into the electrically driven wringer, comprised of two hard rubber rollers turning in tandem. She fed the wringer and watched, one by one, the shirts, pants, and diapers disappear through its relentless press, squeezing out the last of the water and leaving the apparel ready for the clothesline outside. She filled the tub with clothes and started another load.

At eight months, her distended belly pressed against the rounded washing machine. As she dropped the last item into the slush of the agitator, she heard Romeo crying, awakening from his afternoon nap. She walked to the second bedroom where our eighteen-month-old baby stood in the crib anxiously reaching for her.

Three-year-old Baby Gloria had been playing in the living room. Intent upon her coloring, she was unaware that her mother had abandoned for the moment her place at the washer. She headed toward the humming sound on the back porch. She grabbed the doorframe of the porch enclosure. She blinked upon discovering the room empty.

"*Mamá*," she shouted.

"I am here with Romeo," her mother called. "I am changing his diaper. I'll be right there."

Baby Gloria was a child with a curious nature. She enjoyed exploring new objects and sensations. For a moment, she listened to the whirring and whooshing and stared at the round, white tub.

A chair and laundry basket sat next to the tub. She pushed the basket to the floor and climbed on the chair to peer at the churning clothes awash in the white suds and to see more closely the drums hanging above and rolling one into the other. The drums turned, turned, turned. She reached out and touched them cautiously. They were warm and smooth. She reached again and gently pushed the fingers of her right hand into the black line between the rollers. She felt the rubber against her fingernails and pushed a little harder.

Without warning, the rollers grabbed her fingers and held them. She pulled back, but they wouldn't let go. Too late, she understood that the rollers weren't rollers at all; they were a creature, a wild and uncontrollable beast that was eating her fingers and hand. She screamed, but before her scream was out of her mouth, the fiend was dragging her wrist into itself, eating it and moving on to engorge her forearm.

"*¡Mamá! ¡Mamá!*" Baby Gloria wailed as the monster's mouth sucked and its stomach whirred and whooshed. The screams jammed in her throat and became muted shrieks of pain. Blood spurted from the monster's mouth. She pulled against the burning, twisting agony. Her bawling pierced through the beast's brutish noises.

An instant later, her mother was beside her with Romeo in her arms.

"Baby! *¡Dios mío! ¡Dios mío!* What has happened? Oh my God, what have I done?" her mother cried, even as Romeo joined in the desperate cacophony with a frightened screech of his own.

Through a film of tears, Baby Gloria saw her mother place Romeo into the clothes basket and lunge toward the fiend; her body pounded against it, rocking and banging, reaching, bending, stretching her arm downward; all the while Romeo was on the floor beside her, wailing inconsolably.

Baby Gloria heard her mother shouting again and again, "Hold on, *m'ija*! Hold on!"

Elida, at last, jerked on the plug. Instantly, the machine fell silent. She then fought with the wringer's latch, pulling at it, hitting it viciously, and finally releasing it, and with it Baby Gloria's bloodied hand and arm.

She peered at her daughter's wound. The wringer had rolled the layers of skin away, from wrist to elbow, as if it had peeled a too ripe summer plum and revealed its crimson pulp.

"*¡Dios mío!* What have I done? What have I done?"

Baby Gloria wailed, choked on her tears, and fell again into a fit of howls and screams. Elida knew she must find help. Her eyes raked the room. She grabbed a fresh-washed diaper and wrapped the arm, groaning involuntarily with fear and remorse. Romeo's bawl had settled into frantic blubbing.

Elida carried the children to the front room, one by one. A baby buggy sat by the door. She laid Baby Gloria in it, all the while planning her next move. She grabbed Romeo and pushed through the screen door into the late November afternoon. She set him down in dirt and weeds and returned for the buggy. She opened the door again, pushed the buggy over the threshold, and jostled it awkwardly down the step. Even before she had managed to pick up Romeo with one arm and push the carriage toward the sidewalk, she was already shouting over Baby Gloria's continuing and desperate sobs.

"Angela! *¡Ayuda! ¡Ayúdeme!* Angela!" Her voice reverberated along the empty street, high pitched and pleading. Angela Mora sprang through the door of her home and ran toward the bent figure and the crying babies.

"*¡Mira, el brazo!*" Elida cried. "*¡Mi niña!* Baby Gloria! *¡Vamos al hospital! ¡Por favor! ¡Ahorita!*"

Angela stared at the red-splotched diaper. She turned and ran for her car. Within minutes, the two mothers and their four children were driving frantically toward the hospital in McAllister. A few hours later, I stepped through the front door, returning from work. I saw Elida and Angela sitting together. The children were sprawled here and there on the floor.

Junior rose immediately and spoke softly, "Baby Gloria is hurt." He described the accident briefly as I move toward Elida. She stood, but as soon as I touched her, she sobbed mournfully. I held her, trying to comfort her. Angela spoke.

"The doctors repositioned the skin as best they could. She's asleep with a sedative. They said, if the cells live, she'd heal in a few weeks. If not, there must be a series of operations."

I led Elida, still sobbing, into the bedroom to see the sleeping Baby Gloria. We watched her unsettled breathing. The children followed and stared quietly from the hall. My fatherly eyes, also, filled with tears.

"¿Sixto Torres, *que tal, hombre*? How are you?" Memo Corralejo smiled too broadly, holding out a half-empty bottle of tequila. "I think you've had enough of shoveling cow dung today. Sit down, *Amigo*. Warm yourself."

I moved toward the welcoming heat of a fresh fire that popped crisply as flames lipped the edge of a blackened oil drum. I settled into the chair cautiously, mistrusting its squeaky joints and peeling paint. I took a drink from the bottle and handed it back. The burning inside and out made me forget the settling sun and the late-afternoon chill of a Texas December. Corralejo leaned in, forearm against thigh.

"I've been watching you, Torres," he said. "You work well. *¡Fuerte!*" He pumped a fist with his free hand. He was a stout man with large bones and thick biceps pressing against a tight shirt that exposed his chest hairs. He expressed his thoughts in short phrases. His clean-shaven and pillow-soft chin enfolded thick lips. He spoke with the happy confidence of a salesman.

"How many children do you have?"

"Five."

"That's good. That's a good start." He took a quick shot. "I have eight." He pushed the bottle in my direction. "My oldest is fourteen. You'll see him here in a couple of weeks when school is out. I keep them coming. You, too, Torres, you need to keep them coming. That's the only way to make a living here *en los Estados Unidos!*" The last phrase Corralejo rendered in the deep voice and lilting meter of a radio adman. "How old are yours?" he asked.

"The oldest is nine. Then a seven year old, five year old, a three year old, and a new baby," I responded. "The five year old and the three year old are girls, the rest all boys."

"You keep them coming, *hombre*," he advised. "We do real well in the summer. You get so you have three or four and the wife all picking, you can make some good money!"

"Where do you pick?"

"We leave in February before this place becomes a burning shithole and head for California!" Corralejo sang the word "California" again as if he were hawking the entire state. I chuckled at his artistic vocalizing. We continued to exchange the drink in regular intervals.

"In Brownsville," he continued, "every day, people crossing; the *chingones aquí* don't need to pay anything. The day-workers depress the wages. I've been here for twenty years. It was pretty good back then. We make *good* money. About ten years ago—fifty-five—somewhere in there, the farmers, Anglo and Mexican both, began bringing them in from Reynosa, Camargo, you name it." Corralejo took a long *trago*, and exhaled loudly with satisfaction. "You ever hear of this guy, Saul Alinsky?"

"No."

"He's another *chingón*—but a good one. He's a big shot labor organizer in Chicago. He came down to organize us in Rio Grande City. You should have seen it. We lay across the road to stop them from bringing in the *esquiroles*.... Alinsky had the bosses on the run ...but then the rangers arrived and cleared us out.... That was the end of that."

"*Qué vergüenza*," I said. "In California, what do you pick?"

"Mainly tomatoes: '*¡Tomates de* California! *Bienvenidos a* Bakersfield, Visalia, Mendota, Gilroy, *y* Salinas! Welcome all *mejicanos al estado del oro!*" Again, he sang the words, raising the bottle in front of him as if it were a microphone.

He finished the last of the tequila and threw the empty *botella* into the fire. I listened to the blaze crackle and to the distant bawl of cows and calves. I had returned to the dairy after the layoff at the Klaus bakery. I was back to earning the same eighty cents an hour.

I found Corralejo's swagger of interest. I had talked to others who left every year for work in California and Michigan and other far-off places. I had seen them on their return, telling their stories and counting their money. I had decided that it was not for me. I needed steady, year-around work.

"You should try it," Corralejo urged. "Start now, *hombre*. That way, when the kids get older, you'll already be known."

"Where do you live when you get there?"

"Some growers have houses for their workers, sometimes a government camp. Some houses are owned by the *contratistas*. You'll find a place. The secret is to get there early." He rose and walked away. "We see you *mañana!*"

Later that night, I said to Elida, "Maybe we should think about it."

"*You* think about it!" she replied impatiently. "You're going to quit your job? Go to California or wherever and hope that you find something? Didn't you try that once?"

"But we're barely making it here. We can do better."

"And what happens if we don't? What happens to the house?"

"We'll find work, Elida. I always find work. You've heard our friends talking about California. There's always work. We just need to be there when the crop comes in and follow it. You and I and maybe Junior when school's out, we can pick the tomatoes. Who knows what else? Maybe we can bring my mother to help with the babies."

"And what happens with the house? *¡Estás loco!*" she snapped, turning away in frustration.

I knew what was beneath her anger. Two years before, I had traveled west toward Crystal City, I left her alone with the children most of the summer. I found a few pickup jobs, but the pay was lower than what I could have earned in Harlingen and McAllen. After two months, I came home with nothing in my pocket.

The worst part was not the money; Elida must have sensed something more. The long nights away from home were lonely. I sat in the bars, sipping and smoking. One particular night, a woman—*una puta* from the streets—came up to me in the darkness. I took her back to my seedy hotel room. That night, for the first time, I was unfaithful to my wife. It was a stupid and careless moment that, afterward, I regretted deeply. The next day, I determined to return to my home. I promised never again to venture out on my own, looking for work in distant places.

Now, here I was with another idea. I said no more about the move. But then, strangely, Elida talked to her friends and neighbors about California. Many had traveled there for work and claimed to have come home with money in their pockets even after expenses. Elida encouraged me to learn more.

Baby Gloria's arm had not healed well. The skin turned black and itchy beneath the bandage. The doctors warned against infection and prescribed antibiotics. They advised taking skin from the child's leg and grafting it on the wound. Where would we find the money for such a treatment?

Part Two

CHAPTER SIX

Each year, as the late winter fog rose above the Rio Grande and the scant scent of spring hung with it, my fellow countrymen and their families set out to find work. They boarded their station wagons, pickup trucks, tattered coupes, and ancient Chevys. Some headed north to Illinois, Iowa, or Michigan, but most journeyed westward toward California.

Elida spoke to her *comadre*, Angela. Her parents were among those leaving.

"My mother, of course, knows about Baby Gloria's wound," Angela said. "She tells me that, if you decide to head out, you should go to Modesto. The hospital there charges according to what you have earned for the year. They will take care of her."

Once Elida heard this, she was intent on departing as soon as possible. We pulled the children out of school and left our home to the care of her cousins. For the first time, we joined the migrant stream to California. In addition to the hope of finding a treatment for Baby Gloria, we learned that the state's varied climate and soil held greater promise for steady employment and better pay from March to October.

We followed our neighbors and friends from Brownsville and Harlingen; from San Benito, La Feria, Olmito, and Pharr; from Mission, Weslaco, and McAllen. We all traveled on the one road that tethered us to the Rio Grande and led us through the open desert through Grulla and Garcíaville; through Rio Grande City and Rome; through Lopeno, Zapata, San Ygnacio, and on to Laredo; through Catarina, Asherton, Carrizo Springs, and up to Eagle Pass; then to Del Rio, Comstock, Marathon, and Marfa.

We couldn't complete the journey to California in a day, not in two days. Those among us fortunate enough to have more than one driver might complete it in three. For most, it was at least a four-day trip.

Some took an extra day, crossing the border south into Mexico to visit relatives in the ancient towns of Cerralvo and Camargo or Nuevo Guerrero, Nuevo Laredo, Piedras Negras, or Juárez.

In the evenings, we stopped at faded gas stations bordered by grease-stained parking lots. The children scrambled to find the restrooms while the car was filled with fuel and *la mamá* carefully unpacked the mochila heavy with tamales *de pollo y* burritos *de res*. After dinner we napped in our cars and then pushed on.

For four years, with the arrival of spring, Elida and I filled our '57 Buick Caballero Estate with clothes, blankets, and food and headed northwest for the fields and packing sheds of Modesto in the heart of the San Joaquín Valley. During that first year, we followed Angela's guidance and found the county hospital. As advised, the charge for Baby Gloria's treatments was based on our income. The doctors performed the needed skin grafts; little by little, our beautiful child was healed.

Each year, after the harvest was in, we packed up and returned to our home in Mercedes.

During the early years of our journeys, with five children, the station wagon provided ample space. By the fifth year, the children numbered eight, so we hitched a small trailer to the Buick and fill it with everything we needed.

For some of the travelers, these were listless days of driving through a desolate and tedious ground. Weary eyes strained to spot the next *mojonera* that marked the land and measured progress along the tracts of scrunty mesquite, hedgehog, prickly pear, and cholla.

For me, familiar as I was with the tribes and cultures whose destinies were defined by this landscape, the sparse terrain was intense with the phantoms of the nations and generations that had gone before. The very names of the towns called to mind the ancestral stories of the Border and of the Great and Brave River that incessantly scarped its way southeasterly; stories of separation and integration, of battles and of treaties, of murders and retribution, conquest or conversion, reduction and annihilation.

For me, each mile of this trip, tethered as it was to the path of the Rio Grande, called forth images of Fr. Bartolomé, standing before the class and expounding on Mexican history. I remembered his tales of settlement and abandonment, of brash taking and generous giving, love and estrangement, righteousness and depravity, of grafters and gripers. I had never forgotten the exploits of traders and marauders, barterers and thieves, ministers and butchers, and most of all, his stories of the destruction of cultures, the pillage of tribes, and of the remnant that soon disappeared or melded with the newly arrived.

"As a priest," Fr. Bartolomé had said, "I must be all things to all people. But you, *mis jóvenes*, can't assume such a responsibility; you can't be such a person to others if you don't know who *you* are. That is why we study Hernán Cortés de Monroy y Pizarro, First Marquis of the Valley of Oaxaca. That is why we study the expeditions of the other early *conquistadores*, and we study the Aztecs, the Tlaxcalans, the Mayas; and that is why we study the "Discourses" of Captain Alonso de León, the chief governor and captain of the presidio of Coahuila, and his expedition of 1689, and we learn the names of the *indios* whom he encountered there from northern Mexico and what is today southern Texas—the Bobole, the Tetecoara, and, across the Rio Bravo, the Cacaxtles, the Tejas, and countless others.... You, too, will soon become familiar with these tribal names—some long ago disappeared...."

I remembered the grainy woodcuts printed on the thick, yellowed pages and the colored prints from the ragged-edged tomes I pulled from the library shelves at school and consumed with rapt devotion. Since coming to Texas, I had discovered more. I had read of the Comanches, the Kiowas, the Apaches. I had visited the historic sites from the Mexican-American War, the struggle that changed forever the shape of Mexico and the United States and marked the Rio Bravo—the Rio Grande—as each country's *frontera*.

The night before our fifth trip to California, we celebrated our twelfth anniversary. As we lay in the darkness after everyone was asleep, I stroked Elida's soft hair, now cut to shoulder length.

"*Te amo*," I whispered.

I was not surprised that she made no verbal response, only squeezed my hand in hers. With the passing years, she had grown more reserved. I knew that she loved me deeply, but her time and energy were consumed with raising the children. As we made love, I consoled Elida with comforting words about the future. After all, a new opportunity awaited us in the strawberry fields of California.

"*Ay*, Sixto, you're such a dreamer. You think everything is easy...."

She believed that she must do the worrying for both of us. She worried about my health. My ailing liver continued to give me a slightly jaundiced look and drained my energy. She worried about how we would provide for our children. Despite my weakened state, I scratched out a living during half of the year by finding part-time winter jobs. From spring to fall, we took these journeys west, following the tomatoes or working in the grapes of the San Joaquín.

Elida understood that my illness had limited my opportunities with any one of many employers. I could no longer exert myself to the degree I once had. Still, with Junior and Enrique now able to contribute as workers, the annual trek to California had given her more confidence in the future.

Now, on the first evening out of our fifth trip, we pulled into one of the seedy gas stations along the way. The attendant, an *americano* in his sixties, tall and lanky with silver hair, hobbled out to take my ten-dollar bill. He pumped the gas and left to bring change. Unlike some whom we had met on the way, the man showed himself to be *simpático*, cheerfully handing each of the children a balloon, a coloring book, and a box with four crayons.

Elida sat in the passenger seat holding three-year-old Jaime. Mario took his turn in the wagon's most prized seat between his mother and me.

"Pass the mochila!" she called to Junior, who immediately grabbed the food bag and pushed it forward to Celina. Baby

Gloria, Moisés, and she all sat in the middle seat. The attendant bent low to the window.

"Looks like you got your hands full," he said, giving me my two dollars in change. "You need to rest an hour or two. You just move on over there by the water hose and park it for as long as you like."

I had learned enough English to follow the gist of his offer. I thanked him and pulled up to where the desert's dense brush began. From behind came the shrieks of air escaping from two balloons as Moisés and Celina coordinated their efforts in squeezing each opening to just the right tension. The youngest boys draped themselves over the front seat and squealed in delight, as the aroma of salsa and *bistec* filled the wagon.

Elida distributed the evening meal, ensuring that the two oldest boys were held to two burritos each. I peeled the *hoja* from a cold tamale and slipped a lick of shredded chicken wrapped in *masa de harina* and chili into my mouth, savoring the hint of cilantro and garlic. I sipped a Corona and smiled at my wife.

My mother and *Tía* Julia had helped her to prepare for the trip. They made an exact count of what the family would eat at each turn.

"Relax," I had told them. "This time, we have money."

In fact, I still held in my pocket most of the two hundred dollars provided for our trip. A man named Manuel Jimenez opened shop in Mercedes, offering a fifty-dollars-per-head advance for every worker who would sign a contract and show up by March 15 to pick the strawberries in Salinas. With the two boys, we were able to register four workers. The company's name was Pic 'n Pac. Jimenez told us that six hundred acres of first-year berries awaited our arrival.

When I awoke at four in the morning, I opened the car door. Elida was also stirring.

"I need to change Jaime," she said.

I fetched the diaper bag from the rear of the wagon, careful not to disturb Junior, Enrique, and Romero. The two oldest had claimed the rearmost seats, which they reluctantly shared with little brother. I brought a flashlight to Elida's side and held it as she cleaned and re-clothed the sleeping child. Thankfully, a light breeze refreshed the air.

"I have to take a leak," I said. I stepped onto the desert sand, guided by a quarter-full moon. I stood beside a bottlebrush, the plumose blossoms swaying gently. After a moment, Elida joined me and squatted to relieve herself.

"You really know how to treat a woman," she mused dryly.

We wandered for a moment in the dim light among the sweet acacia and desert holly. We stopped and held each other. The morning breeze, cool and moist, whiffled our hair.

"Four years we've been making this trip," I commented, "but this one is different." I kissed her forehead. "The Salad Bowl of the World is waiting; strawberries and lettuce ...I think we'll make more money this time. Do you ever wonder if we shouldn't just stay in California? Stop the traveling back and forth year after year."

"I wonder about a lot of what we do," Elida answered. "I wonder where we'll end up. I wonder about your health and the kids' schooling. You like to pick up and move on. Maybe it's time for that, but I'm not sure that California is the place."

"I feel good about what we'll find in Salinas."

"We'll see...."

A half hour later, I had driven beyond Laredo's empty streets and headed through the darkness toward Eagle Pass. The Buick's headlights flitted across blackened chaparral. Creosote bushes appeared dappled in yellow and green, blending one into the other. Hazy patches of golden poppy and copper leaf in bloom skittered by. The misty whiteness touched upon drifting clouds and distant peaks and mesas. As I drove, I thought again about our destination: Salinas near Monterey in California.

The place names carried my mind back to Fr. Bartolomé brushing a hand through his thinning hair, peering over his thin-rimmed glasses, his black cassock sweeping each student's desk as he paced the room. "Today, *mis jóvenes*, we will review the 'Request from the Municipal Council of Monterrey to the Governor.' You will recall that this document from 1632 was written in the City of our Lady of Monterrey of the New Province of León." The priest had surveyed the seminary's third- and fourth-year classmen. "Cuauhtémoc, please read the names of the Indian tribes mentioned."

Cuauhtémoc immediately sat up straight and wiped his hand across his narrow forehead as he always did when called upon. He peered into the page before him.

"Chichimeco, Cucuyama, Matologua, Tepehuan, Quibonoa, Tacuanama, Icabia, and Borrado of the Valley of San Juan."

"Thank you," said the priest. "And these Indian tribes have been accused of rising up and denying the recognition and obedience that they have pledged His Majesty; have they not, Sixto?"

"Yes, Father," I said. I paused for a moment too long, perusing my notes.

"You will provide a full answer, *joven*."

"Yes, Father. *Dispense*." At last, I found the response. "The request states that many times they have stolen wagons and pack teams, sheep and cattle, and have murdered both the Spaniards and friendly Indians."

"*Muy bien*, Sixto. Now, my dear students, notice that these atrocities take place one hundred and fifteen years after Cortéz. The Spaniards are relentless in their efforts to civilize and Christianize the natives. After more than a century, however, many still refuse to accept the gift that they have been given.

"And these depredations are not isolated. As we've seen, they're constant and everywhere in the North. And the narrative states—in 1632—in the Salinas Valley near the City of Monterrey in Nuevo León, the natives overrun the land and steal and kill more Spaniards and friendly *Indios*, including women and children. And what action will the Council of Monterrey take, Benito?"

"It writes its request," Benito replied. "It wants authority from the governor to impose harsher punishments."

"And to support this request, what do they do, Francisco?"

"They send it to the padre to ask for his approval and support."

"And what does the padre do, Emiliano?"

"He tells the governor to approve the request because God has given the land to the Spaniards, and without more soldiers and stronger punishments, the land will be lost and God's design cannot be saved."

"And as you have read," continued the priest, "the punishments were increased so much so that many of those who would not submit were hanged, or mutilated, or captured and sold to the mines of Zacatecas as slaves. And, as you have read, the *encomiendas* were created, which entitled selected Spanish leaders to the labor of Indian groups; but many of those who rebelled escaped to the mountains of Tamaulipas and from there continued their raids.

"For seventy-five years, the Neighbors—as the Spanish settlers liked to call themselves—were forced to avoid northern routes along the Gulf Coast because of the dangers and depredations of these groups until in the 1740s. What happened at that time, Juan José?"

"The authorities appointed José de Escandón," recited Juan José, "to bring families from Nuevo León and Coahuila to settle the area from Tampico to Rio Nueces in Texas, and he named the area Nuevo Santander and established towns along the Rio Bravo, such as Reynosa, Camargo, Mier, Revilla, and Laredo."

"And, to complete the lesson," Fr. Bartolomé asserted, checking the clock on the wall, "the Franciscans founded sixteen missions in Nuevo Santander. But by now, the central authorities refused to provide adequate support. They gave the land to soldiers so that they would settle down and farm and ranch, and the Christianization of the Indians became secondary.

"Within a few years, the missions of northern Mexico and Texas had failed, and the tribes were ravaged by disease and malnutrition. And the stories that had formed the conquest in the South were repeated in the North. Those who remained saw their children enslaved as *criados*, and their people and cultures soon disappeared."

The priest stood in the middle of the room and spoke to all of us as he turned full circle.

"And now you see why we study these names and places, my dear students. The truth is that the Spaniards perpetrated great sins upon *los indios y los indios* responded in kind; but when this terrible conquest was complete, the Spaniards—who had believed that their *pura sangre* was the root of their presumed superiority—had traded away their identity as much as they had destroyed that of the Indians.

"They had created a world in which the Spanish blood and the blood of the indigenous tribes were mixed over many centuries through schemes of conquest and survival, and a new blood and a new culture were born that we call *mexicano*."

As we drove through the darkness and edged closer to Eagle Pass, my thoughts turned to the Rio Grande itself. In the span of three centuries, the Spaniards had reduced the indigenous populations south of the river through war, conversion, punishment, and disease. North of the river, however, their hold was tenuous at best.

After the defeat of the Spanish by Mexico, the immense region along the border was ruled by the superior horsemanship of the Comanche and their allies, the Kiowa, and by the cunning of the Apache.

But then, a new intruder arrived with his wagons, his rifles, and his lust for land. A new era of war and conquest culminated in 1846 with the invasion of Mexico by the United States. Upon the signing of the Treaty of Guadalupe Hildalgo, tens of thousands of Mexican residents immediately became *americanos* for one reason only: they lived north of that wandering waterway while those still living in the truncated nation of Mexico found their scuppered homeland in defeat and disarray.

With the new *americano* regime came new laws designed to strip the old families of their vast holdings. These offered a claim of democratic rule that, nonetheless, treated Mexican nationals and native tribes not like citizens but like vanquished enemies with few rights. The *americanos* imposed a new superiority based not solely on one's bloodlines but also on one's accomplishments and a new form of justice that was available not only to the wealthy but to anyone who was willing to fight for and hold onto power.

By midmorning, we approached El Paso. The terrain prompted me to narrate to my older children the story of Pancho Villa.

"Just sixty years ago, right over there, across the river in the state of Chihuahua, Pancho Villa rose up to lead the revolution in the North against the people who murdered his friend, President Madero. He was one of the great *caudillos*, or leaders, who was also an *Indio*, he in the North and Emiliano Zapata in the South."

"Why was there a revolution?" Junior asked from the rear of the Buick.

"Because, Son, from the time that Mexico won its independence from Spain, more and more land was in the hands of fewer and fewer people. The rich *hacendados* controlled almost all of it."

Enrique was still nursing one of the popsicles that Elida had purchased during a fuel stop. He wiped purple juice from his lips with his sleeve.

"What happened to Villa?" he asked.

"Unfortunately, he was assassinated just like Zapata by the people who wanted to hold onto the power they had."

"*Papi*," Junior called from the back, "why does Mexico always kill its leaders like that?"

I was surprised by the question. I looked at Elida. She stared straight ahead with her eyes glowing.

"You opened the door," she said, patting Jaime as he lay against her shoulder.

"Perhaps they disappointed and angered the people because they failed to make the changes that they had promised. Of course, not all were dishonest, not all were bunglers. The people loved Porfirio Díaz, Madero, and Lázaro Cárdenas. The people cried when they shot Madero."

When I had completed my tale, Junior called from his rear seat.

"*Papi*, now can we stop talking about dead Spaniards and dead *indios* and dead *revolucionarios*? Can we listen to some music?" Elida smiled and reached for the radio.

We continued to follow the path of the Rio Grande up through Las Cruces and on to Socorro. There, we turned west toward Gallup. We drove for hours through gray sand stippled with boney scrub brush standing stiffly in an arid wind.

By nightfall of the third day, we had crossed Arizona and had made it through the Mojave Desert to the California border town of Needles. There, we found a faded, lemon-colored sign that guided us to the "Route 66 Motel," a stuffy but not too expensive respite from the desolate terrain and dry air. We rented two doubles for the night. Elida showed the four oldest boys to their room.

"Get your clothes off and get into the shower. Put on something clean. We're going to find a place to eat."

"Hamburgers! Hamburgers!" shouted the boys in unison.

Elida nodded in agreement.

"*¡Sí, Sí! ¿Como no?*"

By noon of the following day, we were driving through the Tehachapis. An hour later, we entered the expanse of the San Joaquín Valley. We passed through freshly planted wheat and alfalfa fields and orchards of peach and plum trees. Here, during previous springs and summers, we had turned north at Highway 99 to settle in Modesto, where Elida and I had harvested tomatoes and tended the grapevines.

Now, rather than push northward, we crossed the dry Tulare plain. Barren sagebrush rocked in the dry wind; oil derricks bowed like great gray and steel praying mantises, worshipping the ground beneath. We followed the arching sun through the west side's arid fields of cotton and sugar beets and journeyed toward the coast amidst green rolling hills and canyons awash with seasonal creeks, cooling the March air. As the station wagon climbed to a higher elevation, spring wildflowers enfolded the landscape: violet and yarrow, paintbrush and poppy, baby blue eyes and meadow barley, rabbit brush, aster, and lily.

The children admired the garish spread freckled in yellow and pink, purple and red, gold and white, orange and green. I slowed for a moment so that they might survey the multitude of butterflies and bees flitting and hovering over the abundant blossoms. The car was flooded with competing aromas, sweet and pungent. We exited the foothills at Paso Robles and continued northwesterly up a narrow two-lane road named by the Spaniards *El Camino Real* and now called Highway 101.

By late afternoon, we had traversed the Salinas River near San Lucas. We intersected it again just beyond King City and recrossed it below Soledad. The children observed its nomadic route as best they could through the car windows, pointing at the shallow band of water as it appeared, hid itself among an expanse of wild grasses and coyote brush, and then reappeared for brief moments along its course to the sea.

"Up ahead, where the river ends," I explained, "we'll see the Pacific Ocean."

"Let's go see it now!" five-year-old Romeo begged from his seat behind his mother.

"We can't do that today, *m'ijo*," Elida responded. "We have to stop in Salinas to find the place where we are staying. We'll go sometime soon. Promise."

At last we had entered the heart of the Long Valley. Salinas lay only thirty miles beyond. We fell silent beneath the mottled and dimming light, the sun's last breadth fanning the peaks above the valley's uniform rows of lettuce, broccoli, cauliflower.

A layer of grayish strati stretched itself horizontally along the base of the Santa Lucias, nearly covering the path of now distant river flora. The rope-like cloud pushed halfway up the mountain range, leaving its higher crevices and peaks exposed to the darkening sky. Across the valley floor, high above the Gabilán Range with its wimpling ridges, more clouds reflected the dying sun's amber and burgundy hues as they climbed in tufts, curls, and tendrils above the varied crops and occasional clusters of eucalyptus trees.

"This is a beautiful place," Elida remarked, her smooth skin and dark eyes reflecting the bent light.

"The workers call it '*la crema*,'" I added, "because the weather is so mild compared to the San Joaquín."

In Salinas at last, we found our way to Sherwood Drive and pulled into the trailer park owned by Pic 'n Pac, the company that had advanced us the money for our long journey. A large metal sign on a rusty pole read "La Posada." We stopped in front of the office. A slightly built and balding man in jeans and checkered shirt stepped down from the metal porch of a doublewide mobile home. He approached the wagon with a clipboard in hand and introduced himself.

"I'm Howard Hall, the manager here. Can I help you?"

"My name is Sixto Torres." He checked the name off his list without additional comment and gestured to me to drive along behind him as he ambled down an asphalt road past row after row of buttoned metallic mobile homes, each forty feet long with a small porch stepping up to a screen door.

Children played in the dirt amidst a scatter of bicycles and chairs, irrigation boots and work shoes, brooms, buckets, and mops left idle in the narrow spaces between each of the trailers. Clotheslines were strung among spindly sycamore trees. Family cars, pickups, vans, and flatbeds were parked along the road in assigned slots. Men leaned against their trucks in the evening light, smoking and talking with their neighbors. Mothers, visible through the curtainless windows, stood at their stoves or sinks, stirring their pots or washing their dishes.

Hall stopped in front of a drab trailer with the number seventy stenciled near a slightly rusting doorpost. Elida stepped from the car. She had never lived in such a limited and inflexible space—long, narrow, only about twelve feet wide.

"It's a two-bedroom," Hall said, leading us up the metal steps. "That's all we got left."

Enrique and Moisés pushed ahead, wanting to be the first to examine their new home. They ran from one end of the space to the other and back again. I stepped in, followed by Elida, who was still holding Jaime in her arms. We paused and looked around, trying to imagine how we might fit everyone into the tight space.

"As you can see," Hall continued, "you got your sink, your stove, and a refrigerator here, and some overhead cupboards. That table folds down, and those seats make into a bed."

The whole place smelled like Grandpa's Pine Tar Soap, a bottle of which had been left on the chipped vinyl draining board. Hall stood by, stretching his neck and rolling his shoulders as the rest of the children crowded around us. Although our home in Mercedes needed numerous repairs, it had provided three bedrooms in twice the space we had here.

Elida and I said nothing. We walked the trailer's length and glanced at the tiny bedrooms and bath. Hall was anxious to return to the office.

"Okie dokie," he said, forcing a smile. "Here's your lease and your keys."

He held out the clipboard and a key fob. I briefly scanned the one-page document, written in English.

"Junior," I called, "come help me with this."

Junior reviewed the few numbered clauses.

"It says if you don't work for Pic 'n Pac, you can't continue to live here. If you fall behind in the rent, you have to move within three days." I shrugged, signed the agreement, and handed it to the manager without comment. Hall turned toward the entrance.

"You'll have fifty dollars taken out of your check every two weeks for rent and another fifty dollars until the advance is paid off." The screen door squeaked and slammed shut as he moved to the porch. "The bus leaves from the front gate at seven o'clock sharp."

Elida and I stared at each other. The children stood close by, eyeing their surroundings quietly. I drew Elida closer. No one spoke. Elida gazed out the window at the dreary lines of riveted, sheet metal trailers surrounding our new home, number seventy. I was sure that she was thinking of La Palma, her father and brothers, likely at that very moment, planting the cotton. March, the best time of the year, the wind soothing and the land teeming, the waters coursing through the distant wetlands and on to the Bay of Mexico.

"It's all right," I said. She was startled when I spoke. "We'll be here only a few months. We'll make our money and then we will go home."

CHAPTER SEVEN

In fact, as we soon came to understand, the trailer provided a level of comfort that greatly exceeded what was available to the majority of the valley's farmworker families. The annual inflow of migrants far outstripped the number of available houses. Beyond La Posada Trailer Park, with its 130 mobile homes, lay the crowded jumble of battered bungalows and seedy apartments that comprised many of the neighborhoods in East Salinas, home to most of the workforce.

In time I came to know the back streets of Hebbron Heights and the Alisal: Market and Alisal Streets, Closter Park and North Sanborn, Williams Road, Garner Avenue, and Towt. The area offered a haphazard mix of housing choices from well-maintained, single-family homes occupied primarily by an older generation of middle-class Anglos to successive blocks of high-density, cheaply built, two-story, one- and two-bedroom apartments, hastily constructed for the growing labor force.

Sprinkled among these—along Madeira, East Market, and beyond—sat fading ten-by-ten single-board shacks, built by the migrants from Oklahoma back in the thirties and now home to the more recent Mexican arrivals.

I also learned of the outlying squalor of labor camps that was scattered willy-nilly throughout the valley among the fields and near the railroad tracks, along the foothills and canyons, in the back alleys of Pajaro and Chualar and on the backsides of González, Soledad, and King City. The growers built most of these in the forties to house the newly arriving Mexican *braceros*. The lack of adequate farm labor housing reflected the broader community's attitude toward its field workers: "Be here when we need you, then go back home, wherever that may be."

Six to seven thousand migrants traveled to the valley each year to pick lettuce for local growers, such as D'Arrigo, Hansen Farms, or Merrill Brothers or to harvest the tomatoes for Bob Meyer down in King City.

Single men found shelter in seedy barracks formerly occupied by *braceros* before 1964 when the federal government discontinued the program, designed to bring temporary labor out of Mexico. Since the late sixties, others, like my family and me, found work with the newly entrenched corporations, such as InterHarvest, a subsidiary of United Brands, formerly, United Fruit; Fresh Pict, owned by Purex; and Pic 'n Pac, the property of S. S. Pierce of Boston.

Many workers were unaware of the system of advances that Pic 'n Pac employed to assure itself of an adequate labor force during the peak of the strawberry season. They had come without knowing where they might find a home for their families.

The unattached migrants sought out labor contractors like Manuel Jimenez, a dark and pudgy man with an unceasing frown, black freckles, a protruding gold tooth, and balding head. Jimenez controlled his laborers by providing to them the valley's scarcest commodity: a place to live. In addition to work vouchers, Jimenez offered a fifteen-by-fifteen shack on a scruff of ground along Highway 101, south of Salinas and lying adjacent to Soledad State Prison.

I met Nacho Molina during the first bus ride to the fields. Both of us had our two oldest boys with us. Junior and Enrique were eager to reach the strawberries and test their skills as pickers. All the workers were talking about how the struggling farmworkers' union in Delano was close to signing its first contracts with the San Joaquín Valley's largest grape growers. The hushed daybreak conversation skittered up and down the aisles and across the seats from window to window as the bus rattled up East Alisal Street toward the rising sun.

"Some say, *usted sabe*, César Chávez will be here as soon as the growers in Delano sign.... From what I hear, that could be any day!"

"You're kidding yourself, *mano*, they've been fighting over there for five years."

"Seventy-five cents a crate. *¡Es ridículo!*" Maybe we can get the growers here to pay $1.20."

"I was in Rio Grande City in '66. We refused to pick the *melones*, and the Texas Rangers showed up. *Los brutos* began beating on us."

"Don't be surprised if the same happens here."

In no time, my new seat partner revealed a passionate support for the union.

"Just arrived, eh?" Nacho said, his large balding head bending toward me. "You need to know what's been happening. I assume you're from Texas—almost everyone living in the park is. Five years, farmworkers and growers here have gotten more and more suspicious and angry at each other. We've all been following the fight over in the San Joaquín. You know about that, right? César Chávez and UFWOC—The United Farmworkers Organizing Committee?"

I felt Nacho's fervor and soon discovered that all of the harvesting crew shared his impatience. The workers sensed it: change was coming to the fields and they were ready for it.

A middle-aged couple sat just in front of me on the bus. They turned and said, "We were on the picket lines in Coachella and Delano. We got a wage increase, but the growers wouldn't sign a contract with the union."

Nacho continued feeding me information.

"Chávez didn't have a chance in the San Joaquín or the Imperial Valley until he came up with the grape boycott. Now it looks like they might sign. If they do, we're thinking, why not here? Why not contracts in lettuce and strawberries?"

I had participated in promoting the grape boycott in Texas, leafleting at the Mercedes Safeway. At the same time, during our four summers in Modesto, I had also worked in the vineyards, which some might have seen as undermining the boycott effort. My employer in Modesto, however, hadn't been named among the companies targeted by Chávez, so I hadn't had to choose between going out on strike or joining *los esquiroles*, the scabs.

"This is East Alisal," Nacho continued. "It's the main street through town, east and west. It meets up with Old Stage Road about five miles down. That's where the berries are."

From the beginning, Nacho's son, Mateo, outpaced even his father. He was sixteen, strong and flexible, able to move quickly from plant to plant. He had been working as a picker since he was eleven. He took little notice of my boys. They were four and six years younger, and although they tried to equal his stride box for box, they were no match. Finally, the foreman had to tell them to slow down because, in their haste, they were picking too many "seconds." By the end of the first day, Mateo had filled eighty-seven boxes. Junior and Enrique had tallied only fifty-three between them.

Two weeks after our arrival, I was sitting on one of the worn metal folding chairs assigned to each trailer. A few residents and I huddled beside Nacho Molina's porch, some on chairs, others squatting on their haunches. Molina was a recent arrival from the Imperial Valley, where he had worked for InterHarvest. He, too, had taken the Pic 'n Pac advance payment, having decided to jump from vegetables to strawberries in the hope of making more money.

He introduced me to others: Domingo Ortega, whom everyone called Mingo, and his stepfather, Pancho Vega, Rogelio Peña, and Refugio Cabrera, known as Chuca. They were among the dozen or more in attendance at tonight's gathering. Molina had a round frame, heavy arms, and spuddy legs. At first, he reminded me of a knot on a log, but my new acquaintance quickly disproved his image with high energy and a quick mind. He liked comment and debate and was not shy with his opinion, whatever the subject.

As I became more aware of the tension hanging over the Salinas Valley, I realized that here I might well have to make a choice between striker and scab. My chance meeting with Nacho Molina had set me in the center of the conflict that simmered more and more intensely as the growing season ripened. Molina had taken me under his wing and was pushing me to get more deeply involved.

"You ever work for a union or been involved in organizing?" Molina asked.

"A little, once before in Texas when I worked in a bakery. We ended up winning, too, but then I got laid off for being a leader of the strike."

I explained what the Klaus Brothers had done to me.

"That's not right," Mingo Ortega interrupted sardonically, his heavy eyebrows pressing against the bridge of his nose. "The union should've supported you on that situation. They shouldn't have signed unless the company agreed to keep you. That's what I say about that!"

Before this evening, I had attended only one of the meetings. Now I sat silent and curious. I soon learned that the loose-knit group of would-be strikers had no status either with Pic 'n Pac or the union. They held these meetings to prepare themselves and the other residents for the eventual arrival of César Chávez.

Like Molina, Mingo had the build of a butcher's block: thick, wide, and solid. He was young and brash with defiant eyes. His father-in-law, Pancho Vega, was tall and lean, a veteran strawberry picker with the company. Pancho had seven children, four of whom were old enough to contribute their labor during the summer harvest. For over a year, Mingo and he and others had been quietly fostering support among the two thousand or more berry pickers employed by Pic 'n Pac.

Mingo's prickly nature had limited his effectiveness as a leader on the committee. He was, however, deeply committed to the farmworkers' cause and devoted all of his free time to it. He had no children, having been married for only a few months. With the beginning of the new season, the members had selected Nacho to speak with the union leadership in Delano about the group's organizing effort. In recent days, the union had finally signed its first contracts among grape growers in Coachella.

"I'm telling you, nothing will happen," Peña began softly, intently, "until we get the union over here. The *pinches* growers will never agree to anything unless we go on strike, and even then, we'll probably need to boycott!"

Rogelio Peña squatted on his haunches. He was constantly tugging on a pack of Camel cigarettes. He had been born in Texas shortly after his parents emigrated from Durango, Mexico. He was in his mid-twenties, sometimes rash, with too much energy and never quite enough information. Strangely, when he spoke, his words fell on the ear in a cool, listless, near monotone, as if to disguise the emotion beneath. The tone also served as the perfect vehicle for Peña's dry sense of humor.

"*Mire*, señor Peña, *por favor*, we've talked about this many times." Nacho Molina tolerated Peña because he was born in Texas—Nacho knew his father—and because Rogelio spoke English, which was helpful at times. Otherwise, as far as Molina was concerned, he was just another young Chicano radical who liked to hear himself talk. "The union . . ." Molina continued.

"I don't get why they aren't here right now," Peña interrupted. "You've been talking to Marshall Ganz for months. 'Keep meeting,' he says. 'Keep drawing up your demands.' I'm telling you we need to act now while the growers are most vulnerable! Call me crazy, but I think they have some vegetables and fruit that need picking." Some of the men nodded in agreement with the speaker's opinion. Others shook their head in frustration with his now familiar prods.

Nacho was a patient man with a deep respect for the decisions made in Delano.

"Look, we're doing the best we can," he stated, his irritation growing. "The union isn't ready to come here. It's fighting two wars in the Central Valley and in Coachella. Can you understand that? Ganz has asked us to wait, to get ready. He's assured us we'll have our time, but it can't be now."

Peña, still resting on his haunches, took a last draw on the stub of a cigarette. Everyone watched as he rose, tossed the butt at his feet, and stepped on it with his ankle-high combat boots. As he stood up, he tapped at the air toward Nacho.

"Then we should act without the union. Why do we need the union to submit our demands? We can start the negotiations. We're way behind in wages compared to what they're paying in other places. Every day we're losing money. If we can reach agreement with the growers, the union will have to come over here, ready or not!"

By now I had heard enough. Although I was a newcomer, I could see that nothing was happening to move forward. I had little patience for talk that meandered from topic to topic and for speeches that didn't lead to action. I stood up as if to leave, drawing everyone's attention away from Peña and Molina. I paused and looked around the circle. Molina asked if I had something to say.

"I'm new here, but I'd like to comment if I may."

"*¡Por supuesto!*" he said. "*¡Siga!*"

"I think we have three problems. One, señor Peña here is right. And two, señor Molina is also right." The men laughed and nodded. I continued. "And three, we aren't ready for the union to come here." The group fell silent. "We need to follow both of these gentlemen's advice. I don't believe that the union can help us any time soon, but I also don't believe that we can wait all summer, sitting on our hopes. There's something more basic to think about. As I understand it, this committee has no charge, *ningún papel* to show the growers. We're nothing to them. What we need is a pile of chips for bargaining. We need legitimacy *ustedes saben*, a process to show we represent the workers. As I understand it, we're just a group of La Posada residents hanging around together and talking. It doesn't mean anything. We need an election so that whoever is on the committee afterward can speak with authority to the *jefes*. Why should they listen to us otherwise?"

"It's what I've been saying over and over!" Peña exclaimed. "*¡Órale! ¡Bravo*, Sixto!"

"Listen," I continued, "we can hold an election. Anyone can run to be on the newly formed ranch committee, but it will be the Pic 'n Pac Ranch Committee sanctioned by the residence with authority to adopt a list of demands. Next, we pick one or two issues and take them to the owners."

"Dennis Powell will help us with the election," Peña offered. "Señor Torres, Powell's an attorney from California Rural Legal Assistance. He'll know how to do it the right way!"

"I have another idea," I said.

"*Sí, siga.*"

"We have women in the fields now. Yesterday, my wife started working, but they have no toilets for them. It's one thing to tell a man to go find a tree or a ditch. It's not the same for a woman. The growers must provide toilets."

"That's a good demand to start with!"

Everyone agreed.

After work, Nacho and I sat at his kitchen table.

"I can see you like this kind of work," he declared. "Night after night, going door to door, explaining the need for the union. Some folks are just not interested. Others want to talk your ear off and right away will give you ten grievances to put on the list. It can be drudgery if your heart's not in it."

"I learned from my father," I responded. "He was always organizing the people to make our *pueblito* better. Sometimes he would take me with him to collect the taxes. We often had folks come to our door with one problem or another. He never turned them away."

"Your wife doesn't mind that you're out?"

Nacho asked the question cautiously. I brushed my mustache with two fingers.

"I'm afraid she does. I have a little problem with my liver, *usted sabe*. She worries about my health, especially when she sees my eyes have grown jaundiced. She worries that I work the strawberries all day and then I am out in the evenings. But she has resigned herself to it. I find that picking is exhausting, but organizing *la gente* is energizing. *¡Me da ánimos!*"

Nacho drummed his fingers against the plastic cup.

"You must know that you should stay away from alcohol," he counseled.

"The doctor, my wife, now you . . ." I smiled, unashamed. "Join the long line; or, as Peña would say, 'Call me crazy!'"

"I had to stop," Nacho said, drawing in his upper lip, revealing a gold-rimmed tooth. "As a young man, I was out of control. I had a couple of arrests and spent time in jail. For me, it was stop or die."

"I noticed you weren't joining in and wondered."

"I've learned a lot from watching César and listening," he said. "The people accept their lives. They say, 'What can we do?' They feel helpless. The truth is, it takes someone from outside to make them see. That's the job of an organizer."

Nacho rose, stepped to the stove, carried the coffee, and refilled the cups. The pot was several hours old. The dark liquid's aroma permeated the room.

"I was like that," I admitted. "We traveled through the San Joaquín every year for four years, Bakersfield, Delano, Visalia, and Selma, over to Modesto, Manteca, Firebaugh, Mendota, then up to Gilroy. We followed the tomatoes and cucumbers. In Modesto, we worked the grapes.

"We started out at four in the morning. We'd go for an hour or two, then I'd drive the three oldest to the school and race back to the field. Junior, Enrique, Celina, they sat on the steps of the school every day until it opened. The babies were with us, sleeping in tomato crates. For four years until we came here, that was our life from March to October. We didn't question it.

"In Modesto, the owner, of course, was a gringo, but a good man. He had only twenty acres. We lived in a bungalow on his place. He treated us well. During those years, although I'd worked with a union in Texas, I thought only about the health of the vines. We were happy to return for the next season.

"The large growers over there," I continued, "the ones with thousands of acres—and it's the same as here—to them, the workers are nothing. There's no respect. Until Chávez came along, there was no one to wake up the people. When I was in Modesto, I saw no injustices because I didn't experience it directly and I preferred not to look around too closely."

Nacho sat back in his chair and rested his head against the wall of the trailer.

"Yeah, well, you weren't alone ...and now you have eyes to see," he mused. "But the growers cling to their old habits, the way it was when the *braceros* came under contract and heavy control, then left quietly when the harvest was in, as arranged. Now, with Chávez, it's changing. The people are waking up. I hear them saying 'Get ready! Once César comes, if they don't sign, we walk!'"

A week later, I visited with Mingo and Pancho Vega in Mingo's worn Chevy Carryall. We were drinking a beer at day's end. As we discussed our experiences in the fields, we found ourselves resenting offenses that previously we had hardly noticed. Pancho Vega spoke first.

"I was cutting lettuce at the time with my daughter, Estella. We were working side-by-side, *usted sabe*. It was her first day. I was showing her which heads to keep and which ones to toss. We worked for two hours. She noticed the foreman bringing a five-gallon container of Kool-Aid. He set it on a folding table along the road, same as always. He laid a dipper down beside it.

"After he left, Estella went over. '*Papi*, where are the cups?' she called to me. I yelled back. 'No cups. Just drink it.' I showed her with my hands. She looked around. At that moment, three of the men stepped up. They started taking turns, drinking from the dipper. A woman was waiting. My daughter watched as the woman sipped the juice.

"When the woman finished, she offered the dipper to Estella. My daughter was fourteen. Her mother had taught her hygiene. I could see tears starting up in her sad eyes. She stared at the spoon in her hand. She put it down. She didn't take a drink. She returned to the lettuce, picked up her knife, and started cutting.

"Of course, she was right. I was proud of her that day. But then, I asked myself, why had I been so accepting of that indignity for so long?"

"*¡Ay!* What kind of life is this that the people have?" Mingo asked. "*Mi amigo*, Carlos Carrillo, he has a daughter, too, Guadalupe. You reminded me of her story. She was *una pistola*! You should've seen her. She's gone now with her husband. She married a gringo, you all know him, Robbie Rich, the union organizer. After he left the boycott, he helped the youth here put together the car clubs and got them involved in organizing up and down the valley. Anyway, Lupita could cut the lettuce faster than any of the men. Strong and proud! *Orgullosa, la mujer! Y una chavista de la chingada!*" Mingo's thick brows rose with the words and his lips pulled back from his large teeth.

"I asked Carlos how is it that she's so strong, not only in body but in heart? He told me that when they came here the first time, they lost her. They traveled from Texas. She was maybe five. They stopped somewhere for gas along the way. It was dusk. All of the kids piled out. But then, when they piled back in, it was dark. Little Lupe was still in the bathroom. They drove off, but she wasn't in the car.

"Her parents, of course, were distressed, but with everyone sleeping, they had driven for hours unaware. They returned to the station the following day in hopes she would be waiting, but in the panic another family passing through had offered to take her, thinking that they could catch up, which they never did.

"She lived with that family for two years, crying herself to sleep at night and hanging onto her hope. Sure enough, someone who knew someone else who had heard the story eventually brought them back together. It was right here in Salinas they found each other."

"How many of our friends and acquaintances have died on the roads?" I asked. "They think they're still living in the middle of the Sonoran desert or Tamaulipas. They drink a beer or two and drive or maybe they're walking down Highway 101 or Old Stage or along Williams Road. They roll the car into a ditch or stumble into the night traffic, and a passerby strikes them. You see it in the papers. You hear it on the radio. You go to the funeral Masses. It happened in Texas too. We don't understand the risks here. In our heads, we live a different life. We come unprepared for what we find."

"Every year, two or three workers die under a tractor or by some freak accident," Pancho stated bitterly. "Remember Tereso Morales over in Watsonville? He drove the tractor up a little mound, and it rolled over on him, leaving four children fatherless. Remember Lito, who stood a thirty-foot irrigation pipe on end to move it, unaware of the power lines above him? The pipe touched the wires and electrocuted him. The poor fellow died instantly. I ask again, ¿Qué clase de vida tiene nuestra gente? And we haven't even mentioned the pesticides and the short-handled hoe."

Nacho blew disgust through his teeth. "Bending over all day, thinning the lettuce with that hoe—el cortito—has destroyed the backs of a generation of farmworkers. And the chemicals they throw out there with little thought of who might be working a neighboring field. What will it take to make them stop and think?"

While an unusually hot Salinas summer trudged onward, the other organizers and I felt the momentum growing among the workers. The residents selected a committee. Nacho,

Rogelio, Pancho, Mingo, and I were among the chosen. We culled through the grievances and presented to Pic 'n Pac those demands that we thought we could win.

"I was told that we have to submit them to the general manager, Johnny Simpson," Peña reported. "I took the list to the Pic 'n Pac office. One of the girls promised to give it to him."

"And I called Delano," Nacho stated. "I got a hold of Richard, *usted sabe*, César's brother. I gave him our names. He didn't know what to tell me. He said that they've never had a group elect its own committee before a union contract was in place. 'If management will talk to you, great!' he said. 'Do what you think is best.'"

In the San Joaquín and Imperial Valleys, the workers were much less inclined to take matters into their own hands. Nacho Molina said that Chávez and Marshall Ganz, his chief organizer, had complained often about the lack of strong leadership and initiative among their members in these other agricultural centers of California. We Texan migrants in Salinas admired Chávez, but we weren't in awe of him as were many elsewhere. We didn't want or expect him to call all of the shots. It was, after all, our union, not only his.

The committee submitted its grievances: issues concerning wages, working conditions, supervisor abuses, and favoritism. Johnny Simpson promised to look at the list and get back to us. A week later, Simpson called Peña.

"What we're gonna do is this," he asserted. "We're gonna deliver a toilet to each field. I don't have no authority to discuss any of these other items. You'll have to meet with the top brass for them."

Although the victory was limited, the people celebrated and the committee was encouraged. As it turned out, however, the sanitary units were old and rotten. In one case, a woman sat down, and the poorly built base broke in half, leaving her embarrassed, wet, and very angry. We pressed our demands again, and eventually new toilets arrived.

We weren't alone. Workers at Freshpict, InterHarvest, and other companies had also organized and submitted demands. In fact, these other ranch committees had received stronger support from the union than Pic 'n Pac's had.

"It's because Chávez isn't thinking about strawberries," Nacho said. "No. They're thinking about lettuce. When they come here, they'll go after the lettuce growers first."

The pressure in the valley continued to build, so much so that the union acquiesced and held a rally at the Towne House Motel. I was in the crowd. I watched from a distance and admired César Chávez, this man of both small and great stature, wearing the straw hat of a simple laborer. We saw him as one of us.

He stood at the platform amidst cheering and applause. He appeared animated and confident.

"I praise you for your spirit and determination and for the progress you've made in opening negotiations with management. But I also warn you to expect trouble, anguish, and powerful opposition in your fight."

After the rally, we met with César in one of the hotel's conference rooms. Marshall Ganz led him in and then departed. I stepped forward immediately and introduced myself.

"I've heard your name," Chávez said, giving me a quick glance. "You're one of those Texans, right?"

"*Cierto*," I acknowledged proudly. Chávez motioned for everyone to sit down as he took a chair in the small circle. He wasted no time expressing his concern.

"You guys are moving too fast," he said, speaking in short, quick sentences. "We didn't want to start here yet, you know. We're still fighting for our lives in Delano and Coachella. Once we begin here, these growers are going to come after us."

"We're already signing cards and submitting a list of grievances," Mingo boasted.

"I know that. That's the problem. You're a lot more active and aggressive than the members over in the San Joaquín. I hear it's because you're all Texans. Is that right?" Chávez smiled, and everyone chuckled and nodded in turn. His tone turned more serious. "Listen. The fact is we really aren't ready for a strike here. We don't have the people or the money it takes to support one. Unfortunately, as I said earlier, even if we aren't ready, we may have no choice. There's this rumor that the growers here are trying to cut a sweetheart deal with the Teamsters." He paused and looked around the room. "That's what they're after. They want the Teamsters to be your union. What do you think about that?"

As had happened at the rally, we loudly signaled our disdain for the idea.

"So that's the kind of crap we're likely to be facing. We're going to have to give them one hell of a fight, more than we're ready for, and that's why we've had to hold back. But, at the same time, that's why we came to this rally tonight, even though we're fighting on two other fronts." Again, he looked at each man for a moment before continuing. "Besides, you're not alone. It's also happening in Oregon and Washington State. On the one hand, we are happy to see it. But then, we can't be everywhere at once."

"César," I said, pushing my white Stetson back on my head, "you don't have to be here. We'll take care of the business in Salinas. Everyone here is ready to do whatever's needed. You come when you can. Advise us. We'll manage the rest."

Some of the men nodded their concurrence. Chávez stared at me with his calm chocolate eyes. He said nothing, as if he had not fully understood what I was suggesting, as if the notion that the union might succeed without his direct oversight was unthinkable. I was ready to discuss my idea in more detail, but he gave no response to my statement.

"You have to realize that strikes are going to be very hard on you and your families," he continued. "We've been through it all in Delano and Coachella, and you know what?" He waited as if to give his words more weight. "The grape boycott's a much more powerful tool. You need both strikes and boycotts to some degree, but the growers fear the boycott more, especially these national corporations like Purex and United Brand and your boss, S. S. Pierce. They'll be prime targets for a national boycott and they know it. Strikes take a lot of resources to be successful. So I need you to think very carefully about what you want to do."

"One thing is certain, César," Mingo stated. "No one wants the Teamsters here!"

Marshall Ganz came back into the room. He stood quietly on the edge of the circle of chairs. He listened for a moment, then César spoke again.

"Let's hope the growers don't do something stupid and start a war in Salinas!"

Ganz interrupted the conversation.

"We have to go."

Chávez rose and shook hands one by one with the committee members.

"We'll be back, maybe sooner than later," he said. As he approached me, he paused and observed me keenly for a moment before we reached toward each other. "We need your cooperation," he said. "Right now, they're coming at us from all sides, but we'll be back. In the meantime, stay in touch with Marshall. He'll be coming and going between here and Delano and Coachella as needed." Ganz ushered his charge toward the exit.

"*Seguimos pues,*" I responded.

"*¡Sí se puede!*" Chávez called over his shoulder. "And just keep working!"

"*¡Por cierto*, César!"

"*¡Gracias*, César!"

"We see you soon!"

"*¡Adios!*"

"*¡Hasta luego*, César!"

I watched Chávez disappear out the door. I turned to Nacho.

"Maybe Peña's right," I said. "Maybe we should push forward on our own. Start our own union."

Nacho tilted his head and shrugged his shoulders, dismissing my comment.

"In any case, it's time to meet with Johnny Simpson's boss," he said.

A few weeks later, after we'd had another rally, Marshall Ganz paid a visit. The committee gathered in front of my trailer. All of the members were eager to build on the progress that we had made. We had defined our issues—wages, sanitation, pesticides—and had presented them to Pic 'n Pac's management.

"Señor Ganz," I began, "we've been meeting with the company, and we think we've reached agreement on pay and on some grievances. Now we just need for you to bring the contracts and help us fill in the blanks so that we can get the *jefe* to sign."

Ganz was, perhaps, five feet nine, a roundish man with curly black hair, a bushy moustache, and thick, circle-shaped glasses. Molina said that he was born and raised in Bakersfield and entered Harvard after high school. He left there before graduating to join the civil rights work in the South, trying to help black people vote. After that, rather than return to school, he took up with Chávez and the union cause. Now he was the chief architect of the national boycott. He looked at me for a long moment, as if measuring his response.

"It's not that simple, Don Sixto. Don't get me wrong. What you're doing through the committee is fine. I understand you're making progress. César is very impressed with all of you over here. Hey, when we told him about the toilets, he was even more impressed." He smiled and everyone laughed. "No. It's an important issue," he continued, "and a smart issue. It was exactly the right issue to start with. Who can be against providing toilets? So, again, you're doing good work, but before contracts are prepared, Jerry has to be here and maybe Dolores to complete the negotiations." Ganz was referring to Jerry Cohen, the union's attorney, and Dolores Huerta, its vice president. "They can't come now. They're working night and day on the contracts with the Delano growers."

I was impatient. I wasn't looking for praise or excuses. I was looking for help. The union had told us to get ready. In our minds, we were ready.

"¡Chingados!" I muttered. "That's fucked!"

Nacho glanced at me as if to counsel patience. Marshall Ganz surveyed the committee for other comments. Mingo and Peña said nothing. Ganz spoke for twenty minutes about the union's ongoing struggles with the grape strike and with the national boycott. Then he stopped and looked at his watch.

"I should get over to Freshpict," he said. "We'll see you next time." He shook Molina's hand in passing and headed for his car.

Elida and I spent our days bent over in the fields, picking strawberries on Old Stage Road, a few miles southeast of Salinas. Junior and Enrique paralleled our movement along the furrows. The rows of leafy green plants freckled with sweet red berries stretched broad and wide north and south along the valley floor and eastward to the base of the Gabilan Range. Often, a gray mist drifted inland from the ocean fifteen miles to the west. It blocked the morning sun and chilled our juice-stained fingers as we busily plucked the ripened fruit from its stem and gently dropped it into the basket-lined cardboard trays.

The labor required constant bending or squatting beside the beds. Our muscles grew tense from twisting toward the vines then back toward the waiting trays and from pulling the steel-framed carts that held the boxes of harvested berries. Our thighs and calves grew exhausted and sore from the hours spent stooped over while moving in tiny steps. Our arms and shoulders ached, fingers throbbed, eyes weary but vigilant in our search for only the ripest and largest fruit.

Throughout the early summer weeks, low-hanging clouds eventually lifted, revealing a glow of sunlight tempered by a softening, late-morning breeze. The crews of men, women, and teenage boys and girls were scattered across Pic 'n Pac's six hundred-acre field. Here and there, a toddler ran along the rows, and a young mother stopped her berry gathering just long enough to call the wanderer back to her side.

Across the two-lane Old Stage Road, a group of lettuce cutters also bent low at the waist, swished its knives deftly at the base of each head of lettuce, heavy with the moist air. Five hours into our day, we took a brief lunch break. Elida retrieved our carrying bags from the bus with the other women. She spread a blanket at the side of a dirt road as the boys and I left our harvesting to join her.

Other workers gathered in small groups, dotting the road with their own *cobijas* and reclining next to the verdant leaves, blossoms, and fruit. The aroma of freshly made tortillas and carne asada, chicken enchiladas, and refried beans soon overwhelmed the earthy smell of the rich soil, raising everyone's spirits.

I sat down, hitting the ground heavily and sighing with exhaustion. I noticed that Enrique was stepping on the last of the berry plants along the row.

"No, no, Enrique!" I admonished, "Don't step there. You know better than that. Respect the plants, *m'ijo!*"

"*¡Güey!*" Junior exclaimed, giving his brother a friendly shove as they both settled themselves on the blanket.

"That's enough!" Elida said. She poured a glass of juice for each of them.

"I don't see Mateo Molina out here anymore," I remarked. "What's happening with him?" Junior looked down at the ground for a moment, remembering how Mateo had out-picked Enrique and him during those first days. He looked at his mother and then at me. I sensed that my oldest son, now almost fourteen, wasn't eager to respond. "What's happening?" I repeated.

"He claims he's gotten a better job at a car wash. You know, the one on North Main."

I watched Junior again stare at the ground. I glanced at Elida. I huffed at the idea that Mario could make more money at a car wash than he could make picking berries. I scratched my neck and looked back at my sheepish boy. It was clear that Junior didn't want to continue, but he felt my eyes on him.

"He turned eighteen and moved out," he stated. "I heard that he got involved with a gang in East Salinas."

"Oh my!" Elida groaned and put her hand to her mouth. "I hope you never do anything like that to us, Son."

"Gangs are stupid! Mateo is stupid! Tell them, Junior," Enrique said. Junior pursed his lips toward his brother and looked back at his parents.

"What?" I asked.

"They say he's selling drugs."

"Are his parents aware of what is going on?" I asked.

"I don't know," Junior replied.

"*¡Dios mío!*" Elida whispered to herself.

I pulled a pack of Marlboros from my shirt pocket and lit a cigarette.

"When I was that age," I said, exhaling the smoke, "I lost my father forever. I can't imagine doing something like that to my parents."

"Delia's heart will be broken when she learns," Elida said.

"You're right, Enrique," I said. "That's really stupid! Some of these kids have no respect. No respect for themselves or for their own families. They should understand what it is to watch your father die. They would learn quickly, as I did, what life is about."

In the early afternoon, a strong breeze blew across our bent backs. As the sun found its highest arc, the breeze flew, snapping against our loosely fitting jackets and trousers. The women, wearing ball caps that cupped protective scarves about their faces, pulled the cloth tighter so that only noses and eyes felt the pelting and gusts. We all labored on until, finally, at two o'clock, with the wind sweeping the crop still more fiercely and rustling the plastic sheeting beneath each plant, the foreman honked the horn of the bus and called us back to the main road.

CHAPTER EIGHT

At three in the morning, I awoke to pounding on the door of the trailer.

"*¡Despierta*, Sixto! *¡Despierta!*"

I arose and fumbled my way toward the noise in undershorts and a T-shirt.

"*¿Quién es?* Who's calling?"

"Mingo! I need to speak with you, Sixto! They're here!"

"*¡Momentito!*"

I returned to the bedroom and pulled on a pair of pants, then hurried back to open the door. I stepped onto the porch. Mingo stood below me, out of breath. He tried to whisper but was too excited.

"I've been running from trailer to trailer," he said. "The committee has to meet! Marshall Ganz is here! He just arrived!"

"Where? Why?"

"He's over at Freshpict. Everything's changed. They found out that the growers are going with the Teamsters!"

"*¡No! ¡Pendejos!*"

"*¡Sí!* They've already signed contracts with no workers voting and nobody signing cards!"

"*¡Pura Caca!* Bullsheet!"

"We need to meet at Freshpict now."

A half hour later, five of the committee members, including me, pulled into Freshpict's distribution yard. Marshall Ganz was already addressing the thirty or more workers gathered. He wore a windbreaker and baggy pants. Low clouds hung over the July morning, typical of Salinas in midsummer. The Freshpict packing sheds rose behind him. He spoke in Spanish.

"Now is the hour for these growers!" he called out to the men. "*¡Ahora es cuando!* We have seen this before! In Delano, a couple of years ago, they tried this Teamster trick. They tried to sign their sweetheart contracts. It didn't work there and it won't work here! It serves only to show their arrogance!"

"*¡Viva la causa!*" the assembled all shouted repeatedly. "*¡Viva la huelga!*"

Upon hearing the word "*huelga,*" I turned to a stranger next to me in the crowd.

"They're talking about a strike?"

"*¡Sí! ¡Por cierto!*" the stranger said, eyeing me briefly.

"When?"

"Today! This morning! You should not go out to work!" With the others, the man began pumping his fist in the air and chanting, "*¡Ahora!* This is the hour!"

Ganz held up a handful of union membership cards.

"Who is ready to sign a card with UFWOC?" The men all raised their hands. "Who is ready to go out of here and sign up others?"

"*¡Vamos!*" they all shouted.

"*¡Viva la huelga!*" they repeated. Some began clapping ever more quickly in unison while others waved the union's red flag with its emblazoned black eagle.

When the rally ended, we returned to La Posada. We roused the residents and spread the word that the strike had begun. The people heard the shouts coming from throughout the trailer park.

"*¡Huelga!*"

"*¡Ahora es cuando!*"

"*¡Viva la unión!*"

"*¡Chávez, sí! ¡Teamsters, no!*"

Their voices filled the morning air as the workers, who had been prepared for this moment, emerged into the driveways and pathways. The chants grew into a feverish chorus as others joined in, finally settling on one incantation.

"*¡Huelga! ¡Huelga! ¡Huelga!*"

La gente pushed toward each other and into the trailer park's central thoroughfare. The chanting grew louder until it reached a mesmerizing pitch. At that moment, someone called out above the din, "*¡El nuevo grito es 'huelga!'*" and in our minds, the word "*huelga*" was, indeed, transformed into "*el grito,*" the mythic "shout" that, 160 years before, had ignited Mexico's revolution against Spain. Now, with every shout, the people felt as if Padre Miguel Hidalgo y Costilla himself had risen up from his bloodied grave and was coming to lead them once again with a call for "*¡Independencia!*"

At seven o'clock, the Pic 'n Pac buses pulled onto Sherwood Drive only to discover that they could not take their routine routes through La Posada. The strikers had drawn the chains across each of the five entrances. No one came forward to board the buses on the street. Instead, the agitated crowd greeted the drivers with its chanting, trying to convince them to join the strike. The drivers sat in a line staring silently. Finally, they left to inform their crew bosses that, on this day, they would have no harvesters.

The crowd lingered near La Posada's entrance. Marshall Ganz appeared. Someone had driven to the union office to inform him that Pic 'n Pac crews had declared a strike. The workers gathered around. His presence re-ignited the rhythmic chants. As the committee members and I approached, Ganz showed both enthusiasm and concern at the turn of events. He moved closer to Nacho and me in order to be heard above the clamor.

"You know, this is a surprise to us," he stated. "We were expecting that Freshpict might go out, but not you guys. With you joining, we'll be taking on both the lettuce and strawberry industries at once? It's not a great strategy!" The chanting continued. "Chávez is at the office. I'm going to see if he wants to come over here and talk to you."

Soon we all had heard that César would arrive. When he appeared, the crowd of five hundred men, women, and children had grown still more excited. We greeted him with sustained applause and *gritos*.

"*¡Viva Chávez!*"

"*¡Viva la unión!*"

"*¡Viva la huelga!*"

He spoke in the open air with the people pushing in to hear him.

"I am asking you all to return to the fields!" he shouted. "You're in for a long struggle that the union won't be able to support. We don't have the necessary resources for this fight at this moment!"

"*¡Viva la huelga!*"

"*¡Viva la huelga!*"

Chávez soon realized that he could not convince the workers to give up their belief that they would win by striking now, when the growers were most vulnerable. The following day, a formal vote to strike was approved. Workers at InterHarvest and Freshpict also walked out, and crews from numerous other companies were soon to follow.

We La Posada strikers knew little about what our actions would bring by way of recrimination; still, we voted for the strike willingly and with confidence. Our bravado grew out of ignorance of what lay ahead as much as confidence in ourselves. Neither the people nor we committee members had any idea how we would move forward beyond this bold beginning.

César Chávez moved quickly. He obtained a loan from the Franciscan Friars Province of Santa Barbara to open an office on Wood Street in East Salinas and set up a strike fund. He threatened a national boycott of lettuce if the companies didn't accept UFWOC's demands and recognize its claim to represent all of the workers who were now on strike. The union's chief attorney, Jerry Cohen, arrived to push forward the negotiations. Union staff administered a strike fund, providing a small stipend to those on the line.

The weekend following our walkout, we held a rally attended by thousands of workers, many of whom marched for days to join the demonstration and to pledge their allegiance. Chávez stood before the crowd and recounted the union's successes, but he was quick to cry out against this recent move by the growers.

"On the day..." he declared with indignation, "on the very same day that the grape growers in the San Joaquín acquiesced to our demands, on the very day that they had agreed, after five years of fighting in the fields, to sign contracts with the union ...on that very day the growers in the Salinas Valley and others as far south as Santa Maria announced that they had signed their own set of contracts—not with the farmworkers' union but with the Teamsters!" Chávez sliced the air with an emphatic chop of his hand.

"These sweetheart deals are designed for only one purpose, to preempt the farmworkers—all of you—and to undercut your union by giving to the Teamsters the right to represent the area's farm labor force! These fraudulent contracts cover thousands of full-time and part-time employees. Not one of these employees—not one farmworker—was invited to participate in the discussions. Instead, the companies and the Teamsters conducted their negotiations in secret! Isn't a union something the farmworkers should choose for themselves? These bogus agreements will not stand!"

I had learned that Chávez had always embraced nonviolence and had demonstrated through his fasting and passion his commitment to that ideal. Many priests and other ministers had gathered around him and had supported him. They wanted us to follow the beliefs of leaders like Martin Luther King and of another great man from India named Mahatma Gandhi. On the other hand, the union encouraged us to provoke and defy the growers.

Our walkout pushed emotions and tensions in the valley to the breaking point. Chávez himself told us that he was fearful that a long and aggressive strike would almost certainly lead to more violence, just as it did in the San Joaquín; yet, the drama of a march or a fast or a picket line brought the workers together in great numbers. We believed that people who organized around the single idea of a union could overcome the growers' superior resources and influence.

Nacho Molina had taught me that Chávez was a student of Saul Alinsky, the same man who had organized in Rio Grande City, Texas. He had also organized the workers in the slaughterhouses of Chicago back in the forties. Nacho said that another man, named Fred Ross, in San Francisco, with Alinsky's backing, initiated the Community Services Organization where Chavez, then a young leader from San Jose, learned how to organize. To Alinsky, Nacho explained, all opponents must be viewed as "the enemy," and the only way to bring change was to provoke and defy "the enemy." These ideas were the guideposts of the union's organizing tactics. They had proven to be successful in taming the San Joaquín Valley growers.

Each day, I delivered membership cards from trailer to trailer and retrieved them once the workers had signed. La Posada's strikers joined thousands of *chavistas* from Salinas to Santa Maria and from Watsonville to Gilroy. We gathered on the outlying roads. We waved our red and black flags and banners. We threw up picket lines and called for the scabs to leave the lettuce to rot.

The political lines, too, were drawn. The Salinas Valley divided against itself with the large majority of Anglos on one side and the large majority of Mexicans on the other. The Teamsters sent their enforcers with American flags to patrol and intimidate us. We confronted the growers and their Teamster goons in the north and south near Highway 101 and into the fields along the valley's interior roads.

Our excitement within the labor camps and out on the roads was universal. Our supporters—some politicians, the priests and ministers, and many among their flocks, even some of the press—all were confident that our cause was just and righteous. Equally strong was the outrage and resentment among the growers and their advocates. No upstart Mexican could tell them how to run their businesses.

Just after the growers signed their contracts with the Teamsters, Chávez accused the companies of launching a "Pearl Harbor attack" on farmworkers. The major Salinas newspaper, *The Californian*, reprinted an editorial from *Agribusiness News*. Peña summarized the article for us.

"According to Anthony Harrigan, executive vice president of the Southern States Industrial Council, because of the drive to unionize, farmworkers were becoming 'captives of farm labor bosses,' a condition that would increase food prices and decrease production."

It was strange that Anthony Harrigan said that we were "becoming captives" at a time when most of us felt like we were gaining a new sense of freedom.

Vicente Molina, Nacho's younger brother, washed dishes at The Pub Bar and Grill on Monterey Street. The Pub catered to the grower community. Its décor fostered the Salinas Valley's veneer of cowboy culture that supported the annual "California Rodeo." The bar's dimmed lights and thick, dark-stained wood provided the perfect ambience for smokes and drinks, for the exchange of tips and promises, for whispered gossip and knowing winks, and for sharing the latest stories from out there, beyond the darkness, in the valley's fields and sheds.

Vicente spoke English well. He was easygoing and friendly with a faint moustache and a youthful swagger. He bounced freely from table to table, clearing the glasses and plates and listening, always listening and reporting back to our committee.

On a Saturday night in early September, the Teamster thwackers arrived from the San Joaquín Valley. Twenty or more well-plied and spirited "enforcers," in a ruckus of shouts and laughter, piled out of their pickups and buses. They and their wives and girlfriends thrumbled their way through the already crowded bar and grill. They lined up along the rail and mingled among the tables, noisily greeting the growers and local Teamster field staff already in the room.

Their leader was a brash and blustering bully of a man named Ted Gonsalves, whom everyone called "Speedy." His high-strung persona and seamy entourage quickly gave the place a harder edge. He had dark, bulbous eyes, a tangle of black hair, and a penchant for big cars and pretty women. He was wearing a shiny pinstriped suit set off by a gaudy shirt and tie. Not long after making his entrance, Gonsalves planted himself in the central pathway between the bar and the booths. Raising a mug full of brew, he proclaimed his purpose.

"You all know why we're here! One reason and one reason only: to take care of those sonsabitches and to restore order in this valley! And that's what we're gonna do!" Everyone applauded and raised his glass.

The Teamster gorillas brought with them a reputation for violence perpetrated during the union's battle over grape contracts. Gonsalves was edgy and ostentatious. His tactic was straightforward: spread fear and intimidation. We strikers watched warily as the newcomers patrolled the fields, standing tall in the back of their pickups with rifles held high.

The days passed. The number of depredations grew. One of the ranch foremen took a Caterpillar tractor and rammed it into a car belonging to a picketer. A Teamster goon smashed Jerry Cohen in the jaw, putting him in the hospital for a week with a concussion. A striker, accused of throwing rocks at a scab, was shot and wounded. In Santa Maria, three union members were arrested for shooting and wounding a strikebreaker.

The local press carried stories of bombs detonated in barns and the burning of vegetable crates, of vandalized trucks and severed tractor hoses. Some denounced the picketers. Others claimed that the Teamsters perpetrated the crimes, a plot designed to discredit the *chavistas*.

Rogelio Peña, among the younger and more radical of the La Posada picketers, had taken to wearing a green military jacket set off by rounded dark glasses and a brown beret as if he were Ché Guevara himself. He tucked his pants into the tops of his combat boots. He and nine of his contemporaries— young Chicano organizers like Johnny Martínez—joined under the banner *Carnales Unidos*. Soon all had donned brown shirts, tilted berets, and dark glasses.

Wherever Chávez spoke in the valley, they flanked him, to the right and left, an erect and vigilant security brigade, arms folded behind, feet spread wide. In the evenings, *la cuadrilla* drove stealthily out of the trailer park and into the valley's pocketed labor camps to educate, cajole, and threaten strikebreakers. They carried ball bats and screwdrivers, helpful tools in the work of disabling the cars and trucks of impenitent scabs.

Jerry Cohen recovered from his beating and set up a full-time office in Salinas. Dolores Huerta arrived to take charge of negotiations. Marshall Ganz met with the ranch committees to keep us informed on the progress of the talks.

Fearful that the union would call for a national boycott not only of their produce but of all of their product lines, the east coast companies—InterHarvest's owner, United Brands; Freshpict's parent, Purex; and Pic 'n Pac, a subsidiary of S. S. Pierce's—flew in their executives to meet with Chávez, Huerta, and Cohen.

The union clearly had the allegiance of the large majority of the valley's farmworkers. The executives found themselves squeezed between the demands of their employees and the resistance of the local growers, with whom the national corporations conducted their business.

As the strike spread from company to company and the threat of national boycotts thickened, United Brands' skittish board of directors pushed its executives to sign with the union and its red and black label. The company's own label, "Chiquita Banana," was too susceptible to the union's boycott tactics. The sullied history in Mexico and Guatemala of its predecessor corporation, United Fruit, made United Brands more vulnerable than any local grower. For over seventy years, through bribery, political intrigue, and—with the support of the US government and its military—other heavy-handed strategies, United Fruit Company had maintained its control over railroads, shipping, and vast tracts of land throughout Latin America and the Caribbean.

Within two and a half weeks of seeing its employees walk out, InterHarvest buckled and signed the valley's first UFWOC contract.

Chávez and a thousand farmworkers met at the union office on Wood Street in East Salinas to celebrate the victory. The animated leader trumpeted the contract as the crowning achievement of the long years of struggle. The agreement reflected major concessions on every front: wages, medical benefits, a ban on some pesticides, the power to dispatch the workers—preempting the long-entrenched and much despised labor contractors—and seniority in dispatching the workers out of a union-run hiring hall.

The ranch committee, together with dozens of La Posada residents, attended the rally and cheered with the jubilant crowd. Since the arrival of Dolores Huerta and Jerry Cohen, we had taken a back seat in the negotiation process. I had to admit that the union's experienced negotiators had pushed InterHarvest far beyond the lines that our committee had drawn in our preliminary talks with Pic 'n Pac management.

The locally based owners were shocked and enraged by the unexpected turn of events. D'Arrigo Brothers, Merrill Farms, Al Hansen, and others refused to negotiate with Chávez. They found it difficult to deem him and his "crazies from over the hill" worthy of their attention. It galled the locals that national corporations—outsiders like InterHarvest—had betrayed them and put the entire industry in jeopardy. They turned to local law enforcement, to the courts, and to state and federal governments, institutions that tended to side with the powerful grower community.

In light of the stubbornness shown by these local companies, Chávez called for a national boycott of non-union lettuce. This was the very move that the growers had tried to avoid by signing with the Teamsters and then demanding that their workers join the Teamsters' union or face dismissal.

At eight o'clock in the morning, some of the committee, including Mingo, Pancho, Molina, and me, left the union hall. We piled into Mingo's '59 Chevy Impala. Marshall Ganz had briefed us. We were to drive out to Hitchcock Road almost to Davis Road. A wispy August fog drifted in from the ocean. As we approached the designated target, we could see perhaps twenty picketers with signs and flags and a few feet beyond, a dozen of the growers' supporters. The two opposing groups were shouting at each other. Along the pavement's edge, adjacent to a dirt road, sat three sheriff's cars—presumably to discourage anyone who might attempt to approach the distant crew of scabs cutting lettuce. Mingo drove toward the gathering.

"So we just ignore them?" he asked. I sat next to the window with Peña in between.

"That's what Ganz told us," I said.

"Look!" Nacho pointed toward the opposing crowd. "Over there, some of the Fresno Gang!" Three of the San Joaquín interlopers, surrounded by other local anti-union protesters, waved American flags and held signs reading: "No to unions! No to boycotts!"

"I hope this works," Mingo stated as he arced the Impala to the right and then jerked the wheels sharply to the left just past the vigilant posse. He completed the turn and hit the gas pedal. The car lurched forward along the narrow field road in a slashing fishtail, heading pell-mell toward the lettuce scabs. His foot pressed the floor until the car reached fifty miles per hour.

"Here they come!" cried Molina, who peered through the rear window. A dark green patrol car raced after us.

"Hang on!" Mingo yelled.

Within a few seconds, the Chevy, bouncing roughly along the road's rutted surface, drew near to the harvesting. Mingo hit the brakes and skidded to a stop. We had come for only one purpose, to harass the scabs. We quickly exited the still-shuddering automobile and began shouting and admonishing the gaping pickers.

"Stop working!" we called. "Join us *en la huelga!*" we urged, waving and beckoning. "Don't be the growers' *pendejos!*" We paid no attention to our uniformed pursuers, who soon made their own screeching entrance onto the scene as the cutters stared in amazement, their lettuce knives dangling at their sides.

Two deputies jumped from their vehicle and immediately ran toward us. They shouted their demands to "cease and desist!" We ignored the officers and continued to harass and yell at the cutters until the officers had closed in and were confronting us face-to-face.

"Get off this land!" they screamed. "You are in violation of the law!"

Up to this moment, it had all worked just as Ganz had predicted during the morning briefing. Peña, who alone in the group had a strong command of English, now stepped forward.

"Officers," he said calmly, "call me crazy, but it's my belief that you have no right to demand that we leave this property. We have been advised that only the owner of this land can determine whether we are legally trespassing. To our knowledge, the owner isn't here."

Peña had practiced his part well. One of officers removed his sunglasses and stared disdainfully at the speaker's fatigues and beret. "Smartass!" I guessed he was thinking. But as Peña's words settled in, the deputy's expression changed from scorn to bewilderment. He turned to his older colleague for support.

"What's goin' on?" he asked. "Is that right?" The second deputy hesitated, eyeing the group and considering his options.

"Yeah, I'm afraid it is." Without another word, the two deputies trudged back to their car as we continued our efforts with the cutters and the cutters returned to their scab labor.

In mid-September, a local judge declared the farmworkers' strike to be illegal. With this decision, the sheriff's department had a new weapon against the picketers and new grounds for keeping us away from the scabs. Its officers dispersed or arrested anyone who ignored the court order. Despite the setback, the picketers continued to picket and Huerta and Cohen continued to negotiate, keeping up the pressure on the unsigned national companies. Chávez, concerned that more picketing would only increase the violence, turned his attention to the national boycott.

A month after the InterHarvest triumph, Freshpict—all of whose crews had walked out on strike—acknowledged that it did not have sufficient workers to complete the harvest. It, too, signed with the union. Likewise, Pic 'n Pac soon succumbed to the lack of workers to harvest the ever-ripening berries. Begrudgingly, it followed the others. It also signed with UFWOC.

Jubilant at our success, we Pic 'n Pac workers returned to the fields, earning a twenty-cent-per-box jump in pay, medical benefits, seniority in the distribution of work dispatches, and the right to file grievances. In spite of our victory, however, the organizing work continued.

"Now we'll go after the local companies and their Teamster contracts," Nacho stated. "When we're done picking berries for the day, the union needs us back out on the line."

One evening I stood before the ranch committee near La Posada's office, only twenty yards from the Sherwood Drive entrance to the trailer park. I had become a recognized leader of the families. On more than one occasion, local reporters had printed my comments in defense of the workers, and I had appeared on the evening news.

During tonight's meeting, the committee was discussing recurring problems with the administration of the Pic 'n Pac contract. The union office was responsible for dispatching the workers to the specific fields designated by the company. The committee members were hearing complaints of favoritism in the selection of crews.

Rumors—*chismes*—were circulating, accusing some of secretly paying for their work dispatches. The company foreman complained to the union that one of its staff was engaged in "suspicious dealings" in his distribution of this essential job voucher.

"We have to pressure Beto Garza," I insisted. "He's in charge of the hiring hall, no one else." As I spoke, I caught a glimpse of a pickup on Sherwood Drive and a flash of men with raised rifles racing by the entrance.

"Get down! *¡Al suelo!*" I shouted. An instant later, we heard shots and the distant thump-thump of bullets hitting metal. We lay beside our scattered chairs. I could hear Peña hissing over and over again.

"*¡Chingones! ¡Pinches chingones!*" We got to our feet and ran toward the open gate. We could see the pickup with its riders far up the road headed toward Laurel Drive.

"Crazy Teamster bastards!" Mingo bellowed angrily as the truck disappeared.

We heard a shout from inside the park and turned to see Sabino Montes running toward us up the central thoroughfare. He was screaming and holding something in his hand.

"Who's shooting?" he called. "Who's shooting?"

"We think it was the Teamster goons!" I responded as he approached.

Sabino stopped ten yards away and then walked rapidly to us. He was breathing heavily. His hand was still extended. When he reached us, he dropped the flattened head of a bullet in my hand.

"I found it stuck in the side of my trailer," he said.

"Crazy Teamster bastards!" Mingo repeated.

"*¡Están locos!* They could have killed one of my children!" Sabino barked, coughing to catch his breath. "We should call the police!"

Mingo scoffed at the idea.

"What good is that? The sheriffs are supporting the Teamsters and using their clubs against us! They're not going to come over here and do anything!"

Three days later, Peña, Mingo, Molina, Pancho Vega, and I walked along Hamilton Road, a half-mile outside of Salinas. A late summer heat wave had pushed lettuce production. Some of the strikers could not hold out any longer. They had returned to the fields to work under the Teamster contracts.

Chávez had told them, "Work if you must, but don't sign a Teamster card!"

Sheriff's cars were lined along the pavement's narrow shoulders. We could see the deputies forcefully removing the picketers from the line. We could hear them in the distance screaming "*¡Viva la huelga!*" as the officers roughly shoved them into backseats.

We moved through a large parking area at the edge of the crop. We brushed by the empty cars and trucks, out of the sight of the sheriff's posse and started into the fields, down a wide dirt road. We had spotted in the distance a crew of celery workers cutting and packing.

"Those *pendejos* aren't respecting the strike," Peña muttered. "They need an education."

Fifty yards in, a white flatbed truck with slotted gates on each side approached from behind and slowed beside us. Its wheel frames and fender were encrusted with dry dirt. Three Teamster ruffians occupied the cab. One of them was grasping a walkie-talkie. Five more rode behind. Some of them were shirtless. Others wore black motorcycle vests. They leaned against the clacking side rails. A muscular, ruddy-faced man with a tangle of red hair and thick eyebrows shaded by a soiled ball cap peered down at us. His sleeves were rolled to his elbows. He brandished a thirty-thirty rifle toward me.

"Hey, Torres!" he cried, jabbing the weapon higher into the unusually warm afternoon air. "We've got you fuckers on the run now!"

We stopped and stared upward. We shaded our eyes against the bright sun, catching glimpses of faces with dark glasses and hands holding more rifles and wooden bats.

"*Hola*, beaners!" another voice yelped. A large round and podgy mug appeared over the rail. The man's plaid shirt fell open, exposing a puffy, pinkish white chest. A three-foot link of chain hung around his neck and garlanded his shoulders. He carried a holstered pistol. He glared at Mingo and Molina.

"Go back where you came from. Your union is finished!"

The men laughed as the truck came to a full stop. A Borzoni logo was painted on its door. The image of "Lil' Moll," a friendly girl carrying a tray of fresh vegetables, smiled at me and beyond at the verdant celery fields. Poncho Vega had worked for Borzoni Farms in the past. It was a moderate-sized vegetable producer. Julius Borzoni was proud that his company had cultivated the valley for three generations.

We peered at the truck and its passengers in silence, then glanced at each other.

"Oh shit!" Mingo exclaimed.

We had nothing, no pistols, no rifles, no knives, no bats, no chains. *Nada*. We suddenly realized how foolish we had been to take this walk so unprepared, especially in light of the shooting incident only days before. Although the sheriffs were siding mostly with the growers, their presence nearby had given us a false sense of security from the marauding goons and gadflies.

The men in the cab jumped out and faced us. Backriders lumbered down off the flatbed. They outnumbered and outgunned us. We stood staring at each other. One of the goons looked down the line to his right.

"Hey, Rusty?" he asked. "What do you think we should do with 'em?"

Before Rusty could answer, I tried to lighten the mood.

"*Hola, amigos*, you are carrying a lot of *armas*," I mused. "Where are you going—to war?"

Rusty was not entertained. "What are you doin' out here?" he demanded.

As he spoke, I saw a white pickup speeding toward us from the distant parking lot, kicking up dust. The others turned. The vehicle stopped behind the flatbed. A middle-aged man exited. He was tall, trim, and tan. Despite the heat, he looked fresh and groomed in jeans, boots, and a neatly pressed, green cowboy shirt. He wore a white Stetson, not unlike the one that covered my head. He appeared angry and impatient as he strode toward us.

Poncho Vega recognized him as *el patrón*, Borzoni himself, the son of the company's founder. He stood in silence, dissecting each of us with his eyes. He focused on me for a long moment. Rusty leaned and whispered something.

"What are you doin' out here on my property?"

"*Mire*, señor," Mingo said in Spanish. "We're looking to pick some celery is all."

One of the cab riders translated. Borzoni ignored Mingo's response. He turned toward me, and his eyes narrowed with a hint of recognition.

"Torres," he called out as if exchanging pleasantries, "you're a lucky bastard. From what I hear, you should be dead by now."

I stood only ten feet away. I struggled to understand the man's words. Peña whispered the Spanish. I wondered how one could make such a statement without the slightest fear of recrimination. I called back in English.

"So you are *el chingón* who wants me dead."

Borzoni bowed his head and considered my response briefly. He took a deep breath, shaking his head slowly as if he was disappointed in me. He dropped a lick of spit on the ground. His face grew flushed with anger as he glared at us and over our shoulders at the distant scene of picketers and sheriffs.

"I'd think you'd show a little more respect, Torres," he stated, looking briefly toward his armed Teamster guards. "You're trespassing on my property. You should realize that I can do anything I want with you right now." As his anger grew, he stood stiffly, considering his options and struggling to control himself. He relaxed for a moment and rocked on the heels of his boots with his thumbs shoved into his wide belt. Then the anger flared again and he barked loudly, "I can do anything I want with you, goddamnit! Do you understand that? And when I see all you here like this, doin' what you're doin'," he stepped toward us, the targets of his fury and his disdain, "it wouldn't bother me a bit to see you *all* dead!"

No one spoke. Finally, he turned toward his car. Rusty followed, hoping for further instructions. We watched as he conferred with his crew of henchmen. I, too, was growing angrier as I listened and watched *el patrón*. I couldn't allow the man to leave without a response.

"*Hola*, señor," I called out. "Before you go, please answer this question: Why do you think it's so terrible for us to trespass on your land, but it's okay for your goons to shoot at us in our own homes? That's a real good question for you, no?" My cohorts looked at me with alarm. They weren't anxious to push any further.

As soon as the cab rider completed the translation of my words, Borzoni cut away from the others and came straight at me.

"Turn around and get the hell out of here! Now!" he shouted. The goons quickly moved toward us. "Don't be too rough on 'em, boys," Borzoni said. "They need to live to tell the others to stay away from this ranch."

The back-riders poked at us with their guns, pushing us down the road toward the parking area. We pushed back, brushing the weapons aside. Then, without warning, Mingo turned on the cab rider who had interpreted for Borzoni. He landed a solid punch across his head. The man barreled into Mingo.

"You bastard!" he gasped. Rusty moved swiftly and clubbed Mingo with the butt of his rifle, sending him sprawling on the ground. He lay in the dirt, blood oozing. He rolled onto his knees as if to rise up and attack but staggered and rolled helplessly onto his shoulder. We quickly surround him.

"*¡Suficiente! "¡Suficiente!*" I shouted. "We go now!" Vega and Peña helped Mingo to his feet.

"Fucking beaners!" Rusty barked. He and the others stood with their guns pointed. "Next time we catch you here, you're dead!"

CHAPTER NINE

As I approached our trailer, I saw Junior, Enrique, and Moisés kicking a soccer ball with two of the neighbor's boys. They had placed knee-high irrigation boots in the street, set to the width of a goal. Each of the players was pushing and shoving for control of the ball, kicking and laughing.

"Moisés, you're so slow anyone can take it from you," Enrique teased his younger brother, slicing the ball away with a quick move. "*¡Flojo!*"

"You think!" Moisés retorted. "You're the slowpoke!"

Although the youngest of the group, Moisés refused to let his size restrain his dogged pursuit of the ball. He shouldered his way into the mass of legs and shoes, using his shorter stature to his advantage.

"Shoot, *flojo!*" Junior joined Enrique in razzing Moisés. "You got the ball. Go for it!"

Moisés took his shot, but one of the neighbor's sons, Tabo, caught it easily and threw it to Junior. I stepped between him and the ball before my oldest son—now thirteen—realized I had joined the play.

"No fair, *papi!*" Junior shouted. Just then Celina came out of the trailer.

"It's Celina, Moisés, and I against you boys!" I shouted.

"We'll take you easily!" Enrique said, bumping his way toward a shot.

"That's it, Celina, move in!" Celina intervened and pushed the ball my way. I booted it toward the goal but too far left. Tabo retrieved it and again threw it to Junior. We all scrambled, butting shoulders and elbows and laughing all the while.

Enrique was truly the fastest among us, but Moisés was persistent in the chase, like a sparrow after a hawk. He finally managed to dislodge the ball from both Junior and Enrique's control. He hacked at it desperately, sending it toward Celina, who was away from the action. She had an easy shot and took it. The three of us cheered her goal and raised our fists in triumph.

The play lasted another few minutes until Enrique made a goal through Tabo's stretched-out arms. I was relieved for the opportunity to end the game in a tie.

"I'm going in," I said, fluffing Moisés' hair.

"Let's keep playing, *papi*, please."

"Maybe after dinner," I responded. I was still breathing heavily when I entered the kitchen. Elida sat at the table with Baby Gloria.

"I'm about to feed the children," she said. "Do you want to wait or eat with them?"

"I'll eat now."

"What are you coloring, *m'ija*?" I asked as I took a place next to Baby, now six.

"Caterpillars and butterflies." She showed me her scribbling.

"Aren't you growing up? That's beautiful. Good for you."

Elida glanced at the book approvingly. She set five bowls on the table and poured a ladle of *caldo de res* in each. When Jaime had finished his soup, he ducked under the table and popped up beside me. He climbed onto my lap. His two older brothers immediately left their bowls and huddled around me, as well.

"Look at what I found under the trailer, Papi," Romeo said, showing me a large feather. "What kind is it?"

"Oh my," I said. "That's no ordinary feather. That's a tail feather of the plumed serpent, Quetzalcoatl. In ancient times, he was a mix of bird and rattlesnake. How fortunate you are to have come across this feather, but I must tell you a secret." I looked deeply into the dark and wondering eyes of my three youngest sons. "The truth is," I whispered, "because you and your brothers and sisters are all so very special, you didn't actually find this feather.... In reality, it found you."

"How could it do that?" Mario asked.

"Ah, Quetzalcoatl has many great powers. The Aztecs say that he was born from Coatlicue, who had four hundred children, all of whom now make up the stars of the Milky Way. You remember how we've gone out at night to explore the Milky Way. Quetzalcoatl was also the patron of priests and the inventor of the calendar and of books. He was the god of learning, science, agriculture, crafts, and the arts. You saw Baby coloring earlier. That is because this feather was near."

The children stared at the feather and back at me.

"Is that really true, *papi*?"

I had to admit, Romeo had reason to doubt some of my stories.

"You must decide that for yourself, *m'ijo*." Elida returned from having put Baby to bed.

"Time to say good night," she announced. "Your father is here to tuck you in. *Vamos*."

"What should I do with this?" Romeo asked, showing the feather to his mother.

"Ask your father," Elida said.

"We'll hide it under the bed because if Quetzalcoatl knew it was missing, I'm sure he would come back for it."

"Really, *papi*? Really?" Romeo asked.

"Oh, *sí. ¡Por cierto!*"

As I led the three boys to bed, the older four clomped heavily up the porch stairs and burst through the door.

"What's for dinner?" they asked.

"*Caldo de res,*" Elida answered and served each of them a ladle of steaming soup.

I had met Dolores Huerta only in passing as she brushed through the crowd in a whirl of energy and confidence. Everyone knew of her deep commitment and loyalty to Chávez and her fearless confrontation of the growers during endless negotiation sessions with each of the companies.

When Marshall Ganz told a room full of ranch committee members that Dolores Huerta was now in charge of negotiations, I arose to question why the committee members would not be taking the lead during these important meetings as they had been doing for the past several months.

"It can't work that way," Marshall Ganz had said, sounding impatient. "Certainly the committee members will be there to strategize and advise. However, the growers aren't going to negotiate with a room full of people all speaking at once. Someone has to take the lead; and, believe me, Dolores is tough."

Again I pushed my point.

"I had not meant to bring 'a room full of people.'"

"Sit down, Torres!" someone behind me had called out. "Señor Ganz has answered your question! *¡Siéntese!*" I looked around the room as if to defy the unknown speaker, but Marshall Ganz had already moved on to another raised hand. I sat down, shaking my head in dismay. What was wrong with people that they could not abide questions? You must always question. How else does one learn?

Lately, I had been asking many questions. I had confronted Beto Garza with the rumors of favoritism in the approval of dispatches.

"Some tell me they are giving them away in return for candy, for God's sake," I complained.

Garza had denied that anything improper was happening, but the rumors persisted. I wanted to believe Beto; yet, deep within me, I suspected—everybody suspected—corruption. How could you know the history of your own country and not suspect that *la mordida* was in place? Weren't the *caudillos* of old always taking more than they ever gave?

A week later, the Pic 'n Pac committee members sat in the union hall's small conference room waiting to have a meeting with Marshall Ganz. As we waited, Nacho Molina and I lit cigarettes. Mingo sipped a Pepsi. Pancho Vega drank coffee from a McDonald's cup. I had asked for the meeting. The ranch committee had a proposal for Marshall, the union's director of organizing.

"Do you think they'll go for it?" I asked.

Mingo responded, "Hard to say. They ought to. They're for 'power to the people!'" He smiled. "Of course, everybody is for that when they see themselves as 'the people.' Maybe not so much once they win some battles and hold the power themselves."

"If they say no, we just keep trying until they say yes," I declared.

"Maybe they'll be happy for the help," Pancho stated, blowing on the steaming coffee and sipping slowly from the Styrofoam cup. "They seem overwhelmed with all of the contracts coming at once. I hear that Delano is a nightmare right now."

Marshall Ganz arrived. The four of us rose to greet him. Although Ganz struggled with his weight, he was always on the move and brought a stir of energy into any room.

"Please, don't get up," he said hurriedly as we shook hands all around. Ganz laid a manila folder on the table and bent himself into a metal chair.

"Mingo? That bump on the head is healing?" Mingo nodded but said nothing. Ganz looked at the others. "Everybody is well? Families are all healthy?"

I responded, "*Sí. Sí*, except I have eight children at home and three are nearly teenagers. Some would say that is unhealthy!"

"Your oldest is a boy," Nacho offered. "You can't complain yet. One of my girls is a junior at Alisal High."

"Good luck with that!" Ganz said to Nacho, grinning. "Buy a shotgun and keep it loaded."

"*¡Ya la tengo!*" Nacho countered. "I'm ready for whoever he is!" The men laughed.

The room had no swamp cooler. The screenless aluminum windows were open, but the warm January afternoon offered no breeze to refresh the thickening air. Flies crawled along the vinyl surface of the table. A picture of César Chávez hung on one wall.

"So, what can I do for you?" Ganz asked, looking toward me.

"We've been getting lots of questions," I began. "The members, of course, are aware that all of the contracts provide for three cents per box to fund the union's medical plan. They also know that part of the plan includes the development of medical clinics."

I watched Ganz closely as I spoke. He had won the respect of all of the ranch committees in part because he was highly regarded by César. He was also a very educated and practical man. Ganz opened the manila folder and lifted a pen from his shirt pocket. His thick glasses rendered his eyes smaller than their natural size. An atmosphere of intelligence and precision surrounded him.

"The union has been talking about clinics for some time," he observed.

"Well, yes," I continued, "and maybe that's part of the problem. We have many questions coming about the medical plan and how it will work when everything is in place. Of course, the people know that the money is already being collected, every day, every box, three cents. Many are already using the insurance coverage they have, and they are happy with that. But they also understand that part of the money is to be used to build a medical clinic in Salinas."

"That's the part that they are questioning," Mingo interposed. "They don't understand what is happening with that money. When will a clinic be built? Where will it be built?"

Nacho asserted, "Sometimes, when the people don't see anything happening, *usted sabe*, they begin to wonder." He dropped the filtered butt of his Kent into the now empty cup.

"They are afraid that the money will be used for something else," I stated. "We've never talked to you or Beto Garza or anyone about this. We don't have a lot of information and we don't know what to tell the people. Everything is new to them and to us. So, the questions keep coming: Is the clinic real? Is it going to be built?"

"Of course it will be built," Ganz stated, shifting impatiently and causing the chair to squawk. "We want them in every town where the union is strong. As far as I know, that has always been very clear. We're just not there yet and we likely won't be for a year or two." He paused. "Once again, you Texans are ahead of us."

An unfamiliar sharpness had come into Ganz's voice. He made a notation on the yellow pad. I pushed ahead.

"The point is, we have been talking a lot about the clinic-related portion of the funds for the medical plan. Just that part, *nada más*. We have a proposal for you and César—"

"It's a proposal for César," Ganz interrupted. "He and the board make these kinds of decisions. You're talking about administration. I don't do administrative stuff if I can help it. I have enough on my hands without getting into all that."

"In any case," I said, "here is what we're thinking. The money for the medical clinic—you know—from the three cents per box, the part to build the Salinas clinic, that part should be left in Salinas rather than sending it to Delano." Ganz continued to write. "We recommend that it be administered through an oversight group from here. *Usted sabe, un comité* comprised of representatives of all of the local ranch committees." I waited. Ganz said nothing. "That's the proposal. *¿Entiende?*" I asked.

"*Sí*, I understand what you're saying. *Quedó claro.*" Ganz wrote something more on the pad. "I don't think that I have heard of this idea before," he stated.

Again, no one spoke. At last, Nacho leaned back on two legs of his chair and rested against the wall.

"We recommend it stay here," he reiterated. "People want to know what is happening to it. When they see nothing, they wonder, is the union serious about a medical clinic?"

Ganz stopped writing. He looked up.

"I don't see why this is a problem. When people ask, you just tell them the truth. As I said, it will be a year or two before we have the resources to start building. They have to understand that. Frankly, I believe you should be helping us explain it. Keeping the funds here is not going to change anything regarding the timing of building a clinic." He glanced at his watch. "Look, I'll be happy to let Cesar know of your concern, but this is not something that I can help you with. This is entirely up to him and the board. I apologize. I have about three more meetings before noon." He rose to leave, extending his hand to each of the men. "You all have a good day. Don't worry. I'll let César know. Thanks." He left hurriedly.

Everyone sat down. Mingo was the first to speak.

"This idea is going nowhere without Ganz to push it."

"It's up to us to keep the pressure on," I answered. "We have to see what he comes back with."

Despite the internal squabbles, debates, and administrative hitches, the union's picketing and threats of boycotts slowly wore away the resistance of the local growers. D'Arrigo finally came to the table, as did L. H. Delfino, a large producer of artichokes out of Castroville. Again, the other growers and their supporters were stunned and angered to learn that some among them had capitulated. The strike had been highly effective. These companies, although well established, could not afford to lose what remained of the vegetable-growing season.

The Teamster goons all departed, but only after "Speedy" Gonsalves, armed and likely high on drugs, erupted in a violent parking-lot rage surrounded by his rifle-wielding cohorts. The police soon arrived and carried him off in a straightjacket to a Modesto hospital.

With the approach of fall, berry production waned. Pic 'n Pac laid off its workers. Strike action also faded with the passing of the season. The union leadership dedicated itself to the national boycott of non-union lettuce.

Elida favored a return to Mercedes, but I wanted to stay through the winter, perhaps even permanently. My sister, Licha, had come to live with us. My mother and brothers were also considering making a move west. Licha's husband of only five years had died suddenly of cancer. She arrived only a few days after the phone call came asking for help. She had nowhere else to turn.

Despite the crowded trailer and her grieving heart, Licha was a great help caring for the children, and she had freed Elida to work longer hours in the fields. The older siblings were content with their schooling. They were not eager to move back to Texas. We had done well with the strawberries, especially considering the recent increase in pay. Most of all, I could not abandon my work as a committee organizer, despite the ongoing muddle of issues and changing policies coming out of Delano.

"I'm not sure I understand the role of the ranch committee," I said to Nacho Molina. "We started out with our own ideas, but now with Delano more directly involved, I wonder what they really expect of us. The more they come over here, the more confused it all appears."

"It's not well defined," Nacho responded. "Up to now, they haven't had to be too specific. No one's pushed them the way we are pushing them."

"The people need education," I said. "Delano is creating a lot of new rules around seniority and dues because of these new contracts. The members need to understand how to report any unfair treatment and how to file a grievance."

A week later, Marshall Ganz called Nacho.

"Listen, I brought up your request in Delano," he said. "There's just no way. The union has to be responsible for all of the dues received. They can't and won't share that responsibility with the local ranch committees. There's your answer," he advised without additional comment.

I listened to Nacho's report.

"I think we should let it go," he declared. Mingo agreed reluctantly. I was not so quick to give up.

"No one wins anything important by asking once and walking away," I said. "I think we have to keep pushing."

Early on a gray and drizzly December morning, numerous La Posada residents gathered at sunrise on Wood Street with two thousand Salinas farmworkers and others from up and down California to prepare for a short but solemn march. Marshall Ganz stood with Padre Duran on a flatbed truck parked near the union hiring hall. The crowd spilled onto the sidewalk and beyond, occupying the lawn of Sherwood School. Marshall Ganz began in Spanish, speaking into a megaphone.

"You know why we're here. Bud Antle has just gotten a judge to sign a restraining order against the boycott!" Antle was the largest producer of lettuce in the valley and the first to sign contracts with the Teamsters.

"César has defied the order," Ganz continued. "Today, he must appear before the judge. He will likely be jailed."

Scattered and muffled voices arose.

"*!Viva* Chávez!"

"*!Viva el boicot!*"

"No, no," Ganz cautioned, holding up his hand. "We ask you all to make this march in a peaceful and dignified way. Today, we'll have no shouts, no songs, no flags waving. We'll walk in silence, two by two, down Alisal Street to the courthouse. We'll bear quiet witness to the inequity of a system that punishes those who speak out for justice."

Ganz invited Father Duran to offer a prayer. When the priest finished, he bid the assembly to begin the march. Chávez, his wife, Helen, and their children appeared from inside the hall. They led the group westward along the bleak and empty Alisal thoroughfare through Old Town and beyond to the county courthouse and jail. The beleaguered Chávez wore a solemn expression.

I took my place in line with Molina beside and Mingo and Peña following. We stood for hours in the rain, staring at the drab courthouse pillars from across the way and waiting for the hearing to begin. The months of brash picketing and strident confrontation dissolved in the dewy light. The crowd took its demeanor from its leader, who entered the building in calm dignity, determined to turn this apparent defeat into a public affirmation of the union's underlying triumph: the permanent transformation of the valley's economic and social relationships.

A silent Chávez appeared before the judge and was sentenced to jail for refusing to obey a court order to end the lettuce boycott. The photo of the leader, standing in front of the barred cell just before entering, was published throughout the nation and the world. Dennis Powell stated that for many, the moment evoked images of Gandhi's imprisonment in 1922 for encouraging his countrymen to ignore a law requiring Indians to be registered and fingerprinted. It also evoked images of Reverend Martin Luther King's 1963 incarceration for ignoring an injunction against "parading, demonstrating, boycotting, trespassing, and picketing."

The following day, Chávez published a letter from his cell. It read in part: "At this point in our struggle, there is more need than ever to demonstrate our love for those who oppose us. Farmworkers are being damaged every day by being denied representation by the union of their choice. Jail is a small price to pay to help right that injustice."

The vigil outside of the courthouse continued day after day, even as dignitaries from across the country, including Ethel Kennedy and Coretta Scott King, journeyed to Salinas to trumpet their support for Chávez and his union of farmworkers.

Three weeks later, on Christmas Eve, the California Supreme Court ordered that César Chávez be released from jail.

Dolores Huerta and a young assistant, whose name I did not know, sat behind a stylish conference table at the front of the hall. Perhaps a hundred union members, workers with InterHarvest, Freshpict, and Pic 'n Pac, waited on padded metal chairs, ten across and ten rows deep. To accommodate the size of the group, the union had moved the meeting place from Wood Street to the local carpenters' union hall. The room was thick with smoke and the whiff of the day's fieldwork. Dolores Huerta announced that César would arrive later in the evening.

Once the meeting started, Pablo Acuña arose to express his concern about the payment of dues. The union had published a rule that stated that no one would receive a work dispatch unless he was current with the monthly payment system.

"*Sí*, señora, we understand the rule, but the rule doesn't make any sense." Pablo was in his forties, lean and sinewy. "When the spring comes, you tell us we cannot work until we pay the dues, but the problem is, we cannot pay until we work."

A stirring of agreement moved among the listeners.

"*Mire*, señor Acuña, that's the rule. It must be followed." As always, Dolores Huerta's response was direct and short, reflective of her no-nonsense demeanor and diminutive stature.

"You have to plan ahead," she continued. "When the harvest is still on and you're earning good money, make your payment in advance to cover the winter. That way, you're ready for the spring. The union has many expenses and only a few contracts. It can't survive unless all of us do our part."

Some committee members aired their concerns about the seniority system. A member's seniority began with the first payment of union dues. This new rule, coupled with the union's complete control of the hiring hall, gave UFWOC full power over the hiring process. The union now had replaced the reviled labor contractors and the company foremen. It had designed this new structure to end forever their abuses of the workers.

The seniority rule, however, also served to limit the employee's direct relationship with the company. Although a system known for its mistreatment had ended, the new pattern disrupted relationships among the workers. Many crews had labored as a unit for years. Many had longevity and seniority with their employer. They were experts in certain jobs and had always returned to those jobs with each succeeding year. Now union seniority determined in what order each member was dispatched to a job and for whom he worked.

"I can only tell you," Dolores Huerta stated to an angry questioner, "that we have looked at this. We understand that the system has been unsettling to some, but over time that will take care of itself. In the end, the new pattern will make the union stronger. We all must sacrifice now to ensure that we not only survive but flourish." The complaining worker sat down quietly, but he was still angry. I stood to take up the argument.

"Señora Huerta, as you can see, these rules about paying dues before you can receive a work voucher and about seniority are causing a lot of concern here. We've heard that the reason you have imposed them is that many of the workers in the San Joaquín were never on the picket line. They were *esquiroles*. They came into the union late, only after the long struggle to win contracts had ended. Many had been scabs, who would reap the same benefits offered to those who fought the battles for years.

"Because the scabs never paid any price, it makes sense that the union wants them to pay dues before they receive a dispatch. It makes sense for them to be sent to the back of the line before enjoying the benefits that others fought for and won. Here in Salinas, however, it's different. All of us *aquí*, we were not scabs. We led the walkouts. We put our bodies on the line.

Why are we being treated like *esquiroles*?" A few people behind
me applauded my statement. Others murmured disapproval.
Apparently, they thought that I was brazen. Dolores Huerta
lowered her head for a moment.

"I've given you our reasons," she said without emotion.

I decided to move on. I had actually come to the meeting
specifically to make a different point, and now it was time to
bring it forward.

"Señora Huerta, our committee wants the payment—
usted sabe, three cents per box to create a medical clinic—this
payment should remain in a local account and under the
control of the union and representatives of all of the ranch
committees in the valley. What do you think of this idea?"

As I spoke, I observed Dolores Huerta's features change
from calm neutrality to one of impatience. She and the
assistant were conferring. When I finished, Dolores Huerta
rose quickly from her place behind the table, grabbed her
microphone, and stepped forward to the edge of the front row
of listeners. She met me eye to eye, no more than five feet
away.

"Señor Torres," she began, "I'm disappointed in you. It's
my understanding that Marshall Ganz has already discussed
this idea with you and your committee." She paused and
looked around the room.

"*Sí*, señora, our committee—" I began, but Huerta cut
me off.

"The union is fighting many battles . . ." She paused again
and raised her chin and looked across the room to ensure that
even the members in the back row could hear every word. "We
can't do it all at once."

"*Sí. Entiendo*—" I tried again.

"Many people have ideas," she stated, the tension in her voice building. "Mr. Torres here has many ideas, but the task now is not to come up with more ideas. It's to put in place the victories we already have won".

"*Entiendo*, señora, however—"

"I must tell you, Mr. Torres, it's not helpful . . ." Again, she cut my sentence short even as she turned back in my direction. "...It's not helpful to keep pushing for something when we have told you this is not the time." She looked down at her feet and took a short step backward, raising her head and rubbing her neck.

I felt disrespected; my anger rose. "Señora," I found myself saying, "Why don't you be quiet for a moment so that I can explain ...?" As I completed this request, Dolores Huerta looked up at me. She appeared stunned. The room fell into a fuddle of muted hisses and groans. "Our committee—" I said, but again was cut off.

"You know what?" Huerta shook her head as if chasing away a gnat. "I think we're done for tonight. I think we need to end this meeting right here. We came to listen and we have listened. We'll take what we have heard back to César. We'll let you know what we can do. Thank you all for being here." She returned to the table and laid down the microphone. The assistant reached for her coat. They exchanged a word or two. They waved quickly to the silent crowd and left the room.

I was still standing. I felt isolated, bewildered. We watched as the union leaders departed. Beto Garza, seated in the front row, quickly rose and followed. Many of the workers sat staring straight ahead. Slowly, they realized that Dolores Huerta had ended the meeting. They turned from one side to another to discover what had happened.

"What did Torres say?" they asked. "What was he talking about?"

"I don't know. I think he has upset Dolores Huerta and her aide so they decided to leave. I think he told her to shut up, so they decided to end the meeting."

"Is Chávez still coming? She said he would appear."

"Perhaps, but I don't think so.... Not now."

Still disconcerted, I glanced at Mingo and the other committee members around me. Mingo stared back.

"That was probably not the best time to handle this, Sixto."

I rubbed my moustache in frustration.

"I don't know what our role is if not to make suggestions, to offer ideas," I said. Mingo made no response.

Gradually, the workers in the room rose. The din of their voices intensified. They drifted toward the door. Some greeted me warmly as they shuffled by.

"I like your words," they said.

Others gave me a hard look, as if I had betrayed something sacred. I recognized one of those who glared, Ismael Velez. He was a passionate young man, jimberjawed, with intense, dark eyes. Those eyes now focused only on me. In previous encounters with Velez, I had noticed how, generally, the man's eyes flitted nervously as if expecting any moment to be confronted with danger and deception.

Vélez was in his mid-twenties and among Peña's *Carnales Unidos* who acted as sentinels during Chávez's speeches and rallies. He was also a friend of Mario Molina, Nacho's son. Although Mario no longer lived with his parents, he and Velez often visited La Posada, hanging around with some of the other youth. Vélez's thin frame stopped at the end of the aisle. He pointed his jaw at me and smirked.

"Hey, Torres," he called out. "Why don't you show some respect?" He motioned toward the door. "She left because of you!"

I waved him off and turned away. Peña moved toward Vélez, took him by the elbow, and led him out. Later, on the sidewalk, the committee members lingered. Nacho stepped up.

"You can't challenge Huerta in public like that, *amigo*. You haven't paid enough dues.... I told you to let it be."

"What now?" Pancho asked, looking toward Nacho and me.

I had nothing more to say. I bent my head and pinched my eyes with finger and thumb. A moment later, I noticed Velez thirty feet from us, conversing with Catalina Castillo. I thought it strange. Catalina had always supported my leadership and the committee's efforts.

"You know that she's Ismael Velez's aunt?" Nacho stated.

"No. I was not aware of that."

"*Sí*. I'd be careful with her," Mingo advised. Again, I didn't respond. I was tired from too many angry and suspicious eyes.

"Enough for tonight," Nacho said. "We'll talk more in the morning."

The group turned to leave. As I looked up, others along the walkway were pointing. A caravan of three familiar cars approached. Beto Garza, with the young assistant beside, was driving the middle vehicle, a brown station wagon. César and Dolores Huerta rode in the back seat. Perhaps he was coming after all, we surmised. The cars rolled by. The driver and his passengers took no note of us, only stared straight ahead.

Two weeks passed. A delegate arrived from the union headquarters in Delano. He met with Beto Garza, who brought the news to La Posada Trailer Park. The union would no longer recognize the existing La Posada committee. The committee predated the strike. Its election was not monitored in accordance with union protocol. All of the members, including me, were discharged from our union responsibilities. A new Pic 'n Pac ranch committee would be elected under close union supervision.

A great fire burned the tinder above Big Sur. Smoke meandered along the coast and over the Santa Lucias to the Salinas Valley. The Salinas River's umber brush of sandbar willow, cottonwood, mulefat, and Christmas berry and the furrowed tilth beyond were scrumbled with a thin gray haze. The heavy sky only added to my melancholy demeanor.

The news of the committee's dismissal shrouded me with misgivings about what lay ahead. Through the weeks and months since our arrival, I had rediscovered my talent for organizing, for leading people to some new place, helping them to achieve what they could not achieve on their own. I remembered the bakery and my struggle with Conrad Klaus, how I was quick to assume a leadership position on the negotiating team. There, too, I had risen rapidly only to fall equally as fast. Strangely, the thought gave me a sense of hope. I must trust in my talent and visions, but clearly I had to learn to be more thoughtful in my dealings.

I continued to attend the union meetings. My cohorts and I sat quietly with our arms crossed and our anger churning at our hasty dismissal. We watched glumly as the newly elected ranch committee members hovered around Beto Garza. Catalina's husband, Adalberto Castillo, was among those elected. Garza's eyes scanned the room and met mine briefly. They exuded a sense of self-assurance. He raised his chin and nodded faintly.

"Arrogant . . ." I thought.

In his role as director of the local union office, Garza had prescreened and discretely promoted his slate of candidates. The newly elected committee was not likely to challenge or stir the waters. I knew, throughout the weeks leading up to the election, my hands were tied. The committee's disbandment confused the residents.

"No. No," Garza told them, "Sixto's a good man. They're all good people. They did good work; but their election—how long has it been—a year ago, didn't follow union protocol. And how could it? It predated the contract. They have served well, but we must have a proper election. Perhaps we need new blood, fresh ideas."

Many expressed to me their disappointment that my name and those of Mingo, Pancho Vega, and the others were not in nomination. Again, Garza had a ready explanation.

"Of course, *la gente* can nominate anyone; but, *usted sabe*, we always encourage new people coming forward."

Elida was angry. She felt that the union had not given me the respect that I deserved. At the same time, she hoped to turn the snub to the family's advantage. She had not met Beto Garza, Marshall Ganz, or Dolores Huerta. She had no interest in them or the politics and personalities that had dominated my life for the better part of a year. She saw the dismissal as a reason and an opportunity to return to Texas. Without my committee work, why would I care to stay through the winter?

"We'll come back in the spring and pick strawberries and forget all this grower and union foolishness!"

"It is not that simple," I responded. We spoke softly, trying not to disturb two-year-old Jaime, who slept in a crib next to the bed. Our voices scraped against the late-night silence. "Of course I'm upset about what happened, but I can't just walk away. Who can understand the way people behave? Why they dismissed us. *Por cierto, es pura mierda,* but not all of it."

The turmoil of the past weeks and Elida's readiness to leave behind the valley's endless tensions and confrontations had left both of us resentful.

"No," I said. "Organizing is not foolishness, and the truth is, people in power understand only one idea—power. We need to continue to organize. It's organizing that changes lives, the people acting together, learning how to make a difference. We signed up members and we won a contract. To me, that's what matters. It's not sitting on a committee that matters but organizing!"

The conversation had started late at night after everyone was asleep and after Elida had repeated her plea about returning to Texas.

"I can't walk away," I continued. "I have to keep going, to keep organizing and educating and getting people to sign the cards. We're members of this union, whether they want us on the committee or not. Did I tell you they call us 'the Texans'? They don't know how to handle us because we're not meek and quiet like many of the grape pickers in the San Joaquín. The union members there follow Chávez faithfully, but there are also many illegals over there, migrating back and forth, and many older Filipino and Mexican families who have worked for the same grower for years. Lots of the illegals and older ones are working as scabs. The union has never been able to win their support."

I spoke quickly, trying to convince her, but I knew that none of it made sense to Elida. She took a deep breath and stared at the trailer's rust-flecked ceiling.

"You pick berries all day, and you're out every night at meetings. I worry about your health."

"I'll be okay." I always responded to her concern this way, although I was taking pills and seeing my doctor every few months. "I have to tell you," I continued, "even after all this, any time the red and black flag parades by, I'll jump in line because I love what the union stands for, even if they make mistakes and refuse sometimes to listen to their own. We fought the valley's biggest growers and we won. They had to bargain, and that has changed this place for the better. Anyway, what is in Texas for us?" I answered my own question, "A run-down house, nothing else."

"It was our home," Elida responded gently.

"But it is not anymore. This is our home, Elida. This tiny piece-of-nothing trailer is our home ...and this valley. I feel more at home here than I ever did in Texas. I've found something here. I've found myself here. Forget what I said a moment ago. I *do* hate being thrown off that committee, but now isn't the time to leave." I moved to be closer to her. She rolled toward me. I held her and lightly ran my hand up and down her back. "We have to see it through," I said. "Something good is going to come to make this right. I believe that. There are people in the valley now who trust me, who trust what I say, not just Mingo, Peña, and the other committee members—I mean, former committee members—not just those few, but hundreds of others. They come up to me on the street. You have seen them in the grocery store, at church. Hundreds of people, Elida, are looking to me for leadership.

"Maybe, with the union, I pushed too much. I wanted them to do things right. Do what the people asked them to do. Anyway, beside all that, there's work here. The schools are good. The kids are learning. I can't go back to Texas, Elida. Please understand."

We lay side by side, saying nothing. Elida stared into the room's dense shades painted with distant moonlight filtered through sheer curtains. I could feel her heart pounding softly against the blanket.

"We can't continue living like this, Sixto, on the edge of nothingness."

I knew what she was thinking: Her parents and siblings lay in their beds nearly two thousand miles away, secure at La Palma, still picking and selling cotton, cutting hay. After all these years, her decision to leave them and to come with me and to live her life as my companion still left her in uncertainty and insecurity despite the birth of our beloved children. She missed her family. I could only watch as she struggled to find the confidence and social graces to extend herself to her neighbors. She sensed that some of the residents surrounding her did *not* trust me and treated her as if she were a stranger because of my habit of upsetting people by speaking out.

Rosa Galván had told her about the *mitotes* and their never-ending gossip.

"He's always causing trouble. Why doesn't he sit down? He's just likes the spotlight."

She turned toward me and pressed her face against my chest.

"Give it time, *mi amor,*" I whispered. "We'll find a real home someday."

"I have given it time," Elida responded. "Nothing changes except you latch onto some new dream while your family lives in a rusting trailer."

She turned over and shut her eyes and said nothing more.

I stared into the semidarkness. I knew that she was right. I had wrapped myself in the union and had thought about little else. I found myself at odds with those in power, first the growers and now the union leadership. I remembered my father. My father knew how to bring the people together. It was he who had envisioned the community meeting room and had organized the people to complete its construction.

I didn't remember opposition or dissent when my father stood before the citizens of San Ciro. The naysayers must have been present, but I was too young, too unaware. I remembered only that my father led with ease and command. How could I have been so ignorant of the opposition that surely was there?

Through the darkness, I saw Ismael Velez's youthful, darting eyes and the scowl he wore as he stared at me after the meeting with Dolores Huerta. Impossible to believe ...to Velez, I had become "the enemy." How sad and senseless that was!

Elida and I found winter work pruning grapes for Paul Masson Vineyards in Soledad. Despite my years in the San Joaquín Valley, I knew little about pruning. My employment in Modesto had always started in the spring after the plants had roused themselves from their winter dormancy.

A man named Ausencio was new to Soledad but a veteran at pruning and pulling the latent vines clean of leaves and old growth. With his thin-rimmed glasses and sallow skin, he reminded me of Fr. Valentino—Padre Pesca—from long ago.

"First, remove all of the buds along the main stem," Ausencio explained to the new hires as we stood bundled against the cold in our winter coats. "As you prune, listen to the cutters. The sound and the feel will tell you if the wood is dead or alive. Cut diagonally. Train the cordon to grow on a level plane and bring it up under the wire like this. That will make the picking easier when the fruit comes." The instructor moved serenely along the line of stakes and wire around which the trunks and cordons were trained. "Prune to only two buds on each spur. That will stimulate the maturation process."

Little by little with each passing morning, Elida and I learned the techniques that Ausencio demonstrated. We enjoyed the quiet time with each other as the workday progressed.

"Licha has been a great help," Elida said as we draped the cane around the wire. "I don't know what we would do without her. Did you see Enrique's math test? He got an A-. Licha's been working with him. I left it on the table for you."

"I'll look at it tonight."

"And Celina did well on her report. That's there also. You should look at them both and let your children know you saw them and appreciate their hard work."

It was a gentle prod and I took note.

"I will tonight," I promised.

By spring, we had returned to the strawberry fields in Salinas. Pic 'n Pac management was not happy with UFWOC and its contract. Administrative problems continued to anger both the company and some workers. Management had lost control of its own employees. It sent out its foremen, who attempted to reassert their dominance in the fields. They claimed that the quality of the pack suffered when their watchful eyes were not present. In response, the workers implemented "*la tortuga*"; they labored at the pace of a turtle until the company reconsidered and withdrew the overseers.

During this second year of the union agreement, Pic 'n Pac introduced mechanical harvesters, great monsters with conveyor belts and steel girders that plodded along the rows. Dave Walsh, the new general manager, a tall and chiseled-jaw fellow, instructed the pickers on the proper techniques for laying each ripened berry on the rolling rubber band that carried the fruit to a crew of packers.

After weeks of testing the new technology, Pic 'n Pac was forced to recognize that the experiment was unsuccessful. The machines bruised too many of the berries, rendering them useless for fresh market channels. The company had invested hundreds of thousands of dollars and lost it all. Dave Walsh blamed the workers, claiming they undermined the harvester's effectiveness by handling the sensitive crop too roughly. Despite this allegation, management quickly removed the contraptions, and the workers returned to filling their baskets and pushing their trays along the rows.

The valley's cold August winds brought rumors that Pic 'n Pac was planning to discontinue its Salinas berry operation. For several weeks, Dave Walsh denied the truth of the whispered speculation. In September, however, with the decline of the harvest, we La Posada residents were startled and angered upon receiving notice that the residential camp would be shut down for the off-season. In the past, the company had always kept the trailer park open throughout the year in order to maintain its local workforce for the following spring.

Rogelio Peña and Nacho Molina were among the first to know. They walked quickly through the cold, murky air to tell me that thirty-day eviction notices were being delivered to all the units. I listened, leaning against the doorpost. No one had expected that the company would make this kind of a move.

"It's just their way of getting back at us for the strike," Peña barked angrily. "They never wanted the contract. Their main goal is to destroy the union. Ever since we signed, they've tried in every way to destroy it. The whole thing is nothing but a scheme to get rid of us. They don't like the hiring hall. They don't like *la tortuga*. They want to pay us less so they can keep more."

"What do you think we should do?" Nacho asked me.

"We need a meeting," I answered. "We need to get as many people together as we can."

"I think some are planning to leave anyway," Nacho surmised. "Probably, some are already gone. Let's try for tomorrow in front of the office. I'll call legal aid. I'll also call Delano and let them know what's happening."

Peña continued his angry grumble.

"It's pretty dammed clever, just throw us out and they think they are rid of us. *Pinche* mechanical harvesters! They waste their precious money on those pieces of junk, and now they're shutting down this place. Call me crazy, but I say they're just fucking us over!"

I looked at Peña. I felt a rush of newfound energy.

"Let's not worry about what they do and why they do it. Let's worry about what *we* do," I said. "It's simple. We organize!"

The following day, thirty of the remaining residents gathered in a circle near the office trailer. Dennis Powell, a sandy-haired, young attorney from California Rural Legal Assistance, stood among them. He was a graduate of the University of Notre Dame Law School and had come west to work as a legal aid lawyer. His Midwestern roots showed in his friendly manner and measured tone. He wore rumpled pants, a brown corduroy sport coat, and a rust-colored paisley tie against a light blue shirt. He was slight of build and appeared even slighter standing in the crowd between Nacho's girth and my height. When Dennis Powell spoke, however, the people felt his sincerity and believed his words.

"*Tiene corazón*," they said.

Powell and I quickly became friends. He told me about California Rural Legal Assistance, the nation's first legal aid services program designed to serve rural families. Jim Lorenz, a Harvard Law graduate, was CRLA's founding director. He was a brilliant and restless legal activist who set out to bring justice to California's small rural communities and their long-suffering immigrant workforce.

The agency's founding board of directors included César Chávez, Dolores Huerta, and Larry Itliong; the latter was a fiery union activist in Delano's Filipino farmworker community who organized the first strikes against the grape growers. Government grants supported CRLA's staff. The organization provided its services without charge to clients. In time, it attracted a group of young attorneys from top law schools around the nation, among them Dennis Powell.

I brought the residents to attention. Powell spoke in English interspersed with Spanish words and phrases. Peña translated.

"*¡Buenos días!*" Powell began, his voice breaking through the bracing air. "I know you're all worried about these thirty-day notices. I want you to realize we're doing everything we can to get an extension delaying any evictions from this camp. Lots of people in town are concerned about what's happening here. You can't just throw 130 families out of their homes and expect no one's going to notice. Already, we've had calls from city hall, the county's Office of Economic Opportunity, and the State Department of Housing. They're all working with us to see what can be done." A wave of enthusiasm ran through the crowd as the people heard that others cared about their plight.

"Now you have to know something, and this is important: the law's on their side. Pic 'n Pac likely has the legal right to do what it's doing. Our best hope is to make them understand that we have a terrible shortage of housing in the valley for farmworker families. We have to bring public pressure to bear on them so they'll do the right thing. Of course, they already know that you have no place to go, but we have to get them to care. If they won't listen to you, maybe we can make it so they have to listen to this community. I believe that this community, when it realizes what's going on, will be ready to stand with you."

As Peña finished his translation, the crowd broke into applause.

"*¡Viva CRLA!*" the people shouted. "*¡Viva* La Posada!*"

Despite the suspicions about Pic 'n Pac's motives and the continuing enthusiasm created by the initial organizing effort, many of the idled workers packed and left for their homes in

Texas or south to the Imperial Valley. As the days past, others challenged me as if I had personally decided to shut down the camp and Pic 'n Pac itself.

"What happened, Torres?" Raul Bucio demanded. "Now we're not going to win. We're not going to have work."

Some of the women huddled together at a kitchen window. They glared at me as I passed by on my way to yet another meeting.

"What good was your committee?" they asked scornfully. "We're left with nothing!"

In late October, the eighty remaining families were served with three-day eviction notices. Elida dropped the envelop on the table as I fell into a chair at the end of the day.

"I don't see what alternative we have," she stated. "They're serious, Sixto. They're going to evict us. We'll have to return to Texas."

"It's just a bluff," I said. "It only means more bad publicity for them. Everybody in town is talking about La Posada. How are they going to evict us? We have no place to go."

Elida soon realized what she should have known all along: I had found a new cause to fight. I would not be thinking any time soon about a move back to Mercedes, Texas.

"You know what?" I continued. "The government has just released a housing report—only last week—that said they need a thousand new apartments in this valley for farmworkers and their families. Jerry told me that. He read it in the paper."

Jerry Kaye had started in the fields with Pic 'n Pac in July. He had quickly become involved in union organizing. Few gringos chose to enter the fields to pick berries or cut lettuce with the Mexican crews, and those who did seldom lasted more than a day or two. But Jerry Kaye had made that decision and, more importantly, had survived the initial shock and fatigue to muscle and bone that disheartened most others. Mingo and his family had befriended Jerry and had taken him in. They taught him how to harvest, pack, and move along the rows with minimum stress to his body.

"I saw two families driving out this morning with their pickups full," Elida declared. "Where are they going?"

I lit a cigarette and downed the last of a bottle of *Dos Equis*.

"The county and the city have gotten involved," I explained. "Supposedly the housing authority has found places for two or three. I don't know, maybe they have relatives here. Many garages in East Salinas are being converted. Maybe they have found a garage somewhere. Do you suppose we could find a garage?"

I looked at my wife, hoping for a smile, but none came. Elida arose from the table quietly. She was always the last to eat. The older children were in the back rooms, sitting on beds, doing homework.

"Anyway," I said, "we're talking to an attorney."

"An attorney!" Elida exclaimed. "Where are we getting money for an attorney?" Licha rose from her place on the couch and noiselessly led Jaime to join the other children.

"We don't have to pay him. He works for CRLA. The federal government supports it. A man named Dennis Powell came today to talk to us about the notices. He's very *simpático*. He's already in touch with Pic 'n Pac and thinks they have to back down. A reporter came up to me at the meeting; her name is Elena. She asked many questions. I liked her. She seems very smart. I told her we're going to fight this whole thing. I told her, 'Like a tree planted by the water, *no nos moverán*!" Again, I smiled, and again Elida gave no response.

Nacho and I sat in Dennis Powell's office. He leaned back in his chair behind a large redwood desk that was covered in brown files and stacks of paper. A picture of Pope Paul VI hung on one wall, reflecting the attorney's Catholic background.

"Did you go to seminary?" I asked.

Powell smiled broadly. "No, no," he said. "I thought about it in high school—for about a minute. I liked the girls too much for that."

"I went for three years," I told him. "I don't regret a day of that time; but in the end, I had the same problem."

"I'm not surprised to hear you studied to be a priest. It explains a lot," Powell observed.

"What do you think is going on with Pic 'n Pac?" Nacho asked.

Powell bent forward, loosening his tie. He rested his chin on his clenched fists.

"Rumor is they're going to shut it all down. They'll try to blame the union, but I think it's really about profit margin. You know, when these multinationals got into the ag business a few years back, they looked at the numbers and thought they would make a killing. They assumed they would always have cheap labor."

Powell reached for a book lying on the desk. He held up an orange-colored paperback with a farmworker sketched in red across the cover.

"I've been reading this, just out, *Factories in the Field*. It's all right here. California moguls have been importing cheap labor for a hundred years: the Chinese and Japanese to work the gold mines, build the railroads, pick the fruit, and dig the sugar beets. And the women were excluded to discourage the men from settling permanently," he said.

"As soon as the Orientals started demanding better wages and safer working conditions, the growers successfully lobbied Congress to pass laws that excluded them entirely from entering the United States. Then it was the Filipinos and the Mexicans. Their women were also excluded for the same reason. They brought in Negro men from the South to pick the cotton in Los Baños. Of course when the Okies and the Arkies came, the law couldn't exclude the women.

"For almost a hundred years, as soon as a group began to organize, they'd evict them from their company-owned camps and crush them with court actions, legislation, law enforcement, and armed vigilantes. An alliance called the Farmers' Association paid for it all." Powell laid the book on the desk and pushed it toward us. "I wish I had a Spanish translation for you."

"We don't need to read it," I stated. "We're living it."

"I see your point," Powell mused. "After the *Bracero* Program ended eight years ago, nobody thought about what was going to happen next. The *braceros* all went home, but then they came back legally and otherwise. The growers didn't know what they were going to do for labor until people started swimming the river by the thousands. As far as they were concerned, that was a gift from God. Of course, the only housing available was out in the same old shacks the *braceros* had occupied."

We sat in silence for a while. A breeze swept through the open window and sifted through the paper on Powell's desk.

"It's a shame they're trying to close La Posada," he declared. "It's really one of the better places, at least compared to the shanties in East Salinas, Pajaro, Chualar, and out in the other back-road camps in South County. Those places are hellholes."

CHAPTER TEN

The housing authority's commitment to relocate us out of La Posada and the continuing media stories covering our refusal to leave won us a thirty-day extension. Only a few days later, however, General Manager Dave Walsh announced that Pic 'n Pac, the largest corporately owned strawberry grower in the state, was shutting its doors. The company would terminate its local operation in the coming days and weeks. It planned to sell all of its assets, including La Posada's trailers and the park site itself, to the highest bidders. As Powell predicted, Walsh blamed the UFWOC for the company's demise.

"This means the union contract is dead," I growled toward Elida upon my return from a late evening meeting. The children and Licha were asleep, but I was having trouble containing my anger. "Peña was right!" I hissed. "They've screwed us! Once they sell it all, we'll have no jobs and no homes!" Elida stood at the sink. She remained silent. "I told Powell we should buy the place. I mean all the families together."

"*¡Oye!*" Elida murmured in sudden exasperation. "*Estás loco.* Where do you come up with these ideas?" She stopped puttering with the dishes.

"Powell didn't think it's so crazy. He says we should talk to OEO. The government has loan funds and even grants for that kind of thing." The Office of Economic Opportunity was a federal agency charged with responding to social and economic injustices throughout the country.

Elida threw the dishrag in the sink and gestured in frustration with both hands. Her eyes were afire. Her words came in stifled heaves.

"Sixto, Sixto," she cried, "I tell you again, *estás loco*! It would cost tens of thousands of dollars. No one's going to give that kind of money!"

"Elida, listen to me, Powell is setting up a meeting with the OEO office in San Francisco. He thinks it is a good idea. We lose nothing by asking."

Elida calmed herself and washed the last cup.

"What good is it to argue?" she said. "You will do what you feel you must do. Nothing I say will change that." She squeezed the dishrag until the dripping stopped and brought the cup to the table.

"Do you want coffee?"

"*Gracias.*"

She poured the thick, steaming liquid. We sat together and listened to the boys' deep breathing, asleep on the foldout couch only a few feet from the sink and stove. The small, listless electric wall heater creaked and rattled against the thin cold air.

"I'm ready for bed," she said. She rose and bent to kiss me.

"I'll be there in a minute." I held her hand to halt her departure. "I wish you could see what I see."

"I wish the same thing, that you could see what I see," she said. "Do you want the light on?"

"No. It's okay. You know how I am. I'm not sleeping the way I used to. The doctor told me this would happen."

Pancho Vega, Juan Alemán, and I sipped beer in the early afternoon. Pancho was ten years my senior. Deep channels of cheek flesh bracketed his narrow nose like a barn's angled roofline and fell straight down either side of his thin lips. A green John Deere ball cap covered his balding head. In recent weeks, he had been diagnosed with Graves' disease and was under a doctor's care.

His brown eyes protruded from their sockets and floated as if set on the eggshells of a small bird. The result was an unremitting and, to the viewer, disconcerting look of surprise. Pancho spoke of his condition freely, helping to put his friends at ease. He sat straight with his chin up, enjoying his position as the wise elder of the organizing committee.

"It's dangerous to wait and do nothing," he cautioned me. "Everyone wants to celebrate the victories. Chávez this and Chávez that . . . the union, the contracts . . . It all disappears unless we continue to struggle and to find the next link in the chain of events."

As a newcomer, Juan Alemán kept a respectful silence. He had recently moved from Santa Maria, where he worked in the strawberry fields, and had joined the picket lines during the strike. Juan and his wife, Armandina, had six children. I had grown to appreciate his spirit and believed that he would become a great asset to our cause. Pancho shook his head.

"People come here for opportunity, and some expect it to fall from a tree and carry them forward. No, no, we have to keep pushing the bosses or they will push us. It's all good though. *El jefe* is on the run! He used to tell us, 'I will pay you eighty cents. Take it or leave it.' When we stood up, everything changed. Now we negotiate. We threaten. The *chingones* jeered at us, but we didn't care. We took it all. I was out there on the line. You saw me! When we stood up, everything changed!"

Pancho's teenage son, the product of a second marriage, skirted through the kitchen and out the door. His lanky body, dressed in shorts, a tank top, and new tennis shoes, matched his father's in height.

"*¿Dónde vas?*" Pancho called after him.

"To shoot some baskets with Freddie," he hollered from the pavement below the kitchen.

"He'll be a senior next year. He loves basketball," Pancho boasted. A child cried in a back room. Muffled voices intervened. The crying ceased.

"It's beautiful what we did!" he continued. "Everything in this valley's changed because we stood up." His face again fell into a smile, and his lids closed over his round eyes in contentment.

"*Por cierto,*" I agreed. "The boycott was and is the key. Chávez has always been right about that, a million shoppers saying no to grapes and next, no to lettuce. We have a place at the table because of the boycott."

I looked over my friend's shoulder. The interior of the Vega trailer was identical to my own. Pancho's older children were long departed from the homestead. His second wife, Delia, had given him three more.

"*Es un teatro,* Don Pancho," I declared. "We're players in a political play. It's for us to move the action forward. These past days have been act one. What will be the second act? Everyone is waiting for that."

Pancho handed me another beer. As was my habit, I licked the crevice between my thumb and finger and covered the spot with a dash of salt. I tasted the salt and drank. Pancho stared thoughtfully through the kitchen window. A sparrow flitted from one branch to another in the adjacent sycamore tree. He turned his gaze toward me.

"You're a good man, *amigo*. You keep us all focused on the change. You make us hang onto our hopes. Most of us, *usted sabe*, are ready to compromise; but right now, many people in this trailer park believe in you because you don't compromise. *Cierto*, there are always a few naysayers, but the large majority respects the way you don't let them stop you. From what I can see, those who are staying are ready to follow you to fight this eviction."

The fall weather thickened. The strawberry crop waned. Elida and I found ourselves sidelined until pruning season. Once again I spent much of my time in meetings. Within a few unsettling days, I had moved from my role as head of the ranch committee to that of leader and spokesman for those who continued to occupy La Posada, despite management's letters of eviction.

The Farm Bureau and its members continued to lobby for legislation that would neutralize UFWOC's power. Chávez called their efforts "racist," and a Fresno Farm Bureau representative, Clare McGhan, claimed the statement was "ridiculous."

"The Farm Bureau's bylaws prohibit discrimination!" he stated with indignation. Nacho Molina spit on the ground and shook his head.

"The bylaws prohibit discrimination!" he repeated. "If only we *campesinos* had known, we would never have felt the stings!"

Meanwhile, Chávez had also denied that UFWOC was to blame for Pic 'n Pac's implosion. He pointed instead to its "bad management and political squabbling."

Pic 'n Pac doggedly proceeded with its planned dissolution. Dave Walsh peddled its trailers to a San Francisco firm subject to the rights of the current tenants. It continued, however, to maintain the strawberry fields throughout the dormant season, looking to protect its investment until a new buyer could be found.

With the help of CRLA, the remaining La Posada residents held off the company's management despite all of its threats and legal maneuvers. The eviction dates were extended repeatedly, although some families continued to move on their own.

We told our story to whoever would listen. We picketed the office of Representative Burt Talcott because—according to *The Californian* and despite reports that all of the labor camps in the county were full—he had advised the Rotary Club that an adequate number of vacant units existed to accommodate the La Posada families. He neglected to tell his audience that the list of vacant and supposedly available units that he held in his hand included in its count La Posada and the very trailers that many of the families, having received eviction notices, had already abandoned. Talcott claimed that we holdouts were more interested in "publicity and making political capital" than in finding alternative housing.

The congressman's local headquarters were in the US post office building on West Alisal Street only a few yards from the county jail where Chávez had been incarcerated. More than twenty La Posada picketers stood on the sidewalk. We held splotchy cardboard signs that read "Houses *sí*! Talcott *no*!" We sang songs and chanted, "one thousand homes needed today," a reference to the county's published report, estimating the shortage of family units for the valley's farmworkers.

An aide came outside to inform us that the congressman was in Washington.

"Oh, rest assured," she said, "the congressman is very aware of the situation."

The citizens of Salinas drove by. They heard our music and read our signs. They gestured their support or disdain with thumb or finger pointing straight up.

I moved to the top of the post office steps to speak.

"*¡Vámonos a* OEO! *Este vato* isn't home!" I shouted to the crowd. We marched a block north to the local OEO field office. The director, Mr. Richard Barnes, came out to listen to our plea for decent housing. He was a pasty man in his fifties with thinning hair and a horse-tooth smile.

"Rest assured," he said, "we are doing all we can in conjunction with the regional office in San Francisco to find resources to help."

We didn't put much faith in Mr. Barnes. Not surprisingly, we heard nothing more for a week; then Dennis Powell told us that, despite our doubts, the man had arranged for us to speak to the regional director.

"*¡Vámonos!*" I said again to the people. "To San Francisco for a meeting *con los federales*! *¡Viva* señor Barnes!"

We drove the two hours north to the federal building in the heart of San Francisco. The regional director and his assistant met with us as promised. We presented the idea of purchasing La Posada.

"It's something we are looking into. We plan to discuss it with our regional board."

After another two-week wait, the agency's board agreed to send Rogelio Peña and me to Washington DC to confer with the national director of OEO, Mr. Phillip Sanchez. Upon our return, we two wide-eyed travelers shared our experience with the others.

"A local OEO commissioner assured us that our rooms and meals were all arranged," Peña began, "and that someone would meet us in Washington at the airport and take care of everything. But when we arrived, no one came. No one greeted us. Somehow the messages didn't get passed on to OEO personnel." Peña shook his head to acknowledge our inexperience as travelers. "It was all so new to us—the airport and the flight. Since everything was arranged, we hadn't even thought to bring a little money."

"It was frightening," I said. "There we were without a penny for even a taxi, *ustedes saben,* Rogelio in his Ché Guevara jacket and *boina* and I in my Stetson and cowboy boots among a thousand *corbatas.*"

The people laughed. It was my habit to describe bureaucrats as *"corbatas"* because they all wore ties around their necks. In my experience, people who wore ties made all the rules, or thought they did.

"And we were hungry. We were close to tears. Nothing had been done to prepare for our arrival," Peña interposed. "At that moment, we were about as useless as a pencil without lead!"

"We slept all night in the airport," I continued. "Fortunately, Rogelio's brother lives there in a town near the Capitol, so we called him. He finally picked us up the next afternoon. Then we went to see the national director of OEO. He was embarrassed that we had been abandoned, so he went out of his way to make us feel comfortable." Rogelio, unable to contain his excitement, again broke in.

"He took us to dinner. We told him about La Posada and all of you and our decisions to fight the eviction, and we told him about the committee's work. He asked many questions about the growers and the strike and said he would help in any way he could. He said he had some ideas and we should keep his staff informed." I waited as the people applauded.

"Then we went to see Congressman Talcott, but he got angry that we were there and told us that he didn't want to see us. He shouted at us, 'I don't care what you do, but I won't let you abuse me! Make a spectacle if you like, just don't bother me anymore!' He was still upset that we had picketed him here last month. People were coming into the hallway to investigate the noise, so we left. Then we went to see the statue of Lincoln and some of the other monuments before going back to the airport."

Despite the trip and the good will by OEO's Phillip Sanchez, the $1,300,000 grant that we requested to purchase La Posada Trailer Park was scuttled. We knew why: the Honorable Congressman Burt Talcott had opposed it, although some also claimed that OEO could not legally use the requested funds to purchase land.

Talcott explained to *The Californian* his opposition to the grant.

"These people chose to stay here, and they're looking for perpetuating their cause—*la raza* and *la causa*! They're only interested in disrupting the agricultural community." After that, he called us "parasitic."

"My sister saw us on the evening news," Mingo crowed. "She claims it was on the station from San Jose, not just the local one! The word is spreading, *amigo*! The support is growing."

"Maybe," I cautioned. "It'll take more than a story or two. *¿Quién sabe?*, Look at what's happening with *la unión*. The stronger we get, the more the growers throw at us: the Teamsters still trying to sign up members; the growers still trying to outlaw our strikes, our pickets, the right to boycott. All of our victories are shaky at best."

In early spring, we listened as John Jones, the director of the housing authority, summarized for the benefit of his commissioners the status of negotiations with us.

"We're doing all we can," he said. "The fact is, they won't move and we have no vacancies at the moment anyway. One idea we've been kicking around is to send them out to old Camp McCallum on a temporary basis. It's not a perfect solution, but it may be our only alternative."

The commissioners considered this option, but quickly rejected it as impractical. The housing authority had abandoned the old labor camp at the end of the *Bracero* Program nearly ten years ago. It sat alone in the midst of the lettuce fields five miles south of town, overgrown and deteriorating.

Moreover, Virginia Barton, superintendent of the Alisal School District, stood up and claimed that moving us into Camp McCallum would "create an instant ghetto." She stated that bringing the La Posada children into her district would require "corrective busing, add to the expenses of the district, and place more students on double sessions. You would be really wrecking the Alisal District," she pronounced. Most of the Alisal's Anglo residents in the room applauded her opinion.

"At some point," Jones continued his report, "Pic 'n Pac is going to determine they have no alternative but to evict them. I don't know what we'll do then."

"There must be other options," Commissioner Bob Meyer, a south county tomato grower, stated hopefully. "What about Fort Ord land? Has anyone talked to the warden at Soledad Prison? Maybe he has room."

Union attorneys helped us to file two lawsuits. They claimed that California's three-day eviction notice violated our constitutional right to due process. Eventually, the suits were successfully countered by Pic 'n Pac and dismissed by local judges. They did serve, however, to win weeks of delay in the enforcement of the evictions.

Howard Hall, the manager of La Posada, continuously reminded the residents that the owners were "hell-bent" on completing the sale of the trailer park.

"The day will come when the sheriff will show up with his deputies and a court order," he stated sternly. "All these games won't mean much then!"

"Now we understand why they called their company Pick and Pack!" Rogelio Peña said with a smile. "But guess what? We're not packing. We're staying together no matter what happens. We won't allow them to divide us."

"What should we do next, Sixto?" Nacho asked. "You're always good with ideas, *amigo*. What are you thinking?"

"I do have an idea," I said. "It's a way to do more than just stay together. We learned a lot during the picketing. We learned not to let them have the last say about what is going to happen. We have to take charge of the events. The idea I have will do that. It will show everyone in this town that they can't push us aside, even with court orders."

"Okay, Sixto. What is it?"

The committee listened. They asked questions. They took the idea and examined it on all sides. They poked it and mused about it. They prodded and laughed about it. They imagined the response it would elicit from the *corbatas*, from the media, from supporters and scoffers.

"How will we maintain the element of surprise?" Mingo asked.

"It can be done, but it will require great discipline," I responded.

"The people will understand the need to remain silent," affirmed Pancho. "We must insist on it." The committee adopted the plan and shared it confidentially with the others.

We knew our time was growing short. After our effort to purchase the camp fell through and the lawsuits had played themselves out, we had agreed to a final thirty-day extension to May 16. On that day, according to Dave Walsh, he would deliver the trailers to their new owner.

When May 16 arrived, we were prepared. Our cardboard signs, together with the red and black standard of the recently chartered and renamed United Farmworkers Union, stood upright by the trailer doors. American and Mexican flags were unfurled and positioned nearby. Children and babies were already fed and bundled. They sat on the couches, their expectant eyes uncertain about the change in the morning routine.

The previous night, Peña, Mingo, Pancho Vega, and I had spread the word, "No work, no school tomorrow!"

At eight o'clock, we left our homes to gather at the main gate of the trailer park. We came with thermoses of hot coffee and picnic bags prepared to spend whatever time necessary to confront the arrival of the posse.

"What will we do when they come?" asked Señora Márquez.

"*Momentito*, Sixto will explain," Peña responded. "The important thing is that we do it together."

Dennis Powell and I conferred as the crowd tightened. Mingo began the rhythmic and now ritualistic clap that accelerated into enthusiastic applause and excitement. The people had encircled the leadership committee. I brought them to attention.

"Señores, señoras, *por favor!*" I looked around at the flags and the trailer park's thirty-four remaining families. A morning breeze flowed over us. The people held their signs at the ready: "Justice for farmworkers," they read. "The nation's richest state but no homes for working families," they chided.

"We're not here to fight the police or to fight the evictions," I stated. "We're here to show solidarity. It's important that we don't let them break us apart. A hundred families have already left. They allowed themselves to be pushed aside and forgotten. They've gone back to Texas or who knows where.

We're still here because we believe that it's possible to change the way things are." I stopped, removed my white Stetson, and surveyed the crowd.

"Through the strikes," I continued, "we won better pay and benefits and protection from pesticides. Our message now is simple: we're here to stay, and we need help to make this place our permanent home. We're not sure exactly when the sheriff will arrive, but we all know the plan for what we'll do when that moment comes." I paused again and gestured toward Dennis Powell. "Now señor Powell has something to say."

The young attorney stepped forward.

"It's important to remember our intent is not to provoke the police. When they arrive, everyone will go to his home, pack up his belongings, and drive out as planned. We have agreed to leave peacefully. It's time to keep that promise."

The people applauded respectfully. The meeting ended. Everyone milled about, keeping an eye on Sherwood Drive. As the minutes passed into hours, the mood lightened. The fathers kicked soccer balls to their children, and the mothers sat on the grass and opened their picnic bags to serve their lunches. Mingo reported seeing a sheriff's car pass slowly without stopping.

"I wonder if they're coming at all?" he mused. "Maybe they were thinking we'd all be away and they could just throw our belongings on the road."

At two o'clock, a local television crew showed up, and Robert Miskimon, a reporter from *The Californian*, began a round of interviews. Late afternoon approached. The sun drifted toward the Santa Lucias. The families, too, meandered toward their homes to continue their packing. They guessed that their show of solidarity had given the police reason to delay and, perhaps, to rethink their tactics.

The following morning, we prepared in much the same way as we had the day before, except we rose even earlier and gathered at the gate by seven o'clock. Having waited all day, now we feared we might miss the event all together. What the sheriff had failed to do at the appointed moment, he might well wish to do hurriedly on the day after. Our instincts were correct.

At 7:15 a.m., a posse of twenty men from the sheriff's department and twenty-five more from the city police station arrived in buses. A van with latticed metal windows and no passengers led them past the open gate. Their vehicles parked on Sherwood Drive in a line along La Posada's front wall. The squad exited and formed up. Its ranks were dressed and armed for a riot in black padded uniforms and face-shielding helmets. They carried firearms and clubs. They soberly marched in two rows through the gate, taking little note of the riveted crowd.

The patrol came to a halt twenty yards into the park. A tow truck pushed through the entrance and parked along the curb. An average-sized man accompanied the troops. He was dressed in a dark but trendy suit and tie. He gazed down the park's main road lined with trailers and a scatter of cars and trucks. He surveyed the crowd with an air of dominance. He took a megaphone from a uniformed assistant and called out his order.

"I am Deputy District Attorney Jerrold Mitchell. You will all go to your trailers immediately and remove your belongings. An officer will accompany you. You have ten minutes to leave

these premises! Any automobiles left on the property will be
towed away at the owner's expense!"

The assistant introduced himself as Under-deputy James
Rodríguez. Even before he had translated the attorney's words,
a murmur of protest circulated among the people. We were not
prepared for such a tight timeframe. The crowd reacted with
disbelief and anger.

"That's not right!"

"*¡Es ridículo!*"

"We need more time!"

"*¡No es justo!*"

A few parents ran toward their homes while some of us
tried to convince the attorney to grant more time to depart.

The shouts grew louder and quickly turned into angry taunts
and threatening gestures with some of the men edging toward the
patrol. From somewhere in the crowd, an egg sailed toward the
file of officers but fell just short of its mark. Its yoke splattered on
the pavement; then, a coke bottle landed harmlessly beyond the
file of men. The troops stood erect, holding their position, even as
their eyes darted from side to side and their hands grasped their
weapons more firmly with each goad and insult.

I noticed that Junior had pushed closer to join a group of
teenagers only five feet from the watchful troops. The boys leaned
in toward the line of ominous figures poised to enforce their will
upon the now enflamed group. Their youthful blood was quick
to ignite as the disruptive events of the past weeks and months
came to a head with this arbitrary and unreasonable command
that gave us only ten minutes to depart.

Junior soon forgot all that we had told the people about
remaining calm. He barked insults in words he had not used
before aloud—at least not in front of me—and rashly inched ever
closer.

"*¡Pendejos!*" he yelled, spurred on by older cohorts. "Are you planning to shoot us all, you sons of bitches, if we don't move fast enough?"

Others were pressing in around and behind him. They, too, were screaming and pushing forward. Now the boys stood face-to-face with the enforcers. Their jeers and insults continued. Someone hollered a command.

"Move out!"

Seconds later, a baton fell sharply across Junior's shoulder. He toppled awkwardly onto the asphalt as Tony López and Jesús Urzúa were batted down against his prone body. A tempest of blows fell on all three of them in rapid succession. I was only a few feet away. Immediately, I moved to protect my son. Without warning, that Mitchell fellow stepped into my path and jabbed a finger in my face.

"Stay put!" he yelled.

Who was this *vato* keeping me from protecting my child? I grabbed the man around the neck and pinned him in a hammerlock. I had him positioned to toss him aside when sharp pains ripped through my back and legs. I, too, fell, trying desperately to cover my head and face. Others among the residents immediately scrabbled to help me. The troops pummeled them to the ground, as well.

Within a very few seconds, the fracas had ended. Three other men, Junior, the two underage youth, and I were on the ground, our arms cuffed behind us. One of the sheriff's deputies knelt beside Junior.

"This is the guy I saw throwing an egg at us just before the fighting started," he triumphantly announced to no one in particular. We were marched or dragged still screaming into the paddy wagon to be hauled away.

Dennis Powell, Peña, and Mingo had tried to hold the people at bay during the scuffle, shouting for them to stay calm. No sooner had the crowd settled down than a second tow truck had entered the park. From the paddy wagon, I watched the driver position the vehicle to haul away one of the parked cars. Immediately, some of the men nearby rushed to the scene and threatened the operator, who held up his hands in submission.

"Leave it!" the men shouted. The driver climbed into his truck and sat quietly, unwilling to test the resolve of his would-be assailants. Soon, the car's owner arrived and drove for the exit.

Now the families hurried to their trailers. Dennis Powell went immediately to our unit. He knew, with Junior and me arrested, Elida and Licha needed help packing the station wagon. The officers patrolled the park, badgering the residents to complete their work and pushing them along as soon as their vehicles were loaded. They took no pleasure in their tasks, and some appeared sympathetic to the rousted mothers and children.

"I wish you people had just moved out on your own," Rodríguez told Powell.

We arrestees were hauled to the county jail. Later I learned that the families said nothing as they packed and loaded. They worked with a quiet purpose and dignity. It was their turn to demonstrate their power in the only way they could.

One by one, the drivers slipped behind the wheel of their jam-stowed cars and trucks. They moved slowly along the park's surface roads. Their spouses and children walked beside them. They edged toward the entrance, the vehicles rolling leisurely enough so that the walkers might keep pace. At the open gate, they turned right onto Sherwood Drive. They crept forward, one by one. They found an open space along the road's edge. Now came the big surprise we had been planning.

Each driver claimed a space. Each pulled over and exited his or her vehicle. The family members then opened the car's side doors or trunks, or climbed onto their pickup trucks and unloaded their belongings, piling them along the road's sandy shoulder only a few feet from the trafficked thoroughfare.

With unity and deliberation, the evictees revealed our response to Deputy District Attorney Jerrod Mitchell's haughty ten-minute eviction procedure. The answer fell beyond the reach of his authority. The families of La Posada set up house on the streets of Salinas. The troopers watched from a distance, unable or unwilling to thwart their efforts.

The squatters stacked boxes filled with food, dishes, clothes, and towels. They laid canvas tarpaulins on the moist ground. Some set up tents and stretched blankets from the fence to their vehicles to provide protection from the wind. Folding chairs and barbeques appeared with vegetable crates stacked for tables. Sheets of cardboard that the families had scavenged from commercial dumpsters were hung over clotheslines to provide a semblance of privacy.

Deputy District Attorney Jerrod Mitchell said nothing, nor did he object to those who sought to retrieve any additional household goods from their vacated trailers. At 11:00 a.m., however, he grabbed the sheriff's megaphone to announce that the eviction was now complete. The park was off limits.

"Anyone who remains on this property will be subject to arrest!" he proclaimed.

Howard Hall, the only representative of Pic 'n Pac present during the morning's events, took his turn at the megaphone to reiterate Mitchell's words. The families, busy with their homesteading, paid little attention.

Elida and the children were the last to leave. They settled near the main gate, where Peña had staked a space for them. I had discussed the plan in advance with Elida. She had grudgingly agreed. She found no joy or excitement as some did with the theatrics that my corps of organizers and I had produced. Once I was released from jail, she surmised, I would resume my place as director of the drama.

"I don't understand his mind," she told Dennis Powell as they and the children unpacked and arranged their meager furnishings. "How can he bring his wife and family to this? Why, señor? ¿Díga me, por qué?"

"You can't make an omelet without breaking eggs," Dennis responded.

Later, Powell drove to the city jail to check on the fate of those incarcerated. The clerk informed him that we would be arraigned tomorrow in municipal court.

"They were all brought in for resisting arrest. The four men will face an additional charge of battery. I suggest you be at municipal court at ten sharp." Powell returned to tell Elida that she would not be seeing her husband or son for dinner.

By midafternoon, despite the disturbance, many of the families were in good spirits. Again, reporters and TV cameras appeared, eager to cover this new chapter in the struggle of La Posada's now former residents.

CHAPTER ELEVEN

Junior and I sat in our cell on two metal chairs across from a bunk bed.

"It may rain again tonight," I said. "I wonder how your mother's doing, setting up camp with only the children to help."

Junior didn't respond.

"*M'ijo . . .*"

"*Sí, papi,*"

"I have to ask you something."

Junior raised his head of curly black hair. "*Sí, papi.*"

"I have to ask you, did you throw that egg?"

He looked at the floor. It was scored with black heel marks and scarred with chipped linoleum.

"*Sí.*"

"Why did you do that?

"A bunch of us talked about it. Tito brought a bag of them, but after the first one missed, we didn't try it again. I had a bottle, so I threw it. The others all chickened out. Then, when we missed them both times, we all just got mad at what they were doing and started screaming. I'm sorry, *Papi*"

"You have my temper."

"*Mamá* gets mad too."

"*Por cierto*, but at least so far, she doesn't throw eggs or get in people's faces." We both laughed.

"*¡Dios mío!*" I exclaimed. "I hope they're all right."

"Do you hurt?"

"I'm afraid they beat on my left hip and leg pretty hard. Right now it's feeling bad." I shifted my weight. "How about you?"

"I'm okay. When the others fell over me, I was kind of protected.... *Papi?*"

"*¿Sí?*"

"Why are we doing this? I mean, *mamá* wants to go back to Texas. Why don't we just live there?"

"Is that what you want?"

"I don't know. I want to see her happy."

"So do I, *m'ijo*, but the question is: How long will any of us be happy in Texas? The house there's a mess. We can't make enough money to fix it and to pay for food and clothing and lights and all the rest. The schools here are better and, although your mother doesn't agree, I think that what we're doing is important, helping in the union struggle and now this fight for houses. The truth is, it's what I have to do. I'm afraid I'm not going to be able to work in the fields much longer."

I slouched in the chair and leaned my head against the cold cement wall. My cherished Stetson lay on the floor. Somehow, through it all, I had managed not to lose it.

"I don't know what work I'll be able to do when I get too sick to pick berries." Junior had never heard me speak of my illness so openly. "Think of it this way. What if you're in some deep, dark cave and suddenly you see a light, a way out. You wouldn't ignore that if it happened. You couldn't. You would follow it every step. You would have faith that it's the right way because you can see that light, and if you turn away, all you'll see is darkness and you'll be lost again."

"But what if you're the only one who sees the light?"

"We aren't the only ones, *m'ijo*. That's why thirty-four families are camping on the street tonight. *¿Ve?*"

"*Sí, papi.*"

"You know, when I was your age, I left home to become a priest. In seminary, they taught us to try to live every day in a way that will change the world for the better. I've never forgotten that."

"So why did you leave the seminary, *Papi?*"

I paused to frame my response and smiled at Junior.

"Because I knew that someday I would meet your mother."

The following morning, we were arraigned and then released on our own recognizance. The judge continued the case to May 30, at which time we were to enter our pleas. Dennis Powell and Junior half-carried me to the car. My bruised leg had stiffened during the night. I leaned against the backseat door.

"How is Elida?" I asked as we moved eastward and then north on Front Street.

"People helped them get settled yesterday," Powell answered. "Elida said the babies were a bit anxious. A couple of the older boys slept in the car, but overall, I'd say they fared better than some. I went by this morning. Everyone was up and trying to put together breakfast. You won't believe what's happening. The television coverage is generating a lot of support. Tents and blankets, food, even money is coming in. Trabajadores Adelante paid to have portable toilets brought in this morning. That's a great help."

We crossed East Market Street. La Iglesia Del Cristo Rey, its cement block walls painted pink, rose up on the right. Most of La Posada's residents attended Mass there each week. I peered straight ahead. My heart beat rapidly as the car approached the first tarpaulin that separated the family campsites. It hung along the east side of Sherwood Drive, anchored to La Posada's fence, stretched and gently flapping, held in place by the closed door of a parked automobile.

Rain had come during the night. Soggy cardboard sheets lay useless against the fence. Children sat in patches of mud and clammy weeds, one crying. An infant lay neatly bundled in a walker, only a few feet from passing traffic. As we drew closer, crossing Rossi Street, I saw mothers and grandmothers hovering over camping stoves, their *ollas* teeming with pinto beans or chicken and rice. My first feeling was anger that anyone should be reduced to such conditions.

"Goddamnit!" I muttered.

The car rolled forward. More oily-colored canvas tarps appeared with a camping tent or two scattered in between. We passed a large army green tent with the flaps pulled back. I was startled when I realized the women and child inside were Elida, Licha, and Jaime. A moment later, I saw our other children playing in the spaces between the tarps and boxes.

"Look!" Junior exclaimed, pointing to the shelter. "Where did that tent come from?"

"I had it in my garage," Powell said. "I wasn't using it."

The traffic behind us was getting heavy. We couldn't stop the car safely. Powell continued passing along the line of tents and tarps.

"I'll turn around up at Bernal Street and then park," he said.

"*Gracias,* señor," I sighed.

I noticed each of the families as we glided by: Alemán, Vega, Arrellano, Peña, and others. The campers, especially the men and smaller children, waved to welcome us home, helping to lighten my mood. As I absorbed the meaning of what had happened in my absence, my anger subsided. Given my arrest, the plan to continue our protest by squatting on the streets might well have fallen apart. Instead, the families had held together and carried out the tactic with skill and dignity.

Powell made his U-turn and drove back up Sherwood Drive. He pulled over and parked across the street from the tent that he had provided to our family. Once again, he and Junior supported my painful shuffle as we made our way into the makeshift shelter. The younger children ran to greet us.

"Be careful," Junior cautioned. "Papa's sore all over." Elida embraced me, then hugged her son. My condition alarmed her. She hadn't heard about the beating in any detail. I sat to rest my throbbing leg.

Later in the afternoon, the buses dropped off the schoolchildren, and a few of the men arrived home from the fields. Mingo and Peña came to shake my hand and welcome me back. They stood among the bicycles, chairs, crates, clothes, and dishes of our household.

"Chuca is bringing two steel barrels from the packing shed for a fire. One of them is for you," Mingo said, his thick eyebrows rising with a smile. Peña also had news.

"A man from El Cristo Rey came by and left a truck full of scrap lumber up at the end of the line. You don't need to do anything. I'll bring some of it by later. Everyone will be warmer tonight."

"Señora," Mingo called to Elida, "they're delivering bottled water. Don't worry. We used some of the donated money for that. A group of students from Stanford sent one hundred dollars. We also have extra sleeping bags that some of the people from the church brought."

"Did you hear?" Peña asked. "They're saying that Dave Walsh has taken over Pic 'n Pac. Apparently, they sold the company to him, and he's renamed it Dave Walsh Company."

"*¡Increíble!*" I responded.

"*Sí. Es la verdad.* And a bunch of the workers yesterday staged a walkout to show their support for us. We've been out buying blankets and tarps. There's a lot of activity. The health department, fire, police, they've all been by. They don't really know what to do with us. Someone said that the Red Cross might help."

In the evening, a dank wind rushed up the valley from the ocean, eleven miles away. Our family, like many of the others, had no table, only a chair or two. We ate a hot dinner of fish soup and stood hunched over the barrel of fire set just outside the tent. Junior and Enrique fed the flames with the scraps of wood that Peña had brought. The boys carried a dim flashlight to help them as they herded their younger siblings to their assigned corners of the yawning shelter.

The wind slapped against the tent and rocked the aluminum supports. By now, the children knew that their mother had no answers to their questions about how long they might continue to live in the tent.

"That's something you must ask your father," she had told them without emotion.

As the days passed, we and the other families worked to upgrade our shelters against the chilling weather. Word of our action spread. Church members, nonprofits, and individuals from throughout northern California sent tents, sleeping bags, blankets, food, and money. The women of the camp created food centers along the curb and cooked breakfast and dinner to ensure that everyone had a hot meal. Cleanup committees swept through the grounds daily, clearing it of trash and debris.

The media continued its coverage, detailing life among the tents and tarps. *The Californian* described the residents' high morale and the varied responses from the community. At night, the children were layered in bags and blankets, huddling to stay warm.

"Many of these families are United States citizens," Rogelio Peña told a reporter. "Some of them are registered to vote. We feel like we're a community and part of the broader community around us. If we go our separate ways, the larger families won't find homes. Some of them have ten children and can pay only $90 or $100 per month. What will happen to them? There's nothing out there."

The reporters interviewed Mingo Ortega, describing him as a twenty-year-old fieldworker who dropped out of school at the age of thirteen.

"Before the union came, we didn't have anything. Now we know by sticking together, we can demand a better life. As individuals, we're powerless. They can easily forget about us."

The TV reporters pulled me aside.

"Why have you taken such a drastic action and put your families in so much jeopardy?"

"The truth is, the poor people of Mexico have been in jeopardy for 450 years," I told them. "We've lost our land. We've lost much of our culture. We've come here to the United States to work and find a new opportunity. If we lose this—the opportunity to work and provide shelter to our children—we have nothing left."

The support for our cause continued to grow. The media quoted Juan Valdez, a Soledad candidate for the California Assembly.

"Where are the politicians? What happened to Congressman Talcott and State Senator Wood? Are they going to sit in their big fancy offices in the hope that this whole thing will go away?"

Members of the police department brought coffee and sandwiches. The high school and elementary districts arranged to bus the children and teenagers to their schools early so that they could shower and be ready for their first classes.

The presidential candidate, Senator George McGovern of South Dakota, campaigning in California, sent a telegram addressed to "the sidewalk." He decried the families' circumstances.

"They deserve better than the streets," he announced.

I was determined to prepare for another encounter with gun-toting goons. On Saturday, Junior, Enrique, and I drove to the flea market in San Jose.

"We're too exposed," I told the boys. "We'd better have something just in case they come again."

We wandered through aisle after aisle of second-hand clothes, jewelry, tools, pots and pans, furniture. Finally, we approached a booth with lines of handguns on a table and rows of rifles set in wooden racks. A short, overweight man in his fifties with a flattop haircut and hazel eyes stood waiting, hands folded across his chest. I scanned the pistols and flipped price tags.

"We need something for our house," Junior told the vendor, who wasted no time.

"That there's a real good un. You gonna like it! It's a M1911 semiautomatic and single-action. Magazine-fed and recoil-operated. Takes the .45 cartridge. Been around for decades. United States Armed Forces-issued. Yup, used that un way back in the Philippine-American War, then World War I and II, the Korean War. Over in Vietnam, some of the guys still carry it." The man chuckled, revealing tobacco-stained teeth.

I laid down my money and drove home with the first gun I had ever owned, folded in a paper bag under the seat. "Is this the person I have become, ready to shoot someone?" I wondered. I was ashamed, yet I knew that I couldn't leave my family unprotected. No one spoke. South of Gilroy, the hills that only days before had been matted in plush green now showed traces of brown as spring drifted into summer.

"I don't like doing this," I acknowledged to the two boys, "but that Fresno bunch just might be back. We have to be ready."

Five days later, a drunken motorist hit Delia Pérez as she walked along Sherwood Drive. The young mother suffered only minor injuries, but the incident troubled the families and me. We agreed that the narrow strip in front of La Posada where we had first settled was too dangerous. Across the way, the steel gray towers and transformers of a Pacific Gas and Electric Substation rose behind its heavy chain-link fence.

We decided to pick up our belongings and move there, where the shoulder of the road was much wider and safer. Once we had all packed and moved, a PG&E representative surprised us by announcing that, for the moment at least, the company would not object to the temporary encampment.

On day eleven, US Senator John Tunney visited the encampment. I led him and San Francisco Bay Area TV cameras through the shelters, damp from another late spring rain. When the tour ended, the senator faced the reporters. He called the conditions "deplorable."

"I'm appalled at what I see," he declared.

Clearly, our sacrifices were having a significant impact on the broader community. The whole La Posada episode had become an embarrassment to the city fathers that aired nightly on the news and seemed to have no immediate solution. The tension between Elida and me, however, was also building.

"Look what César is doing," I told her. "Right now he's fasting in Arizona. He's been living on water and nothing else for over a week. He's doing that so everyone will pay attention to the unjust laws pushed through by the growers. Every one of those laws is designed to destroy the UFW! Chávez is putting his life on the line to try to get people to listen! It's the same here! The whole point of this encampment is to get the politicians to listen. Don't forget, they've ignored this housing problem for decades."

"Don't talk to me about Chávez!" Elida responded. "Talk about what you're doing to our children! You know, it's not only you that's suffering. Your children are suffering, and you're jeopardizing their health! They all have colds, and Celina had a fever this morning!"

"Celina has a fever because Pic 'n Pac has kicked us out of our home, bebé!"

"We have a home in Mercedes, Texas!" she retorted, ending the discussion.

Late one evening, Dennis Powell came to visit me. Elida and the children were already in bed. We sat beneath the tent's awning, now expanded into a living area with tarpaulin walls. I had purchased a folding table, chairs, a kerosene lamp, and a bottle of Jose Cuervo tequila at the flea market. Elida, whose father had owned numerous weapons, accepted my decision to purchase the handgun without comment. She focused on the bottle instead.

"Only when guests come," I remarked apologetically.

Flames lapped above the lip of the oil drum and warmed Powell and me against the wind. Before the conversation began, I darted into the tent, returned, and placed the black L-shaped .45 on the table along with the José Cuervo. Dennis gave me a puzzled look.

"Just in case they shoot at us," I told him, pouring two shots from the bottle.

Powell had come to talk about King City, located fifty miles away at the southern end of the valley. For years, the state, through the local housing authority, had operated a labor camp set on the edge of that town. The camp opened every July, just in time for the arrival of the tomato workers, most of whom were seasonal migrants from Texas. Then, as soon as the workers finished with the harvesting and packing, the authority closed the place again.

Powell's blue eyes and sandy hair glowed in the fire's light. "We're thinkin' to sue the state to make them keep it open year around. That way, you and other farmworkers could stay permanently. Of course, the locals have never wanted it as permanent housing."

"What good to sue? *Años y años en la corte*. That no help us."

"You're probably right," Powell responded. "But the point is that camp was built with federal funds for farm labor. I don't believe they can just decide that only a certain predetermined group of workers can live there. They have to open it up to workers on equal terms for all. Right now they're treating it like it's private housing operated for the benefit of a handful of tomato growers who need labor. When the need passes, they close the place. Makes no sense. It's just that nobody's called them on it until now." I poured two more shots. Dennis Powell continued.

"You know, it's been nearly ten years since the *Bracero* Program ended, yet the *corbatas*—as you call them—haven't gotten the message. The migrant trail is dying. We can't keep closing these camps as if everyone's planning to pack up and go home when the work's done." He leaned forward. "So here's the deal; this little trick you're pullin' off with this campout is stirring up a pot of jalapeños, *amigo*. You're makin' every good citizen in this goddamn valley think about the fact that the Mexicans are here to stay and they're here with their families. Agriculture is changing. It's going corporate. You can work for a company for nine months here and a couple more in Coachella or the San Joaquín, then off to Mexico to see family for a month and come back here in time for school. That's what's happening. It's just there's no proper housing. It's all as makeshift as this camp you've set up, and no one's takin' a hard look at that. You're making them look at it."

The following afternoon, Powell came again to announce that the district attorney's office had decided not to prosecute any of us on charges of battery and of resisting arrest.

That same evening, the housing authority held a special meeting to reconsider the idea of permitting La Posada's former residents to move to Camp McCallum out on Old Stage Road five miles south of Salinas. Despite their previous concerns that the place, having been abandoned for eight years, was not habitable, they agreed to permit the move as a temporary solution.

In the paper, a commissioner was quoted as saying, "Whatever the conditions at that place, they can't be as bad as living on the streets of Salinas."

Part Three

CHAPTER TWELVE

My friend, Dan Billings, came to visit the encampment on Saturday afternoon. No one could miss him. His six-foot-five frame appeared on Sherwood Drive. His deeply lined, tawny face carried a drooping, silver mustache. For this special occasion, he was dressed in tapered jeans, a tasseled buckskin jacket and matching knee boots, a red bandana, and a broad-brimmed, whiskey-colored cowboy hat made of felt and graced with a spray of quail feathers pressed into a beaded band.

He doffed the hat soon after making his grand entrance, revealing a silver mane that flowed from his large head. With him, he brought pans of freshly chopped carnitas for the barbecue and two *ollas* full with rice and beans. From the back of his pickup, he unloaded three cases of beer for the adults and three more of soda for the children together with bags of *pan dulce*.

His unexpected arrival created a stir of excitement along the line of tents, especially among the families nearest to Elida and me, for they knew that the feast and festivities would emanate from our space.

Dan Billings towered above everyone. The low timbre and strength of his voice carried across the midafternoon air as he greeted my family, our neighbors, and me with "*¿Cómo* *está?" "¡Hola, amigo!" "¿Qué Tal?"* repeated to all within earshot. The children came running. They naturally hovered near him. The bravest hugged his pants legs and looked up expectantly. He pulled wrapped candy from a pocket and slipped a piece to those closest.

Dan Billings was the grandson of a tall, squared-jawed Texan Anglo who married the Mexican heiress of a modest-sized Spanish land grant near McAllister in 1887. During the decades after the Treaty of Guadalupe Hidalgo, it was not uncommon for Mexican señoritas to assent to marriage with an Anglo suitor as protection against US and Texas laws designed to strip us Mexicans of our land on the theory that we owned too much of it.

Dan's grandfather had been a successful cattle rancher; but his son, Dan's father, lost it all during the Great Depression and Dustbowl disasters that had swept away a generation of Midwestern farmers and ranchers.

Dan carried his Hispanic heritage with great pride. Like his father and grandfather before him, he fell in love with and married a woman of Mexican descent. From his grandmother, he learned to speak a refined Castilian Spanish. From her, he also learned much about the history of Mexico although, in speaking of the revolution, his grandmother was clearly on the side of the *gachupines*, our new and troubled nation's native-born Spaniards who stubbornly fought to preserve their traditional dominance over the land and its people.

After Dan's family lost its ranch and wealth, his father brought his wife and four children west to California. They settled in south Salinas near the home of a great uncle.

As a young man, Dan loved to be around children, but now he lived alone. His wife of nearly fifty years had died just last summer. His son and daughter had been out of the home and on their own for twenty years. They lived in Los Angeles and San Diego. His grandchildren were also grown and working. They rarely visited.

Dan fancied himself a poet and seer. He enjoyed telling a good story. As he narrated his tales, his black eyes, arched by thick, hoary brows, glowed like the beads of a rosary, expressing profound joy and celebration. Sometimes, however, they trimmed down like an oil lamp, turning somber, even morose, or simmered with anger like vigil lights bearing witness to an enraged but distant God.

Now retired, Dan Billings spent his career as a labor contractor. During the late forties and early fifties, he worked for the Salinas Valley Growers and Shippers Association, coordinating the flow of *bracero* labor in and out of the valley and arranging housing and meals in various labor camps, including Camp McCallum.

The memory of those years brought him to Sherwood Drive on this Saturday afternoon. His goal was to celebrate the concession that we had won from the housing authority and toast our impending move to the old camp that he had once managed.

Our common backgrounds touching on the Rio Grande Valley and our common love of history had sealed our friendship early on. One morning, shortly after we met, Dan took me to his home on Katherine Avenue, the same dwelling his father had purchase long ago. He led me, his new friend, into a back bedroom. There, displayed on the wall, were dozens of knives. I stood at the door, surveying the strange collection. Bowie knives, buck knives, boot knives, each pinned in its place against the plaster, some with wood handles, some with steel, some with stacked leather, some with no handles at all, just pieces of sharpened metal.

"All of these, I took off of the *braceros*," Dan said, sweeping the wall with his stretched-out arm. "We avoided a lot of trouble that way. They could be a tough bunch at times." He smiled broadly and moved quickly to a corner of the room. "Here, let me show you something else."

He brought back what he identified as a Colt Walker single-action .44 revolver. The gun was partially rusted. It had been sheathed in a dry and cracked leather holster.

"This gun here belonged to Joaquín Murrieta," he proclaimed proudly. "My great uncle, Toribio Esquivel, left it to me. He told me he got it from a man in Monterey who lived there in 1853. The man swore to him that ol' Joaquín was a friend of his. He visited one night on the run. Left this .44 and his saddle and headed for the San Joaquín Valley incognito. Of course, he never came back for his gear. They gunned him down at Three Rocks near Cantua Creek that year. You probably know that story."

I nodded. "I know it well," I said. "To the *Californianos*, he was a 'Robin Hood.'"

Dan enjoyed sharing his knowledge of local history and relished having a personal connection to it.

After dinner, as a swab of orange edged against the Santa Lucias and the sweet smell of carnitas lingered in the air, the mothers and fathers bedded down the younger children. Those nearest to our tent returned to the barreled fire, for the tarps had been drawn back, and Dan already sat in the midst of twenty listeners. Everyone had carried folding chairs in anticipation. Adults and teenagers sipped their drinks and surrendered themselves to Dan's smooth and resonant narrative.

Elida and I, Junior and Enrique, Celina and Moisés sat nearby as Dan waited until all was quiet except the crackle of the fire and the occasional car passing nearby.

"I wanted to visit today to tell you about Camp McCallum," Dan began. "Names are important. When you hear the name of a place, especially a place where you're going to live, you should learn all that the name can tell you about the past. You should understand the stories that created that name. In that way, you come to appreciate the space and remember and cherish the people who occupied that space before you."

The energy in Dan's eyes drew his audience into his world, and his stately language held them transfixed. The grand poet and seer then began his tale.

"On a scragged patch of sand in the Chihuahua Desert, the Indian children sit and chaw on a twig. This they learned from their parents and grandparents. For centuries, their ancestors chewed the desert scrog and harnessed the extract not only for fuel but for play.

"The first recorded observation of this communal chewing comes from an early sixteenth-century Spanish visitor to North-Central Mexico who described how the children used the product of their chewing—a small black sphere—to play a game not unlike today's tennis. The Spaniards were in awe of the sphere's ability to bounce.

"The bush on which the children gnawed burned readily and provided fuel for warmth and for cooking. Later, the Franciscan and Dominican missionaries again took note of its properties. Throughout the regions of Zacatecas, Chihuahua, Coahuila, San Luis Potosí, Nuevo León, and Tamaulipas, it was known by a variety of names: *xikuitl, ulequahuitl, el copallín, el afinador, la hierba de hule, el guayule*; all of these names may be translated roughly as 'the rubber weed.'

"Now the fact is, an array of scranny yet advantageous bushes and shrubs covers the desert regions of Mexico and grows within the reaches that today we call New Mexico and

Southwest Texas, but guayule's beneficial effect on human lives outstrips all of the others. Humans have chewed it, played with it, cut and burned it to warm and feed themselves and to fuel mining smelters.

"The first American to collect specimens of guayule, as I remember, was some scientist who was part of a surveyor team in South Texas in the early 1850s. American business, however, paid little attention until the early twentieth century with the coming of the automobile."

Dan Billings was proud of his command of these facts, some of which he had learned nearly thirty years before this night and had set to memory. Others he had gathered at the library when he made his decision to visit the families' encampment. He paused to survey the circle of eyes and to re-assure himself that his listeners were ready to hear more. We waited patiently.

"You should understand that during this period, the British monopolized Brazilian rubber. In the late nineteenth century, they controlled ninety percent of the rubber market.

"By the turn of the century, however, American rubber interests had begun to harvest guayule in Mexico. Numerous US extraction companies sprang up throughout its northern desert and in Southern Texas, intent on gathering the endless stands of guayule and processing the precious rubber for the emerging auto industry.

"Mexican entrepreneurs also entered the competition. The most notable and successful company was established by Francisco Madero himself, future revolutionary president of Mexico."

The elders among us listeners were unanimous in expressing to one another our approval at the mention of the martyred president. Dan Billings continued.

"The Rubber Trust, a cabal financed by the likes of John D. Rockefeller and Meyer Guggenheim—these were very wealthy men—owned the Continental Rubber Company. Continental and a dozen other American-financed ventures established processing plants throughout Mexico's northern regions and in Marathon, Texas—I see some of you are familiar with Marathon." A few in the audience smiled proudly.

"Then, just after the turn of the century, Continental acquired *Los Cedros*, an old Spanish land grant covering nearly two million acres of Mexican desert, abundant with the guayule bush. Eventually, Continental bought out the other extraction companies together with their Mexican land holdings. It amassed some 3.5 million acres and thus gained control over 80 percent of the continent's rubber production. Madero's company was among those purchased by the Rubber Trust.

"All this adds up to one fact: between 1906 and 1912, the motley guayule plant gave up nearly 130 million pounds of rubber to the US market.

"Now listen closely to this next fact. A man by the name of Dr. William B. McCallum began working for the Continental Rubber Company in 1910 as its chief botanist charged with studying the cultivation of guayule with its mysterious capacity to produce rubber. Within two years, however, widespread harvesting had nearly depleted the 'endless' supply of the plant.

"Furthermore, the Mexican Revolution and its marauding armies and bands of *pistoleros* increasingly disrupted production and research. It became evermore clear that America's rubber barons needed a more secure and regenerative source of rubber to reduce their reliance on its foreign-grown stock. In time, industry, government, and science combined in the vigorous pursuit of a commercially viable and homegrown guayule plant.

"I knew Dr. McCallum personally. He was a great man. He taught me much of what I am telling you tonight.

"Because of the revolution, Intercontinental directed Dr. McCallum to move his experimentations to the US. Forbidden by the Mexican government to transport guayule plants across the border, the doctor journeyed north with thousands of seeds hidden in a tobacco tin. Upon his return home, he developed a number of test sites in search of the ideal soil and the ideal weather to tame and tailor the guayule plant for a fast-growing American rubber market.

"He settled first in Arizona and then San Diego but eventually established a research, production, and processing center in Salinas, where the sandy loam and Mediterranean climate might bring greater success.

"Now, World War I came along. That, of course, boosted interest and investment in the study of guayule and the production of rubber. By the late twenties, the Salinas Valley had become the center of McCallum's research. Farmers were under contract to plant eight thousand acres of guayule.

"The good doctor made significant strides in his quest to increase the yield and improve the quality of the latex produced by the plants.

"Japan's growing belligerence in Southeast Asia and the subsequent bombing of Pearl Harbor prompted the US Congress to authorize the Emergency Rubber Project. A wide variety of federal agencies was enlisted to push forward aggressively on the production of rubber in support of the war effort.

"The US government purchased the Intercontinental Rubber Company. Through the Department of Agriculture, it continued the company's work in Salinas, retaining McCallum as project consultant. Once again, guayule grew on thousands of acres of Salinas Valley land.

"Doctor McCallum spent over thirty years of his life in meticulous research designed to transition the guayule bush from its feral and scruffy origins to the groomed and ordered fields of agribusiness. Through precise breeding and tracking, he led the national effort to engender higher and more predictable yields. His work was essential to the Allied victories in Europe and Asia."

Once again, Dan Billings paused. The audience members murmured among themselves, repeating some of what they had heard. Pancho Vega sat tall and attentive.

"When I was a boy," he explained to the whole group, "my father and I gathered up the guayule near our home. We burned it to keep warm."

Dan Billings acknowledged his testimony and pushed forward.

"What I've told you so far is only the first part of my tale. You must now listen closely to the second part.

"With the country's entrance into World War II, the federal government was concerned not only about replacing Japanese rubber but also about the supply of domestic labor to harvest the nation's crops. After President Roosevelt's declaration of war, millions of American workers enlisted in the military or soon found themselves employed in the making of war materiel. Labor in many sectors of the economy was in short supply.

"Under pressure from California farmers, Roosevelt traveled to the city of Monterrey to meet with Mexico's President Manuel Ávila Camacho and seek agreement for a bold plan to bring hundreds of thousands of Mexican men to the US to pick the crops.

"In early August 1942, the US and Mexican governments initiated the *Bracero* Program. Maybe some of you have heard of that." Dan smiled wryly.

The older men nodded. "*¡Sí. Por cierto!*" they exclaimed.

Dan Billings continued. "With the expansion of the US war effort, thousands of Mexico's rural farmers and day workers sought to contract their labor as *braceros*. They left their scanty scraps of land and traveled to processing centers in *La Ciudadela*, Mexico City, and *El Trocadero* in the city of Chihuahua. Riots broke out in these faraway places as men with nowhere to go stood for days, struggling to hold their place in line against recently arrived challengers. After a cursory physical and an examination of hands, which served to determine their fitness for fieldwork, those selected were taken to way stations in Juárez or El Paso or to Calexico across the border from Mexicali to complete the processing and await the offer of a contract from a US grower.

"During the wait, they slept in sterile barracks and experienced their first taste of American cuisine: cold bologna and mayonnaise sandwiches."

We all broke into laughter at the description of the odd and unfamiliar foods that *americanos* seemed to love so dearly. Dan Billings sat silent only briefly.

"Every *bracero* signed a personal services contract identifying his rights and responsibilities. Both governments approved the form of the contract and required that it be translated into Spanish. Many of the *braceros*, however, were illiterate. They had no idea what the document demanded of them, nor did they understand the protections it provided.

"Upon signing, each worker was transported at no expense to himself to the cotton fields of Texas; the vegetable farms, vineyards, or fruit groves of California; the potato patches of Idaho; or the apple orchards of the Northwest.

"Before departing the processing center and boarding the bus that would take him to his worksite, each man was made to suffer one last indignity. He and his fellow compatriots were lined up and required to strip naked; then, one by one, they were sprayed or dusted with DDT. Unlike the *americano* who administered the 'cleansing,' they were given no protective covering during the dousing, although they were advised to close their eyes. They were also informed that this peppering was necessary 'to kill the Mexican fleas.'"

We shook our heads and silently cursed the stupidity of those who had designed such measures. Some of the older men gave each other knowing looks.

"Now listen to this quite astonishing fact." Dan Billings raised a finger and held us in suspense for a long moment. "They say between 1942 and 1964, over the life of the program, some 400,000 *braceros* signed 4.6 million work contracts with US growers.

"For many, like your own situation, the trek *al Norte* represented the start of a new life as a migrant farmworker and provided a new source of income needed to support their families back home. For others, whom duplicitous, overbearing, or abusive employers had victimized, the experience was a source of anger, resentment, and distrust."

The pace of Dan Billings's speech hastened with his growing indignation.

"In some locales, they encountered blatant and often vicious discrimination. At the end of the workweek, they were bussed into the nearest town to purchase goods, send letters and packages home, or seek some form of entertainment.

"Most towns, especially in central and northern Texas, made little or no provision for the influx of thousands of laborers looking for a place to bathe, eat, use a toilet, or entertain themselves. Local retailers and owners of restaurants, hotels, laundromats, and theaters systematically excluded them.

"Signs reading 'No Niggers and Mexicans' were common, despite the importance of the local and migrant workforce to the community's financial wellbeing. Often, the locals complained about the workers' filthy clothes and unhealthy personal habits, although they conspired to deny them access to shops and essential facilities. They berated *braceros* for living in conditions that these very people had designed for them.

"A few helpful merchants, of course, were willing to serve the men's needs for goods and services, despite the prevailing culture of racial discrimination." The storyteller stopped to calm himself. He took a deep breath and drew on a half-empty beer.

"Finally, I must narrate something of the terrible events that occurred here only ten years ago and not ten miles from this spot.

"Undoubtedly, some of you are aware of this already. A train loaded with sugar beets collided with a hooded flatbed truck as it crossed the tracks in Chualar. In that false and ill-fated bus, fifty-nine unknowing *braceros* sat within a covered sepulcher on rocky wooden benches.

"They were headed toward home at the end of a day's work in the celery fields, home to the squalid labor camp across the tracks. The train engineer saw the hesitating vehicle poised to make the crossing. He blew his whistle repeatedly, but the driver's view was blocked by his passenger, who himself was preoccupied with the daily time cards, and the noise of the truck's engine covered that of the whistle.

"The unsuspecting driver rumbled on over the rails and, within seconds, sent thirty-two unwary children of God to their graves. The carnage of broken bodies entangled with twisted metal was an absolute, unmitigated disaster that those who witnessed it can never forget. You all know Johnny Martínez. He was only ten at the time and living in González . Johnny and his father were among the first to come upon the scene. It was the bloodiest traffic disaster in the history of California."

Dan Billings spoke this final sentence with a tone of indignation and sorrow. He then fell silent. At last, the seer was ready to end his narration. He sensed that his time with us must also end. Some of us shifted in our chairs. Only a few moved to leave. Once again, he raised a finger, bidding them stay a moment longer, and then concluded.

"Throughout the forties, fifties, and well into the sixties, the *braceros* were the strong-armed men of two nations, providing their labor to help feed America and contribute to the winning of its wars. At the same time, they supported not only their families at home but also the chronically crippled Mexican economy.

"As I said at the outset, I came to narrate the story of Camp McCallum. Now, I trust you understand what sort of place it is; it is a place touched by the lives of thousands of immigrant workers, for the most part single men who came to care for the guayule and to harvest the sugar beets, sorghum, and lettuce."

"I knew these men," the seer stated. "Never forget them. Continue to tell their story. Do that and you also will make a great contribution to *la historia de los campesinos* in this valley."

We gave Dan Billings a respectful applause. Everyone stood and stretched legs and arms. We were ready to return to our tents, but first, we thanked him for giving us an understanding of the new home we were about to occupy.

The teenagers, who had listened keenly throughout the tale, stared at him from a distance, perhaps too shy to come closer. I could see that the barrel fire reflected in their eyes as brightly as it reflected in his.

CHAPTER THIRTEEN

My family and I led the caravan. Another thirty or so cars and trucks belonging to La Posada families followed. The sound of laughter carried through the windows and into the street as we drove east on Alisal. Radios sang out their *corridos*. For the moment, we had left our tents, tarps, and household goods sitting on Sherwood Drive, signs of our fourteenth day of living on the street.

On the edge of Salinas, we turned south, passing Bardin School through open fields extending northeast to the Gabiláns and southwest to the Santa Lucia mountain range.

We drove four miles down to Old Stage Road. There, we turn east for half a mile, along a narrow lace of black pavement. We slowed to make a right turn onto a rutted layer of gray asphalt and dry dirt, the long driveway into the abandon site of old Camp McCallum.

The state and the housing authority had offered us a ninety-day lease. In return, we had to abandon the tarps and tents, occupy the camp, and move again as soon as they found alternative housing for us. We had no choice but to accept their terms. We knew that the city was already planning to remove us from the street.

The neglected thoroughfare into the old camp ran some eight hundred feet from Old Stage Road. A field of dried weeds lay to the right. The road brought us to a sagging gate. The sign warned the public to keep out, but the gate was partially open.

I looked at Elida, who stared ahead without comment. I glanced into the rearview mirror. Our children gazed at the towering eucalyptus trees that lined the camp's westerly edge. Celina, Romeo, and Baby Gloria chatted, anxious to see our new home. Jaime bounced on the middle seat, humming and trying to whistle.

I got out of the Buick. Junior, Enrique, and Moisés opened the back door and escaped. They darted past me, intent on exploring the dense grove. I dragged the gate farther back against the weeds to allow the caravan to enter, then stood smiling and waving to the following drivers. As they passed, I shielded my eyes from the dust rising with the June breeze.

The last car in the line belonged to Dennis Powell. He and I had become good friends over the weeks while planning our response to the next issue or the next crisis. Powell paused at the gate. He looked ahead at the rows of gray barracks and wild foliage. He leaned across the passenger seat and rolled down the window.

"John Jones was right," he called. "It's a mess!"

I nodded agreement, then returned to my car and followed Powell. We parked with the others wherever we could find a patch of dirt that was free of tall grass and bramble. Elida and I got out of the car. Our younger children followed our two boys into the grove. Dennis Powell greeted Elida with a firm handshake. She smiled faintly and nodded. She still appreciated the support Powell had given her on the day of my arrest.

The families, gathered in a half-circle, stood with their backs to the foremost building, a disheveled community center, and its flagless pole. They waited for us and peered cautiously down the property's middle road, bordered on either side with rows of raggedy barracks. Thin gray exterior siding wrapped the buildings, each covered with a low-pitched roof, its asphalt shingles slapping in the breeze.

Each building was lined with large lattice-paned windows, many with broken glass. Tilted doors hung from their hinges at awkward angles. Wild-growing trees and foliage engulfed the siding and the roofs and overflowed across the roads and between the rows of structures.

"*¡Vamos!*" I called out. "Keep in mind, two families in each barrack."

The people broke their polite silence and fanned out across the site. The late morning breeze grew stronger, roughly brushing exterior walls and disturbing the layered dust. The children ran willy-nilly. They scavenged through each of the barracks, rolled on the cold cement floors, peered through the broken windows.

The wind rattled against the loose casements. The smell of eucalyptus mingled with that of rotting wood and corroded metal. The children hid among the tall, stately trees, and chased one another. They threw small branches like spears. They grabbed handfuls of leaves and tossed them in the air. They called to each other with each new discovery: an old tire, a faded magazine, the shell of an abandoned car. Weeds and rust had assaulted the large water tank toward the rear of the property. It stood precarious on its flaked moorings.

The parents cautioned, "Don't touch."

"*¡Cuidado!*"

"*¡Déjelo!*"

"*¡Es peligroso!*"

Mingo and his family had quickly selected a unit close by. He approached Dennis Powell and me.

"I can't believe we're here! Once we get it cleaned up, this will be a good place for us." He surveyed the scene, the line of barracks, the fields beyond, the Gabilán Mountains to the east. "Congratulations to both of you." Mingo shook my hand and then Powell's.

"Everyone worked hard to make it happen," Powell declared.

I watched Elida enter and exit one building after another. I had thought it best to let her decide which one would be ours. Each of the barracks was 120 feet long and 22 feet wide, providing some 1,300 square feet of living space when divided between two families. The first of the gray structures on the west, however, stood alone, only half as long as the others.

Elida entered, our younger children tagging after. I knew she was ever wary of the direction our lives had taken. She had suffered through the insecurity and indignity of living on the street. Everyone around her celebrated the housing authority's approval for the move. She doubted that we had gained anything worth the effort.

Was this our reward: a ninety-day lease on an abandoned labor camp? It was an improvement over the dirt and tarps, but still, it wasn't security.

Elida approached. She pointed toward the first, half-sized barrack. After all our years together, I was still in love with her dark eyes.

"That one's fine," she told me without enthusiasm.

"Are you sure?"

"It's fine," she repeated. "It has some broken windows in the back. They'll need repairing."

Powell turned to me.

"I'm going to look around. What did the county say? Thirty-two buildings, constructed with redwood? Incredible resource!"

I had walked the property the previous day with a Mr. Ames, the chief maintenance man from the housing authority. We examined the barracks, the T-shaped dining halls with common showers and bathrooms attached. The structures extended across the site with generous space between, some facing north and south, others east and west. Mr. Ames, who had helped manage the camp ten years ago when it still housed *braceros*, assured me that he could have the water, gas, sewer, and electricity running again within a week or two.

"The larger problem," he surmised, "is the trash and overgrowth of trees, bushes, and weeds, and the broken windows and doors." He expressed his regret that he had no idea how we might take care of those issues. "Somebody else is gonna have to figger out that one," he said as he climbed back into his truck. "I'll tell you what, this place doesn't look like much now, but it was very well built, redwood studs, tongue-in-groove redwood ceilings. Can't beat that!"

He closed the door and started the engine. "We'll be out here in the morning to fire up the pump and the boilers. We'll let you know how it's goin'."

I was pleased with Elida's choice of living quarters. The location allowed me to monitor access into the property. I walked with her to view the space. I pushed open the dirt-streaked door and stepped aside to let her pass. We entered and stood in silence. The air smelled of weathered and wet wood. The recent rain had puddled portions of the cement floor. The gray paneling also covered the interior walls and ceiling. Vandals had poached some of the sections, leaving jagged-edged holes and revealing the unit's redwood studs and exterior siding. Other sections bulged with weather damage, broken corners dangling. Some of the ceiling panels had partially detached. They hung precariously above. Many of the windows were broken, and bird droppings soiled the drab cement.

"How are we to live here?" Elida asked. "No water, electricity, stove, gas. We have no money, Sixto. How are we going to fix this place?"

"The housing authority will help us. They told me they're not going to let us move in until the utilities are repaired and the doors and windows fixed. Powell says he's gotten calls from people who want to volunteer. We'll work something out. We've gotten this far."

"And we'll continue on the street for another month or two. Is that your plan?"

"It won't take a month or two, bebé."

She turned and stepped into the bright morning sun. I followed. Junior and the other children exited the grove, saw us immediately, and ran in our direction.

"*Mamá*," Mario yelled, "we found an empty bird nest!"

"Those trees smell like medicine!" observed Celina, who bent to pick up Jaime.

"Is this where we're going to live?" Enrique asked, looking through the open doorway.

They all pushed into the space as we watched in silence.

"Everything is broken!" cried Moisés.

"We have to fix it, *papi!*"

"We will, *m'ijo*. We will. Don't worry."

Before our arrival, we had heard that the overgrown property had been closed for eight years not only because the *Bracero* Program ended but also because local grower families, especially the Bardins and Fanoes—who owned the adjacent land—didn't want the camp encroaching on their farming operations ever again. Undoubtedly, they were closely monitoring the county's decision to allow us to live at the camp.

Dennis Powell came to visit on Sherwood Drive.

"You're not going to believe what just happened."

"*Dígame*," I said, inviting him into the foyer of canvas tarps.

"OEO has announced that your friend, Mr. Phillip Sánchez, has approved a grant of $50,000."

I rose from the table.

"*¡Maravilloso!*" I exclaimed.

"Obviously, your trip to Washington made an impression on the national director. And get this: part of the money will be used to fly the Green Berets from Fort Bragg, North Carolina, to Salinas to help clean up Camp McCallum!"

"*¡Es increíble!*" I stammered as Powell reached out to shake my hand.

"Absolutely, it's unbelievable! I just got the call from San Francisco. The Green Berets Fifth Special Forces Group from North Carolina is coming to Salinas! They'll be here this weekend!" The attorney smiled excitedly, delighted at the turn of events.

"They said Sánchez personally intervened with the administration. He also got the county, the city, and the state housing department to back his request. Even the state national guard is sending people to help. They'll all coordinate with officials at Fort Ord." Fort Ord was the local army base. Powell continued, "And if they need any equipment, they can bring it from there. Senator Tunney had a hand in the whole thing. I can imagine Talcott's not real happy about it."

I sat down again to absorb Powell's words. Sanchez had promised to help, but I had no idea he had the power to pull this off. Junior stepped toward the tent to translate the news for his mother, who stood at the open flap with Jaime beside. The child was coughing badly. Elida wiped his nose with a towel as she listened. She and Jaime then disappeared into the shelter.

Powell continued, "This special forces unit rebuilds villages over in Vietnam after we or the Vietcong have strafed them or whatever. They pick up what's left and try to put it back together. They'll arrive on Saturday. Only in America!" he said, shaking his head.

Precisely at nine o'clock on Saturday morning, two hooded troop carriers arrived at Camp McCallum from Fort Ord bringing the Green Berets and the national guard. A dump truck and supply vehicle followed. We and the other families were already moving through our chosen barracks, sweeping and scrubbing. Some of us had brought our first load of household goods and furniture. We stepped away from our cleaning to watch the convoy pull up in front of the community center. The soldiers, in fatigues and boots, disembarked. The officers shouted their orders, and two dozen troopers began their day's work.

For two weeks, the troopers and we labored side by side. A mutual respect grew up between us. We were impressed at the soldiers' focus and efficiency as they moved from one task to the next in orderly sequence. The soldiers admired our work habits, especially the endurance of the women.

The troopers bivouacked on site. Each morning, while they shouldered up for their daily orders, they observed the animated residents already engaged trimming trees and bushes or mending doors and windows. They also applauded our habit of working long after the captain had dismissed his men at the end of the day.

The State Department of Human Resources delivered a truckload of building material, beds, and wallboard. Fort Ord contributed surplus chairs. The residents scrounged at the flea markets for used couches, lamps, dining tables.

When the troops and we had completed the work, we stood together surveying the site, half of its thirty gray buildings useful once again. We had repaired windows, rehung doors, covered holes in walls and ceilings, trimmed trees, and removed trash and brush. We called for a celebration.

Caravans of local and Bay Area media arrived with their cameras and reporters. Captain Thorne, who led the Green Beret unit, claimed his men carried forty truckloads of debris to the dump.

"We finished a week sooner than expected," he told the press. "These folks know how to work!"

I stood before the television cameras. A young female reporter, named Phoebe, brushed back her blond hair and pushed a microphone toward me.

"This is what we feel: *orgullo*, pride," I declared, responding to her question. "This is what we fight for: opportunity for our children, an education so that they can, at least, defend themselves, and a career for them, work that is better. We know that such things are out there because we've seen them. We've seen others win them."

"Mr. Torres," the reporter asked, "you have overcome a great deal already to be standing here in this place. What do you think lies ahead?"

"The parents here are from the fields, always in the fields," I stated. "We'll die in the fields. The growers, they want our children to be the same, to be in the fields, to crawl in the rows. In the future, our children won't crawl the way that we have had to crawl. We fight for our rights to organize, to live in a good home like others, but these things are denied us.

"Somehow, the growers think that we're not normal people. It's true, they are white, we are brown, but I believe that our blood and their blood are the same red color. So why do they think that we're different? We work to live. They work to live. In that, we are very much the same." The reporter listened intently. I continued, "In the beginning, everybody was against us. The Pic 'n Pac company told us we had three days to leave. The county officials said the growers had all the power and they could do nothing for us. OEO helped us with a grant, but then Talcott denied it. We asked the county counsel, 'Why could they not use the money to provide us with housing?' He said that it was taxpayer money and the taxpayers didn't want to use the funds for that purpose. I responded that we are also taxpayers. When we buy cigarettes or purchase a car or truck, we pay taxes. When we buy clothes for our children, we pay taxes. We have taxes deducted from our paychecks like everyone else."

Later, I returned to the house and found Elida among the children and the unpacked boxes. A recommissioned sink from one of the old refectories was set into the worn plywood along the back wall. Celina lifted pans onto a makeshift draining board that the troopers had built from scrap wood. They had set two shelves, six feet long, below the sink.

"Moisés," Elida called, "put those towels on our bed. I'll find a place for them later."

Moisés carried the towels to the rear of the barrack, where a sheet strung from the ceiling defined his parent's bedroom.

"Celina, I want you to take all of the food from those boxes over there and put it on the shelves."

"Where is Baby Gloria?" Celina asked. "Why isn't she helping?"

"I sent Romeo to find her. Just do your work. They'll be back in a minute."

CHAPTER FOURTEEN

We had been living at Camp McCallum for only a week when Saul Alinsky died of a heart attack in Carmel, twenty miles away. Peña brought the newspaper to me and translated the article. It read in part: "Alinsky had inspired a generation of community organizers with his writings and his efforts to teach the powerless how to gain political power. He and his cohort, Fred Ross, had mentored Chávez during his years with the Community Services Organization."

I had no formal training in Alinsky's organizing principles: "goad them, confuse them, irritate them" and "rub raw the resentment in the community." But I had experienced the successes of the union's confrontational tactics. I had a talent for goading, confusing, and irritating *los corbatas*.

As the weeks passed, the housing authority continued to transfer a few residents to available rental apartments. A month into the ninety-day lease period, it had found alternative housing for seven of the original thirty-four squatters. Some of us, however, quietly resisted the planned transition out of the camp.

Elsie Burton, the authority's longtime board chair, a large woman with a large presence in the county, wrote to Senator Tunney, "The families do not appear to be interested in submitting their applications for an apartment...."

A local reporter phoned Rogelio Peña at his home.

"Can you help me understand why?" he asked.

Peña answered with his own questions.

"What should we do? They have no houses for families with five, six, or eight kids or for extended families. Do they expect us to abandon our babies or our parents who may live with us and move into one of their two-bedroom apartments?"

At night I lay in the darkness behind the hanging blankets that separated Elida and me from our children. I listened to my wife's uneasy sleep. The crickets beyond the windows chirped impatiently. The restive wind cuffed the eucalyptus branches.

"It all happens for the convenience of the *corbatas*," I thought. "They do nothing until they are forced to act. We can't win unless it is to their convenience that we win. We must leave them with no alternative but to help us. The shortage of houses can't be an accident. Either it's planned or it's the result of negligence."

I sat in the community center with the remnant of families. Everyone was anxious because the lease period would end on August 31, only a month away. Perhaps, once again, we would have to squat on the streets of Salinas.

"I have been thinking," I said, "we need to resist. We need to stay here, not allow them to push us out."

Juan Alemán was surprised to hear me suggest this new strategy. We had made a promise to cooperate, to relocate.

"I've been talking to my friend, Dan Billings," I explained. "He told me that the government decides what housing can be built and where. The government decided to shut down Camp McCallum and to keep it closed for all these years. He asked me, 'Why not push them to keep it open permanently?'

"Dan Billings says they would have moved us to this place even if we hadn't signed that agreement. They would've done anything to get us off the evening news. I asked myself: What is best for our children—to be pushed into a small apartment in Salinas or to stay here where we have more space?"

Aldolfo Zúñiga raised his hand. He was from Yucatán. His round, elegant moon face reflected the afternoon light.

"Don Sixto, *usted sabe*, I gave my word. That is important to me. If they offer me a house or an apartment to rent, I will take it as I promised."

La señora Catalina Castillo nodded in agreement.

"Some of us here are tired of fighting," she stated. "We want a home, a permanent home. Everything depends on that, the job, the schools. By the end of August, the parents will need to know where their children will go to school."

I was not surprised that Catalina had challenged me. Lately, she had changed. At one time, she supported my opinions and ideas without question. Now she was looking always to contradict me in one way or the other. More and more, I had seen her enter the meetings with one or two others who shared her criticisms.

Amparo Contreras rose to make her statement. She wore a purple apron over a black housedress imprinted with yellow flowers.

"When we arrived, we were all very happy to be off of the streets. *Gracias a Dios*, we had help from the soldiers and from the volunteers. We made these barracks livable, but we all know it's not a fit place for a permanent home. We have no hot water. The sewer system is barely working. We don't even have a streetlight at night. With our cars rumbling up and down the worn-out roads all day, the dust is everywhere. I have heard that the principal of Bardin School doesn't want to accept our children in the fall."

"*Mire*," I said, "you have to decide to stay or to leave on your own. I'm not trying to convince you one way or the other. I'm only telling you how I feel, and I believe we must negotiate a different agreement with them."

Voices reverberated around the room's shabby walls and ceiling as the families reacted to the statement, some concurring, others opposing.

"As I said, I've been talking with my friend, Dan Billings. Some of you remember his stories when we were on the street. He's been telling me more about the history of this place and this valley. He's told me about the people before us, from Oklahoma, and Arkansas, and Texas, who came here forty years ago. They were migrants just as we are migrants, but they arrived in the thirties.

"Dan has told me that it was the same then as it is now. The growers and the government built as few camps as possible and shut them down when the crops were picked so no one could stay permanently. When the people tried to organize and create a union, they crushed it, same as they are trying now, with the goons, the police, and the courts. There were too many workers and not enough houses then, same as now.

"When the Oklahoma migrants arrived, some of them were able to squat on a piece of land outside of Salinas across the tracks. They set up tents along Madeira and Woods Street, Market and Alisal, *usted sabe*, near where the fruit stand is located. Back then, nobody ran them off the way they were ready to run us off for camping out.

"After a while, they put a little money down on a lot and built a little house to replace their tent. That is how the migrants were able to stay, and today many are still there in the Alisal."

I paused and sat down behind a folding table at the front of the room. I lit a cigarette, inhaled, and exhaled before continuing.

"I've heard some of you say that we should call César to ask him what to do. If you want to call César, you should do that; but, I must tell you, I don't believe that he can help us with this problem we have. The union has been good for us and we must continue with that fight, but it can't solve all of our problems. We can all see what's happening. The union is struggling just to stay alive. The growers haven't changed since the thirties. Every day, it's a new fight. They're trying to stop us from picketing and from boycotting. Chavez has to spend all of his time fighting court cases in California, in Arizona, in Texas.

"Maybe we'll win them, maybe not. Someday we'll know, but this is what I know now: we can't expect the union to fight this battle for us. This we must fight on our own, and this *campo* is an opportunity, an opportunity to make a permanent home right here. If we don't hang on, we'll lose it forever."

Juan Alemán listened. He and his family had arrived at La Posada only a few weeks before Pic 'n Pac issued the initial eviction notices. He was a baker by trade, but his family had been picking strawberries in Santa Maria when the strike began. Over the months, our two families had developed a close friendship.

Juan was a short, muscular man with a wave of thick hair. He spoke in rapid, staccato phrases as if his tongue and lips couldn't keep pace with his feverish thinking and conclusions. In the few months since his arrival, he had grown to trust me. He saw it as his role to help build understanding and consensus among the doubters.

When I had finished, Juan stood to make his statement.

"*Amigos*," he began, "I support what Don Sixto is saying, *ven*. He has led us through so much already. He organized the protest on the street. He was jailed just for defending his son. He pushed for a solution that led us here. He's a good man, *ven*. We should listen now to what he says."

Juan pulled a blue, wrinkled handkerchief from a back pocket and wiped his forehead.

"I think maybe he's right. The agreement we made is *chueco*, crooked. We had no choice but to sign or face another eviction. When we signed, we knew nothing about this place. They told us that it was unfit for human living, but now we can see that it can be put in order, *ven*.

"What Don Sixto is saying is we shouldn't look only at what we see today. We should look at what it might become. Perhaps the government can help us to repair the sewer and the water and the barracks. Perhaps this camp presents a better solution than moving into a tiny apartment in Chualar. These barracks are large and well built. We have space for gardens. We can repair this center for meetings. We said that we would stay together, especially the larger families. We must stay together.

"Don Sixto explained it already. It's the government that decides what houses can be built, and it is the same government that now says that the valley needs a thousand new homes for the farmworkers and their families. This same government that helped to create the problem, *ven*, has made us sign the agreement to leave the only housing available after ninety days. That's not right and that's why the agreement is *chueco* and that's why we should renegotiate."

As the days passed, we felt less and less threatened with eviction although our lease was to expire on August 31. The housing authority seemed to know that we would not leave so easily. In the end, John Jones and his commissioners gave us another ninety-day extension. We felt that we had triumphed again.

Summer rolled into fall and the harvest waned. Many families throughout the valley reentered the migrant stream as they had always done. Some at the camp had had enough.

Chino Camargo shyly knocked on my door to advise me of their families' departure.

"We're headed for Yuma. We may come back. *¿Quién sabe?* I hope you find a way to stay and rebuild. That would be a good work." We shook hands. "*Adiós*, Sixto," he said.

To my surprise, Rogelio Peña, who still sported his army jacket and beret, was also among those moving on.

"*Dispense*, Don Sixto, *pero mi papá* has decided to return to Texas. I have to go with him. He plans to work up in Michigan next season. He says this place is too full of politics. Call me crazy, but maybe he is right."

I was saddened to lose such close friends and supporters. I embraced them all warmly.

"*Adiós*, Sixto."

Other families also came to bid me farewell.

"No. It's time to leave," Rigoberto Amaya sighed. "They offered us a two-bedroom, but we're not going to live like that again. We are too many. We'll go to Mexico *para la Navidad* and then back to Wasco in the spring. *Adiós*, Don Sixto. Maybe we'll see you again. *¡Buena suerte!*"

The second ninety-day lease period was near its end. Only fourteen tenants remained. We asked the commissioners for another extension. When we arrived at seven in the evening, the agency's small boardroom was packed with supporters and opponents of our request. Residents of the East Alisal neighborhood, together with the Alisal Chamber of Commerce and the school district, submitted a petition with a thousand signatures, demanding that the agency close the camp.

"It doesn't sound like the people of Camp McCallum are doing their part," claimed Mrs. Bonnie Alvarado. "It's been two years since Pic 'n Pac folded, and we feel this is going on and on!"

Mrs. Walter Bardin also spoke, indicating that the farmers in the area of the camp opposed any extension.

"We've had trouble with the ones already there!" she claimed.

We came prepared with our own petition, gathered by walking the neighborhoods of East Alisal and signed by three thousand individuals. Our petition requested that the agency permit us to stay at the camp.

"Our biggest concern," I stated, "is the education of our children. If you evict us, we'll have to take them out of school. As you know, we adults have little or no formal education. We're servants of the field. We have realized the importance of ensuring that *los chavalos* are able to stay in school. I'm sure you understand by now the struggle we have had, trying to become part of this community. We're not looking for a handout. We want to pay our own way, but we need more time. A few months more is not too much to ask."

Arvin Carvel, an East Salinas resident, stood up and announced to the commission, "This Torres fellow here is nothing but a scallywag! He promised to move out. You jes got to go there with the sheriff and evict, just like Pic 'n Pac done before."

Jason Corbett also rose and came to the microphone.

"We all know what Torres's game is," he stated, "but don't underestimate him. He's fearless and smart. He'll have the Farmworkers' Union out in force and CRLA, and another lawsuit, and a bunch of radicals and TV stations from San Francisco broadcasting how unjust the Department of Housing and all of you are to these poor folks. We've been through this before. We know what's gonna happen."

The commissioners listened, but made no decision. York Gin owned a grocery store in East Salinas. He sat at the front table, looking over his gold-rimmed glasses.

"What are they thinking?" he asked. "They must realize they can't stay. Despite the improvements, the conditions out there are still deplorable."

The winter deepened. John Jones, as promised, continued to offer the few vacant units available to the remaining residents. By the New Year, only ten families lived at Camp McCallum. We waited to see what would happen next.

In February, the state extended the lease for 150 days. At the same time, however, the housing authority delivered thirty-day eviction notices. A state housing official explained that the additional time it had granted would give the authority the time it might need to clear the camp.

A few days later, the housing authority, apparently in an effort to avoid having to evict us, decided to sell Camp McCallum to the highest bidder.

CHAPTER FIFTEEN

Billie Leo Briggs loved to talk about himself. After we became friends, he shared with me the story of how it happened that he purchased Camp McCallum.

He was born in Big Spring, Texas, in 1938. His daddy was a cowboy out of Crystal City. His momma was a preacher—the first woman in Texas to be ordained in the Pentecostal Church—and a singer and musician. She was a beautiful and spirit-filled evangelist who knew the bible verse by verse. She was the host of her own radio show and became well known in Central Texas.

Billie Leo's momma had laid her hands upon his head on more than one occasion. He felt himself called to greatness, but a snake intruded into Billie's paradise. When he was six years old, his daddy walked to the back of the house and hollered for him and his seven brothers and sisters to come to the table. They gathered around a long row of two-by-eight planks laid across three sawhorses. His father sat at one end and his mother sat at the other.

"Me and your mom is splittin' up," his daddy declared. "Four a you is gonna come with me and four a you is goin' with her." He let the announcement rest for a while on the seedy planks. He eyed each of the dazed offspring. "You talk among yerselves and decide whose goin' where. No sense squawkin' about it. That's jes how it is."

Billie knew right away that it was a bad bargain. No child should have to choose between his momma and his daddy. It would be like having to shoot one of them, so the scrappy child slipped through the window that same night and set out on his own. He took with him his three-legged dog, a shorthaired collie mutt named Rooster. No one came looking for either of them.

Even at six, Billie was aware of and enjoyed his own God-given talents. Tall for his age, he had handsome features, wavy jet-black hair, a cherub smile, and eyes blue and forceful as the shooter marbles in his pocket. He soon found that he could beguile most anyone with his easygoing confidence, charm, and wit.

He sold newspapers on the street with an arm slipped out of his shirtsleeve so that he appeared to possess only one such appendage. It was 1944, all the men were away to war, all the women working and lonely.

The young beauties coming out of the bars and the housewives pushing their shopping carts found Billie Leo irresistible. They took him home, fed him, clothed him, and gave him money. He was having a grand time until two years later when the law nabbed him on the sidewalk one morning. They sent him off to his momma, who lived in a place out in California, called Salinas.

Billie Leo started fifth grade at Roosevelt School, having no knowledge of the alphabet, numbers, or the written word, but the crafty boy was ready to learn. The teachers enjoyed his outgoing nature, his high energy, and his willingness to do the work.

By eighth grade, he had caught up to his age group academically and entered Salinas High eager to show his athletic talents as a football player.

Billie Leo Briggs was a natural salesman and a quick study. Fresh out of high school, he hooked up with a friend who had experience in starting health studios. They opened two establishments, one in Fort Wayne, Indiana, and the other in Des Moines, Iowa. Once launched and successful, they sold their interest.

Back in Salinas, he landed a position with Spreckels Sugar, where he charmed his way through the ranks until he was offered a management position. He read books about how to run a business and applied the ideas to his daily work. The company paid attention when his division reduced costs and increased profits. He was asked to implement his ideas company-wide. He soon found himself sitting in Spreckels's central office on Market Street in San Francisco and living high in a posh suite.

All the while, Billie Leo kept smiling and shaking hands. He left Spreckels and started his own management consulting business. He provided management services to the county sheriff's office, a contact that would serve him well in future years. He heard about a start-up company named Mobile One, a synthetic oil product. Its developers claimed the viscous substance would increase motor efficiency and reduce engine wear. He traveled to Texas to negotiate a buyout on behalf of a group of California investors.

When he returned, he and the investors owned a Mobile One franchise. He sold the product's virtues to Governor Ronald Reagan, and soon all of the state's official vehicles were gurgling cans of the oily concoction.

At one point in his rise, Billie Leo Briggs was pocketing $25,000 per week. He bought a 360-acre ranch in Carmel Valley and started raising koi fish and investing in real estate. He made money at both. He bought homes, developed lots, and made a practice of contributing to the political campaigns of every elected official in the county. He soon learned that such generosity could ease the permitting process for most any building project he might undertake.

Billie Leo Briggs retired to his Carmel Valley ranch at the age of thirty-three.

"Not bad," he said, "for a poor six-year-old runaway."

In retirement, the savvy businessman learned to fly his private plane, hustled folks in chess or in a local pool game, and enhanced his reputation as a guitar player and great talker.

In midsummer, a friend gave him a tip about a new real estate opportunity.

"Rumor was," he later said, "old Camp McCallum was going on the auction block. The county was looking to dump it. Could be someone might just slip in there and make an offer before the auction ever got rolling. Rumor was they'd take $53,000 hard cash."

Billie was not one to pass on such an opportunity. He drove through the property, estimated the number of residents and the additional space still to be filled. To Billie, Camp McCallum was a gold mine. The following day, he submitted an offer to the county housing authority, full payment in cash. The purchase agreement stipulated one important condition: the residents must clear out before the close of escrow.

I slammed the phone in a fit of anger. Celina and Moisés were playing cards at the other end of the kitchen table. They jumped at the sound and looked at me with alarm.

"That was someone from the county! They called to say the camp is going to be sold to a Señor Bricks."

Elida stood at the sink.

"Sold? Why would they do that?"

"Same as Pic 'n Pac. They don't want to deal with us."

I picked up the phone again and dialed Juan Alemán's number. While I waited for a ring, I continued to speak to Elida.

"They claim the guy who bought it might want to tear the place down for the lumber ...¡Juanito, *venga!* And call Mingo, Pancho, and Chuca. Call the whole board. *¡Más problemas!* We need to meet!"

The following evening, all the people gathered in the community center. The drooping sun cast the gray building in shadows. The eucalyptus leaves fluttered against each other, sending a muted rattle across the camp. Some of the men hung by the door, one foot in the room, one foot out. The women all sat, apprehensive, speaking quietly.

After our hastily called board meeting the previous night, rumors of another eviction had spread through the homes. Now Chuca had arrived ready to take the floor. He was a lumpish man, generally quiet and disengaged, but now he was a little drunk and irate. As soon as I opened the meeting, Chuca stood.

"I want to say something," he began. "My friend, Mr. Torres, is going to give us all the latest news. Isn't that right, Don Sixto?" The portly man bowed slightly toward me. He then shifted his weight and surveyed the room. "He's going to tell us how we have been screwed again."

As he finished the sentence, he swayed in his cowboy boots ever so slightly. He steadied himself on the metal chair. Again, he looked around the room.

"I want to say something," he proclaimed once more as if he had forgotten his previous opening sentence. "This is not acceptable!" His voice pelted the chilled June air. "Not acceptable!"

As he spoke, Chuca eased his chair against the adjoining one, on which his spouse was sitting. The maneuver allowed him to depend on the chair by leaning a knee against it without having to take a hold, thus freeing his hands to gesture in broad, swinging motions.

"They are selling the camp!" Chuca announced as if the news were both fresh and devastating.

The people commented to each other, "We already know this, *hombre*." Chuca continued, unperturbed.

"It is rumored that the new owner will be here Sunday to evict us all. I say again, this is not acceptable!" I watched my cohort carefully. So far, despite his heavy tongue, he was handling himself well, even making sense. I let him carry on but remained vigilant. "Now this is what I propose. I propose that we greet this man, whoever he is . . ."

"Señor Bricks. Señor Beelie Leo Bricks," I interposed.

" ...I say we meet this man as a group, all of us, all together, right out there. Men, women, and children, right out there." Chuca pointed faintly toward the flagpole. It stood naked just beyond the center's front door. "And I propose that all you men

. . ." Here the orator held his audience in suspense until he had their full attention. " ...that all you men bring your rifles! Yes, everyone bring your rifles!"

Chuca now entered into a kind of a chant, his arms beckoning and thrusting forward with each phrase.

"And again, all you men bring your *pistolas*! Yes! Everyone, bring your *pistolas*! And all you boys bring your baseball bats! *Sí* . . ." The people now joined in "*¡Todos los muchachos traigan sus bates de béisbol!*"

Chuca's head bobbed in rhythm as he hit the last word of each phrase and as the younger boys shouted, "*¡Dale!*" and "*¡Órale, Chuca!*"

"And all you women and girls bring your kitchen knives and frying pans! *¡Y todas traigan sus cuchillos y sartenes!*" echoed the crowd. Chuca prepared for a final flourish. "And all of this we do and we do it together! Why? As a show of our strength! *¡Una muestra de nuestra fuerza!*" With the final words, Chuca's eyes grew large and ominous and his mouth stretched open as wide as the round edge of a beer can. He pounded a fist into a palm on the word "*muestra*" and on the word "*de*" and on the word "*fuerza!*"

The speaker's audience bellowed with laughter and broke into an enthusiastic applause. Chuca sat down heavily. He folded his arms and maintained an intensity of purpose by pursing his mouth and glaring straight ahead.

I smiled when I saw the response from the people. It was not a bad idea. As Chuca accepted the applause, I stepped forward.

"Señor Chuca, you should speak more often at these meetings. You've given us something to think about."

When the residents settled down, Pancho Vega stood.

"This idea that my good friend, Chuca, has described is a very good one. We can't allow this newcomer, Señor Bricks, to push us around. He has to understand that we're here to stay. What better way to welcome him than for all of us to gather and demonstrate our intention to stay?"

On Saturday, a pickup truck with the logo of the Housing Authority of Monterey County printed on the door stopped in front of the shed adjacent to the community center. One of the agency's maintenance staff loaded tools into the truck. Francisco Galván walked over to chat with the worker, who was a *compadre* of Galvan's cousin. They exchange greetings, and before long, Francisco described our plan for welcoming Mr. Briggs.

Later, Billie Leo told me how that afternoon, the worker mentioned the conversation to his boss, Mr. John Jones, who called to alert the new owner of the plan.

A lesser man might have heeded the warning from the authority's CEO; but Billie was a one hundred-proof Texan, who never backed away from a challenge. He thought about how he would counter our scheme to intimidate him.

On the following Sunday, as the sun approached its highpoint, Billie arrived at the old camp gate in his red Mark IV Lincoln convertible with the top down. He pulled onto the property. We watched the car crawl forward. We men held our guns. The women clutched their brooms and pots. The children shouldered their bats and sticks.

Billie Leo stopped the grand town car ten yards in front of the crowd. He exited and stood for a moment behind the open door. As his tall frame cleared the door, we stared in astonishment. Billie Leo was dressed in tight, black charro pants with gold lacing. He wore black gloves and black and gold knee boots. The suit's matching jacket featured two dancing horses stitched in gold on each pocket. He immediately placed a large matching sombrero on his head.

Most impressively, he carried two matching pearl-handled Colt 45 Peacemakers holstered on each hip.

The Texan strode forward with a sharp jingle of spurs trailing each step. He paused just seven yards from us and stood as still as a puma poised to pounce. Incongruously, like some modern Billie the Kid, he wore an easy smile on his face.

He spied me standing forward and center of the rest.

"Sixto Torres?" he called. I nodded slightly.

He raised a finger and beckoned me toward a knobby pepper tree a few feet away, near the drooping fence. He stepped toward the tree. I also walked in that direction. The people looked on intently, not sure what might happen next.

Billie Leo faced the tree and bent slightly, reaching for a Bowie knife sheathed in one boot. He pulled the knife, deftly grabbed it by the pointed end, and, with a quick snap of his wrist, sent the weapon hurling toward the tree's soft trunk, where it stuck with a thud and a quiver.

The people watched in silence. Then Billie Leo turned toward me. I had previously shoved my United States Air Force-issue 1911 pistol under my belt buckle.

"Here's the way I see it, Mister Torres," Billie said affably. "I can probably take out ten or twelve of you before you get me. I'm almost sure that's the case. So what's it gonna be? We can start shootin' and killin' each other or . . ." Billie Leo Briggs paused and gave me and the anxious residents his best Texas smile, " ...or we can have a party."

I looked into the man's cunning eyes and saw my own reflection. I realized that Camp McCallum's new owner had trumped our ploy with a superior stunt of his own. I gave him the faintest smile that I could manage. Billie Leo continued confidently, "What's it gonna be? Cuz I got a truckload of beer and food and a band waitin' just up the road. So you choose for all of us, señor. What's your pleasure, shootin' or party?"

I huffed, shook my head, and smiled broadly. "We party!" I said, turning to the residents and gesturing with both hands in the air. "*¡El jefe me dijo, tiene comida, cerveza, y una banda! ¡Vamos a celebrar!*"

My life and that of Billie Leo Briggs were very different. Our personal stories and cultural ties should have driven us apart. From the first moment we met, however, we recognized in each other a kindred view of the world and our place in it. We were both practical men, yet we were also searchers with dreams and visions. Neither of us was afraid to oppose whatever *los corbatas* might throw at us to punish us for our boldness, our impulsiveness, and our occasional disrespect.

"We're wily men with good hearts!" Billie Leo told me later. "That's what sets you and me apart. To some, we're fools and to others, heroes."

By midafternoon, we had eaten Billie Leo's roasted chicken and downed his kegs of beer. The children ran about happily, high on his sugary soda. The band played its *ranchera* and *salsa* tunes, and couples swayed with the eucalyptus trees in the Sunday afternoon breeze.

Billie Leo and I sat together near the now distinguished pepper tree that Billie's Bowie knife had wounded. We communicated directly as best we could in our different languages. Junior translated when necessary.

"Why did you buy this place?" I asked.

"Because I could," Billie responded, "and because the price was right. I really didn't know nothin' about the troubles you all have had. I guess I thought I'd fix it up, bring in more families, rent all the units. I figured the redwood studs and ceilings have to be worth what I paid. I didn't see how I could lose."

"They told you it needs permit?" I asked.

"Hey, I don't worry about that kind a thing. I can usually handle the planning commission." He grinned. "You just have to know the right people on the board of supervisors." I didn't respond, yet Billie Leo seemed to know that I was after something. "What do you think I should do?" he questioned.

I remained silent. He sat, deep in thought. Suddenly, he smiled.

"Ah! I got it! You want to buy the place, don't you? You want me to sell Camp McCallum to you and your families."

I stared at him and nodded. "You sell. We buy." I stated.

"Where you gonna come up with the money?" he asked, not hiding his skepticism. He probably believed that I had drunk too many beers. I pointed toward the couples dancing.

"These families and others. I know many who will want to live here. You give good price. I find *el dinero*."

Billie thought some more.

"The place is yours for $150,000!"

"How long to pay?" I asked.

"Let's see. I'd have to have at least $20,000 down." He watched my eyes. They didn't change. "And the rest in four or five years." Billie now knew that I was serious. "What the hell," he declared. "I triple my money in a few years and still give you all a break. How much can you pay a month?"

"Maybe two, three thousand dollars."

"Just a minute," he said. He went to his car and returned with a tablet and pen. He sat and scratched out numbers. "Make it $2,500 per month. Divide that into $130,000. That's fifty-two. Fifty-two months. That's four years and four months."

"And Señor Bricks," I stated, intending to seal the transaction, "we no pay interest." Billie affected a huff, but he knew he had just struck the gold he was hoping for.

"No interest," he affirmed, "but I hold the mortgage!"

I looked questioningly at Francisco Serna. "Mortgage," Francisco repeated. "*Hipoteca.*"

"Oh, *sí, hipoteca.* You have mortgage!" I said. We shook hands.

My heart was pounding with excitement. It had all happened so fast and with such little effort. I had hardly thought about the idea before the moment came, but then I knew in an instant that it could be done. Fifty families could pay an *enganche* of $400 each and then put in only $50 more each month to make the $2,500 payment. In four years, they would all own their own homes.

"Now, there is just one problem." Billie Leo was talking again. "Just one problem; and that is, I don't own the camp yet. I have to close escrow with the county. And here's the deal. They won't sell me this place unless you all are out of here. It has to be empty, and they're gonna check. They told me that."

"We have no place to go," I said.

Billie's chin rested on one hand.

"Look, I know how this works. They'll come out once and inspect the barracks. They'll see you're gone. Then they'll leave and they won't be back any time soon. You all just have to move out on the day they show up. Just take everything and get outta here for the day. They'll do their checkin'. They'll leave. You can return. You can sit in your cars down the road for a couple of hours. I don't care. You just have to disappear when I say it's time, they're comin'. *¿Comprende?*"

Two weeks later, on the given day, we played Billie Leo's gambit. In the morning, we loaded our cars and trucks just as we had two years before. Some rented trailers to carry their household goods to Salinas where they left them with friends. In the afternoon, the county inspectors came, looked around, affirmed that the camp had been vacated, and left. By evening, the remaining nine families were back in their barracks.

On the following morning, Billie Leo Briggs deposited $53,000 in escrow. John Jones deposited the signed deed, and promptly at 11:00 a.m., First American Title closed the transaction. Billie Leo became the new owner of old Camp McCallum.

I set out immediately to raise the money needed to purchase the camp. I had only sixty days to collect the down payment. Half of the remaining camp residents were wary; but

Juan Alemán, Efraín Zavala, Francisco Galván, and Juan Miranda all signed their names to the freshly minted list of *socios*.

I invited whoever would listen to join in the great adventure: the purchase of the property. The valley farmworkers knew my name. They had seen me before the cameras. They had stood beside me on the picket line.

"*Oh sí*," they said. "*Este es el vato* who led La Posada, who fought Pic 'n Pac, who camped on the streets for so many nights. He's a good man. He fights *por la gente!*"

Others said, "Oh no! *¡Es un busca pleitos!* He's a troublemaker. Be careful with that one!"

I ignored the naysayers. I traveled the valley. I walked the streets of East Salinas: Towt and Williams, Fairhaven and Garner, Acosta and Alma. I knocked on doors, extending invitations to come and see. I catalogued the names of friends and acquaintances and collected more names and addresses as I spread the word about the deal that Briggs and I had struck. I drove the back roads to seek out the residents of labor camps in South County: Metz Road in Soledad, Campo Jimenez, Villa Camphora, *Campo* 21, and *Campo* 17.

At *Campo* Jiménez, the children played in the dirt between the cars crowded along the line of drooping cabins. They ran to their mothers to say that the large man was back, knocking on doors again.

I traveled farther south to Greenfield and King City and approached strangers in their yards on Sunday afternoons. Back in Salinas, I climbed rickety staircases to second-story apartments to seek out a prospect or called from the sidewalk to people on their porches. I passed out flyers at la pulga on Sanborn Road and buttonholed shoppers as they exited Monte Mart and scurried to their cars. I shouted to be heard over the noise of passing automobiles and trucks out on East Alisal Street.

"*Mire, amigo*, this is a great opportunity for you and your family. If you want to become *un socio*, it is a simple thing. You will pay only $400 immediately and $50 each month for four years and four months. As soon as we obtain a permit from the county, you can come to live at the camp."

The people arrived and I greeted them. Many scrutinized the still shabby buildings and pocked roads, the teetering water tank and the peeling roof shingles, and the diminishing number of residents. They noted with concern my words about the lack of proper permits. They thanked me for the information and they left whispering to each other that I was fooling myself.

"*¡Está loco!*" they said. "Don't waste your money. Nothing will come of it."

Others appeared, as well, and they had eyes to see. They believed in my dream somehow to rebuild and restore life into the decrepit bones of old Camp McCallum. They walked through the spacious buildings. They admired the towering eucalyptus. They smelled the camphorwood air. They envisaged the future and, unlike the doubters, they said it was good. When they had completed their visit, the believers also left; but, unlike the others, they promised to return and to bring $400.

"*Primero*," they said, "*usted sabe* I need to wait until my paycheck arrives." Of these, some actually did return and they laid down their money.

When I was a boy in San Ciro, no banks existed there. In Mexico City as a young man, I lived well enough with the money I earned by moving furniture. I held the bills and coins tightly in my wallet. Even now, I had no reason to enter a bank. Why would one need such a place? Why would one leave his money with a stranger? Everyone I knew agreed; keep it close and safe in your pocket or in your home. Always buy what you need with cash. Banks cannot be trusted.

As a boy, I had followed from house to house and from business to business as my father collected the municipal taxes.

My *papá* had said to me more than once, "Never accept money from anyone, *m'ijo*, without providing a receipt in return, and be sure to obtain a signature."

I had watched as my father carefully had placed the carbon paper behind each receipt; had printed in the book the name, the amount, the date; had required the payer to sign— even if it was with only an "X"—and then had torn out the original slip to give to the signer.

When my father organized the building of the community room—a space for the *ejidos* to meet—again, he had collected money house to house. He stowed the money by placing it on a shelf, in a coffee canister, in the kitchen of the Torres home until the day came to forward the people's taxes to the authorities or to construct the *ejidos'* meeting room.

Now I purchased a receipt book. I carefully recorded each *socio's* payment. Sometimes a friend approached me in the store saying, "Ah, Don Sixto, you are here. I have the money. *Por favor*, take it before I spend it on my truck."

Then, remembering my father's words, I would respond, "No, señor, I don't have the book. You must come to the camp. Come tomorrow in the afternoon, and I will accept it and give you your receipt."

Over the course of sixty days, the believers came one by one. They laid down their $400 and committed to continue to pay their monthly *cuota*; and I gave them each a receipt, obtained the signature, and registered the name in the ledger until I had found fifty *socios* and had collected the required amount of $20,000 for the down payment.

With each signed receipt, Elida and the children watched in silence as I stowed the money on a shelf in a coffee can in the kitchen of our home until the day came to close escrow on the purchase of Camp McCallum.

Dennis Powell often visited us in our new makeshift quarters. He drove to the camp early in the morning before going to the office. Today, he carried a special package. Elida greeted him amiably at the door. The oil drum stood upright, its top half sliced away and a screen hanging over the opening. A wood fire, vented through a rusty stovepipe, warmed the house.

Powell and I sat at the kitchen table. The children scuttled about, preparing for school. Elida brought the visitor *chorizo con huevos* and freshly made tortillas and coffee.

"Don't sign anything without calling me first, okay?" he said. Powell had cautioned against the purchase of the camp, but he knew that he'd already lost the argument. I was determined to follow through on the deal that Briggs and I had discussed. "Here are the incorporation papers. You need to sign there at the bottom. I'll be sending them to Sacramento today." Powell handed me the manila envelope. I looked at the documents with little interest except to note the name, "San Jerardo, Incorporated, a public benefit corporation." Powell sat back. The chair's loose frame creaked. "I still don't see why you're spelling Gerardo with a 'J' instead of a 'G,'" he commented.

"I want it to be the only one of its kind in the world," I responded with a smile.

"Who was he anyway?" the attorney asked.

"In Mexico, he's the patron saint of gamblers."

"Yeah, that makes sense."

When escrow closed, the word quickly spread throughout the valley. Briggs had transferred the property to San Jerardo, Inc., and I was the signatory on the mortgage.

The farmers out on Old Stage Road were enraged. The Alisal School Board was livid. The merchants and the churchgoers of the downtown set were quite upset. The Anglo community generally—most of whom still disdained the picketers—scorned Chávez, and decried the union's shenanigans, was suspicious.

"That Torres fellow has bought Camp McCallum!" they asserted.

"I never heard of such a thing. They say he put $20,000 down. Where'd he get that kind of money?"

"I can only imagine!"

"You ever heard of such a thing—farmworkers owning a labor camp? I don't even think that's legal. I think you have to be a farmer or maybe a labor contractor to own a labor camp!"

"And another thing, that Briggs is a slick fellow, tripled his money in a couple of months. He sure took those poor bastards. They ain't got nothing. County's still gonna kick 'em out anyway. From what I hear, the place don't have its permit anymore!"

"I'll tell ya something else; it's gonna be a hotbed for breeding union radicals!"

"You got that right!"

Others, Mexicans and Anglos alike, who supported the farmworkers' cause, were skeptical at the news.

"It sounds fishy. They're paying three times the appraised value. I wonder about the guy whose organizing the whole thing, if he knows what he's doing."

"Collecting money from people who can hardly afford to eat, on nothing but a whim; somebody should look into that...."

CHAPTER SIXTEEN

As the months passed, we struggled to pay Señor Briggs. Everyone was anxious. Only the Alemáns, the Galváns, and we still lived at the camp. Fall had brought with it cold weather. We had no money. We were running out of canisters of gas for cooking. The electric company had cut the power. We had no lights, no running water. We carried our water from town in bottles.

We had been living this way for the past eight months. Walter Wong had come from county health. His inspectors spent hours assessing each building and noting page after page of violations: the water system, the sewer ponds, the electrical panels and poles, the roads, the barracks, the bathroom and showers; nothing met the county's modern codes.

The inspectors sent demands that we apply for a use permit and make needed repairs. They delivered a pile of papers that I couldn't understand. I knew only that to occupy our homes fully and permanently, we would have to rebuild everything. Dennis Powell reviewed the papers. He advised that we couldn't meet the many requirements without raising a great amount of money.

Some of the *socios* dropped out. They wanted their money back. I told them that it was impossible. We had spent their money to pay the mortgage.

The days of celebration were over. We thought that we had done a great deed. I had proclaimed to everyone, "What has happened is good and wonderful!"

From one point of view, perhaps, it was great and good and wonderful, but not from another—not now that we understood more deeply all that was required of us.

Some sneered at me. "No way," they said. "It's impossible. We're wasting our money." I continued to pour my heart into keeping our dream alive.

Francisco Galván knocked at my door in anger. He wore a ball cap. His hair pushed out beneath it in thick, coarse strands. His lips were pressed together and his eyes puffy from lack of sleep.

"How can we live in this *mugrero*?" he asked. "This jungle is a mess!"

"Come in," I responded. "We'll talk." We sat at my table.

"I'm not angry at you, Don Sixto, but what am I to say to my children that will explain why we live like this?"

I tried to console him.

"You mustn't see it that way. Don't you remember when we were there on the streets with cars racing by, with *gabachos* and other *pochos* who have no shame yelling at us that we were worthless? Many things happen in one's life. We were in a rusty trailer, then a leaky tent. Does your roof leak now? No, it doesn't. *Usted sabe*, we gain only by struggling. This is just another fight. We have already won so much."

As I spoke, I saw him glance around our home. He observed how we lived, with sheets dividing our rooms, an oil drum for our fire. Elida was at the sink, pouring water from a saucepan to cook, pouring water from a large vat to bathe the children. We all carried water to the toilets so that we could flush them. With his swollen eyes, he took in our threadbare couch and half-broken chairs. He noted our candles and kerosene lamps. We lived just as he lived.

"Don't think that I am blind to what is happening. You're right. In some ways, it's a mess here. There is much to be done; but still, in other ways, it's a beautiful place, *verdad?*"

After a while, he left to return to his half-barrack and his own half-broken chairs and his own kerosene lamps and rooms set off by hanging sheets.

Some of the women who lived in town, although they and their husbands were *socios* and continued paying their *cuotas*, treated us as if we were nothing, like we were on the floor, like we were invalids. They followed Catalina Castillo and strutted about as if they were superior. They blamed us for the delays and the lack of progress. They drove from town in the evening to spread their gossip and rumors. Instead of supporting us, they grew angry, claiming that we were causing problems for the Mexican community and the farmworkers. They came to my door and yelled at me.

"*¡Estás tonto!* You told us that it would be easy, that we could all live here. You don't know what you're doing! The county will soon come and throw you all out!" They shouted so that my family and the other families could hear.

I had grown to respect Dennis Powell deeply; he visited almost every day. Sometimes he brought his coworker, Luis Jaramillo. We sat and talked in the mornings over coffee before they had to go to their office. They told me to ignore Catalina, that I was doing a good and important work. They wanted to take on more of the burden, but they were both attorneys with caseloads to attend. They could only advise and encourage.

Elida cried often. "We have nothing but an illusion," she said. "Sixto, we must do something."

"What could we do that would be better?" I asked. "One day, you're going to see that, after all, this truly is a very beautiful place."

"I know what I'm looking at now," she countered. "I'm looking at a man who is lost, who doesn't know how to find his way because he lets other people lock him into their problems and ignores his own. What are you seeking that you do this?"

"I'm not lost, bebé. This is something of my soul, my machismo, something I must do."

Junior, Enrique, Celina approached me in the evening as I sat beneath the moonlight and smoked a cigarette.

"*Papi*, please let us move into town," they begged. "We're tired of this. We're tired of the people fighting you and saying bad things about you. We hear it all of the time."

I said to them the same words that I had said to their mother.

"This is something of my soul, my machismo, something I must do."

We sat in silence for a long while.

"I'm going to help *mamá*." Celina said. She rose, and the boys followed her into the house.

We found a little work with International Vineyards near Chualar. Finally, we made a bit of money; but then, my liver started to give out. Once again, I had been drinking too much. I had been spending my time hanging with those who supported me and continued to believe. Together, we downed *Tequila Cuervo*, *Rum Castillo*, *Tequila Viuda De Martínez*, and when those were gone, we had our beer. This too is why Elida became *muy desconsolada*. She no longer badgered me, but I knew that I made her sad.

I usually didn't get very drunk, except once when I awoke on the kitchen floor with my face in a pan of dog food. That was bad enough, but something worse was happening also.

On Saturday evenings, Héctor and Jesse—two old friends from my days with Pic 'n Pac—sometimes came to pick me up. We'd drive into Salinas and sit in Maida's, drinking. On one of those nights, a comely *puta* asked me for a dance. In no time, she invited me to a back room. I didn't know why I committed these sins against God and Elida and all I had worked to build. I said to myself, I deserve an escape from the coyotes that nip at me constantly; but deep down, I knew that someday I would pay for my transgressions.

On Sunday, we went to Mass and then to Monte Mart. We needed clothes for the children. School was to start in two weeks. They must have pants, shirts, socks, and underwear. Moisés needed new shoes to start first grade. They must have pencils, paper, and notebooks....

In the evening, we all sat outside with the brightening moon. I played an old Victrola that I had purchased during better days. We cranked the handle. We listened to worn records from the thirties. They came with the machine, some in English, some in Spanish.

We cooked corn on a grill with the children all around. The box of records held a strange collection: love songs like "Moon Over Miami" and "*Aquellos Ojos Verdes*" and others from Mozart to "*Allá en el Rancho Grande*." The music relaxed us. Even Elida enjoyed these moments together.

I had met Juan Morales one afternoon outside of Monte Mart. He accepted a brochure and expressed an interest in becoming a part of San Jerardo. He invited me to his home, which turned out to be two trailers on a ranch not far from Camp McCallum. He introduced me to his wife and family.

Juan was a small, tight-muscled man with pointy features who dressed most often in dark brown workpants, a light brown short-sleeve shirt, and scruffy brown shoes. On Sundays, he changed to more formal attire: dress shoes, slacks, collared shirt, jacket, and fedora—all brown.

In time, Juan Morales and I became good friends. He was a strong supporter of my work throughout the trials still to come. During that first visit, he told me his story.

"I am from Jerécuaro," he said. "Carolina and I married when I was twenty-two. Together we had thirteen children."

"What did you do to manage?" I asked.

"We used to farm a patch of land near our home. You know how it is in Mexico; you do whatever you can to get by. Over the years, we peddled produce, bought and resold towels, cups, and glasses, *usted sabe*, things for the kitchen and tools for the garden—whatever we thought our neighbors might need. One year, we purchased a machine to grind everyone's corn. We ran a candy concession in a movie house. We even set up a café in the *salón* of our home and served breakfast, but it was never enough.

"So, in 1957, I decided to join the *braceros* who I saw going north. There were hundreds at the processing center; but I was very lucky, getting a contract that took me to Salinas. I came back to this same ranch every year. Then, in the sixties when the program ended, they put us all on a bus and sent us home—I guess they thought we were gone for good; but most of us came back. We had to. We needed the money. I started crossing the river, back and forth for six years, crossing and re-crossing with all the other *mojados*. It was easy to find work. The growers—*mi jefe aquí*—he and the others were desperate for us to come back.

"Finally, after a few years, I was able to bring Carolina and my family. Our last baby was born here, which meant that I could apply to be a citizen, and that's what I did."

A week later, Juan brought his $400. I went out to greet him near the old gate.

"You know," he said, "I have followed the stories in the paper. You and your family and the others are suffering much for this dream." He looked at me with the eyes of an attentive brother. "But you're right not to give up. Many people—the growers, the farmworkers, those who work in the stores and the offices—all are watching."

Juan's youngest tugged at his coat. He stopped to pick her up. He kissed her cheek and said, "We need a larger house. This is our one opportunity to have it, but that's not the only reason I'm here. I want to see you succeed, Don Sixto. I want to help you. If you truly make this happen, if we all succeed, it will be another sign that change is coming. The growers continue to resist the union. Some of them will throw everything they have at you just as if you were another Chávez, but not all of them are against this place. The union is one thing, but most of them know the workers need houses. They have no reason to oppose this place."

Alfredo Navarro came to see me on a chilly morning in November. Navarro ran a nonprofit, community-based organization: Central Coast Counties Development Corporation. Everyone called it CCCDC for short. He brought with him another young man named Eduardo. He was a *gabacho*, but he spoke Spanish.

I knew Alfredo because he had successfully organized farming cooperatives for farmworker families. During La Posada, when we were trying to purchase the trailer park, he spoke to us about starting a cooperative farm and buying Pic 'n Pac's 600 acres of berries on Old Stage Road, which were for sale at that time. This was not just a pipe dream. Because of his organization's work in Watsonville, creating the successful *Cooperativa Campesina*, Navarro actually had the funds to make the purchase. The federal government had already approved the proposal. He and Dave Walsh had already reached agreement.

The families, however, were not ready to undertake such a large venture. They and their advisor from Delano said that it was too risky to move from being a farmworker to becoming a farmer. After that, we watched as Dave Walsh disked the berries into the ground.

Now, Alfredo told me that he wanted to support the development of San Jerardo. He offered me a full-time position with his organization as an intern in community development and organizing. CCCDC would pay me $200 per week to lead the San Jerardo development project and complete the work to obtain the permits we needed. Alfred was in the midst of hiring twelve interns.

"You'll all meet in the mornings," he said, "to discuss strategies for bringing change to communities: how to work through the political systems, how to raise and administer public funds, how to approach foundations, how to run a meeting properly—a lot of different topics that will help you with the work you'll be doing as you organize San Jerardo. We've got a library room over at the farm. That's where the classes will be held." Alfred was referring to CCCDC's one hundred-acre farm just up the road from Camp McCallum. "In addition," he said, "if you agree, I will assign Eduardo to assist you."

I couldn't believe our good fortune. I would have a full-time position, and San Jerardo would benefit from the help of one of CCCDC's professional staff.

Eduardo hadn't said much. I wondered about his background, but the more I talked to him, the more I learned that he had experience with permits and loans for houses. He told me that he had developed homes for farmworker families in the San Joaquín Valley. He knew how to obtain funds from *el gobierno federal*. Before the morning had passed, I felt reborn. At last, because of Alfredo Navarro and his organization, we had a path forward.

CHAPTER SEVENTEEN

In her mind, Catalina Castillo must have thought that she was a brilliant woman and that she alone could see through me. She alone could decipher the many mistakes and speak the truth to the people. This was her calling and her duty: to watch every move, to read the signs of what she saw as my ineptitude and corruption, and to voice her opposition in the name of reason and justice.

She was a short, scrunty woman with a roundish face and challenging eyes made beady by thick glasses designed to correct her nearsightedness. Her hair fell to her heavy shoulders in dark wisps and ringlets. She dressed always in bright-colored slacks and flower-print blouses, which stood in contrast to her often doleful attitude.

When she spoke, she displayed complete confidence in all that she had to say. Once she formed an opinion on a subject or event, her aggressive self-reliance took over, belying the need for additional information and revision.

When we first met, Catalina and I were friendly toward each other. She told me about herself. She was born in Edinburg, Texas, in the forties. She had learned English in school. Later in life, however, she found it more useful to feign ignorance of the language. As a teenager, she had grown shy toward others and

avoided company except for a few schoolmates. She married
Adalberto at the age of seventeen. Although she was pregnant
at the time, the baby was stillborn. She was later diagnosed with
a tumor that required her to have a hysterectomy, so the couple
remained childless.

According to some, after the operation she grew more
distrustful of all but a few close friends who could appreciate
her tormented soul and her special comprehension of
human behavior.

Catalina Castillo was proud of her combative nature.
Throughout her life, she had stood up to authority when
it attempted to impose itself upon her. Although generally
reserved, she was eager to tell a new acquaintance how, from
first grade forward, her teachers had victimized her; how as
a teenager, working in the fields, her bosses had victimized
her; how her doctor, who, she was sure, had misdiagnosed her
medical condition, had operated on her unnecessarily; and how
the police had stopped Adalberto for drunken driving although
he had had only two beers.

According to her account, the authorities had again
victimized the couple when the district attorney issued a bench
warrant for Adalberto's arrest only because he hadn't showed
in court to dispute the DUI charge, nor did he present himself
for sentencing or payment of a fine. Why should they submit
themselves to the harassment of the court? It made more sense
simply to move out of Texas and find work elsewhere.

Like our family, the Castillos signed with Pic 'n Pac's
recruiter as he made his annual circuit through the Rio Grande
Valley. Within a few weeks, Catalina and Adalberto were living
at La Posada and ready to pick strawberries. When the strike
came, they joined the picket lines and felt the glow of impending
victory. They had not known Elida or me in Texas, but because

of our common roots, initially Catalina was disposed to support my organizing efforts.

After the eviction from La Posada, Catalina chose to live with her sister in East Salinas rather than join the families beneath the tarps on Sherwood Drive. The Castillo couple, however, was quick to reassert its place among the refugees during the move to Camp McCallum. Catalina and Adalberto were also quick to pay their *cuota* and become *socios* of San Jerardo, Inc.

Catalina plotted with my foe, Beto Garza, trying to discredit and replace me. Garza traveled to the union's administrative offices at La Paz in the Tehachapi Mountains on the east side of the San Joaquín Valley—for many, the center of the farmworkers' universe. He whispered in Cesar's ear that I was a bad man. Perhaps it was because I questioned him about selling union dispatches and spoke my mind on many other issues. Perhaps it was because of my confrontation with Dolores Huerta.

I had seen this coming. He and others spread rumors to destroy my reputation among the people. They said that I was stealing money, that I was a tyrant, a dictator, a communist. They said that I was "fucking over" farmworker families. Those were the very words. Ismael Velez and Catalina Castillo were now like rabid dogs. I was their target as they stumbled down the dirt road that was their lives, frothing at the mouth.

I had been drinking too much. I admit it. I had become very sick. I couldn't sleep at night. I was jaundiced. I went to the doctor. He shook his head and told me that it was bad and that he could do nothing for me. He told me that I must stop drinking. I must stop smoking. He told me that only a miracle could save my liver.

Each day I drove the two miles to the farm where Eduardo
had his office and where we planned our work. I had grown to
respect him and his knowledge. I had taken to calling him Lalo.
In Mexico, that is the nickname we used for someone named
Eduardo. Together we visited the county officials to discuss the
use permit. We had met with the director of planning and with
his assistant. They had discouraged us from proceeding. The
director, a Mr. DeMars, said that it would be impossible.

"That place has too much history and too much political
opposition. The planning commission, the board of supervisors,
I can't see them voting to reopen it," he said.

When Lalo and I were out the door, I grew angry, cursed
the *corbatas*, and said that we would organize a protest against
them. Then they would have to give us our permit. Lalo told me
that I must change my attitude about the *corbatas*.

"It's a process," he said. "To be successful, we have to
follow the process. Unless you have filled out all of the forms
and answered all of the questions, you don't exist to them.
Your anger means nothing. Demonstrating on the steps of the
courthouse will be useless. You think that it's only political. It's
not. It's also technical."

We held monthly meetings with all of the *socios*. We
gathered inside an empty barrack. We sat on wobbly benches,
our boots and work shoes brushed against the rough cement.
We built a wood fire in an oil drum to cut against the icy air. We
explained our plan to *la gente*, our campaign to win approval for
the use permit from the planning commission and the board
of supervisors, our strategy to seek a loan from the federal
government. We searched for ways to neutralize the opposition
of the Alisal School Board and of the growers who owned the
land around us. Lalo stepped to the front of the room.

"We have one very difficult problem that we must discuss with you." The people fell silent. "We know that all of you are looking forward to owning your own home here someday, but we have now learned from our meetings with the county that it's impossible. I'm sorry to have to inform you that you will not be able to own your homes as individuals here at San Jerardo." A murmur raced through the room. Lalo continued, "You will not be able to own your homes as individuals because the zoning doesn't permit this." Some of the people grew angry. They leaned toward their neighbors and spoke in rapid phrases.

"Please, wait a moment. Let me explain." Lalo said nothing until the room was quiet. "This property is zoned as a labor camp. According to the county, labor camps must be owned as one parcel and one parcel only. That means we can't divide the camp into fifty parcels, one for each *socio*." Again, the people murmured. "If we propose that each of you owns his own home, we'll violate the zoning because we'll create an illegal subdivision in the middle of agricultural land. The county has informed us that it will never allow this. If we push for it, the supervisors will not give us the permit we need."

Lalo had brought an easel. He drew a neighborhood of lots on its large white paper and explained how the zoning ordinance governs the creation of parcels and subdivisions.

"This is something all of us must understand clearly: We must own the property as a corporation, as one single entity. If we try it as individuals, we will lose everything."

I was angry at my own ignorance. I should never have told the *socios* that once we obtained the permit, they could come and own their houses. Back then, the county had given me a stack of papers. *Los corbatas* said, "Fill out these forms; answer these questions; when you have done that, we'll issue you a permit." I understood nothing of these matters. I couldn't read their papers. Only later did Lalo help me to understand. Only later did we discuss our options with the planning director.

Lalo had studied the alternatives with CRLA's attorney, David Kirkpatrick. He and Kirkpatrick recommended to the board and me that we create a housing cooperative. Now it was time to bring this idea forward to the members.

Catalina stood and demanded that I be removed from the project.

"Torres has lied to us!" she proclaimed. "He said, 'Pay your *cuota* and you will have your own home!' Now what does he and *este gabacho* say? They say, 'You can't own your own home!'" The anger was building in the room. A few were shouting for me to resign as *presidente de la mesa directiva*.

Juan Morales stood to calm the people. He was now a member of the board and very aware. My friendship with him had continued to grow. More than most of us, he knew how the government worked; after all, he had been here *en los Estados Unidos* for many years and he was now a citizen. It was Sunday. Juan Morales looked very distinguished, dressed in his Sunday clothes and brown fedora.

"Señores, señoras, *miren*, don't be led astray. I've been to our board meetings, and I've read the letters sent by the county. Sixto and Lalo are telling you the truth. They are learning of these new demands every day. You must understand. Sixto *es un campesino*, like me, like you. You know how it is. You can't get an answer until you ask the question. Sixto and we on the board are learning what questions to ask. Sometimes the answer that comes back isn't what we want to hear, but still, it's the answer. Some answers, *ustedes saben*, we can't change them. Everyone, please listen to what Lalo is going to tell you."

Catalina would not stop her ranting. Encouraged by two of the women sitting near her, she continued to demand my removal.

"Torres is making many mistakes!" she called out. "He should have understood these things before we paid our money! I have been telling all of you how he has lied to us, and now you can see it for yourself!"

The people were growing impatient with Catalina. They wanted Mingo, who was the sergeant of arms, to quiet her. Mingo made a move in her direction. Adalberto barked at Mingo to go back to his place, but then he whispered to Catalina and she ended her tirade.

Juan Alemán suggested that we go to La Paz and ask César for help. Lalo responded.

"When it comes to zoning issues, the board of supervisors listens to only three groups of people: its planning staff, its planning commission, and the voters. How many here are registered to vote?"

Of the seventy people in the room, six raised their hands. Most, like me, were Green Card holders. Some, of course, had no documents at all.

"That's the problem," Lalo stated. "As a group, we have no vote. How can we win if we can't bring pressure as voters? We must convince the planning staff to recommend approval to the planning commission. That will happen only by responding, point by point, to the issues raised by the staff. We must explain the need for housing. We must show them how much value is here. We must make them understand your lives and your dreams for a decent home. We must answer their questions, all of them. If we leave one question unanswered, they will have an excuse to recommend denial. Lastly, we must launch a campaign to convince the voters in Salinas and the county to support us.

We need at least three of the five supervisors to approve the permit. This will be very difficult."

"But we can hold a march and bring three thousand." Juan Alemán was unwavering.

"I'm sorry to say it," Lalo responded, "but this isn't a strike or a boycott. These are locally elected politicians. Without staff approval and voter pressure, a rally of mostly nonvoters won't do any good and may cause us harm."

"Chávez has defeated many politicians!" Juan proclaimed.

I was growing impatient with Juan Alemán. He and I had discussed this in private, but he was *cabezón*. He would not give up. I rose from my chair and demanded that he explain his reasoning.

"Why would we talk to César?" I asked. The people knew that I was no longer a welcomed guest at the union hall. They looked at Juan and then back at me.

"César has 40,000 members to worry about," I said. "He's building a union, not fighting for a use permit. They're two different things, *amigo*! The union battles are in the fields, in the courts, and in the grocery stores. The board of supervisors does not make decisions in the fields, or in the courts, or in the grocery stores!"

Juan stared at me. He must have known I was right. I should have stopped talking, but I was agitated and weary.

"If you want to be with Chávez," I said, "take your goats and go to La Paz!"

The people stared in silence. Juan sat down and said nothing more. I saw Catalina and her brood of gossipers exchanging glances. Tomorrow, they would repeat my words to Beto Garza, but I didn't care what they said or what Garza thought about me.

At night, Juan Alemán and I, despite our differences, patrolled the property, looking for vandals. We wondered if the growers or some of our own members who opposed our leadership would attempt to burn us out. Rumors surfaced constantly of plots and intrigue to wrest control of the project from my hands. Juan sometimes carried a shotgun for protection. Perhaps we were growing paranoid.

The youth who hung around the fruit stand on East Market Street sometimes came in their lowrider cars. They dimmed their lights and crept to the rear of the property to make out with their girlfriends. More than once, Juan and I had to tell them to leave. Others less amiable also arrived.

One evening, we were making our rounds when we heard a muffled cry in a rear building. First we saw the car, then through a side window in a back barrack, shadows moving, hovering. As we drew nearer, we heard a stifled and desperate moaning. The very air was tense and twisted, fraught with the wretched, muted sobs.

We spied two young men, hunched and watchful, a flashlight wobbling through the darkness. Juan raised his shotgun in the air and fired. Three figures ran from the building's backside and flung themselves through the vehicle's open doors. It screeched up the road toward the exit. Juan's wife, Armandina, cared for the distraught girl until parents and police came to take her home. The girl's name was Lydia Abrego, the oldest daughter of Carlos and Hortencia Abrego, friends and faithful members of San Jerardo.

The boys were later prosecuted for rape and convicted. Juan and I were called to testify. The judge sent them to jail for ten years.

When, in the fall, a vigilant mother heard the honk of geese flying south, she hastened to lift and wrap her baby, sheltering against the biting October wind. She pressed the child to her breasts and pushed for the door. She stopped only long enough to snatch a silver spoon from the cupboard. She stepped onto the porch, straining to hear the tootle of the migrating fowl.

She searched the heavens and the moment she spied the flock, she raised her infant toward it as the geese labored across the flossy sky. Immediately, she touched the spoon to the child's lips; in this way ensuring that her baby would grow to speak in sweet and clear tones throughout its life.

The people knew of many such antidotes to protect against an uncertain world. For a lonely child who is desolate or terrified and who cannot sleep because of the fearsome darkness, an egg bathed in holy water and passed over the innocent's body while praying will dispel the *susto*, and the child will return to peaceful rest. Medicinal herbs provided by *la yerbera* or *el curandero* will cure disease and relieve the pain of injury or old age. Floral waters of rosemary and sage will cleanse the body of its impurities.

Those who are acquainted with the healers and their remedies diligently communicate the names of the ill and suffering so that their treatment and recuperation may soon come to pass. It was not a surprise, therefore, to discover that one such devotee, upon taking note of my jaundiced eyes, provided my name to her most trusted *curandero*, a man whose name I was soon to learn was Juan de Dios.

CHAPTER EIGHTEEN

I was in *el hospital*. The doctor told me that he had to intercede. He said that I had to stay here for at least a month so that my liver could find some relief from my bad habits. Elida visited me with the children. She bent to give me a kiss. She wiped my forehead with a cloth, but I saw anger and resentment in her eyes. She told me that she had applied for food stamps.

"We have no choice," she murmured. The children stood silent and fearful. My sister, Licha, stepped into the room.

"There is someone here to see you," she said. To my surprise, *mi mamá* followed. She had come from Texas. My eyes filled with tears when I saw her. It had been four years.. Her hair was grayer and thinner. Her dress hung on her slumping shoulders. She, too, bent to kiss me.

"You must take better care," she said. Her black eyes were, at once, accusing and forgiving.

I was mortified because of my behavior. In one of the back barracks, under a canvas, I had stashed a dozen or more bottles. Elida must have known this, but she had said nothing. I resolved to sell them or give them away when I returned.

After my family left, I lay in the shaded room, depressed and full of self-revulsion. I had been unfaithful to Elida. I thought about how I had slipped away into the darkness of

Maida's Cantina to sit at the bar until the *puta* brushed against me and led me to the dance floor. Elida must have sensed these violations also, but she had said nothing. Padre Hermosa came into my room.

"How are you, Don Sixto?"

"I am well, Father."

"Can I do anything for you today? Do you want to receive Communion?"

"I think not now, Padre, perhaps tomorrow."

This was our routine, day after day; but today when he arrived, I asked him to stay. I told him that I wanted to confess. He sat and took my hand. We talked as if we were the oldest of friends.

"Do you remember your time as a boy in Mexico?" I asked. I felt tears welling.

"Of course."

"How simply we lived then," I said, "and how confident that we would change the world. I think often about a promise I made to myself always to seek beauty and truth just as Padre Benito had insisted." I stared up at the priest from my pillow. "I have failed," I confessed. "I have defiled my body and harmed my family." I asked forgiveness.

On a Sunday afternoon, Lalo visited. His sandy hair had grown to shoulder length, and he had sprouted sideburns, as had become fashionable. I was happy to see him. He explained that he had continued to compile an application for a loan through the Department of Agriculture. He had submitted the paperwork to the county, requesting the use permit.

After weeks of confinement in the hospital, I demanded that the doctor release me. I vowed to stop drinking, which I succeeded in doing. I took the stash of bottles to *la pulga* on Sanborn Road and sold them. From that moment, I drank only juice and an occasional beer. I knew that I had to do better or I would lose everything. I never returned to the nightlife on Soledad and John Streets.

I stepped into the eucalyptus grove. I stood in silence among the trees staring into a gauzy and starless night. I savored the last drag on a Marlboro, blowing smoke into the cool air, dense with the smell of rotting leaves. In the settling darkness, the breeze brushed through and around the lanky trunks and lipped its way into the loose-fitting bark.

The camp's barracks lay a few yards away, surrounded by stands of bougainvillea and pepper trees, now only clumps of black, brushed at the edges with the glow of distant bedroom lamps. I tossed the cigarette into the matted ground and pushed the dull glow into the dampened pods and branches beneath me. I had come to be alone, away from *los niños*, away from Elida and her doubts about my visions.

"*Sus visiones*," she had said, "are leaving us penniless."

I had come, as well, to put space between myself and Catalina and her constant nagging and poking at my decisions. I was tired of her and some of the others. I was their leader, their organizer, their dreamer. Without me, this opportunity would not exist; yet, I had made mistakes. Lalo told me that it was a mistake publicly to disrespect Juan's opinion regarding help from Chávez. Lalo cautioned me to be smarter.

"You must treat the members—even Catalina— with respect."

I should have known better than to invite Catalina and some of the others to become *socios*. "*Pinche ruca,*" I muttered as I moved deeper into the trees. "They treat me like an outsider," I thought, "as if I'm harming them in some way, as if I'm a goddamned alien." I smiled bitterly at my own joke. We are all here with our *pinche* Green Cards. We are all aliens, *mojados*. We know nothing.

My internship at CCCDC had begun. All of the others were younger than me, mostly Anglo and college graduates. Every day, we met in the old farmhouse set in the midst of the hundred acres where CCCDC ran its program to help farmworker families learn to farm in a cooperative setting. The first day of our discussions, we introduced ourselves. I explained in my half-English how, because of Alfredo's interest in helping with San Jerardo, I came to be among them.

"I haf proyect," I said. "One mile, old Camp McCallum." I pointed northward. "We need permit from county.... Money to build new."

Afterward, one of the interns, David Foster, approached me. He had shaggy blondish-red hair and a bit of a beard. His eyes were blue and pure with the clarity and confidence of youth. I learned later that he had recently graduated from the University in Santa Cruz, forty miles away.

"*Quisiera ayudarle,*" he said with a self-conscious smile. " ...Work with you on your project." His Spanish was as labored as my English. Over the coming weeks and months, however, that would change as we learned from each other and conspired with Lalo on how we would overcome the power of the growers and others lined up against us. After the break, Lalo had called us back together.

"For the next few weeks," he had explained, "we'll spend a lot of time here discussing what we mean by community development, social change—how to create and sustain it— social justice, community organizing, institution building, corporate structures, the process of creating and filing of articles and bylaws, the duties that board members owe to their organization, fiscal responsibility and oversight, budgets and financial reporting."

Even after Lalo's words were translated for me, I had only a vague idea what he was talking about, but I was determined to learn.

The members of San Jerardo also had little or no knowledge of these grand concepts. As time went by, it fell to me to teach them; yet some did not wish to learn from me. I feared that the more I grew in understanding and in mastering this new knowledge, the more I would become strange and threatening to Catalina and her followers.

Now, in the eucalyptus grove, I peered through the cluster of leaves and branches jutting from the shadowy poles. Even as I watched, the valley's fog lifted slowly, revealing a filmy moon that tinted the open fields surrounding the camp with a whisper of light. Then the fog was gone, and the moon appeared in its fullness, illuminating the barren Gabilán Range and the rows of lettuce that lay between it and the McCallum barracks.

My wandering had brought me to the property's southeast edge. Just ahead lay the bent and rusty chain link fence that separated the camp from the surrounding farms. I stood at the fence, eyeing the brightened Gabiláns. There in the distant hills, I could see a tiny light staring back at me from Jim Bardin's home.

For a long time, I had thought of old man Bardin, along with the other neighboring growers, as the enemy. They had been opposed to the camp since the day the government decided to build it at the outbreak of the war. Now, thirty years later, the Bardins and the Fanoes were organizing again, trying to obstruct its reuse as a place to house workers.

I hadn't noticed the Bardin light before tonight, but that morning, Lalo and I had visited the old man. We had called ahead to request the meeting. *"Este* gringo *tiene huevos,"* I had thought when he told me he had arranged to visit the man in his home. We made our way up the long drive in Lalo's van, admiring the Mexican-style adobe hacienda set before us on a plateau against the brown hills and overlooking the valley floor.

We rang the bell and waited. A middle-aged woman opened the door. Clearly she was expecting us, although she said nothing as she led us across the red tile floor and into the broad expanse of the living room with its exposed-beam ceiling and large bay window overlooking the valley.

Bardin sat in a rocking chair, his legs covered with a woolen blanket. In his late eighties, he appeared fragile. The morning light reflected off of his taut skin, a mixed hue of burnt orange, splotches of purple on white. A wisp of yellowed hair lay across the brow of his skull. His aqua eyes were fixed on the window with its imposing vista.

The woman offered us a seat and then left after a brief, "They're here." Lalo introduced us. Until he spoke, Bardin had stared straight ahead without acknowledging our presence.

"We've come to discuss the camp and the families...."

The man's frail demeanor immediately disappeared. He straightened up and turned toward us, the drawn skin of his forearms revealing the intensity of emotion running through the exposed veins as the blanket fell away and as a clenched fist jerked upward with his first words.

"That goddamned camp's been nothing but a pain since the day it was built! I fought it then, and I'll fight it now. It doesn't belong there. You have no idea what we've been through. There was twelve hundred *braceros* out there in the fifties! They ate our crops, stole our cattle, our equipment, you name it!" Bardin's fierce eyes blistered us. "And every goddamned *Cinco de Mayo*, shootin' off their fireworks and stealin' my cattle for their goddamned barbecues!" Lalo waited to respond until the man calmed himself.

"We're not talking about twelve hundred men, Mr. Bardin. We're talking about sixty families."

"Yeah, and their kids will be jumping that fence and trampling my lettuce!"

"Their kids, perhaps, will be working for you some day."

"Not for me, they won't!" Bardin retorted. "Don't think you'll have my support!"

He said nothing more. He covered himself with the blanket and stared straight ahead. Lalo stood. I remained silent throughout. I had grasped Bardin's words only dimly, but there was no mistaking their emotion and meaning. My gut bawled like a butchered calf in my uncle's shop. I knew that I would explode if I tried to say a word. I had no words that this man would know or hear.

Agitated, I rose from the couch. I stood for a moment and peered intensely over the old man in his chair and out through the large window. I could see the camp's eucalyptus grove. I realized that Bardin had been sitting there, bedridden and bitter, staring at the camp for weeks, perhaps for months, just staring and brooding since the day the news broke that we had purchased McCallum.

I thought about all of the children who might someday live in the camp. My own children attended Bardin School, located on Bardin Road at the very edge of the Alisal in East Salinas five miles from where I stood. We were living in the middle of the Bardin Ranch; and here before me was *el mero patrón* himself treating me like some *pulga* that was sucking his blood and that he would crush with pleasure if he could.

"*Estás enojado, cabrón?*" I thought. "You are angry? You with your *hacienda* and your name on public buildings and roads, with all your land, you are angry?"

The words raced through my brain. Lalo saw my eyes and gestured as if to say, "*Cálmate, hombre.*"

Now, in the living room of Jim Bardin's *hacienda*, Lalo grabbed me by the arm.

"We should go," he said quietly. "Don't say anything."

The woman who had greeted us at the door came to show us out. On the porch, she said in a low voice, "I'm his daughter. You have to understand, we've been through a lot with that place." Lalo nodded in silence and we left.

On the way back, Lalo said, "You know, you and your temper have a reputation in this town. If you want to be successful with *los políticos*, you'll have to change. The politicians have to trust you. They have to believe that you're not going to embarrass them. That means always being on your best behavior, even when you want to scream. You did well today. You didn't scream."

A fresh cloud moved across the moon and brought me back to the camp's shadowy property line. I turned away from the distant point of light still shining from Bardin's *hacienda* and walked back to my family among the darkened barracks.

I opened my eyes at first dawn. I heard a slight tapping on the window. A man was calling in a low and comforting voice.

"Sixto Torres! Sixto Torres!"

I had not slept well. I was still groggy, thinking that perhaps it was only a dream. My liver still kept me awake although I had stopped drinking and smoked only rarely. The tapping came again.

"Sixto Torres," the soft voice continued. "Sixto Torres, I am Juan de Dios, and I have come to heal you." I didn't know this man or his voice. He repeated, "Sixto Torres, I am Juan de Dios. I am informed that you are sick and I have come to heal you."

I rose, dressed, and went to the door. The visitor was slight of build, about my age in his mid-forties. He was *un guero* with wavy light brown hair, a broad forehead, and pointed brows above keen eyes. His mouth and the lines down his chin were surrounded by a drooping mustache. At his feet lay a rumpled sack. He spoke to me in long, slow, musical phrases as if he were chanting, yet his words were very simple and to the point. He was dressed in the garb of a peon with white shirt and pants and a colorful, thin serape. Perhaps because I was not fully awake, I found myself drawn into the space that was his eyes, lured by the movement of his spindly arms and his incantation.

"Sixto Torres, I bring you herbs from San Luis Cabrillo, Colorado. They will alleviate your pain, and after a time, they will cure you."

He looked at me with great kindness, the way a father may look at a son. I felt a tremor run through me—a chill—as if I were in the presence of a supernatural visitor.

"I am Juan de Dios and I come from the border, San Luis Cabrillo Colorado" he chanted again with utmost sincerity. "I have come to heal you."

"*Cierto*," I said. "But how? Who sent you?"

These questions Juan de Dios chose not to answer. Instead, he picked up the cloth bag and handed it to me. As I took it, I heard a rustle and guessed that it was full of herbs.

"I have brought you these," he said. I stared at him. The shiver continued to run through my whole body. Juan de Dios continued, "Place a handful into two gallons of water and boil it until there remains only one gallon. Pour this solution into a jar. After dark, set the jar, still open, on a knoll so that it cools in the night mist. In the morning, drink a cupful. Keep the liquid in the refrigerator and continue to drink every day." With that, Juan de Dios, still facing me, backed away toward his car. At the door, he stopped. "The bag should last six months," he called. "I will return to bring you more."

I watched as he drove away. I followed the instructions faithfully and drank the *curandero's* concoction daily. I continued this discipline for five years. As you will see, it had its effect....

CHAPTER NINETEEN

The following week, Lalo and I drove my beaten GMC van homeward, south from Gilroy to Salinas. Lalo rolled down the window a few inches. A stream of fresh January air rushed across us.

"Look at the hills," he said. "They are already turning green." We had just left a meeting with the regional representative of Farmers Home Administration, a division of the US Department of Agriculture. "What did you think of Quiros?" Lalo asked.

"*Es un cabrón*," I responded.

"It's hard to imagine," Lalo observed, "we spent two months putting together an application for a USDA loan. We followed the agency's instructions and gathered all the required documents. We sent them to the proper person in the specified office. We gave him time to review the application and requested a meeting to discuss it. First of all, the guy doesn't look at the package. Then, he tells us that the 515 loan program doesn't exist. Unbelievable!"

"He just wants us to go away," I said.

"Well, he's going to have to learn we aren't going away. When we get back, I'm writing a letter to his boss in Woodland, documenting the submittal and his statement that the program doesn't exist. We have a copy of the *Federal Register*, verifying that the Congress reauthorized it!

"The problem is, they know Talcott won't care if they ignore us. The Republicans have said they want to kill all of the government's housing programs."

We passed through the hills south of Gilroy and entered the northern plateau of the Salinas Valley. Swatches of dark earth scraped with brown furrows and lined with bluish-purple and green rows of endive, lettuce, and broccoli, and white-dappled clumps of cauliflower extended full circle around us.

In Salinas, we exited Highway 101 and turned eastward on Alisal Street, through a wide corridor of small and seedy flat-roof structures leftover from the thirties. They housed cafes, *tortillarillas, tiendas de ropa*, beauty parlors, and payday lenders. We sat at Sanborn Road waiting for the light, newly developed commercial buildings on all sides: Monte Mart's megastore, Safeway, fast-food establishments, reflective of the Mexican community's growing economic power. We turned south at Bardin School.

"By the way," Lalo noted, "I've made an appointment with Virginia Barton. She finally got back to me. At first, she said there was nothing to discuss because, last week, the school board met and voted to oppose reopening the camp."

"They voted without even giving us a hearing!" I snapped.

"That's what I thought too," Lalo said. "I told her we wanted to come in and talk anyway, so we got the appointment." Later in the week, we met the superintendent in her office on East Market Street.

Virginia Rocca Barton was a middle-aged woman, high-strung and charismatic with strong opinions. Although she was slight of build, she filled the room with her powerful voice and air of authority. Her hair was dyed autumn amber and cut short. She wore a pink business suit. Her makeup was applied with scrupulous precision.

"Oh, I know Camp McCallum," she said. "I started a school out there back in the fifties when it was leased by the growers and shippers, after the war prisoners left and before the *braceros* came back. They housed families at the time. We heard that the teens out there weren't going to school because they worked the fields all day. I organized the whole thing. Got the Office of Adult Education involved, helped to hire and train all of the teachers. That's when I started to learn Spanish and made all those teachers learn it too. I taught there three nights a week—all volunteer."

"Mrs. Barton," Lalo said, "we plan to rehabilitate the old barracks and—"

"No need to explain. I know all about your plans, and don't go thinkin' I'm personally opposed. But you have to understand something. My opinion on it doesn't matter. I work for the school board, and the school board is absolutely against what you're doing, not to mention all the old families who live out that way!"

Lalo and I drove back down East Alisal and made the now familiar turn at Old Stage Road.

"Tell me something, Lalo," I said. "Why are you here, doing this?"

"It's real," he answered. "If you can put a family into a decent home, you've changed their lives forever. The parents are proud. The children grow up in a stable environment. What's the alternative in this valley—people doubling up in garages, ten individuals sleeping on a crowded floor in Chualar? We need more housing for the workers. If San Jerardo can succeed, perhaps more will follow."

We designed a campaign to win our use permit. The Alisal School Board continued its opposition, saying that we were creating a ghetto, that we would bankrupt the district, that the district's residents were opposed to our plan. Lalo and I traveled to Sacramento to meet with the State Department of Migrant Education. Its representatives sent letters to the school board outlining all of the financial support it would receive because of the influx of additional migrant children.

Juan Alemán, David Foster, our older children, and I walked the neighborhoods of East Alisal. As we had with the housing authority, we collected more than a thousand names in support of our use permit. We investigated the many rural subdivisions that the planning commission and the board of supervisors had approved in recent months and found that hundreds of homes had been authorized in the county area, most all of which were built for and occupied by upper- and middle-income Anglo residents.

"Why are these housing sites not also called ghettos?" we asked.

We learned that a large farming company, Bruce Church, had once proposed one hundred units of farm labor houses at Camp McCallum. The planning commission had denied the permit, but had indicated that it might look favorably on a proposal for sixty-five units. Our proposal was for only sixty units. This discovery renewed our hopes.

We appeared before the Alisal School Board and chided its members for passing a resolution against San Jerardo without having provided us the opportunity even to make a presentation. We countered their arguments one by one. We presented the thousand names and signatures, urging the district to support the issuance of our permit. Lalo stood before the trustees and pleaded our case.

"The people of San Jerardo, like all people, need homes. They are lucky in that they have found a means of acquiring this dream. They have worked hard and sacrificed, having already spent over $40,000 of their own money to make payments on their mortgage. They know, as you do, that government resources are available to assist this district in meeting the impact of their children on your budget. They are neither cynical nor suspicious, but place their faith in the letters you have received from the state, telling you that this support is available. They have presented these petitions and are grateful for this affirmation from the very people that elected you."

The Californian's Helen Manning was present with her notebook. Her front-page stories about the district's continued opposition despite all we had done to answer their stated concerns had helped to turn public opinion in our favor. I watched her writing. The television cameras were also present. Lalo continued.

"Our society, our laws are founded on the belief that reasonable people, when presented with a reasonable choice, will choose reason. We have done all we can do. We leave it to you, reasonable people, to respond in kind."

Neither our work nor our words moved the trustees. The board denied our request. The next day, *The Californian's* morning headline read, "Despite Promise of State Aid, Alisal Still Says No!"

Although the rejection was a setback, the media coverage
tended to neutralize the board's opposition. A feeling of
sympathy grew among the good citizens of the valley. We learned
that the growers had retained a lawyer by the name of Brian
Finnegan to speak for them before the planning commission
and the board of supervisors. Lalo told me that this person
was well known and well respected in the county. He worked
in a large firm that represented many of the valley's growers.
We decided to hire an attorney. His name was William Bryan.
He, too, had a strong reputation and was from an old Salinas
family. He knew everyone among the powerful people who sat
on commissions and boards and made important decisions.

Lalo and I stood in the community's meeting room on a warm
September day. We had invited the planning commission to
visit and to learn about our proposal. The members sat in one
of the barracks. Its redwood siding and tongue-and-groove
ceiling surrounded them. My fellow CCCDC intern, David
Foster, had taken photos of the 140 broken-down, yet legally
operating, labor camps in the valley. He and Juan Alemán had
visited the sites and had interviewed the residents. They had
documented fifty additional camps that were operating without
any permit at all.

We showed the slides of the single-room hovels in which
some of our *socios* were currently living. We showed their
receipts, $130 a month they paid to rent these tiny shacks. The

dreary black-and-white slides passed before the commissioners' eyes. They revealed patchwork quarters crowded with one or two families, parents and children, grandparents, aunts and uncles. They revealed the decades of willful blindness and neglect on the part of public officials. The inhabitants' accepting eyes stared at the camera. One man, standing in his shabby doorway, was wearing a shirt showing a US flag waving and the words "God Bless America."

The slides displayed exposed wiring, leaky pipes, and rusting sinks. In one case, David had photographed a broken sewer line spewing raw sewage into a camp's muddied parking area, children playing in the background. The commissioners fell silent. Clearly, the county planners and the building inspectors were failing in their duty to monitor the continued use of these scarred shanties from the past. The planning commissioners' bosses, the board of supervisors, had done nothing to improve the conditions in the camps or to demand their removal and replacement.

We described our plan to obtain a government loan. We presented sketches of the McCallum barracks, as they would appear after they were transformed into modern three- and four-bedroom homes. The architects and engineers were present to confirm that our plan was feasible. A building contractor validated that the camp's redwood framing and ceilings were structurally sound and held significant value. To replace these assets throughout the thirty-two buildings, he stated, would cost nearly a million dollars.

"Who will own the property?" the commissioners asked. "How will it be managed?" "Can we see your financial statements?"

Lalo explained that like most other labor camps in the valley, San Jerardo would be owned through a corporate entity—in this case, a cooperative corporation. Residents would not own their own units; rather, they would own a membership in the cooperative. A professional management company would ensure proper maintenance and fiscal integrity.

"You asked for financials. Yes, of course, we have them right here." Lalo smiled in my direction and winked as he distributed the statements. From the beginning, he had insisted that we retain an accountant to keep the books. I thought it was an unnecessary expense. Now, I saw how important it was to take this step.

By the end of the meeting, it was clear that the commissioners' tidy world of political convenience was shattered. They didn't come expecting to be convinced that the proposal to rehabilitate old Camp McCallum was sound.

Douglas Ziegler, the only son of Abraham and Thelma Ziegler, married Lydia Abrego at Christ the King Church on an overcast Saturday morning. The bride's parents, Carlos and Hortencia Abrego, were, as I have mentioned, *socios* at San Jerardo and supported my work strongly.

Because of Lydia's dreadful experience that night—now months ago—in the shadows of the rearmost barrack, her parents had shared with me their fear that no man would take their oldest daughter for a bride. Douglas Ziegler, however, was a romantic young man who had fallen deeply in love with Lydia. He refused to allow himself to be dissuaded from proposing marriage by the girl's frightful suffering.

On the night he asked Carlos Abrego for his daughter's hand, he stood before their apartment in East Salinas and sang to the girl in his clear tenor voice. Carlos readily blessed the union and Lydia eagerly accepted.

At the church, the twenty wedding *padrinos y madrinas*— Elida and I among them—readied ourselves for the procession. We were all dressed in matching beige suits and gowns.

Abraham and Thelma, having just the day before flown in from New York City, wheeled into the parish parking lot and exited their rented town car. Abraham, a large, gregarious, and pleasant man, immediately lit a cigar and, like the salesman he was, greeted the arriving guests.

"I'm Abe Ziegler, the father of the groom," Abraham acclaimed to all who passed by on their hurried walk toward the church's side door. Thelma Ziegler stood awkwardly near the car, tall and fulsome in her waist-length jacket and long skirt, also beige.

Abraham's extended hand bewildered some of the passersby. They pinched his fingers weakly and moved toward the church, waving away the trailing curls of cigar smoke. Others simply ignored him, pretending not to notice.

Unlike her husband, Thelma was reserved and wary in these strange surroundings among a quite alien population who, as she had learned the night before, spoke little or no English, ate unpalatable food, and—at least on this occasion— appeared strangely joyous despite their lack of material wealth and comfort.

Because of the language barrier, she had barely endured the rehearsal dinner, straining to make conversation seated among us, the group of sponsoring couples. Thankfully, her future daughter-in-law rescued her with the timely delivery of a talkative and bilingual aunt.

The church's garish pink exterior walls rose twenty feet above Front Street in East Salinas. Its interior was adorned with spiraling columns, tinted in pastel shades. Plaster statues of the Virgin and the Saints in thick-folding gowns, blues and yellows, ribboned in gold, cast their fervent eyes to the heavens. Spanish baroque paintings of the Ancient Fathers hung amid the columns and the statues. Above the altar, surrounded by colonnades, the haggard and bloodied crucified Christ hung on the cross.

At the request of the bride's parents, *los padrinos* had accepted the burden of paying for the wedding. As was customary, each couple was responsible for a particular expense: the use of the church, the services of the priest, the playing of the organ, etc. Thus, among the ten couples, all of the wedding costs were covered.

At the appointed time, we sponsors marched to our appointed seats at a dignified pace. When we arrived, however, we found that the rope reserving our rows had not been removed. No usher stepped forward to detach the obstructing cord, so we men simply stepped over it and then lifted it to the extent possible so that the women—some with no small difficulty—might duck under it. The viewing congregation squirmed and teetered sympathetically, but the cord remained anchored in place.

After this precarious beginning, Abraham and Thelma were led to the front of the church and sat alone in the first pew. An usher then escorted Hortencia Abrego to her place of honor.

Douglas Ziegler worked for the UFW. He earned five dollars a week as a union organizer, investigating complaints of contract violations among other duties. At five foot eight, he stood slightly taller than his pretty, dark-eyed bride-to-be. He was among the scores of educated and young *americanos* from across the country who had joined Chavez and quickly found themselves far from home and deeply engaged in the farmworker union's continuing struggles.

Now an usher walked to the pulpit. He announced that the church's pastor, Father Hermosa, had taken ill and would not be able to perform the wedding Mass. He explained that a retired priest, Father Charlie, from the diocese would fill in. The usher also thanked the organist for playing on short notice. "Lots of people seem to have caught *la gripa!*" he observed.

The priest, a tall and elderly man with pale skin and a shaggy circle of hair around a balding pate, stepped from the sacristy and took his place front and center. He greeted the congregation with a smile and a loud "Mornin'!" and then asked how many of the attendees "might could speak English." A dozen hands went up. The priest bowed his head in resignation to his plight.

Douglas Ziegler stood to Father Charlie's left in his tuxedo, tails, and yarmulke, waiting for his bride. He looked out at his parents in the front pew and beyond at the *padrinos*— some of whom he knew—and still farther at the few union friends who had come: Beto Garza, Mario Molina, Ismael Velez, Catalina and Adalberto Castillo. He was proud that they had made the effort, almost as if they represented César himself; yet their presence also made him anxious, even fearful about what, perhaps, lay ahead after this joyful day.

The organ began the wedding march. The young man's eyes met those of his beloved as she stepped slowly up the aisle, Carlos Abrego at her side. Carlos extended his daughter's hand to the groom and then took his place next to Hortencia. Father Charlie bid the couple to come forward. He began the Mass.

"En el nombre del Padre, y del Hijo, y del Espíritu Santo . . ."

This opening prayer, Father Charlie called out in his slow and songlike Oklahoma drawl. Initially, he was embarrassed by his lack of command of the Spanish language, yet he appeared determined to grit through the text of prayers and readings that lay ahead. After the first sentence, however, the aged cleric lost heart. His voice dropped beneath the organ's continuous recital of popular love songs—"Strangers in the Night," "Love me Tender," "*Bésame Mucho*," among others—and he switched from his attempted Spanish to Latin and then, on occasion, to English as he saw fit.

This pattern continued throughout the Mass—drawled Spanish, muted Latin, an apologetic spate of English—all cradled by the organist's unremitting underlay of familiar strains from the fifties and sixties, including "Moon River," "The Twelfth of Never," and "April Love."

The young organist had not previously played a Catholic Mass. Apparently, the church secretary had told her, simply, to show up and bring music appropriate to a wedding; and that is what she did, innocently lending a new dimension to the cultural jumble already in progress. The culmination of her work came during the communion when she followed the priest's invitation to the table with a heart-warming rendition of "The Love Theme from the Godfather."

As the ceremony ended, Douglas Ziegler and his new bride walked down the aisle toward the exit, smiling and greeting friends. The groom's glow dampened as he passed Beto Garza and his followers. He knew that he must choose; he could no longer remain silent. He must tell Carlos Abrego—now his father-in-law—what he had seen a week ago.

Unexpectedly, he had paid a visit to the home of Beto Garza. Ismael Velez and Mario Molina were there. He had sat in the kitchen, chatting casually. The door to the garage inadvertently had been left open. He said later that he could see clearly a table with jars lined up, a gasoline can, and rags. He stared, disbelieving: Molotov cocktails for God's sake! Can it be true? He had heard a rumor but had thought it to be exaggeration. The rumor persisted; *chismes* describing a plot to set fire—to bomb—some of the barracks, the back barracks, to intimidate, to discredit, to destabilize, to gain control. His loyalties divided, he had said nothing to me or to Carlos Abrego. But now, he knew that he must warn us.

Lalo and I were always learning and teaching each other. At one moment, he taught me so that I could teach *los socios*; at another, I had to instruct him so that he better understood the people and how they would respond to all that had to be explained.

I was learning about articles of incorporation and bylaws, motions and seconds, revenue and expense, files and audits. I had to show the government that the people and I understood these tools so that the *corbatas* would approve our loan. I no longer kept the payments in a coffee can. We had opened a bank account. We had retained a bookkeeper. I taught the people everything that I had learned.

I repeated Lalo's words: "We must follow the process, step by step. We can't be reactionaries, thinking that we can simply show up at a public meeting and chant and clap. You can't intimidate them the way you might have intimidated

some of the growers with threats of boycotts. We must address
the issues or we'll lose at the hearings for the permit."

We had gathered new *socios* to replace those who had
drifted away and those who could no longer keep up with their
cuotas. Some of the original members, especially Catalina and
Adalberto, continued to oppose me. They had persuaded a new
member, Nicolas Machado to join them. They were against
forming a cooperative. Now they were pushing to sell the
property, to split the money. I believed they were looking to
get their hands on the proceeds. In any case, Catalina's nephew,
Ismael Vélez and Mario Molina were not clean. The rumor was
that they were dealing drugs on the sidewalks of East Alisal and
East Market Streets.

Nacho Molina lived in town. He was not a *socio*. He told
me how disheartened he was at his son's behavior. At the same
time, I heard that Beto Garza was planning to leave the union
and would soon be replaced. Perhaps, at last, its leaders were
catching up with his antics.

The nation had elected a new president, señor Jimmy
Carter. He was very much in favor of building more homes
for working families. Within a few days after the Democratic
victory, Mr. Quiros from the Farmers Home, the man who had
told us that he could do nothing to help with our loan package,
called to invite us to lunch. He brought his manager from the
state office.

"Rest assured," the manager said, "this agency will
do whatever it can to assist you with this approval." It was
this experience that, for the first time, made me think about
becoming a citizen so that I could vote in the future.

I continued to drink the concoction that Juan de Dios
had given me. I continued to avoid José Cuervo. My eyes were
no long jaundiced. My energy returned.

We had formed a committee of local business people to advise us as we prepared for the hearing on our use permit. We gathered letters of support from many local organizations. We even found a grower or two who was willing to speak on our behalf. We met with the county supervisors one by one. We strategized often with our attorney, Bill Bryan, to devise our presentations before the planning commission and the board of supervisors.

I admit that I was surprised that so many gringos were coming forward to help: Mr. Briggs, Dennis Powell and another CRLA attorney, David Kirkpatrick, the architect and the engineer, Lalo and David from Central Coast Counties. Some, of course, were paid for their advice; but others, like Sal Solinas, who was a Quaker, volunteered to stand with us and give us their ideas.

The great majority of our *socios* were also faithful allies. They understood that what we strove to accomplish would take time. They paid their *cuotas* and trusted that we were faithful in making our payments to Mr. Briggs. Some others, however, did not trust.

Somehow, Beto Garza and his *locos* thought that they were invisible and invulnerable, that no one could see their foolishness. They believed that wrapping themselves in the union's aura would shield them from recrimination. They trusted no one, least of all a person like me: not under their thumb, someone who in their minds had usurped a leadership position among *los campesinos*.

On Sunday, the chilled air lay on the old camp's shallow roofs. The sun licked the distant hills. Cloud puffs padded the sky. Juan Morales and I walked through the eucalyptus grove together. We worried about the growing opposition.

"Beto Garza and Catalina Castillo continue to feed on the distrust among the *socios*," Juan commented. "Those who listen to them, first they grow reserved, then angry. They are upset at the delays and at all of the issues we must yet resolve."

"It's a sickness," I agreed. "I see it in their eyes. They learn nothing from my words because their distrust makes them afraid. Their fear disrupts their ability to learn. Remember when I explained that Alfredo's organization pays Lalo and me a salary. Immediately, they wanted to know how much. 'I am paid $200 a week,' I told them, 'but I receive nothing more.'

"'No, no,' they insisted, 'we know how this works!'

"I couldn't convince them that there is *no mordida*, no bribe. I don't blame them. Who could trust such a statement? Who lives in a world in which no one is taking something under the table? They think that I'm lying or that I'm ignorant and don't know what's going on. You've heard me when I explained how we would obtain a loan from *el gobierno*, from *los federales*.

"'We understand,' they said, 'but whose palm must be greased? Whom shall we pay? The loan will not come until we pay the right official. Is it Lalo? Is it Alfredo? *Por cierto*, we will have to pay Alfredo something.'"

"The *desconfianza* feeds on itself," Juan Morales stated. "Those who can't trust, they are defenseless against Catalina's confused ramblings; and those who listen to her ramblings lose their ability to trust."

I thought constantly about this; why is it that some of the people are so easily misled, so ready to suspect? Is it because they carry the scars of our nation's history in their very blood? Can we never escape these shadows of our past that would have us killing each other the way the gangs in East Salinas kill each other still. Will these shadows make us forever ready to assassinate our leaders in one way or another?

At last, they came late at night with their Molotov Cocktails ready to light and hurl against a back barrack. Juan Alemán and I were watching. We saw them lower their car's headlights as they trespassed up the long driveway. We followed the vehicle's silhouette. It stopped in front of the sagging gate.

Despite the darkness, we could distinguish two agile forms dart past our homes into the grove of eucalyptus. We moved away, out of the shrubbery, and paralleled their passage toward the rear of the property. We eyed them as they exited the grove, holding in each hand their jars filled with gasoline and rags. As soon as they were in the clear and headed for the last barrack, Juan raised his shotgun and fired into the air. Immediately, the startled shades wheeled and scooted back into trees. We saw them running feverishly toward the front gate. Their arms pumping, their hands now empty.

We followed as best we could, but they were too fast. By the time we reached the community room, they were in their car and backing hurriedly from the gate, spinning in a circle. Juan fired his second shot again into the air.

"¡*Vatos locos!*" he yelled through the darkness. The driver lay on his horn and yelled obscenities at us. The vehicle dashed back toward Old Stage Road and Salinas. The next day, we found their spilled jars and rags scattered about in the eucalyptus grove.

I continued daily to drink the tea from *las hierbas* that Juan de
Dios has brought me. I found that I was sleeping better and the
jaundice in my eyes had disappeared.

On a raining September afternoon, our attorney, William
Bryant, Lalo, the families, and I gathered in the planning
commission's chambers wearing red and green lapel buttons
proclaiming *"¡San Jerardo sí!"* Twenty or so members of the
opposition were also present.

The meeting lasted two hours with testimony from both
parties. At its conclusion, the commissioners voted five to three
to approve the use permit. We had won the initial skirmish
in our fight to rehabilitate Camp McCallum's barracks and to
create sixty three- and four-bedroom homes on the property.
Our excitement didn't last long. The growers—Bardin, Fanoe,
and others—immediately filed an appeal to the board of
supervisors designed to overturn the Commission's decision.

Six weeks later, in the midafternoon, I stood before
the five-member board, each of who represented one of the
county's diverse districts. Three hundred of San Jerardo's men,
women, and children had crowded into the chambers, again
wearing our lapel buttons. We and the same two dozen members
of the opposition—growers, school district representatives, and
East Salinas residents—filled the room. The air was heavy with
the smell of cigarette smoke and the sweat of hardened bodies
fresh from the fields.

Lalo and others had helped me to prepare my speech. I had decided that, despite my limited understanding of the language, I would express my words in English. I stepped to the podium a full two hours into the hearing after the staff reports and a presentation from each side's attorney. As always, I was dressed in slacks and shirt of a distinct western cut, including boots and Stetson hat. Before beginning, in a gesture of respect, I took off the hat and laid it on the podium.

"Señores, I thank you for dis opportunity."

I spoke into a microphone. My amplified voice cut through the din in the room. The supervisors stopped browsing through their stacks of paper. They stopped glancing about as if anxious for the hearing to conclude. My decision to communicate with them directly rather than through an interpreter captured their complete attention. By now, they knew me well enough to understand the effort I had to make to prepare my speech in this way. The *socios*, too, were surprised, as were those who opposed us. The chambers fell silent. I continued reading from my sheet of paper.

"You have already heard from Meester Bryan, our attorney. Meester Bryan tol you about how we will own and manage San Jerardo as a *cooperativa*. You have already heard from our architect, Meester Barstad. He tol you that these barracks can be remade into good, safe homes for our members and our families.

"You have already seen the peectures of how our people live in these labor camps with no place for the children to play and no quiet space for our teenachers to do their homework in the evening. You have heard how, for over a year, we have stroggled and sacrificed to make the payments on dis property. These payments now total over $40,000 out of our own pockets.

"You have received the letters from the agencies and others who support us. The representatives from the State Office of Migrant Education have given their promises to help the school district.

"One of the people who opposes us has said that if you approve our homes, the school district will fail, the taxes will go up, and the nearby people will want to move out of Salinas. Isn't it true, however, that in dis county, every year, you approve many, many homes for the wealthy? So, I must now ask you something. Have the schools around these new homes failed? Have the taxes increased? Have all the people nearby decided to move away? I don't think that is the case.

"Why would these disasters happen just because our homes are approved; yet such disasters have not happened when these other homes were approved?

"I ask, what more can we do to convince you to approve our permit? What more must we say? The ones who are against us, they have their houses and their land. They live in comfort, but they tell us that *we* must continue to live in the old, temporary camps. If you approve, the ones who oppose us, they will still have all that they have now; but if you disapprove, you will leave us with nothing, *nada*. To approve causes no injustice to them; but to disapprove causes a great injustice to us.

"Whatever you decide, please understand one truth. We are not going to disappear. Three years ago after Pic 'n Pac evicted us from the trailers, we didn't disappear. After we lived on the streets of Salinas for eighteen days, we didn't disappear. After the lease on Camp McCallum ran out, we didn't disappear. Most of the *socios* here today, they are the families of La Posada. They have not disappeared.

"For the moment, they have been forced to move out of San Jerardo. They now live in East Salinas garages. They live in tiny apartments on Laurel Drive, on Garner Avenue, and on Towt Street. They live in *Campo* 21 and *Campo* 17. They live in *Campo* Jimenez and *Campo* Villa Camphora.

"Some of these spaces in these *campos*, they are not homes. You have seen the peectures. They are more like sheds. They are tiny and worn out. They were built as temporary houses for the migrant workers a long time ago. But now it turns out that the old sheds and barracks and cabins from long ago have become the only alternative for us farmworkers, even though we no longer are migrants; even though we now have permanent jobs here in Salinas; even though we are here to stay; even though we will not disappear after the crop is in.

"As you have heard today, when San Jerardo is completed, when all has been rebuilt, it will not be anything like the labor camps that are scattered all over the valley. Our new homes will be warm and safe for our children; with paved roads and streetlights; with a playground, a community center, a daycare center.

"With your help, our families will never again have to live *en un campo*. With your vote of approval today, we will win greater stability and control over our lives. We will occupy and care for these homes with even greater pride.

"Thank you for your vote of approval. *"¡San Jerardo sí!"*

The moment that I finished my speech, the *socios* stood and applauded. What surprised me more was that the supervisors themselves also stood and applauded me. That left only those who opposed us still seated. The hearing lasted for another half hour. When the time arrived for the board members to express their comments, Supervisor Dusan Petrovic, an immigrant and former World War II German prisoner of war, made his statement.

"There is nothing more important for a human being than to own the roof above his head. I don't think that I could say no and live with myself."

Supervisor Sam Farr declared, "I support the right of the people to help themselves."

Supervisor Warren Church observed, "The property has value. It should be restored and utilized."

The chair of the board, Roger Pointer, upon counting the votes—four to one in favor of upholding the planning commission's approval—congratulated the families. "You have worked hard for this victory. We trust that you will work as hard to preserve and maintain the community that you are about build."

After the hearing, the county sent the permit with its conditions: the owner must be a single entity, such as a corporation; only members of the corporation may reside on the property; no one may own a unit as an individual; only farmworkers shall live at San Jerardo—now officially deemed an approved farm labor housing site—and, finally, the rehabilitation of the camp must begin within one year from the date of the permit approval.

With my position at CCCDC, I was out of the house nearly every day, attending strategy meetings and often out of town. Lalo and I traveled to secure funds from the state for the school district and for the rebuilding, to push for approval for Farmers Home Administration financing from its national office.

Lalo had explained, "We must go there and resolve the issues face to face. It's the best way to get results."

Elida grew weary of the routine. She snapped at the three youngest children.

"I need to sweep." She waved them out of the barrack. At seven years old, Jaime was the youngest.

"I don't want to go outside," he whimpered. "I'm afraid. There are ghosts in the trees." He wiped his eyes and stood by the door.

"Stop being silly! *¡Váyase!*"

Eleven-year-old Baby Gloria led them through the opening.

"It's okay. Come on," she said.

Mario, two years younger, carried a stack of tattered comic books under his arm. The three children immediately headed for the bench near the community center.

"What's going on with Jaime?" I asked. I sat at the table writing a weekly report for my work.

"Are you surprised? Of course he's afraid," Elida responded. "They're all afraid. The older ones fill their heads with silly Halloween stories, not to mention what is happening in this place."

"What do you mean?"

"You think that they don't see and hear? Every night, you and Juan out wandering around, watching with your guns. Every time a dog barks, they look at me. They ask me if someone is coming. Is it any wonder they see ghosts? They think the grove is haunted! Then when you're not here—off to your meetings—they're more afraid. They don't understand where you are when you spend the night in Sacramento or leave for three days to go to Washington. It's the first question they ask in the morning and the last at night: 'When will *papi* be home?'"

I stopped writing and looked at Elida. We had both aged. I had gained weight. Elida had kept her youthful figure, but the strain of her daily life showed around her eyes and mouth.

Catalina Castillo continued to push the board. She wanted to sell Camp McCallum. Her friend, Nicolás Machado, and three or four others supported her. Once these *socios* learned that they could not own their homes individually, they lost interest in continuing. Catalina insisted that we call a special meeting and place the issue of selling on the agenda for discussion and a vote. The board members reluctantly agreed.

With Lalo's help, the board and I prepared for the meeting as carefully as if it were another formal hearing before the supervisors. We knew that Catalina had been busy talking to whoever would listen, promoting the sale of the property.

Many of the original La Posada families were still active *socios*. For six months after we won our use permit, I visited them in their homes in Salinas or in the outlying camps. In addition, every month, we held a meeting to report our progress to the whole membership. At these gatherings, Catalina spoke out against our plan for the property's rehabilitation. At these meetings, Nicolás Machado flapped an extended finger through the air, insisting that we had a moral obligation to sell the property and to repay everyone immediately.

On this night, the community room droned in anticipation of the debate. This was the first time that an issue had divided us so deeply. By now, at least a dozen *socios* were challenging my leadership. I knew that. The rest of the board knew, as well. We were uncertain how many more might join them, although because of my conversations with the majority, I was hopeful. Still, I suspected that some members would say one thing to my face but act quite differently at a later date. The vote was to be held by secret ballot.

As always, the families sat in rows on the now familiar metal chairs. Catalina took a seat near the very middle of the room. Her group sat nearby. Machado and his adherents took their places just behind her. Juan Morales, Jesús Miranda, Juan Alemán, Marcos Zavala were all seated in front with other board members. I stood beside them, ready to start the meeting. Lalo was also present to answer questions.

"*Buenas tardes. Buenas tardes a todos.*"

Nicolás Machado immediately jumped to his feet. He was average in height with a round face, a bald head, and menacing eyes. He wore a thin mustache and a short scruff of hair planted below his lips. He was in his fifties and wore dark glasses no matter the hour of the day.

"The only way we'll get our money back is to sell the property!" he proclaimed, surveying the room. "It's time to ask, is this a good investment? At first, I thought that it was. We all thought that it was, but now we see that it isn't. Twenty-one months is a long time to keep our money and have so little to show. Yes, we've won a permit, but it's taken too long and we have no money to rebuild the camp. We hear that a loan is coming, but who knows when. Why not sell it to someone who can rebuild it, someone who has the money? With the permit, the camp is worth more now than when we purchased it. You can all make a profit. With this, you can buy a home in Salinas."

Catalina and her group applauded Machado's statement. Juan Morales then stood.

"*¡Momentito, amigos! ¡Momentito!*" He waited until the room was silent. "Perhaps unlike señor Machado and his group, the rest of us didn't join San Jerardo to make money. We joined to give our families a home. It's my understanding that some of these men who are pushing to sell already own their houses in Salinas. We have learned that they invested in San Jerardo with the idea of renting out the house here once the work is completed. Isn't that right, Señores? "Perhaps, it was a mistake to invite these people with their different ideas. They have their houses already."

Machado and the others didn't respond.

Morales continued, "If we sell, it's true we'll have a little money in our pocket, but it won't be enough to buy a home. Don't be fooled. Lalo has looked at this idea. He has reviewed it with the board: First of all, there are very few houses for sale in the valley. Second, the interest rates, as we know, are very high. And third, many of us couldn't get a loan because of our seasonal work. No, no, don't be fooled by this man's clever words."

The discussion continued until, at last, we were ready to take a vote. Catalina made the motion to sell. Machado seconded it. I instructed the *socios* to write *sí* or *no* on their ballot. Lalo recorded each vote with a mark on the easel pad. In the end, the count was twenty-three *sí* and thirty-seven *no*. For the moment, we had silenced those who had opposed us.

A month went by. At last, we received good news. We had won approval for a loan from the Housing Assistance Council, a nonprofit in Washington DC. The winning of the use permit had triggered this approval. The money allowed us to pay off Mr. Briggs and repay each family the money that it had invested. We didn't have to pay back this new loan until we started construction.

As soon as they received the repayment of their investment, Machado and his supporters resigned. Catalina and her followers did not.

CHAPTER TWENTY

On Christmas morning, the children moved from bed to bed awakening their younger siblings. They giggled and whispered excitedly, trying not to disturb Elida and me before the appointed time. Junior and Celina, however, couldn't corral Jaime and Mario for more than a few moments. The two youngest pushed back the sheets that cordoned off our sleeping space and threw themselves toward the bedside yelling, "*¡Feliz Navidad! ¡Despierten! ¡Feliz Navidad!*"

The family gathered around a small tree set between the couch and the barreled fireplace. The children tore open their gifts, one each from Santa and others that had arrived from distant grandparents, aunts, and uncles. By now, my mother had moved with Licha and two of my brothers to San Jose. *Mamá* had found work there packing tomatoes. She and the others would arrive in time for dinner.

Today alone, with great fanfare, the children illuminated the Christmas tree. My continuing employment with CCCDC and Juan's work at the bakery had allowed our two families to restore electricity to our homes; still, we could not afford to be extravagant in its use.

Despite the holiday cheer, the struggles to bring San Jerardo to fruition continued. Lalo and I knew that we must begin the rehabilitation work within one year of the issuance of the use permit or the board of supervisors would likely rescind it.

"We must 'drive a nail' to meet the condition!" Alden Barstad, the architect, had stated.

Farmers Home Administration, however, was a slow-moving federal bureaucracy. Both the state and national offices had to review and approve the cooperative's governing documents: articles, bylaws, the use permit and its conditions, the architectural and engineering plans, the project's operating budget and management team, the proposed water and sewer facilities, sources of gas and electricity, the contractor's and sub-contractors' qualifications, on and on. The list of issues was extensive.

Lalo and I met with Jim Rathbone, the director of Farmers Home's state office. Like many of the agency's top personnel at the time, Jim was a southerner. He was tall and friendly. He had an effortless smile, but he didn't abide soft-headed thinking on the one hand or too much rigidity on the other. He liked to start hard and then grow into an easy relationship once you understood the limits of what he could and couldn't do for you.

"Now, this here cooperative, what's that about?" he asked.

"It's the only way that the families can be owners," Lalo answered. "Other structures, like a single-family subdivision or a for-profit or a nonprofit corporation, either don't fit the zoning or don't provide any kind of real ownership. With a nonprofit, for example, essentially the residents would be renting. With a co-op, they own a membership that gives them the exclusive right to a unit; and it's run democratically with each member having one vote in the affairs of the project."

"Well, you know, you boys are buckin' a trend here. I mean, the law may say we can make a loan to a co-op, but we've done it only once in our thirty-year history. That was back in the forties, I think it was." Rathbone shook his head with its white and thinning hairline. "And these are all farmworkers? How are they gonna manage the place?"

Lalo explained the plan for contracting with a professional management company.

"Now, what's this I hear? You're over budget?"

"That's why we've come, Mr. Rathbone."

"Please, call me Jim."

"We've gone over our costs with the contractor. We even have the families volunteering to do some of the work—some of the painting and a portion of the landscaping—but prices just keep going up."

"The national office seems to think the whole thing's too expensive," Rathbone stated. "They're not used to California's cost of living. Have you thought about what more you can do?"

"The only item to cut is the playground," Lalo offered. "We'll have to get rid of that or perhaps the community center."

"If you do that, where will the kids play?" Rathbone asked. "Where will you hold your meetings? You said this place is gonna be democratically run. Gotta have a meeting place."

"Then we need your help with the national office," Lalo said.

"Well, as a matter of fact, our boys here looked at your numbers and they think they're good." Lalo realized that Jim Rathbone's questioning had given him the answers he'd needed to convince those above him. "I'll talk to the staff back there in DC and see what I can do." A week later, we received a letter from Jim Rathbone's assistant indicating that DC had approved our budget with the playground and community center intact.

Day after day, Lalo and I worked to resolve policy conflicts among federal and state jurisdictions and to win approval of the construction plans and related financing. We soon discovered that many of the agencies were quick to respond "no" to our proposals. One had to push back gently, but persistently, to win approval.

Even as we made progress, we learned that San Jerardo's surrounding neighbors had filed a lawsuit challenging the supervisors' approval of the use permit. One member of the San Jerardo Advisory Committee, David Kirkpatrick, was an attorney with CRLA. He and Lalo worked for weeks to prepare for the court date.

The opposition contended that a labor camp could not be owned by farmworkers. Farm labor housing was permitted in agricultural zoning; but, according to the challengers, only growers or labor contractors could own and manage such housing. This first argument tied into a second contention: ownership of the housing by its occupants would effectively subdivide the parcel, a change not permitted under the property's agricultural zoning designation.

In the end, after hearing the testimony from both sides, Judge Harkjoon Paik ruled in favor of San Jerardo. The law did not preclude farmworkers from owning their own farm labor housing. And owning a membership in a cooperative corporation did not create an illegal subdivision of the land. Still, the growers persisted. They threatened to file an appeal of the superior court's decision.

For our fifteenth wedding anniversary, Manuel Santana invited
my family to be his dinner guests at his restaurant in San Juan
Bautista. Manuel was the founding chairman of the board of
CCCDC. Alfredo Navarro, Lalo, and a few other CCCDC board
and staff members were present. We sat in a small building set
apart from the main restaurant, the restored remnants of an
ancient adobe, with its thick ceiling beams and red floor tile.
The buildings were located only a block from the grounds of
Old Mission San Juan Bautista.

Manuel was a short, round man with a large head,
muscular arms and legs, and eyes that gleamed with cheerful
energy. He wore a brush mustache. He loved to entertain and to
sit like a Hindu guru among his friends and customers, advising
on the day's political and social issues.

He was an excellent cook and generous host. He had
studied art in his youth. The walls of his two restaurants—one
near Santa Cruz and the other here in San Juan—were graced
with prints of Mexico's greatest artists and with stylish *artesanía*
from our native country. They also featured his own statues
and paintings.

Although the lights were dimmed, candles set in
wrought-iron holders brightened the colorful walls and threw
shadows with the movements of waiters and guests. The food
and drink flowed in abundance from the adjoining kitchen.

At first, both Elida and the children sat in awkward
silence. The children, especially, stared wide-eyed at the strange
and mystical surroundings. The dinner tables were arranged in
the shape of a horseshoe. Elida and I were invited to take our
places on either side of Manuel at the main table. Manuel's wife
Alicia sat to Elida's left. The children were lined up next to her
along one side of the tables. Manuel eyed each of them.

"You look like the oldest, so you must be Junior. Where are you going to school?"

"Alisal High. I'm just a freshman." Junior smiled, embarrassed to be singled out. His brothers and sisters watched.

"So how are you doing?"

"Okay, I guess. I just got a B in math on the final."

"I don't think I ever got a B in math. Good for you," Manuel said, laughing.

Alicia looked at Celina, sitting next to Junior.

"What about you? What grade are you in?"

"Ninth at El Sausal. I like English."

"I like history!" Mario suddenly offered. "We visited the Old Mission here last week!"

"That must mean you're in the fourth grade," Alicia said. "My boys did that when they were your age."

She turned back toward Celina.

"Why do you like English?" she asked.

"I like the stories. We're reading *Twenty Thousand Leagues Under the Sea.*"

"I read that book in high school," I said. "Now my daughter is reading it in junior high."

Mario reclaimed the spotlight. "At the mission, we saw old wagons and tiles like these," he pointed to the floor, "but with paw prints in them from a coyote or something."

"We just went to sixth-grade science camp!" Moisés called out. "I slept in a tent all week!"

"What did you make?" Manuel asked.

"Nothing. We went on hikes and learned about trees. There was a lake. I can almost swim now!"

"I wish I could swim," Manuel said. "I'd sink like a boulder."

All the children laughed as he cupped his arms, puffed out his cheeks, and stiffened his generous torso.

"And what is your name?" Alicia asked our younger daughter.

"Baby Gloria."

"And how old are you?"

"Um, eleven."

"What is your favorite thing to do?"

"Um, make cookies with *mi mamá* and Celina!"

"What kind of cookies?"

"What kind of cookies, *mamá*?"

"We make sugar cookies, *m'ija*," Elida responded.

Baby Gloria looked back at Alicia. "Sugar cookies!"

The chatter continued with each of the other children given their moment to shine. Alicia turned to Elida.

"You have a beautiful family."

"*Gracias*, señora."

"We have two boys. They are much older," Alicia sighed.

"Sixto," Manuel asked, "what's this I hear about delays and opposition?"

"*Usted sabe*," I said, "it doesn't end. The government wants my flesh and the people want my blood!"

"That sounds about right." Alfred Navarro dished himself a serving of rice.

"Listen to this, Manny," he said. "Farmers Home requires them to file the cooperative's articles of incorporation before it will approve the loan. Meanwhile, the state's corporations commission claims they can't file the articles until the cooperative's membership list is established and the members have signed their documents. At the same time, the State Department of Real Estate won't permit them to sign their documents until the financing is approved; which, of course, requires a Farmers Home loan.... It's an endless circle!"

"The families are restless," I said. "They keep asking, 'How can it take so long?' 'When will we be notified that the loan is approved?' Lalo tells us to be patient."

"He's exactly right," Manuel said. "If you don't do it right, you let them off of the hook. You make it easy for them to say no."

"I understand," I responded, "but in the meantime, I have to find money to pay the taxes on the property, and the people grow restless, suspicious."

"We do have some good news," Lalo declared. "We just got a small loan from a nonprofit lender to rehab the first two barracks. That means we'll start construction in time to meet the one-year deadline required by the use permit. We think the growers are planning to appeal the supervisor's approval of the project. But our attorney says if we can start construction, they might finally give up."

The waiters distributed fluted glasses, then poured champagne for the adults and Seven-Up for the children. Manuel stood and lifted his drink to offer *un brindis*.

"Everybody, let's take a minute here," he said, quieting the group. He surveyed the room and then turned his focus toward the children.

"Kids, we enjoyed meeting all of you tonight and learning about what you're doing—books, math, field trips, and Moisés over there trying to swim." The children giggled. "So, it's your parent's anniversary, a special day. I hope each of you will take care of them, your *mamá y papá*. They're doing some hard work right now." Our host glanced back at Elida and me.

"Believe me, we understand what you two are going through. When we started CCCDC six or seven years ago—and I should say, it was Alicia's idea—we had the vision of helping farmworker families become strawberry farmers.

We went through the same progression. We had to create the right vehicle—the right institution—to carry the human and community development process forward. Just like you, we decided on the cooperative structure. The cooperative became what we call 'the developmental vehicle' needed to sustain the aspiring farmers through the tough transition from worker to farm owner.

"San Jerardo will serve that same purpose. Despite the challenges, the fact is you're creating an institution that will not only meet its members' need for housing, but through the process of owning and maintaining that institution, those same members will gain new skills and a new understanding of themselves and of their place in society. It's hard work to make that journey, but don't be discouraged. You're well on your way."

Manuel hesitated. "Look at the children," he said. "I'm putting them to sleep! Okay, it's time to wrap this up." He raised his glass. "Congratulations to Sixto and Elida on their anniversary and *salud* to San Jerardo and its future!"

With the small bridge loan in hand, we started construction on the first two units just in time to meet the use permit's one-year deadline. A few months later, as these units were completed, we closed the larger Farmers Home Administration loan and pushed forward on the rehabilitation of the remaining barracks, creating an additional fifty-eight homes.

The attorney, Mr. Bryan, called Lalo.

"They've given up," he crowed. "The growers have withdrawn their appeal of the superior court's decision. Your permit is safe!"

Again, we rejoiced at our victory, yet the struggles did not cease. Material prices continued to rise. Everett Sánchez, our contractor, came to me time and again.

"There's not enough money, Torres! Looking ahead, the budget is going to be very tight. I don't see how we pay for it all. *Usted sabe*, I have a family to feed. You need to find more money."

What was I to do? Lalo had squeezed all he could from Farmers Home.

"I'm telling you," Lalo said, "they won't put up another penny. The members may have to do more of the work than we'd planned. There's no other way."

I spoke to the *socios*. "We must make a greater commitment. Not only painting inside and outside, but the men will have to help to finish the roofs."

Armendina Alemán stood to speak. "No, Sixto, you're wrong. We women can climb ladders. We will lay the roofs, as well!"

Throughout the years, even at La Posada and as we pushed forward with our permit and now with construction, the women—except for Catalina and the few who only gossiped and sowed dissension—had driven much of the progress among the people. They had cooked the meals along Sherwood Drive to ensure everyone was cared for; they had organized our fiestas to celebrate the victories; they had held not only their own families together; they helped to keep all of us together, even when some of the men were ready to give up. And now they were on the roofs with hammers in hand, nailing down the asphalt tiles.

It was time to establish the formal membership of San Jerardo Cooperative, Inc. We had to submit each of the family's credit and income history to Farmers Home to prove their eligibility. Juan Alemán and I sat in the newly renovated community center. Sunlight reflected from the beige Formica tables and bathed the new metal chairs in a warm sheen. A steamroller floated past the windows, compacting the freshly poured blacktop just outside the center's new glass doors.

We reviewed the stack of applications. Many of the members had been with us since La Posada and others had been making payments as *socios* for two or three years.

I looked at Juan and shook my head. "It's clear that some of our families are not going to qualify," I said. "The ones with older children ...sonamabeecha ...they work hard to make good money until the crop is in; and then, it turns out they've earn too much to qualify. They're over the income limits...."

In mid-April, five hundred people arrived to celebrate the community's grand opening. They parked their cars along the newly paved entrance road, now lined with young poplar and juniper trees. The smell of freshly poured asphalt mingled with the aroma of freshly cut lettuce carried by the breeze from surrounding fields. Camp McCallum's torn and drooping gate was gone. The visitors stood silently to marvel at the property's full rebirth.

Each of the barracks had been transformed into modern duplexes with stucco siding painted in bright pastels and featuring white-trimmed windows and doors, topped with earth-toned roof tiles. The circle of roads and walkways through the property—asphalt and cement—lay clean and crisp in the late morning light. The yards, swept and fertile, awaited the flowers and fruit trees yet to be planted by each new occupant. The interiors of the homes were bright with the scents of tape, texture, and paint still lingering above the recently laid linoleum tile floors. Children yelled excitedly, running from room to echoing room.

Twenty-one of the original thirty-four La Posada squatters were now official members of the cooperative. The balance had either left the area or was unable to qualify under Farmers Home Administration or the county's criteria. Employment information and documentation of twenty new applicants were still under review by the board and the financing agencies. Another nineteen new applicants were still in the screening phase.

Farmworker families from throughout the valley sauntered among the homes as a mariachi struck up its first song of the day. Some of the gapers knew little of the site's storied history. Others understood the years of struggle that nurtured this dream and made it real. Newlyweds sat hunched together among the newly purchased tables. They thumbed a brochure entitled ¡San Jerardo sí! and wondered if they might still make an application for membership.

The former residents, many of whom had contributed to the wad of dollar bills first stored in my tin coffee can, came from all parts of the valley to celebrate the great triumph. Those who had lived at Camp McCallum for a month or for six months stared in disbelief at the transformation before them.

I stood proud and happy in front of the refurbished community center with its bright flagpole, displaying the American flag, the flag of the State of California, and the Mexican flag. The initial board of the cooperative had already met for the first time and had named me its first president. The members and I would hold our positions for one year until the membership of the cooperative was fully established and ready to elect a new board on a one-member-one-vote basis.

Workers and dignitaries crowded together near the other board members and me. Women scurried in the background, preparing for the meal. They carried *ollas* of beans and *caldo de pollo* and stacks of fresh tortillas into the center's renovated kitchen. Juan Alemán stood with Marcos Zavala and Juan Morales. The rich smell of carnitas rose from the freshly dug pit barbecue.

"*¡Bienvenidos a todos!* Welcome! Welcome!" I called out, shaking hands and embracing well-wishers. County supervisors and planning commissioners milled about with the planning director and his staff, all of whom had played their parts in the drama of La Posada and San Jerardo's unlikely emergence. Representatives from the federal and state agencies, whose resources had made the rehabilitation possible, walked the site. The music played, the crowd ate and drank its fill, the politicians made their speeches, praising the families for their patience and perseverance.

After several weeks of waiting, the board and the financing agencies approved all of the sixty families for membership. At last, the cooperative was fully established and every family had moved into its new home. The joy that I felt in what we had achieved should have been boundless. We had never lost hope. We had held firm to the dream. We had followed the process and now the dream was a reality.

The children were excited to be sleeping for the first time in such spacious bedrooms. Elida and I, at last, had our own room. Despite her years of doubt and uncertainty, she was contented to stand in her bright kitchen and cook on her new stove. She cared for it as if a new child had arrived to stay with us.

My joy should have been without limit, but I felt dread and disquiet. My spirit was heavy with what had to be done, what I had a hand in doing. Why were all blessings mixed? Why could my happiness never be pure?

We had followed the process as Lalo advised; but we had never fully understood that some would win and others would lose. Now, many of the La Posada families were angry because they had not qualified to live at San Jerardo. Some of them now cursed me and berated me and said that I was *chueco*, crooked, that I had invited only my friends and *compadres* to take a home or that those who were chosen must have paid money.

These statements were far from the truth. With the county's permit came conditions. With the government loan came many more. Many of us had assumed that, in some way, we would be able to maneuver around these government demands. This was how it worked in Mexico. But we learned that it was different here *en los Estados Unidos*. The income limits were rigorously applied. The *corbatas* were not flexible in these matters. They disqualified some whose earnings exceeded the limits by only a few dollars. There was no one who might be "convinced" to bend the rules.

I didn't screen the applications alone. A committee of the board performed this task in all cases but one. An applicant was qualified first by the committee and then by the funding agencies.

"Everyone in this room knows that we followed the rules," I told the board. "Some of you were on the committee and made the selections. You saw the list from Farmers Home of those who could not qualify. I admit I accepted the Álvarez family without your review. But what was I to do? Robledo and Alemán were out of town. Farmers Home called to demand the final list immediately or the take-out loan would not close on the appointed day."

Even Juan Alemán was angry at me for accepting the Álvarez application in his absence. He said that I disrespected the role of the committee. Of course, Catalina and Adalberto also came to the board meeting and chastised me.

A few months after we occupied San Jerardo, CCCDC terminated its internship program. Suddenly, I had no job, no income. The annual harvest was completed. What was I to do to pay my bills? I felt justified to reimburse myself and Junior. In truth, the amount covered only a fraction of the many hours that we had spent over the nearly ten years it took to bring this dream to fruition. The checks I wrote totaled less than $3,500. In my mind, it was small payment for all of that I had contributed and my family had suffered, and it was our sole means of support for several weeks. Juan Alemán scolded me some months later.

"You shouldn't have drawn that money without our approval."

"*Amigo,*" I said, "you know very well that you, Robledo, and some of the others were away to Mexico. What else was I to do?"

Many of the new members were strangers to us. We knew them only from our initial interview with them. They hadn't lived at La Posada. They weren't with us from the beginning. They knew little or nothing of the struggles and the years of uncertainty. They understood little or nothing of the cooperative, of articles and bylaws, of occupancy agreements, of Robert's Rules, of loan payments and record keeping, of bank accounts and financial statements, of reports and audits.

We had to educate these new members. My heart was heavy because I knew that Catalina, Adalberto, and others who had opposed me from the beginning were already moving into the void of information. Their lies skittered from door to door much more readily than the burdensome truth.

Adalberto was running for a seat on the new cooperative board. The first elections were now only a few days away. He and Catalina were working to ensure that I was not reelected as *presidente*. Adalberto was more capable than his wife. He was quieter, but he was also hot tempered. Turbulence lived behind his eyes. I understood his constant struggle to control and subdue the anger within.

Despite these problems, it was beautiful to see the children and teenagers with their soccer games at each end of the open field that bordered the entry road, all playing on the green grass in their separate groups, shouting and laughing as children should. On weekends, the parents watched. By late morning, they returned to their homes, content to sweep and mop their floors and tend to their freshly planted gardens.

When the cooperative's one-year anniversary arrived, the members cast their ballots for the succeeding board of directors. I had not prepared well for this event. Perhaps I was too exhausted from the long months of stress and from all the issues we had confronted.

As it turned out, less than half of the membership voted for me to remain on the board. It was not enough.

"Why didn't you go door to door, Don Sixto," Espiridión Rodríguez asked, "to respond to Catalina's accusations?"

I had no ready answer. Undoubtedly, he was right, but why should I have had to defend myself against the *chismes*, the rumors? Why were some people so willing to hear whatever is said that is negative and to overlook the reality in front of them that is a blessing for their lives? The reality was this community, their homes, and the great obstacles that we had overcome. These all disappeared before the rumors that I was crooked, that I had taken money, that I was a tyrant.

Although I was distraught at the loss of my position, I offered to assist the new board in learning all that it needed to know, but the members preferred to rely on Juan Alemán, or Marcos Zavala, or José Avila for information. Jaime Robledo was the new *presidente*. He was a salesman, selling his smile and his easygoing nature.

"Señor Robledo," I said, "this community and you have much to learn about your responsibilities. If I—"

The new president interrupted me.

"Don Sixto, *dispense*, you have done enough. It's time for others to step forward. Juan here, señor Castillo, and señor Ávila, they are all supporting us immensely."

Later, as I lay in bed, I concluded that some of my former cohorts on the board had turned away. They still smiled to my face, but they weren't willing to struggle against the likes of Catalina and Adalberto. Juan and some others accepted the opinion of whoever spoke the loudest, spreading their false but easy answers. I feared for the future of this cooperative.

My thoughts turned to my friend, Efraín González. He was one of the newer members. Almost immediately after he and his family moved in, the trouble began. Efraín worked long hours. He had little time to manage his household. He himself broke the rules and shouted down anyone who tried to confront him.

Aurora, his wife, was a caring but docile person with only a dim understanding of the goings on around her. She spent her days struggling to maintain not only her house, but an uncontrollable brood of children who came and went willy-nilly. Efraín was an irrigator for Hansen Farms. He left in the early morning and returned late in the evening, tired and short of temper.

At age nineteen, the couple's oldest son, Crescencio, had dropped out of school and had become friendly with Ismael Vélez and with Mario Molina. Crescencio soon joined them and their drug use and dealing. On Saturday nights, the González boy and his cohorts scudded along San Jerardo's central thoroughfare in their lowrider cars with their noisy pipes. They and their buddies partied behind the wooden fence that defined Efraín González's small patio. They played their loud music. They and their girlfriends drank, shouted, cackled into the night, and stumbled about among the neighbors' flowers.

I had liked Efraín when I first met him. I had promoted his acceptance into the community. Now I felt badly that he and his family were in trouble with the new leadership. "Perhaps," I thought, "I should try to be more supportive and help him keep his boy in line."

"They have no respect! They're savages!" Juan Morales had come to me complaining and waving his arms in frustration. "They're endangering the children, the way they race through the streets! They're selling drugs right here on the property! I've seen it!

"I am told that Robledo and a committee of the board paid them a visit, but Efraín only got angry and threatened them. I don't think the board knows what to do," he continued. "You know—you were there—we've discussed evicting him for months, but the attorney insists on approving every move we make."

I listened. "I've heard that the board sent a warning letter," I said.

"I'd be surprised if Efraín bothered to read it," Juan Morales retorted. "Miranda tells me that González has been invited to a hearing. After that, the board will decide on whether or not to evict."

"I may go just to observe," I said.

CHAPTER TWENTY-ONE

I appeared at the board meeting to witness the seating of the new officers and to hear the discussion on the fate of the González family. The community center was brightly lit and still pristine with white walls, vinyl flooring, and its rows of shining metal chairs.

It was hard for me to make my plea for Efraín before the very members of the cooperative who had plotted my defeat. I should have known better; yet, I remained optimistic. In seminary, all those years ago, we had learned to believe in every person's ability to change, to be redeemed. We had learned that one must never be governed by hatred and distrust. For these reasons, I had come with hope in my heart as I stood before them. Perhaps, now that they held the power, these men would weigh the eviction action more carefully.

Efraín González was slouched in a front row in one of the new metal chairs. His legs were crossed. His hand bounced on one knee with nervous energy. Twenty other members were in attendance. González stared at the board with an air of defiance.

At the front of the room, behind the board's Formica table, Jaime Robledo was flanked by the six additional members, which included Juan Alemán, Marcos Zavala, Samuel Ávila, and

Adalberto Castillo. My friends, José Miranda and Espiridion Rodriguez, were also present. Robledo opened the meeting.

"We have just two subjects this evening to discuss: the seating of the new officers and the status of the González family's membership. We have sent written warnings to Señor González that his membership may be terminated because of violations of the occupancy agreement."

Jaime was in his fifties with pudgy jowls and thick gray hair. Although generally easygoing, he was very businesslike once he called the meetings to order. Without further comment, Zavala nominated the slate of new officers. Robledo called for the vote, which was approved unanimously. I was now officially unseated as *presidente*.

Adalberto sat between Marcos Zavala and Juan Alemán. Marcos leaned against the table with his head in his hands. After a moment, he raised his eyes and surveyed the other board members.

"We've already heard from the attorney that we have good reasons for acting," he said dejectedly. "We have no choice in this matter, and we have already waited too long. I make a motion that we evict the González family. The father disrespects our community. His boy races through our streets, endangering the lives of our children. Will we wait to act until after one of them is dead? We've warned him for months, and nothing has changed. Only last night we heard the pipes rumbling by the windows, tires screeching; and two days ago, one of our residents saw drugs and money exchanged among his friends and him on *la* Calle El Rosario. What more evidence do you need? The people want action. It's our duty to act."

Juan Alemán spoke directly to González.

"Señor, we have a witness who saw your boy hanging around the tool shed the night the chainsaw was stolen. Do you know that? Do you have the chainsaw? If you do, *ves*, you should return it. It belongs to the people here, not to you or your son, *ves*."

González stood and hissed through his teeth.

"He hasn't stolen your saw! It's all lies and rumors! If you do this, if you evict us, I'm saying it again: you'll have to pay for the skylight that I installed." He sat down, still smirking defiantly.

The board was unmoved. They voted to deny any payment for a skylight, which they claimed had no value because, reportedly, it leaked. Marcos Zavala made his motion to evict Efraín González and his family from the cooperative. Adalberto Castillo, who had said little up to now and appeared to have been drinking, seconded the motion.

That was the moment I stood to defend Efraín. As soon as I spoke, Adalberto Castillo went into his drunken rage against me and called for the vote to evict the González family. The board immediately voted in favor of the action. Then Efraín González began to rant against the members. I moved forward to escort my friend from the room before violence would erupt.

As I have already described at the beginning of my story, I sat outside next to Efraín in silence and shadows. I took out two cigarettes and gave one to him. I raked a match across the rough wooden bench. The smell of sulfur surrounded us.

"They're after you next, you know," he stated. "They won't stop until you're gone too."

Jaime Robledo called a special meeting of the board for October 1. A window in the community center had been broken. Esteban Padilla had witnessed the incident from his living room, but the light was dim. He could not be sure. He thought he recognized Sixto Torres Junior and Horacio Amézquita and their brothers. They were fighting Paco Alemán. He thought he saw Crescencio González with Paco and his brother, and maybe Ismael Vélez and Mario Molina.

The two groups had tangled near the spot where the crack of the glass interrupted his quiet evening. He saw sticks and swinging chains, he said, and maybe flashes of bottles and knives. Some of the youth he didn't recognize. He assumed that they were from Salinas; more of that *Madeira Barrio Locos* gang of teenage thugs—they called MBL—who had invaded the community and for weeks had stirred up trouble with their drinks and their marijuana and cocaine. The board members knew that this was not the first such rumble and it would likely not be the last. Something had to be done.

A committee comprised of Jaime Robledo, Juan Alemán and Esteban Padilla had come to our door. They brought an affidavit submitted by Esteban. They wanted to ask Junior, Enrique, and Mario a few questions.

"We need the names of all who were there the night the community center's window was shattered," they said. I listened.

"*Momentito*," I answered and disappeared into the house. I thought that Elida might know something about the matter. Elida came to the door. She stood, wiping her hands on an apron. Our three teenage boys gathered in the shadows behind her.

"What do you want?" she asked.

"We would like you to read this. We have some questions for your boys." She took the paper and glanced at it. "People are upset with the broken window and the continuous fighting," Jaime said. "If your sons were there, perhaps they can identify who else was present."

The conflict among the community's youth reflected the growing division among their parents. The violent confrontations had increased with the arrival of the MBL thugs and their drugs.

Horacio Amézquita, whom everyone called Lachos, was Junior's friend. He was a high-spirited eighteen year old who fought with a fierce abandon. To bring him down, you had to take him by surprise, and that is what happened at Pancho's Nightclub on East Market. Checo Caballero and his friend, Memo, were in one corner, eyeing him. Lachos sipped on his drink with complete disregard. Before he knew what had happened, Memo slipped into the booth behind him and, without warning, hit him across the side of the head with a long flashlight. A week later, his head still wrapped in a rag, Lachos encountered Checo and Memo kicking back and smoking pot in the shadows of San Jerardo's community center. It took only a few moments for the opponents to gather their forces and begin the fight.

Elida knew nothing of the occurrence and, in any case, didn't care to hear from this delegation of board members who, in her mind, had plotted the removal of her husband as *presidente*. She had had enough of the *chismes* and finger pointing. How dare these *güeyes*—these buffoons—come to her door and accuse her children?

In an instant, the years of pent-up frustration and anger surged to the surface. She wadded up the affidavit and threw it at Esteban's feet.

"Señora, please—" he objected. Elida stepped from the porch before he could finish his sentence. Her dark eyes turned to molten lava. The anger spewed forth as she reached out and slapped Esteban across the face.

"Get out of my yard!" she cried. He grabbed her arm to restrain the attack, but she scratched and clawed at him until I burst through the door.

"Don't touch her!" I yelled and pushed Esteban away. He quickly disengaged and retreated with Alemán and Robledo. Elida and I reentered our home. Our stunned children stared at their mother. The older boys cast their eyes to the floor contritely.

Now, a week later, the center's large meeting room was abuzz when Jaime Robledo pounded the gavel on the table. Elida and I sat among the other residents in attendance. *El presidente* began with a speech in which he demanded that all of the parents take control of their children or the destruction would never cease.

"We have to do something so that *los muchachos* don't inflict so much damage as happened last Sunday," he said. "After señor Avila's family enjoyed its fiesta, they closed the *salón*, and then a fight ensued and a window was broken. These damages cost the entire community! They must cease!"

As always, Adalberto Castillo appeared slightly drunk. His droopy eyes cast about the room.

"We should close the center until these problems stop!" he proclaimed.

Juan Alemán stood to beg everyone's cooperation.

"This is a problem that affects all of us. We must take responsibility to care for one another!" Esteban Padilla took the floor.

"The committee of the board has been attacked by Elida and Sixto Torres!" he announced. "Elida Torres slapped me in the course of carrying out my duties as a board member. They have refused to cooperate in the investigation into the window!"

Padilla was a small man in his late twenties. He had been appointed to the committee as one of Castillos followers. Elida's action and his accusation had ripped open the scabbed wound—the tensions between Catalina and me—that had festered for years beneath the life of the community.

Immediately, Elida rose to respond. Once again, her heated gaze fell scornfully on Esteban Padilla.

"You came to my home to accuse my children of something you thought you saw. I am sick of your rumors. We have witnessed many misdeeds over the past months. Go investigate those! You scurry about like cockroaches trying to place the blame on us, always pointing fingers at our family. Don't come to my door again to accuse my children or you will receive the same treatment!"

Juan Alemán stood and shouted in response, "You're to blame because your children are always causing problems, fighting and threatening all the others! Don't pretend that you don't know Junior attacked my son, Paco, only two weeks ago!"

"Your son is no angel!" Elida retorted. "I have no doubt he deserved whatever he got!"

A woman named Susanna stood to speak. She gestured toward Elida and me.

"These people lack respect and do not take responsibility for their children. They shield and coddle them, which only gives wings to their misconduct!" I sat in disbelief. I hardly knew who this woman was. I could manage only three words before Robledo gaveled the meeting to a close.

"*¡Estás loca, mujer!*"

Despite the signal to end the meeting, the anger and shouting among the families continued. Elida returned home without further comment. Outside, everything happened very quickly. The people pushed through the center's glass doors. An October chill had settled on the darkened community. I saw shadows moving nearby. It was Junior and the Amezquita boy, Horatio, rising from the porch bench. Castillo half-stumbled through the open doors.

"You need to show more respect, *cabrón!*" he mumbled as he brushed by me.

"You're the burro who has no respect even for yourself," I said to Castillo.

The last of the crowd was drifting away. Across the way, Guadalupe Amézquita was in a heated discussion with his wife and one or two other sons. As Castillo passed me, he looked up to see Junior and Horacio standing in his path. My son, Moisés, had also joined them. He stopped, realizing that he was surrounded. He thought that we were going to hit him. Suddenly, he reached under his jacket and pulled out a pistol and pointed the gun around the circle.

"Now we will see," he said. "I'm going to shoot you all!" With that, I pushed him forward hard from behind. As he fell, he dropped the gun. The three boys pounced on him and pommeled him. I started to yell for them to stop, but at that moment we heard a shot. We realized that the gun had been kicked to one side. Esteban Padilla had picked it up and had fired into the air. As the three boys rose, Esteban once again threatened us with the pointed gun. He backed away, moving slowly up *la* Calle El Rosario, and then turned to run. Horacio and Moisés chased after him. In the dark, Padilla tripped on a speed bump and was suddenly sprawled on the asphalt, the gun skipping forward. I saw Moisés kicking Esteban. I yelled for him to stop. Horacio retrieved the gun.

I turned back toward Adalberto Castillo. His head was bleeding from hitting the pavement when I had pushed him. Juan Alemán knelt beside. He had given him a paper towel to stem the flow. They rose and walked toward Adalberto's home.

The police came and asked many questions. At first, Castillo denied that he had a gun. When confronted by the testimony of many others, he admitted he was carrying one but denied he pulled it out or pointed it.

"It must have fallen out of my waistband when the Torres boys beat me," he claimed.

The police decided to press charges for assault and battery against my sons, the Amézquita boy, and me. The report was turned over to the district attorney, who soon dropped all charges for lack of evidence.

As had become my habit, I wandered through the eucalyptus grove alone. My mind raced in a flurry of thoughts and emotions. For months, I had continued to seethe with resentment over my removal as president of the cooperative.

I felt lost and untethered. I could not contain myself, knowing all that had yet to be done. I could not stand by, silent and disengaged.

Some of the residents failed to control their children. I saw a child ripping the branches from one of the saplings along *la* Calle El Rosario.

"Look at what he's doing!" I yelled from across the road to the mother who was tending her garden. "You need to watch more closely. He's destroying the tree." Later, the woman reported to the board that I had accused and threatened her. When I heard this, I realized that I could do nothing to improve my situation or the cooperative's.

I seldom attended the meetings, but my friends, José Miranda, Juan Morales, and Espiridión Rodríguez, kept me up to date. It was difficult to observe from a distance as the board called its weekly meetings to deal with the many struggles of the young community: delinquent payments, unauthorized guests, disruptive teenagers, and squabbling children. The list was endless.

The sixty families were required to contribute their labor to the maintenance of the property. The board monitored the hours and issued fines for slackers. After several months, I had to admit that the new members were taking their responsibilities seriously and doing a better job than I had expected. Still, after the October meeting, I had grown even more distant from Juan Alemán. My old friend did not come to visit. Others told me that Juan now questioned some of my decisions and actions taken during the years that we had struggled together. It was convenient now, I thought, to find fault, especially when I was not present to explain why I had acted as I did.

The morning light fell through the trees stippling the dry ground. I thought, how far I had come only to find myself, once again, drifting into an uncertain future. I missed Lalo. His position with CCCDC had ended a month before I had lost the election. He had not been there to advise me during the struggle. Without him and David Foster and Alfred Navarro, the cloak of authority that had shielded me had been torn away. Before the election, I wanted to lash out because of the accusations and suspicions that drifted through the community like rancid air. I had managed to control myself during those difficult days. But perhaps my friend, Espiridión Rodríguez was right when he said that I had not fought hard enough to hold onto my place of leadership. Now, I smiled sadly. I knew that, in the end, nothing would have made a difference.... As I walked, I thought I could hear the cackle of distant blackbirds and see their shadows flitting among the branches of the towering eucalyptus.

Espiridión—who was my strongest insider on the board—continued to warn that my foes were after me. The Torres family, they claimed, was the source of the community's many problems.

"They have an attorney," he said, "They've asked her to prepare a summary of your supposed violations of the cooperative's governing documents. Beto Garza is also advising them."

I was not surprised to hear this. As the weeks and months passed, the board members met repeatedly in closed sessions. More and more, I was told, they focused on the few decisions that I had made that were not to their liking. Over and over, they reviewed the events of October 1. Each retelling strengthened their resolve to hold the Torres and Amézquita families responsible for the melee. Eventually, they drew up a list of grievances against my family and me in preparation for the issuance of an eviction notice. I imagine the self-serving document is still archived among the pages of the cooperative's books of minutes. It read in part:

"It is affirmed that the sons of Sixto Torres assaulted a member of the board of directors.

"It is affirmed that Sixto Torres took cooperative funds in the amount of $3,403.43 for his personal use.

"It is affirmed that Sixto Torres admitted the Abel Álvarez family to the cooperative without following the procedure."

Elida and I and our supporters attended the formal board hearings to answer each and every charge. By then I was on disability with a bleeding ulcer. With our three oldest boys working the fields during the summer months, we managed to repay the money that I had taken to feed my family during that last difficult winter. My opponents, however, continued to push for my eviction. Our efforts to defend ourselves were to no avail. For the alleged wrongdoings, my family and I were evicted from San Jerardo Cooperative, Inc. within four years of its founding.

CHAPTER TWENTY-TWO

On the night before we packed our family's limping Dodge van and moved out of San Jerardo, Lalo and I met at Maida's Bar on East Market Street in Salinas.

Lalo and I embraced. "I'm sorry to hear about your problems," he said.

I shook my head. "It has been a long struggle. I don't know if I'll ever fully understand it." We ordered two beers.

"How is your health?" Lalo asked. "Is it okay for you to drink that?"

"Believe it or not, my liver is fine. Do you remember how the doctor told me that I needed a miracle? Now he claims that a miracle has happened! He says I'm cured, but he has no idea why that should be. I told him about the visits from the *curandero*, Don Juan de Diós, and *las hierbas* he had given me. Every day for five years, I drank that strange tea. The doctor scoffed, but he also admitted he had no other explanation for my recovery. I smiled at Lalo and we raised our glasses.

"Where will you stay now?"

"We've found an apartment near Closter Park."

The plastered walls of Maida's Bar were brushed with a musty orange paint, accented with yellow windowsills. Outside, an August sun labored behind a low layer of midday fog, bringing a gray and dust-speckled light through warped and faded blinds. I sat for a moment eyeing Lalo. I moved closer to the table, scraping my cowboy boots across the chipped linoleum floor.

"What will you do?" Lalo asked.

"I'm on disability with an ulcer. Perhaps you will hire me, huh?"

"I wish we could, but we don't have money for an organizer. Reagan has killed all of those programs. He's even trying to shut down CRLA. I don't think the Congress will let him. We'll see. How are Elida and the kids?"

"Junior, Enrique, Moisés, they work in the summer. We manage."

I looked at my friend. I remembered our first meetings in the cold barracks with the families gathered near the barreled fire, preparing for the hearing before the planning commission.

"I've heard about what you're doing now," I said. "It's good, taking what you learned during, how many, seven years, and starting a new nonprofit. It's very good. I like the name, CHISPA; how you say ...spark?"

"Choosing the name was the easy part," Lalo said. "Finding the words to match the acronym was more difficult, but I won't bother you with that. Our goal, of course, is to spark more development of farmworker housing in the valley."

Again, we raised our beers and toasted.

"In any case," Lalo stated, "you and I know that the real spark was San Jerardo."

I wiped the beer from my mustache with the palm of my hand.

"The group from King City, La Buena Esperanza, they came to see me," I said.

"I know. I suggested they do that."

"They wanted to know about cooperative housing. I guess they have an option on two acres."

"Yes, CHISPA is doing the pre-development work. We've got Farmers Home involved, as well. Of course, the neighbors are fighting us every step."

"They won't be able to stop it," I observed. "The people know now what can happen if they hold on, if they dare to dream the way we did. They know now to trust...." I reached for a cigarette and realized I had none in my pocket. "I've stopped smoking. Elida finally convinced me, and the children were after me, as well. They learned in school it causes cancer and insisted I quit." I waved to the waitress to bring two more drinks.

"The neighbors are fighting against La Buena Esperanza?" I asked. "I guess that's no surprise.... The 'neighbors,'" I repeated. "How strange these words, '*los vecinos*.' That's the same name the Spanish *conquistadores* gave to themselves. They insisted that the indigenous tribes call them 'neighbors'. The Spaniards, however, were not very good as 'neighbors.' In any case, they couldn't keep the people from rebelling against their power. The 'neighbors' in King City will find the same is true for them."

"Tell me something," Lalo said. "What happened with Beto Garza?"

"I heard he moved to San Luis Obispo. Supposedly, he's managing an apartment building, but who knows? Some say he's dealing drugs there the way he did here. That *cabrón* plotted with the board to get me thrown out. He came to San Jerardo for weeks in the evenings, meeting with Jaime, Juan, and Adalberto. They finally came up with the claim that I abused my authority. *¡Ridículo!*"

"It's hard to be a leader," Lalo observed. "If you're not strong enough, the people will eat you up. And if you are too strong, they will eat you up as well."

"But why must they feast that way?" I asked. "Is it jealousy? Is it envy? I don't know. I made mistakes, *es cierto*, but that doesn't explain why they did what they did. When Juan Alemán turned on me, I couldn't believe what I saw. He came after me one night in front of the center. He seemed to burn with such anger and passion. When I think how we were, almost fifteen years ago now. How little we understood; how far we had yet to come ...what more we might have accomplished if we hadn't wasted so much energy on mindless squabbles among ourselves."

"Much more *will* be accomplished, Sixto," Lalo said.

"I agree. I'm sure of it. I think of the children at San Jerardo. They already know much more than we knew. Oh, they're the children of farmworkers, certainly, and some may choose to stay in the fields. They'll become strong and proud workers just as we were. But some will become doctors and lawyers, and teachers and shopkeepers, and soldiers and nurses. I can see already; a thousand homes will grow from San Jerardo. The children in those homes also will find the opportunities that we all came here to provide them."

We sat for another moment in silence. The waitress came with a second round of beers. As she placed them on the table, I licked the crevice between my thumb and finger and covered the spot with a dash of salt.

"*¡Salud!*" I said.

"*¡Salud!*" Lalo responded.

For the third time that afternoon, we toasted the past and future.

Twelve years after my family and I left San Jerardo, I stood at the pump of an East Alisal gas station, filling my faded yellow pickup truck. I wore my one rumpled suit and tie along with my best Stetson and boots. I felt proud. I was on my way home after a swearing-in ceremony at the courthouse. I was now an American citizen.

Elida and the children waited for me at our home on Towt just a few blocks away. Jaime and Mario still lived with us, along with Enrique and his wife. They all helped pay the mortgage. Most of our other children were married and on their own. Moisés was single. He had joined the navy.

As the pump whirred, I noticed a homeless couple, perhaps in their sixties, riffling through the station's trash bin. The man wore jeans and a smudged white T-shirt. The woman was dressed in a flower-print smock that fell over her jeans. Their taut skin and wrinkled faces reminded me of the pictures I had seen of the Oklahoma migrants who had come to the Alisal in the thirties.

A white, late-model Cadillac pulled up to one of the pumps across the way, blocking my view of the couple. A man stepped out of the driver's side, wearing white pants and a black shirt beneath a white sport coat. His dark glasses were tucked into waves of blond hair. He looked around, then entered the station's convenience store.

The car's passenger door opened. Beto Garza stepped out. He was dressed in a purple shirt with an open collar and black pants. He sucked on the stub of a cigar. He shut the door, stretched himself, and turned. Immediately, he and I locked eyes.

"¡Hola, Torres!" he called. "Hey, bro, what's up?" We stood perhaps twenty feet apart.

It had been a month since I had run into Garza's father. He had told me that his son was still in San Luis—he was ashamed to say—still dealing drugs.

I stared at Garza but made no response. Garza called again over the hum of traffic and through a stiff, late afternoon wind, "What's up?"

"*Nada*," I replied. I didn't like his too-friendly tone. "You make any Molotov cocktails lately, *vato*?" I asked, turning away toward the gas pump.

"No, no," Garza responded. "Come, Torres. That was a long time ago. 'Forgive and forget,' no? What say, *deme un abrazo*! We go have a drink together!"

"Not now," I said without looking back.

"Suit yourself."

Garza climbed into the car and waited for his cohort to return. I walked into the store to pay for the gas. The man in the white suit pushed past me and out the door. I paid my bill and rummaged through yesterday's *Californian* until I saw the Cadillac pull away.

When I returned to my truck, I noticed that a large bag of fresh yellow corn had been set in the bed of my pickup. A peace offering, I thought. The first fresh corn of spring would be good to bring home for dinner. I stood for a moment, then shook my head. I picked up the bag and carried it across the pavement toward the trash bin where the desolate couple still scrounged.

"Here, you have." I offered them the corn. They smiled through dried lips.

"Thanks," they said. "We got a cook stove down at the creek. This'll be good eatin' for a day or two."

I returned to my truck and drove home to spend the evening celebrating with my family the beginning of my new life as a citizen of the United States of America.

EPILOGUE

Sixto Torres lived for another eighteen years in East Salinas. Eventually, the family lost its house on Towt Street during the mortgage meltdown of the mid-2000s. A few months later, Sixto died of congestive heart failure with his wife, children, and grandchildren at his bedside.

For many years afterwards, Elida Torres lived on Laurel Drive in Salinas, renting a small back-alley bungalow with her son, Mario. On a certain Sunday afternoon, Lalo came to see her. She sat on a rusty metal chair placed precariously on a narrow slab of cement at her front door. Her sons and daughters and grandchildren came and went as she and Lalo talked. She was slight and fragile, showing all of the wrinkles accumulated during her eighty-five years of a life dedicated to the raising of eight children, the keeping of a household, and the taming of a husband.

She was happy to see Lalo, yet she expressed bitterness about the past.

"He left us with nothing, just as my parents said he would," she stated. Lalo was gentle but insistent.

"Please, Elida, you must not see it that way. Just look around you; he left you with eight beautiful children and now how many grandchildren. All of you paid a price. But for the people of the valley, you must know, great progress was made. Without you, Sixto could not have succeeded in his life's work. Without Sixto, San Jerardo would never have succeeded as it has. Without San Jerardo, CHISPA would not have completed the thousand plus homes in Salinas, González, Greenfield, King City, and Watsonville that are now occupied by farmworker families."

After many years, Beto Garza returned to Salinas permanently. He had overcome his addiction to drugs and had left behind his life as a dealer. He took a position in a local nonprofit drug-counseling agency and spent his final years helping struggling East Salinas youth overcome their dependency on drugs.

After a difficult youth, Horacio Amézquita and his family managed a successful farming venture in the Salinas Valley. Eventually having earned a bachelor's degree, Horacio took a position as manager of San Jerardo Cooperative, Inc.

Marshall Ganz spent sixteen years working with César Chávez and the United Farm Workers Union. He continued in community organizing for another ten years before returning to Harvard University where, in 2000, he earned a Doctorate degree in sociology. He became a senior lecturer in public policy at Harvard's Kennedy School of Government.

After the death of César Chávez in 1993, Dolores Huerta continued to work for the United Farm Workers Union. Eventually, she established the Dolores Huerta Foundation. Its mission is "to create leadership opportunities for community organizing, leadership development, civic engagement, and policy advocacy in the following priority areas: health and environment, education, youth development, and economic development."

In due time, the sixty families of San Jerardo Cooperative, Inc. learned the hard work of self-managing their housing cooperative through systems of democratic governance. Eventually, the board of directors refinanced the property, obtaining a loan from a private bank and fully repaying the United States Department of Agriculture for its Section 515 Loan.

ACKNOWLEDGMENTS

I express my deepest gratitude to Cary Neiman, whose friendship and clear mind were invaluable in the writing of this book. I also thank the following individuals: Alan Rinzler for his sage advice as consulting editor, the staff of Mill City Press and Hillcrest Media Group, Elida Torres and her children, especially Mario Torres and Sixto Torres Junior, Rogelio Peña, Marcos Zavala, Jorge Gomez, Jerry Kaye, Roberto García, Juan Martínez, Maria Luisa Alcalá, Virginia Barton, Hector de la Rosa, Dennis Powell, Horacio Amezquita, and Sabino Lopez, all of whom I interviewed for background. Thank you, as well, to Marc Moncrief, Father Ray Tintle, OFM, Dan Haight, Jose Flores and my wife, Judi, for their help in proofing the manuscript. I also thank Mara Tubert, the translator of the Spanish edition of *Raising the Blackbirds* and Susanna Suaya for her support in editing the translation.

In my research, I consulted the works of Juan Bautista Chapa's *The First Official History of Texan & Northern Mexico, 1630–1690*; Carey McWilliams's *Factories in the Fields*; Mark Finlay's *Growing American Rubber*; Enrique Krauze's *Mexico, Biography of Power*; Oscar Martínez's *Border People*; Dewey Bandy's doctorate dissertation on San Jerardo; Frank Bardacke's *Trampling Out the Vintage*; and Miriam Pawel's *The Union of Our Dreams*.